"YOU PAYS US NOW, OR WE BREAKS MUCH!"

The two ogres towered over Cymric and Leandra. The ogre who had spoken raised his club and swung at the swordmaster. His blow missed Leandra by two club-widths; Leandra parried the second, then instantly followed up with a deep cut across the ogre's weapon arm. Leandra whirled away from the ogre, and he and his companion turned to face her, leaving their backs turned toward the wizard.

Turning his sight inward, Cymric chose a spell. The threads of his matrix appeared blue. He started to slide the spell pattern down the thread. The spell slipped neatly into the matrix.

"Cymric!"

Leandra's shout brought him back to the external world. The ogre with the wounded arm was charging down on the wizard, swinging his club wildly. Cymric cast his spell even as the club smashed into him . . .

EARTHDAWN: PROPHECY

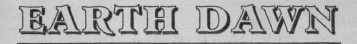

EARTH DAWN

PROPHECY

by

Greg Gorden

A ROC BOOK

ROC
Published by the Penguin Group
Penguin Books USA Inc., 375 Hudson Street,
New York, New York 10014, U.S.A.
Penguin Books Ltd. 27 Wrights Lane,
London W8 5TZ, England
Penguin Books Australia Ltd, Ringwood,
Victoria, Australia
Penguin Books Canada Ltd, 10 Alcorn Avenue,
Toronto, Ontario, Canada M4V 3B2
Penguin Books (N.Z.) Ltd, 182–190 Wairau Road,
Auckland 10, New Zealand

Penguin Books Ltd, Registered Offices:
Harmondsworth, Middlesex, England
First published by Roc, an imprint of Dutton Signet,
a division of Penguin Books USA Inc.

First Printing, July, 1994,
10 9 8 7 6 5 4 3 2 1

Series Editor: Donna Ippolito
Cover: Joel Biske
Interior Illustrations: Joel Biske

 REGISTERED TRADEMARK—MARCA REGISTRADA

EARTHDAWN, FASA, and the distinctive EARTHDAWN and FASA logos are trademarks of the FASA Corporation, 1100 W. Cermak, Suite B305, Chicago, IL 60608

Printed in the United States of America

1

No one has work for a wizard with holes in his shoes.
Cymric paused briefly to weave a delicate illusion. Holding his staff stiffly enough for show, he strode down the second hill in now-gleaming boots, down into the village of Twin Chin. The wizard rotated his shoulders and shook his thin arms to expand the sides of his robe. The breeze was too light to catch the cloth, but the sunlight glinted brightly on the robe's rich blues. The young wizard swept his hand through black hair, trying to keep it out of his eyes. He then took deliberate steps down the dusty slope. He wanted to give Twin Chin's residents time to see him. Cymric also wanted a chance to survey the town.

The breeze shifted, bringing with it the scent of cinnamon. Cymric smiled; cinnamon rolls were a favorite, despite the difficulties he'd had with the Bakers Guild in Tuakan. Cinnamon also meant some of the villagers had enough coin to afford the occasional indulgence—an important bit of information when the wizard came to setting his prices. Cymric counted the buildings—sixty-five of them, eight of brick or stone. Two of the outermost buildings were burned, but the rest of the village looked in good shape.

Cymric's smile widened until he caught himself and adopted a sterner, more wizardly expression. Drawing nearer, he saw three little girls loudly playing Hobmen in the Field. One in a yellow smock was the first to glance up in the right direction, then the other two followed her gaze, until all three were staring. Cymric paused, leaning on his staff for effect, then made broad, theatrical motions with his right hand. Squealing in excitement, the girls took off toward town.

You might eat well tonight, lad, thought Cymric, and increased his pace to time his entrance appropriately. Just then, a woman rounded the corner of building carrying a full pail of water. Seeing Cymric, she stutter-stepped, sloshing enough water to cause a solid *splat*! Villagers glanced from out of the doorways of their shops. A few, emboldened by their second-story vantage point, followed Cymric's progress toward the well that stood at the center of Twin Chin. The well was rimmed by good gray stone, and a dusty bucket hung from the rope wound around the crankshaft. Opposite the crank was a peculiar statue. Carved from rose quartz, the statue showed a young girl, her left arm extended, right arm across her body. The statue girl held the palms of both hands face up, as though she were inviting the traveler to drink at the well. Cymric thought it odd that the statue had no face: the head was hollow, narrowing to a pipe that disappeared down into the statue. He stopped by the statue, twice thumping his staff upon the ground.

"Gentlefolk, I am Cymric! I am a far traveler, a man of magic!" As he spoke, he began to walk a large, slow circle around the well, at the same time spinning in smaller, tighter circles. His movements were smooth and relaxed, his staff held up and out. As he spun, the wizard Cymric sized up those who watched him. Standing by the roadhouse he saw a woman armored in crystal chain; strapped to her side was a broadsword in a leather scabbard adorned with enamel writing. Cymric's smile faltered slightly under her dark-eyed gaze. Probably she was an adept. Possibly a swordmaster. Perhaps the sheriff of Twin Chin? She could pose a problem.

"I have descended into Kaer Irisoi and returned," he went on. "I have solved the riddle of Chandler's Cross." He turned past the couple who were obviously the village bakers. Middle-aged, disciplined enough not to grow fat on their goods. Standing there in flour-covered aprons, they gazed upon Cymric with looks of poorly concealed anticipation. They would not be a problem.

"My flames have routed trolls, and my will has broken wraiths. I have learned spells coveted in the halls of

Throal," Cymric said. He spun past a blacksmith. The blacksmith's arms were crossed, his eyes closely following each of Cymric's moves. He began to trail the wizard, perhaps to better hear every word he said. The blacksmith was going to be a problem.

"I have talked to the spirits. The spirits told me that the gentlefolk of Twin Chin have a problem," Cymric said. He slowed slightly, beginning to weave an astral thread for a spell. As he was doing so, a man in a red-dyed linen kimono patterned after those of the dwarf merchants of Throal moved into Cymric's field of vision. The silver threads looked genuine, but the kimono's dwarven-looking runes were nonsense rather than a list of family accomplishments. The man's cologne was spicy in the dwarven fashion, far too liberally applied to his jowly face. He was breathing heavily and beginning to perspire, probably from the simple exertion of getting here from wherever. This man was going to be a gold mine.

"So I now ask the spirits for a sign. Show me, oh spirits! Show me who understands best the problem that I might learn what services are required of Cymric the wizard!" Cymric's face masked the strain his patter caused his spellcasting. He tied off the thread to the spell pattern, and cast a flame flash on the tip of his staff. The flame arced toward the jowly man, the fire coming close enough to make him stumble backward, his mouth open and working in inarticulate protest. The gathered villagers gasped. Blast, thought Cymric, the flame was too close and looked nothing like a sylph. He took one long step forward toward the jowly man, then nodded curtly and thumped his staff twice.

"So it is you, sir, whom the spirits have chosen. I only hope they have chosen wisely. You are . . .?" he asked, sustaining the "are" for two beats.

His kimono reacting to the jiggle underneath, the man waddled forward. "I am Drofin," he said. "I am mayor and glass merchant for Twin Chin." Cymric smiled and lowered his eyelids a notch, hoping to create an expression that conveyed only a modicum of approval and a minimum of respect. In response, Drofin straightened his shoulders and tried to instantly grow three inches taller. Cymric's mouth twitched as he restrained a grin.

"Mayor Drofin, if you would be so kind as to tell me the details of your problem, I am ready to put my skills at your disposal," said Cymric.

"Didn't your spirits tell you?" said the blacksmith. Cymric turned his head left to see the blacksmith casually walking over to the mayor. The mayor glanced at the blacksmith, than back at Cymric.

"Drofin, you are mighty impressed by a wizard whose robes have so much blue and whose hair has so little white," said the blacksmith. As Cymric squared to face the man, the bakers also walked up to join the mayor. Then four other villagers, farmers arriving fresh from their fields, strolled over to the mayor's group. The swordswoman, however, stayed put. Good, thought Cymric. I'll take what help I can get.

"I think we need to know what sort of wizard he is," said a farmer. Another nodded. The mayor caught the nod, and puffed himself up to full size.

"Yes, um, Cymric, we have heard tales of a magician in Havel town who, um, perpetrated a dastardly . . .," said the mayor.

"Burned a man's bones while his flesh was still on him. Did the same thing to the man's two brothers," finished the farmer. Cymric blinked. He had debated whether to cross the river and try his luck in Havel. Now he could imagine what kind of reception he might have received.

"No, friend, I haven't come that way at all," said Cymric. He glanced at the bakers. They wore no guild symbols. "I have most recently come from Tuakan," he said.

"Oh! They have master bakers in Tuakan," said the baker man. "I myself began apprenticeship under Hensworth. Have you heard of him?"

Yes, I heard him quite clearly as he bellowed for my arrest. Unfortunately, I was most of the way out a window, and couldn't catch everything he said, thought Cymric.

"No, baker, I have not. But the loss is certainly mine, especially if his work smells half as delicious as yours," Cymric said. At least the compliment was genuine; it was nearing the dinner hour. The baker man beamed, and gave the baker woman an affectionate nudge in the ribs.

"Returning to the problem?" prodded Cymric.

"My problem," said the blacksmith, "is that magicians are known for their elixir talk, their flashy spells. They can get everyone to ooh and ahh and then throw them their silver." The blacksmith crossed his arms, revealing that the man's left forearm was hairless, probably from a recent accident with fire. "Young wizard, I mean no disrespect, but seems to me magicians go throwing spells at everything. They don't have to know what the problem is or whether spells are the answer. They just do it. Spells are no substitute for a clear head and a good eye." The mayor and the bakers looked unsure. Two of the farmers seemed to be in stubborn agreement with the blacksmith. The blacksmith gained confidence and volume from the set of their faces.

"So, wizard, before you laden your pouch with our silver, we would like to see some proof that you can do something other than song and flash," said the blacksmith.

Cymric's face scrunched into a mask of annoyance, then softened slowly into a more neutral expression. The smith wanted some evidence as to his clear head and good eye, a challenge that had cut off Cymric's wizard patter as surely as his hammer cracked a faulty blade. Cymric's gaze quickly touched on each farmer, the two bakers, the mayor, and the blacksmith. The bakers and the mayor might be persuaded, but the deal would have to be argued out and haggled over with the smith and the others. Damn, thought Cymric, I was so close to a decent dinner, I could almost taste it.

Then the solution struck him so swiftly that he had to laugh. The loud sound startled all but the blacksmith, who might only have flinched ever so slightly. Then again, maybe that was just wishful thinking on Cymric's part.

"Blacksmith," he said, regaining his composure. "I must plead guilty to an occasionally muddled mind. That is a hazard of filling it up with spells and mystical facts," said Cymric. He again began to spin in a slow, tight circle, staff held above his head.

"There is nothing wrong with my vision," said Cymric. He stopped his spin, holding the staff in his right hand, pointing in the direction from which he'd come, "and my reasoning is still clear. Coming into town I startled a woman carrying water, causing a spill." He then swung his staff to hit the bucket of the well with a satisfying thunk.

"When I arrived in the center of your village, the bucket was dry. That the dinner hour is near, yet no one draws water from the well merely confirms my reasoning that your well has gone dry," said Cymric. Now he gently knocked his head with his staff.

"All of this was obvious to me. I apologize for not making myself clear to the mayor," said Cymric, nodding and smiling at the mayor. Mayor Drofin beamed back. "I meant to ask for details on the well. How long has it been dry? What are the circumstances surrounding the loss of water?"

"A warlock cursed the well," said the baker woman.

"Or a Horror inhabits it," said the baker man.

"Clearly an act of perfidious, um, supernatural origins," offered the mayor.

"The well went dry two days ago. When I lowered the bucket late on the first day, the bottom was powder," said the blacksmith.

Cymric thought about it for a few moments, then said, "I believe the mayor is right. This problem has supernatural origins. The blacksmith has offered evidence that the well dried up with unnatural speed." Cymric turned away from the villagers. He looked down into the well, scooped up a pebble, tossed it in to hear the rattle and clack as it bounced on the bottom. He then turned back to the bakers.

"I don't think a Horror infests your well. I am no expert on Scourge lore, but legend suggests that if a Horror did inhabit your well, it would want you to use it," said Cymric. The baker man seemed both disappointed and relieved.

"A curse makes the most sense. I have no specific remedy for curses, but curses are magic. And I can dispel hostile magics," said Cymric. He kept to himself the knowledge that a competent curse might be only temporarily removed by his skill. *Do not advertise your weaknesses before the deal is closed.*

"You should know something of the well," said the mayor, "My grandfather was a magician, an elementalist, who enticed a water sprite to live in our well. He promised her safe haven from some of the river's dangers in return for her keeping our well water pure."

To confirm a guess, Cymric asked, "Does she use the statue to talk to you?" The mayor bobbed his head enthusiastically.

"She would make requests, asking for dandelions or meadow wings, that sort of thing. We would leave her small treats, such as fresh marion berries or kilm. During holidays, she would make the well sing for our night dances," said the mayor.

"What is her name?" asked Cymric. The mayor looked around at the farmers, then the bakers, and finally the blacksmith. He took a deep breath, but the blacksmith cut the mayor off before the man could speak.

"We don't know. We have never known. Phraetun told us that the sprite would leave instantly if anyone tried to learn her name," said the blacksmith.

Cymric nodded his head. Perhaps someone in town was a fledgling magician, trying to learn the sprite's name in order to command it. The sprite could have left in a huff, drying up the well in retribution. Or it really could be a curse. To find out, he would have to get to work. There was one very important item to clear up first.

"About my fee," said Cymric, "I customarily charge three hundred silver pieces for curse removal." Cymric remained impassive as the mayor looked aghast, his right arm flopping about like a fish on a deck, seemingly caught in the confusion of his thoughts.

"I simply cannot . . . that is, we simply must not allow . . . this is to say . . .," said the mayor. The baker woman moved over to the mayor, taking his right arm and more or less confining it to his side. Then the blacksmith stepped in front of Drofin, silencing him.

"Lower your price, wizard. We can still get water from the river," said the blacksmith.

"Yes, you can. Today. But whatever cursed the well might not be through with this village. It might still be hiding in the well," said Cymric. The baker woman looked directly at him. The look was watchful, not intimidating.

"You said there was no Horror in the well," she said.

"I told you that I *doubt* a Horror inhabits the well," Cymric said. "There are more creatures in the world than just Horrors."

"What guarantee can you give us that your remedy will work?" asked the blacksmith.

"Smith, spell magics are an uncertain craft," said Cymric.

"Uncertain skills wanting certain coin," snorted the blacksmith.

Cymric leaned his staff in the crook formed by the elbow of his bent left arm. He used both hands to smooth out the wrinkles in the front of his robe. He tugged on one sleeve, then the other, until the cuffs rode evenly. The wizard glanced at the villagers. The mayor and one of the farmers looked nervous. The baker man blinked once too often, a sign of indecision. Only the blacksmith looked calmly committed to haggling a better deal. Cymric decided to strike the deal now.

"Gentlefolk, the issue is simple. You either pay me to descend into the well, taking the risks for you. Or you save your silver and test fortune yourself," he said. The villagers huddled. Cymric smiled slightly, secure in the outcome of their frantic meeting. Tonight he could start living again. If he were careful, he'd have no money worries for five or six weeks. He adopted his most open expression, all the while thinking that the mayor's nervousness seemed inappropriate for the sum Cymric had asked.

"We can offer you twenty-four and a half silvers. Most of it in copper," the mayor said. Cymric's face froze between expressions, until he realized his appearance must be most unwizardly. He opened his mouth, but thought moved quicker than tongue, so he closed it again.

"An ogre band struck a little over two weeks ago. They demanded gold. We refused," the blacksmith said.

"Then they burned Jenkins' house and Old Chula's place. Old Chula went up with her home," the baker woman said.

"They asked for money again. We paid . . . what we could," the mayor said, "Trade between Tuakan and

Marrek is slow this time of year. So our coffers are low . . ."

"So you haven't got the money," Cymric said. The villagers nodded in ragged unison. Fantastic, thought Cymric. Now what, oh-high-priced but hungry wizard? The baker man approached him.

"Luwen has agreed to let you stay free of charge at the Greens," the baker said, indicating the roadhouse, "until the Marrek trade picks up again." He nodded toward the baker woman. "Gerl and I are just starting to bake our specialties, the ones we sell to the Marrek trade. We will give you the pick of the best, each day, until the trade comes in."

While weighing the offer in his mind, Cymric's stomach rumbled up an important vote. He straightened, smiled his broadest smile, and said, "Never let it be said that Cymric the wizard does not appreciate hospitality as much as gold. Done, gentlefolk, done. Now, let's see to this well."

He turned to the well, making a few large passes with his staff while speaking four mystic words. He, of course, was the only one who realized that, in this context, the words meant nothing. Next, he was peering into the shaft, muttering an occasional word or two under his breath. Then he gazed up at the sun, using the staff to estimate its inclination. This was all part of the show, theatrics to convince casual onlookers that he was a knowledgeable wizard. It also bought him time to think.

If the problem was that the sprite had simply up and gone, the well would still have some water in it. But seeing that the well was completely dry, Cymric knew that a spell or a curse had to be the most likely cause. And the most likely caster was the sprite herself—perhaps because of some irritation with the villagers. Cymric could remove the curse or spell, though probably not permanently, but the only way he could make the remedy permanent would be to talk to the sprite, persuade it to again favor the villagers. Then Cymric's reputation would grow, at least for a few villages in either direction of Twin Chin. He made his decision.

"Mayor Drofin, I require a personal item of your grandfather's. Best would be an item he used while working one of his spells," Cymric said. The mayor's head bobbed in acknowledgement, then off he went as fast as his duck-stride could carry him. Cymric then turned his attention to testing the rope attached to the bucket, which was apparently strong enough to lift a full bucket, but seemed too frail to hold a wizard.

"Smith, get some rope. I want you on the other end when I go down into the well. I'll tug once for 'stop lowering', and twice for 'get me up quickly, thank you'," Cymric said. The blacksmith grunted, then went to fetch the rope.

Cymric used the errand time to cast a real spell, one to heighten his sense of changes in the astral plane. The magic of the well would surely be creating a flux in the astral plane, and Cymric hoped to use his astral vision to get a better idea of what spell or curse he was working against. Again reaching into astral space with his mind, he tied in the threads of his spell, filling and strengthening the pattern he knew by heart. The spell flowed around him, then through him. His vision now tied to the spell, Cymric waited a moment for his astral sense to adjust to the flux at the bottom of the well.

But there was none. No images, no disturbance, not even the faint orange-brown curlicue filaments associated with living earth. Just black, unnatural black. Someone or something was in the well but it had defenses preventing astral sight from perceiving it. There's something down there that doesn't want to be seen, yet doesn't care that I know it's there, Cymric thought. Not what you'd expect from a curse. So what could it be that was down there?

Twenty-four and a half silvers now seemed less appealing. Cymric was still peering into the well when the blacksmith tapped him on the shoulder, offering him one end of a rope.

2

Cymric dropped into the well, the crossbeam creaking loudly as his legs bounced against the rock of the well wall. His feet crushed to powder the dry residue hiding in the cracks or clinging to the rougher portions of the rock; the blacksmith continued to lower him.

The well was perhaps twenty strides deep, much deeper than it had looked from the top. The low late afternoon sun left the middle portion in shadow and the bottom completely dark. A borrowed lantern hung from a knot not quite two feet above Cymric's head, its light just enough to cast a lumpy shadow of Cymric on the walls below. Finally, Cymric could see bottom. About six or seven feet above it was a ring of greenish stones, each one the width of his palm. One particularly unnerving noise from the crossbeam, and then Cymric landed on the bottom of the well a bit harder than he would have liked.

He checked his side pouch. Mayor Drofin had given him one of his grandfather's quills and a vial of ink. Cymric expected that the quill would have taken no damage from his banging against the wall, but the vial was of very thin glass. He smiled to see that the vial looked intact, then began to explore the well.

When Cymric found his movement constricted by the rope, he was about to tug on it for more slack, then changed his mind. They'd agreed on one tug for "stop lowering," two for "up quickly," but had made no provision for more sophisticated signals. Cymric shook his head ruefully. Must be fatigue and hunger.

"Blacksmith, give me five feet of slack," he shouted. After a brief pause, the rope loosened enough for Cymric

to kneel and examine the well bottom, whose surface was
rough and covered with lime deposits. Standing up again,
he knocked some of the deposits loose with his staff, then
knelt once more. The powdery dust made him sneeze, but
he could see the glinting spot he'd just cleared away. The
stone was wet. Cymric reached out to touch it, then froze
in mid-motion as the water slid off the rock and sank from
sight.

Cymric took a slow, deep breath and hauled himself up
slowly. Holding his staff in both hands, he leaned his forehead against the staff, thinking hard. This did not seem
like a curse at all. Or if it was, it was more sophisticated
than any Cymric had ever seen. It might still be a vengeful
sprite that had dried up the well, but whatever it was, it
had not reacted aggressively to Cymric's probing. Let's
see how this thing reacts to a challenge, he thought.

Cymric lifted his staff off the ground, his mind slipping
into an old pattern, a familiar pattern. His skill quickly
plucked an astral thread, one he saw as a deep, quiet
green. The thread matched the green of his native forests
on that early morning when he'd first cast this spell. The
thread slipped easily into the pattern, making it whole.
Cymric released the pattern, casting the spell to dispel
magic.

Four beats later, Cymric could breathe again. Nothing.
He tried the spell once more, putting extra energy into it.
He strained to expand his perception, reaching out into as-
tral space once more. He tried to place the thread *just so,*
preserving the symmetry of the pattern from all angles.
With a sharp exhalation, he unleashed the spell.

In the next instant Cymric was lifted off his feet and
hurled against the wall, then repelled again with even
greater force. His breath knocked out of him, he could
only give out a strangled whimper as he hit the other side.
His wrist bent awkwardly upon impact with the cold stone;
his face bounced hard. Stunned, Cymric grabbed his staff
for balance. Looking down, he caught his breath.

The clear spot on the floor burbled, a small spring spilling water onto the dry-caked bottom of the well, then the
spring suddenly died as the water vanished into the well

bottom. Cymric had no doubt this time. The water disappeared too quickly. It was as if something were pulling it.

Maybe the sprite was being held prisoner by a powerful enchantment? Or an entity? Cymric's spell had not been enough to counter the magic, but it had provoked a counterattack. His spell might have weakened the enchantment, or perhaps the creature's attention had been diverted when making the counterattack. The sprite, held captive, might have sensed her chance. She might have tried to free herself, causing the jet of water. That made sense.

To Cymric it also suggested a course of action. *Learn; most of all learn how to turn your knowledge into power.* The aphorism was one of the few guild teachings Cymric ever heeded. He decided to start learning about the ring of stone above his head; it was the most unusual feature of the well wall. He needed to work whatever he could learn of the well's history, and of the sprite, into his spell. With the additional power, his spell might give the sprite a better chance to free herself.

"Hallo, the wizard!" The blacksmith's voice startled Cymric as the man rattled his staff against the side of the well. Cymric looked up at the blacksmith's broad frame silhouetted against the well opening.

"How goes it?" called down the blacksmith. "Sounded bad just a bit ago."

"Well enough," said Cymric. "I believe your sprite is being held captive. I am working to free her."

"Luwen sent word to ask you how long you're going to be. The dinner hour is near," said the blacksmith.

Cymric looked down at the lime deposits to hide his annoyance. These crude villagers he was forced to work for seldom understood the delicacies of spell magic. They assumed that wizardry was easier than farming. Cymric wiped his expression clean, then looked up and said, "Wizardry is a complicated matter. One cannot state with certainty what is needed, nor when one will be finished."

Cymric saw the silhouette hold its hands out and up near its shoulders. "Calm, wizard. Calm. Luwen only asks because he thinks you would want your dinner hot. Food cannot cook forever."

Cymric closed his eyes and gave himself a silent rebuke, then said, "Tell Luwen I might be a while. I would appreciate a hot meal, and won't mind waiting for it once I'm finished."

"Do you want the mutton or the pork?" asked the blacksmith.

Cymric was distracted by a sudden gurgle of water. He looked down to see an arc of water splash against the stone, then quickly get sucked back in. It looked as if the sprite were struggling. Cymric realized he had not answered the blacksmith's question.

"What do you recommend?" he asked, but had already knelt down to examine the lime. Not even damp

"The pork is more tender, but Luwen has a hardworking sauce for the mutton. I like the mutton," the blacksmith said.

"Fine. The mutton then. Give Luwen my thanks," called Cymric.

The blacksmith grunted, then the silhouette backed away from the well. Cymric heard what he thought was "Here, woman. Take this." No, no, thought Cymric. I didn't mean go tell him right now!

"Blacksmith?" shouted Cymric. A new silhouette appeared at the top of the well.

"Gone, but he'll be back," said the shadow in a woman's voice. Cymric said nothing, looking up with a perplexed expression. The shadow laughed.

"Don't worry, wizard. I can pull you up fast enough to leave your scrawny legs behind. Two tugs, right?" she said. Cymric gave an exaggerated nod. The shadow moved away from the opening.

Cymric looked again at the green ring of stone. Closer examination showed that the stone was actually white, covered by a layer of algae. Taking slack in the rope, he reached up and began to scour one stone clean. The rubbing left a green smear, but Cymric had removed enough to see writing on the stone. He moved methodically to his right, similarly cleaning each stone. The writing bore similarities to the dwarven magician script, but was more fluid, the harsh angles rounded like a stone polished smooth by a swift-running stream. Was the script a combination of the letters used by the old village elementalist and the language of the sprite?

The script was etched only lightly into the stone, and even more difficult to read because of the algae and low lantern light. Cymric blinked and rubbed his eyes. If the writing were magical, it might have an astral component that would be easier to read. He recast the spell to heighten his sense of astral space, then waited, lips pursed in frustration. He still saw nothing but the same black as from the top of the well. But he had another idea that just might work.

He uncapped the vial of ink then carefully applied the ink to the letters using the feather-end of the quill as a crude brush. Darkened with ink, the letters became easily legible. To his surprise, Cymric heard a slight hiss rising from the surface of the stone, saw the ink etching the letters deeper into the stone. This ink must be what Phraetun had used for his enchantment, thought Cymric. It followed the course of the magic.

Though clearly legible, the letters still did not make much sense, even though they obviously formed words. Cymric could make out the word "Phraetun" three times, but he couldn't read the rest because the letters were not in any language he knew. Given time, the wizard would be able to translate them, but that much time he didn't have. Cymric sat down.

What did he know so far? Phraetun and the sprite had made an agreement: the elementalist would protect the sprite from river dangers in exchange for pure water. If anyone ever learned the sprite's name, it would leave the well. Now the sprite was being held prisoner by some form of magic. Perhaps its name was the piece of knowledge Cymric needed to gain the power to free the sprite.

Experience suggested that the ring of stone was the agreement between Phraetun and his sprite, her copy of the contract. Or the contract itself. If that was true, then her name should appear on the contract. In fact, from what Cymric knew of standard guild contracts, the agreeing parties were always mentioned the same number of times. Of

course, sprite contracts might vary, he thought, but he had
to start somewhere.

Cymric read the circle closely, trying to find those
words that appeared only three times, matching the
number of times "Phraetun" appeared. Most likely the
name was part of the phrase "Orichalcer Phraetun Ab
Aquiliria Tisibia Linil," which appeared exactly three
times. Cymric knew that "orichalcer" was derived from
the same magic root as "orichalcum," the most precious of
elemental substances. Was "orichalcer" someone who
worked with orichalcum, such as an elementalist?
"Orichalcer Phraetun" could be "Elementalist Phraetun,"
or another such title. Made sense. Contract symmetry
meant the sprite should be similarly titled. This language
seemed derived from dwarven. If syntax followed that
tongue, "linil" was most likely a verb. The sprite's title
was either "ab aquiliria" or "aquiliria tisibia." But what
kind of title would "ab" be? Going on sound alone, Cymric decided it had to be "aquiliria tisibia." The sprite's
name must be "Tisibia."

That solved part of the problem. Now he had to figure
out a way to survive the backlash from whatever was im-
prisoning the sprite. He could put up a spell to shield him
from attacks from astral space, but such spells did not last
very long. Besides, Cymric wasn't sure he could create a
thread from his knowledge of the sprite before the shield
faded. Again, lacking other options, he decided to cast the
astral shield.

Cymric began to weave the pattern for a spell to disrupt
or eliminate the magic it was cast against. He added the
usual, necessary thread, then turned the word "Tisibia"
over in his mind, combining it with memories of water
sprites. Word and memory spun into a coarse thread,
which Cymric's skill continued to spin until the thread was
fine. He then sought for ways to incorporate the thread
without disrupting the fragile, dimly glowing pattern. He
turned the pattern one way, then rotated it another.

But he must have rotated the pattern too fast. It began
to blur in his mind, lines and discs diffusing into an indistinct glow. Clamping down on his panic, Cymric managed

to relax just enough to touch up the image in his mind's eye. Eyes closed, licking his lips, he stabilized the pattern. A faint smile tugged at his lips.

Now Cymric saw a possible point to start the weave, a spot near the center of the pattern where it most resembled a rounded latticework of tightly packed triangles, something like the center of a queensflower. His first attempt was uneven, and the thread tangled itself.

Burn in netherflames! he thought. Cymric coaxed the thread free, and looked at the pattern from another angle. Though dimly aware that his astral shield had now lapsed, he was too deeply involved in spell-weaving to worry about it. He tried further out along the pattern, putting the thread through a simple over-and-under. This time, the weaving took. Cymric carefully applied the thread along the whole pattern, fusing the name, the image, and the idea of "someone knowing the name of Tisibia the water sprite allows her to leave this well" with his magic. Weaving finished, Cymric cast the spell.

Water suddenly roared around him, surging past him in a rush toward the top of the well. The torrent knocked the staff from his hands, carrying it toward the surface. The flood also shattered the sides of his lantern, leaving him in darkness. Water spun him, tangling him with the rope, but he somehow worked one arm free and tugged twice on the rope, as hard as he could. Immediately he began to rise to the surface.

Then, just as quickly, he was pulled back down to the bottom of the well. The pull was so powerful that the only thing that kept him from losing consciousness was the cushion the water provided against the blow to his hips and back. The pain was enough to suck Cymric's attention from all his other senses. An involuntary gasp ended in a choking snort of water.

Gradually he again became aware of his astral sense. The spell still functioned, and now he had something to see. Extending several paces in either direction was an astral construct glowing like burnished copper in the noonday sun. It resembled a seven-limbed starfish, except that the limbs made a sweeping curve as they radiated outward.

The limbs consisted of three helices woven closer and closer together until they joined at the tips. Inside each limb was a faint yellow glow that sloshed around within the confines of the limb. The center of the construct formed a series of barbed branches, like a stylized rendition of a row of barren rose bushes. The astral images of dozens of the branches pierced Cymric's body, the branches curling backward to form hooks.

The creature thrashed its limbs twice, releasing some of the yellow ick. The area where the yellow ick spread became black to Cymric's astral senses. He was left with only his normal senses, pinned under dark water at the bottom of a well.

Another determined tug on the rope from above jerked Cymric up from the stones. Again, the creature yanked him back down against the pull of the rope, the impact knocking some air out of Cymric's lungs. He watched as bubbles of his life's breath broke from the darkness, rising through the cool blue near the top of the well.

3

Another sustained pull from the rope shot splinters of agony through Cymric's body as he rose a few feet in the air. Pinwheels of painful light arced across his field of vision. He struggled against the desire to scream, a small corner of his mind fiercely reminding him that he was underwater. Water moved through his crooked fingers, flowed past his face. He was still, unmoving. Water pressed against his ears, and his hair streamed backward as he was lifted upward. Cymric felt stretched taut in the front, stretched somehow thin. Sparks ignited in his back as muscles clenched. His muscles were trying, and failing, to hold something in place.

The pull on the rope stopped. An air bubble escaped Cymric's nose with a ticklish pop, rolling up his cheek on its way to the surface. His body floated slowly back down to the well bottom. The tautness in front released; simultaneously he felt the muscles in his back relax.

What was happening? Cymric's awareness had split, as if there were two of him rather than one. One of him rose with the pull of the rope. The other stayed where he was at the bottom of the well. Cymric felt his body settle, legs first, onto the well bottom. He sensed that he was once again whole.

The creature has hold of my spirit. The villagers have hold of my body. Freeing the sprite had given the other entity an opportunity to capture another victim, and it had seized the closest available spirit. Cymric thought of what he had seen of the creature. The jagged hooks in the center of its astral body looked too big to be intended for human spirit—or the spirits of water sprites. Unfortunately, they worked quite well against smaller prey.

The villagers and the spiritcatcher are involved in a tug of war. Cymric easily imagined the villagers' increasingly desperate efforts to pull him out of the well, lifting his body while his spirit remained in the maw of the creature. Each renewal of the contest would strain the life threads that bound Cymric's body to his spirit. The physical efforts of the villagers would have no effect on the astral spiritcatcher. They would never be able to pull him out, not until death separated his spirit from his body and the entity had Cymric's spirit forever. Then the villagers would pop his corpse from the well like a cork from a bottle.

Cymric readied a spell. Disrupting the magic had freed the sprite; perhaps it could also free him. Another wave of pain interrupted his casting; the tug of war was on again. The spell unraveled in his mind, dissipating with no effect. Pain made the work impossible. This time the contest was much shorter. The pulling stopped. Perhaps the villagers were giving up on the idea of saving the wizard.

Now Cymric tried a quick spell, pulling a pattern whole from his mind, one that did not need astral threads to complete it. A sliver of light formed in astral space, and Cymric flung it at the creature. The mind dagger struck the spiritcatcher.

The creature began to thrash wildly, tossing Cymric around the bottom of the well like a seal in the mouth of a shark. He managed to protect his head, but the rest of his body was less fortunate. Water churned violently. Reverberating sluicing noises punctuated by the thump of a knee hitting stone or the crack of a wrist flung against a wall.

Cymric convulsed once, expelling stale breath in a burst of bubbles. Concentration was becoming more difficult. His heartbeat became a thick, physical presence in his chest and ears. His desire to breathe weighted evenly with his common sense at the folly of inhaling underwater. Cymric knew the balance would soon tilt. He had time for one, maybe two, spells.

Learn to turn your knowledge into power. What did he

know about the entity? Not much. It existed soley on the astral plane. It relied on magic to affect the physical world. It had hold of his spirit. Cymric tried to relax, to conserve air. The arrangement of hooks in the entity's maw were set into a complicated pattern. Perhaps the pattern in the maw matched the pattern of a specific spirit. If so, the spirit-catcher had captured a spirit it was not meant to capture. Unless the bakers of Tuakan had superior magics to those Cymric had seen.

Let me go, you've got the wrong spirit, he thought. This knowledge might be too frail to spin into a thread, but it was all Cymric had to work with.

The knowledge produced a thread so wispy and elusive that Cymric could barely distinguish it from the surrounding blackness. His skill allowed him to detect a bend here, a weakness there; the thread did not look strong. Cymric clamped down on his thoughts. Adding the weight of his doubts to the thread could snap it before thread ever touched pattern.

Cymric again called up the pattern for dispelling magic. The pattern was blurry, particularly around the edges. But, no, the pattern never changed, only his perception of the pattern. He must better focus his mind. Ah, now the pattern looked a little clearer. Cymric placed the thread where he could, using fewer knots than would normally be prudent, but he was in a hurry.

His fingers objected to being spread in the right way to release the spell, and it felt as if he had to lock each digit into place individually. There. He had it. Cymric poured every scrap of mental energy he had into the spell.

The spiritcatcher reacted as if shocked. There was a brief stab of pain, then Cymric felt the creature release him, then back away. The wizard's muddled mind enjoyed the sense of relief, while another firm corner of his thoughts tried to remind him there was still something very important to do.

Get to the surface. Cymric kicked off the bottom of the well. He rose several feet, then his legs cramped violently. Fighting panic, he remembered the rope. Two tugs and they would pull him up. He tugged once, pulling three or four feet of loose rope down to him. Another frantic grab produced more rope.

This isn't happening. The villagers can't have given up. Desperately, unable to think clearly, Cymric panic-climbed the rope, going nowhere, pulling yard after yard of rope down to him. His right arm cramping as his legs had, Cymric tried to swim with just his left arm, but he didn't have the strength to move. He began to settle back down to the bottom.

Something lashed his face. Dimly he thought the spiritcatcher had returned to reclaim him. Then a hard jerk pulled him upward, and Cymric realized the lash had been the slack rope being hauled up with considerable speed. But he couldn't hold his breath any longer. Involuntary reactions won. As the last of the air exploded from his lungs, Cymric inhaled a choking gasp of water.

He broke the surface at good speed, his right shoulder catching against the crossbeam, which sent him twisting around. As momentum swung him, his feet rose above the crossbeam. The twisting motion spun his legs out, over the rim of the well. The villagers stopped pulling. His legs hit against the wall, and his head and torso began to fall back into the well.

"Pull! Don't lose him now!" shouted a woman. The villagers pulled. Cymric slapped up against the crossbeam, pinned by the force of the pull.

"Easy. Don't crack his skull after all this," said the woman. "Hold him there. I'll lift him out." As Cymric coughed up water, he heard the sound of approaching boots. A strong arm encircled his the waist.

"I've got you," said the woman in crystal chain. "Let go of the rope," she commanded the villagers, and they did. Then she lifted him up with a smooth motion, trying to land Cymric on his feet. The lift was good, but Cymric's legs refused to work and he slumped to the ground. The woman made sure the fall was slow enough to do no further damage.

Cymric gasped, his lungs working like the bellows of a dwarven weaponsmith. Legs sprawled, he leaned his head against the well, his eyes lifting wearily toward the woman. The rings of her armor caught and bent the fiery red of the light of late day. He couldn't read her shadowed face, but those arms and the runes on her sword spoke plainly enough. An adept. Definitely a swordmaster. Probably a very good one.

"Is he going to live?" bubbled a voice. Cymric turned his head in the other direction. He looked at the face of the sprite, set into the statue. Its face moved with the sound of thick syrup pouring from a narrow container, reforming at a different angle, the better to look at Cymric.

"I am no physik, but I think our wizard's going to make it," the swordmaster said.

"I asked the water not to drown you. I did my best, but water is water," the sprite said. There was that syrupy sound again, and the sprite was studying Cymric closely. "I think the creature is gone. I know what you had to do to free me. My thanks." The sprite continued to stare at him.

Cymric guessed that the sprite knew he knew her name. Cymric wanted to say that her secret was safe with him, that he had no desire to bind a water sprite to his service. He also wanted to thank her for her help, to talk to the sprite, to ask her about the spiritcatcher. But he didn't have enough energy. Instead, he said, "I'm leaving soon. You may stay."

The answer seemed to satisfy the sprite. The sprite smiled at Cymric, her expression turning itself inside out with a slurp as she went back down into the well.

The blacksmith came over carrying Cymric's staff, which was still wet. The woman hauled Cymric to his feet. Dizziness laced with pain moved in a wave down his body, but he managed to remain upright.

"This came up a little before you did," said the blacksmith, handing Cymric his staff.

Taking it gingerly, Cymric said, "Sometime's a wizard's staff knows when to quit before the wizard does." He sagged against the staff for support.

"Thought we'd lost you, wizard," said the blacksmith, inspecting Cymric as closely as the swordmaster was doing.

"Before you paid me? Never," said Cymric. His smile wouldn't bend quite right, but he was determined to tough it out. At least until the villagers no longer provided an audience.

The swordmaster looked doubtful. "Wizard, I've pulled boys from bear baiting pits who looked better than you do," she said.

Cymric dismissed the comment with a wave of his hand, saying, "We wizards are a resourceful lot." He gave the swordmaster a firmer smile. In return she cricked the right corner of her mouth and raised her left eyebrow. Cymric decided not to waste any more energy trying to convince her. He had a show to close. He gathered his thoughts, tailoring old words to new circumstances.

"Gentlefolk of Twin Chin, hear me! A fell creature indeed inhabited your well, holding your sprite prisoner. Cymric the wizard descended into the well to battle the creature. Down there Cymric learned wisdom from your own elementalist, Phraetun! Cymric forged Phraetun's wisdom of years past into a mighty enchantment. Cymric and the creature smote each other, but in the end, Cymric's enchantment won out. Cymric the wizard has returned, triumphant!"

"Only 'cause we hauled you out like a pig stuck in quickmud," said a farm hand. Cymric's vision wavered, but of those whose expressions he could see, most looked decidedly unimpressed by Cymric's rhetoric.

Perhaps this is not an event upon which to build the legend of Cymric. Smiling ruefully, he nodded to the farm hand.

"I'll tell Luwen to get your supper ready," said the blacksmith. He turned away, took a stride, but then turned back again. "I'll go see Mayor Drofin and the others too. I'll have your money for you by morning."

Cymric nodded, and the blacksmith went on his way. The wizard closed his eyes for a moment. He hurt. He couldn't face a tavern full of people yet. He needed a few moments by himself.

He saw a boy laboring to carry a pair of full buckets across the center of town. Then the boy paused, lowering the buckets for a rest. He glanced at the well, did a double take. Then slowly took in the soaked wizard leaning on a wet staff.

"You got the sprite back?" asked the boy.

Cymric nodded. The boy grinned. "Mama told me to go down to the river to fetch some water quick. I told her the wizard was fixing our well, but she sent me anyway. Mama was wrong."

"Apparently," said the weary wizard.

The boy kicked up some dust with the first four steps of a sprint, then reconsidered, going back to the buckets. The wizard blinked.

"Where were you off to?" Cymric asked. The boy grunted, lifting the two buckets before replying.

"Davil and some others are still down by the river, filling barrels in a cart. I was just going to tell them they could stop," the boy said.

Cymric saw his chance. "You go on home with your water. I'll go down to the river and tell the others," he said.

"Just wait until I tell Mama you did it," the boy said in high-pitched excitement. Then his expression clouded. "If I do, she'll cuff me for talking smart to her."

"She probably already knows about the well," Cymric said. Then he lowered his head and gave the boy his best conspiratorial smile, "In case she *doesn't* know, you might want to fill up your buckets with the fresh, clean well water. Don't say anything to her. Just give her the water. She'll know the difference."

The boy took a moment to puzzle this out, then his face brightened again. He kicked over his two buckets, then began drawing water from the well. Cymric began to walk out of town in the direction of the river.

His slow pace changed to a hobble when he reached the gentle incline at the edge of town. His right knee was flaming with pain, and his right wrist couldn't take much weight. His calves continued to cramp. His back refused to bend. Neither hip seemed inclined to move. Cymric paused for breath. The rest was welcome, but breathing still produced a raw burning in his lungs. He set his eyes on the top of the hill, gauging the number of steps it would take to reach the crest. He began to count.

At thirty-one steps, the slope reversed. Cymric hobbled, then stumbled downhill. Once out of sight of the village, he stopped. Sliding his hands down his staff for support, Cymric dropped to the ground cross-legged. He had to wait a few moments for the ragged gasping of his breath to calm down. Then, still holding his staff with his left hand, he reached for a side pouch with his right. He winced; his wrist wouldn't bend enough for him to put his hand in the pouch.

Cymric laid his staff across his knees, then fumbled through the pouch with his left hand. When he found what he was looking for, the herbs had become a sopping wet wad. The silver-green leaves had been tied off into the proper dosages, but were now hopelessly matted together. Cymric pulled off what he thought was a single dose, reconsidered and pulled off half-again as much. Taking a mouthful, he wondered if the soaking might have diluted the power of the herbs, whose bitter-burnt taste was less offensive than usual. The wizard closed his eyes and waited for the pain to ease.

Stupidity rarely has to be invited twice. The villagers had said the well was inhabited by a sprite. He'd known the well would still have contained water if the sprite had simply left. Which meant something had to be holding the sprite. Cymric hadn't been prepared for it, and it had nearly killed him. He grimaced.

The beating the spiritcatcher gave me was plenty, thank you. No need to add to it myself. Cymric lay back against the ground. It could also have been a curse on the well— the spirit holding a petty grudge perhaps. It really shouldn't have been an enormous astral spiritcatcher. Astral entities didn't make a habit of lurking in the wells of small villages.

Cymric's knee now signaled a persistent, but distant, ache. He tried his wrist and flinched; better wait a little longer. He thought more about the spiritcatcher. He'd have thought an astral creature of that size would have to be magically summoned or could only exist in areas of high enchantment. Phraetun's pact with the sprite couldn't possibly have been a sufficient point of entry for a spiritcatcher. Unless Phraetun was more of an elementalist than Cymric imagined, but he still didn't think so.

He sat up. Pain no longer dominated his senses, but was reduced now to an occasional, throbbing reminder of injury. He stood up, powering his rise primarily with his left arm and leg. After gingerly tested his right leg, which seemed solid enough, Cymric continued his walk to the river.

I freed the sprite. I freed myself. I'm getting paid . . . not a fortune, but I'm getting paid. The smile started on the right side of Cymric's face. By the time he reached the river, the smile had evened out. About forty yards from the river he saw seven adolescent boys and girls hauling water to a large two-wheeled cart, which already held four huge barrels. A series of deep ruts closer to the river told Cymric that they'd parked the cart on soft ground during a previous trip. Dozens of footprints and churned-up mud surrounded the ruts. It must have been some task to free the cart.

On the way to the river, Cymric had refined his speech to make it sound more impressive. He opened his mouth. Seven pairs of muddy feet stopped moving. Seven tired, dirty faces regarded him with varying expressions. A girl pushed an errant strand of brown hair behind one ear, but the strand only flopped forward again. She let it go.

Cymric realized just how tired he was and exhaled loudly. "I am a wizard," he said. "I freed your sprite. Your well works. Go on home."

The cheer caught Cymric by surprise; then the group tipped and emptied one barrel and sent a couple of buckets flying into the air. One of the boys turned to Cymric, giving him a stiff-armed salute with his fist from the chest into the air. It was one of the worst imitations of the Throal honor salute Cymric had ever seen, but he enjoyed it anyway. The youngsters grabbed the cart, urging him to join them in a chorus of voice. The girl with the brown hair was pushing on the back of the cart. She patted the back of it and waved to Cymric to take a seat. Cymric jogged to the cart. He jumped in with a half-twist, landing with a thump. The youngsters whooped their approval, but Cymric's body was pointedly reminding him of his injuries. The cart lurched forward.

Cymric blinked. Out on the river, the current eddied to form a pool that continued to expand. As the young people joked with one another, working up the courage to question the wizard, Cymric cast a spell. They heard the casting. Quieting suddenly, they became very attentive about pushing the cart. Cymric again enhanced his astral sense. He ignored the cart's jostling to see a blot of black beneath the water. As the cart's wheels creaked toward Twin Chin, Cymric watched the spiritcatcher travel south along the river.

4

Cymric slumped happily against the padding of a high-backed chair, his left arm dangling off the chair arm, the fingers of his right tracing circles around the rim of a drained beer mug. The light spell he'd cast inside the mug dimmed and brightened in accordance with his concentration, which made his face tingle pleasantly. Cymric experimented with the touch of his right hand, trying to produce a matching tingle in his fingers. Just then an ork with a leather collar, probably a tanner, shouted his name and pointed to a mug with a full head of foam. Cymric bent from the waist, sweeping his left hand back in mockery of a courtier's bow.

A serving girl grabbed the mug, clacked it onto a tray already laden with a loaf of bread, and delivered both to his table. While serving, she showed a bit more shoulder, a little more movement of her hair, than before. Cymric's smile grew to a full grin to see that she'd certainly cleaned up well from the river-mud. *Just practicing her wiles on some new blood.* She turned away, but first gave him a quick over-the-shoulder smile. Her glance met his for perhaps half a heartbeat, then slid away as her smile grew; the move ended with a head-turn and a spirited toss of her hair. Cymric felt a few tingles not inspired by the beer; it looked like she'd soon be giving the boys of Twin Chin a bit of trouble. A few more beers and I could be in trouble too, he thought, still watching the girl as she reached forward for the bread.

But as quickly as he picked up the bread, he dropped it again, flinching at the three rapid stabs of pain penetrating points in his upper chest and back. Changing hands, he

carefully hooked his beer mug with his right thumb, then
slid it across the table toward him. Lowering his head to
drink, he slurped noisily at the foamy head. It was all a
show while he tried to calm his ragged breathing, give his
eyes time to stop watering from pain. The spiritcatcher had
injured him far beyond what a few good beers could
numb, but with his room and board here at the Greens, a
few days' rest should take care of everything.

Cymric looked again at the serving girl. *A few days
should be enough as long as he did nothing to make things
worse.* Probably best to slow down on the beer, too. He silently recited one of his teacher's most frequent proverbs:
Tattered judgement causes more hurt than a battered body.
His body hurt enough.

Shifting his weight as he reached with his left arm got
Cymric the bread. He held it in his right hand, tore a piece
free with his left. The bread was warm, a little doughy and
underdone, the taste good, familiar. As a young apprentice,
how often Cymric had braved a hot oven to carve out a
hunk of loaf even before Master Iveston had pronounced it
ready. He'd prided himself that the holes he made would
not be visible to the baker simply by looking into the
oven; Cymric had considered it a special talent. Apparently Master Iveston did not, for he sold Cymric's apprenticeship to the troll-wizard Brathaks.

Cymric sipped his beer, contemplating his next stop.
The jowly dwarven merchant had told him of Theran trouble upriver near Hadis Town, although tavern regulars dis-
agreed as to how far south the trouble went. Ogres had
been seen moving across river to Corthy. Leather-ork had
mentioned scorchers roaming the eastern road. Havel was
already out because of the oft-mentioned evil-magician rumors. Downriver lay Marrek, a city-state nominally allied
with Throal, but open-minded enough to trade with everyone. That sounded like a promising destination, but Cymric lacked coin for the boat downriver. He sighed. Walking
seemed an unwizardly way to travel.

"May I join you?" Cymric's eyes flicked up to meet the
steady gaze of the woman in crystal chainmail, the one
he'd earlier thought was sheriff of Twin Chin. Her expres-

sion was stolid, too neutral for him to read. Her brown hair was tied back from her face with a silver ring, her sword tied to its sheath with a peace bond. Cymric put on a mock frown.

"I believe the owner has reserved this table for solitary spellcasters," he said, leaning forward while trying to favor his left side to avoid pain. In his best conspiratorial manner, he whispered, "But I think we can break the rules, just this once."

The woman's mouth twitched upward only on its right side, and only for an instant. If that's a smile, Cymric thought, this could be a long conversation. The woman nodded, then took a seat opposite him. Opening her eyes wide and arching her brows, she gestured to the bread with her left hand, palm up and out. At Cymric's nod of permission, she broke off a big piece, then swallowed a third of it in one bite.

Cymric took an exaggerated swig of his beer, watching her chew hungrily and noticing a small brass medallion worked into the left shoulder of her armor. Some Throalic noble must have thought highly enough of her to buy her that crystal chain. He observed that her lean face was tanned and weathered; she might be seven or eight years his senior. A white scar curved from her upper right lip to her nose. Sinewy hands tore off another piece of bread. She regarded Cymric intently while taking another bite. Of course, he thought. A long conversation required someone to start talking.

"I don't believe we've been introduced. I am Cymric, the wizard who just today destroyed a fell creature infesting the well of this fair village."

The woman hurried to wipe the crumbs from her mouth, perhaps to conceal a sudden smile. She turned toward the serving girl, snapping her fingers loudly enough to attract the girl's attention and startle Cymric. The girl hurried over, her smile now neutral as her eyes shifted back and forth from Cymric to the woman. The girl's attention finally settled on the woman.

"Bring two whitewaters for the wizard and myself." The serving girl's smile brightened. Whitewaters were expensive drinks, implying the possibility of a decent tip. The words piqued Cymric's interest as well. This conversation might turn out to be worthwhile after all. If nothing else, he'd never tried a whitewater, and someone else would be paying for his new experience.

The woman turned back to Cymric. "I am Leandra. I am interested in hiring a wizard." She stood and extended her hand. Cymric half-rose to shake it, noting that the muscles of her arm were well-defined from what must be an indecent amount of work. Calluses protected her sword hand as armor protected the rest of her.

Aggravating injury as little as possible, he pulled his hand away slowly. "Are you a swordmaster?"

Leandra sat back down and nodded. The serving girl returned with two tall, partially filled glasses, a bowl of whitewater crystals, and a decanter. She took the empty mug, and placed the new items on the table. Leandra three-fingered some silver pieces from her money pouch, then dropped seven of them onto the table. Several of the coins rang out as they bounced against the mug. The girl curtsied to Leandra, and bounced happily away.

"I need a wizard who can read, a wizard who can decipher ancient texts." Leandra split the whitewater crystals into two even piles. "I need a wizard who can stand a little taste of danger," she said, plopping the crystals into the liquor in the two mugs, then adding fluid from the decanter. The drinks began to fizz and bubble, foam spilling over the rims. Leandra pushed one toward Cymric. "Think you're qualified?"

Cymric touched his left hand to his forehead in salute, taking the glass with his other hand. Whitewater had a mysterious reputation; everyone said you had to understand it rather than merely drink it. He resolved to try it slowly. "More detail about your needs would help me decide whether I am qualified for your task," he said.

Leandra nodded, then took a solid swig from her mug while Cymric took a less ambitious swallow. When she had taken her big drink, Leandra laid her hands on the table, the fingers cupping, but not really touching, the glass.

Cymric thought the intensity of the energy in those hands could shatter the glass with one finger if she happened to brush it. "I'm after a calendar, a ritual calendar. The writings on that calendar contain a history that is very important to me. I need a wizard to decode that history."

Cymric tilted his whitewater back some more. There were the standard questions he should ask, but they dissipated in the bubbles of his drink. He looked down at the glass and back up at Leandra, then nodded sagely to cover his confusion. "Anything you wish to ask of me? About my qualifications?"

"Perhaps a little something about your travels."

Cymric hesitated the merest fraction of a second. What was it he'd said during his spiel by the well? It would be best not to contradict earlier claims. A look at Leandra's eyes convinced him that she would tolerate less embellishment of his past than the townsfolk had.

"I solved the riddle of Chandler's Cross when I was but an apprentice."

"Wizards' puzzles mean nothing to me."

Great, Cymric thought. So much for my most legitimate achievement.

"I descended into Kaer Irsoi and returned. Of the six in my party, I was one of only three survivors."

"Did you learn anything from the kaer? Secure any treasure?"

Yes, I learned that shadowmants move too fast to let you carry much treasure out of a kaer. I was happy to get out alive. Cymric gave Leandra his best cryptic-wizard's smile, "I secured enough to content me."

Leandra finished her drink. "Kaer Irsoi is just on the other side of the Throal Mountains. Travel much outside of this area?"

No, but I've probably read more than you have traveled. "I have traveled over much of Barsaive, from Parlainth to Jerris, even south as far as Skypoint."

"Skypoint? Tell me about it."

Cymric took the bare threads of his knowledge and started to weave a bold fabrication. "The Theran outpost is a monstrous city suspended above the ground on three colossal metal legs. The city is limited to Therans, their slaves, and a few chosen representatives from the people living below. All the tribes and other peoples who ally with the Therans live in a ramshackle city built underneath the sky city. Theran skyships dock at all hours of the day and night. Elemental magicians scour the ships clean of impurities, dumping the residue overboard onto the undercity. Only the rich can afford to keep their buildings free of the fine ash from the ships, but very few of them live in the undercity."

Leandra's eyes hooded and fluttered. Cymric halted his tale. Was she envisioning the scene? Her face tweaked into a smile, which then widened to become a sharp gasp. Her armor jangled from a jerk of her body. Then her eyes snapped open. She stared hard at Cymric, closing her mouth into a rueful smile.

"Sorry," she said. "I'm back . . . You were saying? The undercity?"

. . . is not nearly so interesting as whatever you just saw.

"The most fascinating part of the city is the dark market, which is held in a spot constantly shadowed by the sky city overhead. There are the usual slaves, gaudy wares, and opiates. Swarthy dwarfs sell basilisk organs, some of which are genuine." Cymric fell into form, hunching to play the part of a dwarf merchant, miming the transaction.

"Tattooed Uzhbek shamans hawk summoning tomes from before the Scourge, with blood magic contracts to assure proper use. Troll-crones urge you to take a look at recently acquired 'heirlooms.' Your eyes behold silver braids silver gleaming with enchanted crystals in the elven style, your ears fill with ork entreaties to buy, while the basil and cumin of the Azvan cooking fires carry on the breeze."

Cymric stopped. A moment ago, he had felt a fresh breeze on his face. He looked at Leandra. She was speaking, but the words were lost in a sudden roar coming from all around him. He blinked, then opened his eyes just as he hit the water face-first. The bracing chill sent a jolt along his limbs and spine. *Where did the tavern go?* The wizard bobbed to the surface, sputtered, tried to get his bearings.

The rapidly moving water carried him along, bouncing him from rock to rock, spinning him in the current. The roar thrummed in his head. The current kept him whirling. Not five body-lengths away, a huge fall of water was pouring over the edge of a precipice. Cymric knew that he screamed, but couldn't hear the sound over the water's thunder. He windmilled desperately as he plunged down with the water, then hit the pool under the waterfall.

Bubbles tingled off Cymric's skin as he sluiced along the bottom. Finally the roar of the waterfall dulled, and he found himself in quieter water. Light rippled across the surface a few feet above him, and he swam toward it, not so much moving through the water as the water sliding over his skin. It seemed to carry away his fatigue and much of the pain from his injury. Breaking the surface, Cymric took a deep breath of the freshest air he had ever inhaled. He splashed both arms out of the water, and let out a joyful whoop.

He blinked water from his eyes and when he opened them again, he was braced against the back of his chair, arms raised over his head. Leandra was sitting with her head down, eyes studying the hawk's-head pommel of her sword. Every one of the patrons in the place was staring at Cymric when suddenly the leather-ork began to applaud loudly. Others joined him. Cymric lowered his arms, and shrank into his seat at the hooting that accompanied the applause. He glanced over at Leandra. *Damn.* Her expression looked one part angry and two parts ugly. The prospect of walking to Marrek suddenly looked more likely. As the crowd quieted down, Leandra exhaled, long and slow. Cymric cleared his throat, swallowed, and tried to salvage the situation.

"My sword lady, I congratulate you on your good fortune. Embarrassed wizards have been known to work for reduced rates."

Leandra's face locked into an expression that instilled quiet terror in Cymric. *Sorry, sword lady. Thanks for the drink, but how about you just let me slink away with all my fingers still attached?* That Leandra's left hand was tapping the pommel of her sword didn't make Cymric feel any better.

"You could have told me you'd never tried whitewater before."

The wizard's glib response died on his lips, impaled on Leandra's gaze.

"Cymric, I need a wizard. The wizard I need will not tell me what he thinks I want to hear. He will not tell me what he feels like saying. He will tell me the truth."

Cymric's head buzzed. Apparently whitewater had some aftereffects. Perhaps it was the alcohol and the injuries. His embarrassment faded, replaced by dull anger. Emotion added an edge to his voice.

"The truth is I sell knowledge," he said. "When negotiating a deal, it's stupid to open with an admission of ignorance. When making your sellsword pitch, do you begin with a confession of all the strokes and moves you *cannot* do?"

Leandra considered for a moment. "It's not the same thing, wizard." She raised a hand to cut off his reply. "But I see your point. Perhaps we should just start over from the beginning."

Leandra turned and snapped her fingers at the serving girl. "Two tall ales for the wizard and myself." She turned back to Cymric.

"I am the swordmaster Leandra. I am looking for a wizard who can read an ancient calendar. A knack for killing well-dwellers would be a plus."

Cymric bowed, a move that made his head swim. "You are in luck, swordmaster. I am just such a wizard." The serving girl replaced the whitewater glasses with tankards of dark ale. Leandra hoisted hers, clanked it against the unsteady one in Cymric's hand. She drained half her mug. Cymric did the same, realizing only several swallows too late that it was the wrong thing to do.

"I can pay well."

Uh oh, thought Cymric. Another one of those questions I forgot to ask. Your brain must be really addled, wizard, he scolded himself. The smile on his face felt lopsided. "I would be most interested in knowing the amount of that payment."

Leandra pulled a necklace from her pouch. The silvery chain gleamed, reflecting light from unseen sources. Hanging from the chain was a gold and silver hand grasping a crystal sphere. He leaned forward, ignoring the pain in his side. Inside the sphere was a rune, green as the shallow sea. As he watched, the rune slowly changed shape, a rhythmic motion that fascinated him. The necklace was not flash-and-spell magic. It was deep magic, and it stirred an equally deep hunger within Cymric. The sphere wavered, and Cymric realized his vision was losing focus. He forced his eyes to work again, but his efforts to sit back up were unsuccessful.

He heard the scrape of a chair, felt Leandra's grip steady and lift him. She continued to hold the necklace in her other hand. Cymric found his feet.

"Cymric, you find out what I need, you bring me to the fulfillment of this mission, and the necklace is yours. But you must see me through to the end. Do you understand?"

Cymric nodded vaguely. Leandra shook her head and slipped the necklace back into her pouch. Cymric was still leaning against her, his cheek mashed up against the crystal links covering her shoulder. The armor was cold and sharp, indenting and scraping his face.

"Luwen, have you the key for the wizard's room?"

The innkeeper tossed a key to Leandra. She caught it with her left while using her right to guide Cymric toward the stairs. He straightened a bit, then stumbled on the first step.

"Where did the necklace come from?"

Leandra's grip tightened. "I don't know," she said. "I've had it for as long as I can remember."

5

Cymric slid the chamber pot into the corner of the room near the foot of his bed, then looked about for the pitcher of water to rinse out his mouth. He looked past his wizard's robe draped over his backpack and staff near the head of his bed, then glanced too quickly over his shoulder. Swiveling his head so abruptly brought the dizziness back, but Cymric spotted his quarry on a small table near the door. The pitcher shone brightly in the morning sun streaming through the bedside window. Cymric couldn't remember anyone entering the room to bring him the pitcher, but then he didn't remember taking off his robe either. The young wizard thanked his unseen benefactor, then plotted his approach to the pitcher.

Sliding his fingers along the rough plaster wall, Cymric covered the distance in four unsteady steps. Then he grabbed the pitcher with both hands and held the cool metal to his forehead. That dulled the ache, but didn't cure it. Thinking more coolness would help, he leaned his back against the wall and poured some water over his head. All that did was drive a wedge of pain from his temple to his jaw, forcing a short, sputtering cry from Cymric that was as much indignation as pain. Water dripped from his black hair and trickled down his bare chest, warming a little by the time it soaked into his codpiece. Not the best start he'd ever had to a morning.

Cymric took three or four sips from the pitcher. Encouraged by the refreshment, he drank until his stomach sent up a gurgle and a ripple of nausea. He was trying to decide between going back to the bed and curling up in the sunbeam by the door when he heard two firm, loud knocks followed by a third, more tentative one at the door. Cymric huffed, shook a shower of drops from his hair, then opened the door.

Sunlight danced and reflected from the hundreds of rings in Leandra's armor as though it were woven from rainbows and ice instead of crystal chain. Reflections also flared from the pommel of her sword, and sparks of sunlight played along loose strands of her hair. She stood in the doorway, left arm bent and up, hand curled around the doorframe, the light framing, accentuating, the darkness of her eyes. She was a strong, lovely vision, for which Cymric decided to hate her at least until noon.

"Sorry if I woke you. I heard sounds from your room. I thought you might be up."

"That was me retching, a sound very few people take to mean 'good morning, won't you please come in.'."

"Foolish when drunk, nasty when hung over?"

"Oh, this has *nothing* to do with a hangover. I accidentally dumped a pitcher of water on myself. After yesterday, I'm just a little testy when wet."

"Ale and whitewater don't mix. Especially if you're not used to it. I've ordered breakfast for us."

"Thank you so much, but nothing for me."

Leandra dropped her hand from the doorframe, and began to tap the pommel of her sword. Her expression remained soft, but something about the tapping made Cymric decidedly nervous. She was looking past him, out the window, then slowly returned her gaze to him. Cymric countered with as much of his foul mood as he could get his face to show, but Leandra's only response was one of her quick-tic smiles.

"I thought we made a deal last night."

"My impressions of last night are less certain."

"If we have a deal, get your gear together. And if you plan to eat, better hurry; the cinnamon things are going fast. Then again, if we haven't got a deal, I wish you good times while waiting for the Marrek trade to arrive." Leandra clicked her heels together, bowing curtly before turning to leave. Cymric leaned his head against the door as she strode down the hall. It was not until one of her boots had thumped hollowly on the first step that Cymric called out to her. She paused, turning to face him.

"I don't remember all of last night, but I remember your saying something about needing a wizard and the truth."

Leandra nodded, then creaked back up the stair to face him. She stood staring for a moment, and Cymric decided he must look almost as bad as he felt. She took a few steps forward.

"Truth is . . . truth is the wizard you want to hire was mauled by that thing in the well. It left no physical marks, but it tore through me. I'm not in traveling shape. Not for another couple of days, that is."

Leandra shifted her weight, looked across the hallway for a few heartbeats, then back at Cymric. "My truth is that I am in grave need of a wizard's help. I don't know how much time I can spare. My instinct says not much. If I could shake some healing salves out of Mayor Drofin, would you be willing to travel?"

Cymric thought. Healing salves sounded very appealing. Traveling today did not. Unraveling ancient texts for a tidy profit sounded good. Waiting for the Marrek trade to resume did not.

"How far are we going?"

"First stop, Corthy. Four days' walk. Five, if we take it easy. I'm willing to take it easy."

"Done." Cymric extended his hand. Leandra gripped it, smiling for longer than Cymric had seen until now.

"One request, and then I shall become your humble wizard. Could you ask the kitchen to send my breakfast up? I'd like to rest as much as possible before we leave."

"Consider it done." Leandra turned to leave, again pausing on the first step down. Cymric caught that tic-smile of hers even before she'd turned back to face him.

"Better get some clothes on before somebody comes, though. Wizards are more impressive when wearing their robes." Cymric snorted. Leandra shook her head. "Nothing personal. Your feat in the well earned you a few coins of reputation. No need to spend it on the giggling gossip of the kitchen help." She disappeared down the stairs as Cymric turned the advice over in his mind.

Cymric descended in boots and robe made fresh by a new illusion, which also helped hide his surly mood. He must have just missed the last cinnamon roll, but the bread had been good. The pepper sausage, on the other hand, wasn't doing his digestion any favors.

Waiting for him were Leandra, Mayor Drofin, and the tavern-keeper. The mayor wore a shiny new kimono, but the tavern-keep had on the same dirty smock and greasy clothes from yesterday. Mayor Drofin thanked Cymric in a speech that wasn't too long and misused only a few words. The tavern-keeper handed him an ale skin, and said that Leandra had the bread and cheese. Cymric slipped the skin into his pack, noting that Leandra's was bigger and better stuffed than his. As they were leaving, Cymric decided to make it a dramatic exit by casting another flame flash— and this time it did look like a sylph. The image even managed to blow a clumsy kiss to the mayor, who looked as though he might turn the experience into a week's worth of preening.

Following the path that led from town out toward the river, Cymric and Leandra were on their way. The late morning sun had warmed the ground, and flying insects swarmed around them in a feverish buzz. Then the breeze brought up the smell of water even before they caught sight of the river. They were descending toward a spot marked by wagon ruts when a thought caught Cymric up short. He waved Leandra to a halt. Moving his staff like some oversized needle, Cymric mimicked the motion of the thread of his spell. A moment later, he was looking into astral space, the river become a friendly swirl of brown, white, and green. There was no sign of the spiritcatcher. Leandra looked at him questioningly.

"I spotted something unusual in the river when I came down here yesterday," he said. "But it seems to have left during the night."

"An 'unusual' I should know about?"

Cymric shrugged the question away, not ready to admit that he hadn't killed the creature in the well. "Did you get those salves from the mayor?" was all he said.

Leandra drew two glass vials from a side pouch of her backpack, then handed them to Cymric. "I have one more."

Cymric nodded. He opened one vial, which immediately released a powerful scent of roses and revealed a salve that was clear rather than the blush color Cymric would have expected. He wriggled one arm out of his robe and began to smooth the salve over his upper back. The initial sensation was cool and surprisingly grainy. As he worked the salve around his shoulder blade, the salve warmed and the grains disappeared. *That should help ... unless the mayor obtained the salve from a magician like me.*

He knew that Leandra was watching him closely, but he caught only glimpses of her over his shoulder. Then he stuffed his arm back into his sleeve and turned to her with a bright smile. Leandra wasn't smiling back.

"You haven't a single mark on you."

Cymric's smile narrowed, but did not falter. "I told you so as much this morning. The creature didn't injure my flesh, though the pain is physical enough."

Leandra bent to snatch up a five-petaled wildflower, took a sniff, then sent it into the river with a quick toss. Blue petals spun downstream, bouncing off the moss-covered rocks lining the shallows. The drone of insects and the burble of the water defined the silence between wizard and swordmaster before Leandra finally spoke again.

"I need to trust you, but I can't. I need you to show me things I cannot see. But I don't think you're telling me everything you know. Yet I can't always tell *when* you're not talking straight."

Cymric pursed his lips, rubbed them back and forth. He looked at Leandra, flinched at her gaze, then made himself look back.

"My sword lady, are you telling me everything?"

"No, because I don't think I can take that chance. Not until I sense that you're willing to do the same."

"I see. Is this farewell then? We shall always have the whitewater to remember each other by." Cymric bowed low, staff held down by his side, keeping his gaze on Leandra. She crossed her arms.

"Do you always walk away from problems like this?"

"No. Sometimes I solve them. Sometimes the problems walk away from me."

"Well, *I'm* not walking away. I still need a wizard. You still need money."

Cymric stood and reached over and behind his back to scratch. The salve must be working, for now he was starting to itch. The insect buzz seemed uncomfortably close and loud. He sighed.

"So, what do you suggest?"

"We travel to Corthy. When we get there, you let me know whether you're willing to be completely honest with me. And you can start with what it was you saw by the river."

"And if I do?"

"I tell you what you need to know."

"And if I choose to keep my own counsel, we part ways?"

Leandra nodded, and Cymric did the same to show his acceptance. The few days to Corthy would give him a chance to determine whether the necklace would be worth any risks of traveling with Leandra. Without further discussion, the two resumed walking along the river in the same direction as the water.

It was some time that afternoon when they caught sight of a rafter. The man's wild red hair framed a broad face that was matched by equally broad shoulders and arms twice the size of Leandra's. His raft was piled with crates overflowing with linens and the smell of cheap toiletries. He was on his way back upstream with the load, and perfectly willing to ferry the two across the river for a copper apiece. The fare was cheap; the man wanted conversation more than coin. Had they seen ogres along the river? Heard of the horrible goings-on in Havel? The scandal about Prince Gustav and some woman of the Outriggers Guild? Ever thought about purchasing a fine linen nightshirt?

Leandra said little, watching the river instead. Cymric

stepped in to fill the gap, telling of his encounter with the well creature in Twin Chin. When he seemed to hesitate at the ending, Leandra looked over sharply. Damn! thought Cymric, then finished with a rousing tale of a fight in which he managed to banish the creature with a powerful and rare spell. The rafter's face radiated astonishment. Other villages are going to hear this tale, Cymric thought with some satisfaction, but decided not to check Leandra's reaction. The rafter let them off with a wave and a small vial of his best bath freshener, which Cymric slid into his pack. He tried to match the rafter's enthusiastic wave, then hurried after Leandra. The set of her shoulders made him decide it might be wiser right now to follow a few paces behind.

Soon they came to a well-worn trail that Leandra said led to Corthy. After perhaps a quarter of an hour along the trail, she stopped to scan the area, then pointed to a wooded rise.

"We can camp on the other side of the rise. From there we can keep an eye on the trail."

Cymric's injuries had tired him. Though a few good hours of daylight still remained, he was glad for the chance to rest. Leandra took a couple of long strides, leaving Cymric to scuttle through the tall, young grass as well as his long robes and short wind would allow. But Leandra continued to outdistance him.

"Are you hoping to arrive far enough ahead of me to eat your evening meal alone?" he shouted in annoyance.

Leandra stopped and stood staring at the rise. When Cymric caught up, she slowly turned to face him, her arms crossed.

"This is a good place to camp. Maybe other folks thought the same. Maybe folks are still up there. I thought I'd check it out first. Give you a little time for spells if things go bad."

Cymric threw up his arms in exasperation, "A really good idea. Too bad mind-reading isn't in my contract."

Leandra drew her sword, pointing its tip up the rise. "Shall we go together? The noise we've made should have alerted anyone already up there."

"Certainly. It's not polite to keep one's host waiting."

They trudged up the hill together, caution slowing them as they neared the crest of the rise. Then they stopped, Leandra glancing over at Cymric. The wizard took a deep breath, exhaled, then grinned. Thumping his staff for emphasis, Cymric strode over the crest.

6

Cymric saw the campsite first. Stumps from six trees surrounded the firepit in the center of the clearing. Wood was stacked, the logs and kindling in two different piles and separated by an old axe. The ashes in the pit were cold. The camp looked as though it saw frequent use, but was currently unoccupied. A rasping whoosh told Cymric that the swordmaster had sheathed her sword.

He laid his staff on the ground, then shimmied out of his pack. Leandra watched, the tic-smile flashing occasionally. The pack hit the soft ground with a thud.

"Nice to see travelers around here have road manners," Leandra said, pointing to the axe and the piles of wood. She slipped off her bigger pack one shoulder at a time, then laid it soundlessly on the ground. Kneeling down, she began to rummage in a side pouch. Finding whatever it was she'd been looking for, she pulled it out and tossed it to Cymric. As it flew, he saw that it was a flint and steel.

"Would you please start a fire?" Leandra asked. "I must perform my ritual." She'd already gone a few steps back up the rise before calling out over her shoulder, "I'll chop wood to replace what you use. No need to strain your wizardly wrists."

Cymric snorted. He looked down at the flint. *A flint and steel?* His disdainful look caught only Leandra's back as he walked over to the logs. He selected one that looked recently cut, then added an older, drier log. He struggled back with the wood, wondering if smaller loads might not be more in order for an injured wizard. He made three more trips, one log at a time. The last log had just thudded into place in the pit when a booming laugh rang out over the camp.

Leandra's laugh startled him, but he enjoyed the sensation. The laugh filled him with warmth as well as some confidence. It made Cymric remember a swallow of hot rum on a cold night and some kind words from his master about his student's problems with thread-weaving. *A little more perspiration, a little less sophistication, that's all it takes, lad.*

Cymric went to join Leandra up the rise, and found her in a low crouch, sword held over her head with both hands. The late-afternoon light caught the edge of the sword near the tip as Leandra parried a blow from an imaginary attacker, shifting her weight to spring up in counterattack. She used light and dark to her advantage, sunlight gleaming off her blade for feints, shadow concealing her actual attacks. Her moves were rapid, her blade impossibly quick. Cymric could sense the magic in her; it flowed between her and the blade, then back again. The pattern of swordmaster molded and used the magic within Leandra. It wasn't a magic as intricate as Cymric's matrices and spells, but Leandra's had a flow, a power-in-motion that Cymric's did not.

By her moves, it seemed to him that Leandra was fighting and reacting to more than one foe. One foe delivered a clumsy overhead attack, another delivering a head-blow from behind that Leandra deflected just in time, while a third was downed by a savage cut across the legs. The longer she fought, the faster and more intricate her moves became. During one complicated maneuver, Cymric thought he saw Leandra outline a pattern, like the pattern of a spell. Her sword flashed in and out of the sunlight. The pattern was briefly defined by reflected light surrounded by shadow, as if dozens of stars winked and rippled across a dark pool. Cymric couldn't quite catch the pattern, for it disappeared as Leandra skewered another imaginary opponent. In a whirl she was on to the next foe.

The spectacle fascinated him, but he found watching it just a little fatiguing. His own injury reminded him that physical action also had its price. He walked back down to camp, then sat down cross-legged, staff across his lap. Turning his senses inward, Cymric focused on a spell pattern, tracing it with mental fingers, envisioning the areas of the pattern. The first white gossamer thread looped over and under, then held. The second attached in a zigzag, but grayed as Cymric worked it. Another thread held. The last thread coiled around lines of the pattern, drawing energy from astral space to strengthen and reinforce the pattern. The weaving complete, Cymric cast his spell. A gentle, refreshing wave suffused his body.

He lay down to give the magic time to help his body's own healing powers. Resting like this felt so good, even with that small rock under his shoulder blade. Cymric closed his eyes, attentive to his breathing. He played at separating and identifying the smells from the camp. Ash was easy, with log and grass not far behind, and Cymric might even have detected foxglove.

A twinge told him it was time. He concentrated. The rush of energy started in his chest, then spiraled out. Magic knitted broken bits of his body together again—not into a seamless whole, but better. He smiled, stretching his repaired body. Jabs of pain told him he still had a bit to go.

"Nice fire."

His eyes snapped open to see Leandra wipe sweat from her forehead, then shake her head. Cymric cursed himself as she walked over to the pile of kindling. She rebuilt the fire, thudding logs into place with special emphasis. Then she added the kindling, all the while muttering complaints about the uselessness of wizards. Cymric junked the relax spell, tried to reattune another in its place. His first attempt failed. His next succeeded, and he smiled as the pattern slid into place.

"Just going to lie there?" Leandra looked at him incredulously, then bent to retrieve the flint and steel still resting undisturbed where it had landed.

Cymric rolled over onto his stomach. Yawning to suppress the slight effort of the spell, he snapped his fingers and pointed at a log. A jet of green flame the length of his forearm hovered, then struck the log, igniting it instantly.

Leandra's shoulders dropped an inch or two. Cymric sat up. He repeated the spell with each of the other logs until the pit was ablaze with strong orange flame.

Leandra pursed her lips, wiggled them a bit, then returned the flint and steel to her backpack. She pulled out a cloth bundle, which turned out to contain bread and cheese. Drawing a knife from a concealed boot-sheath, Leandra then proceeded to carve the bread and cheese into manageable chunks. With a sigh as she looked over at Cymric, she reached into her pack to withdraw a smaller bundle. She tossed it to the him. The cheesecloth was sticky, making it difficult to undo. Leandra pointed at it with her knife.

"It's one of those damn cinnamon things. Probably a bit smashed from a day in my pack. Smelled good this morning, so I saved you one."

Cymric carefully peeled off the last layer of cheesecloth, licking his fingers when he was done. He broke off a piece of the roll, drawing in a full, deep breath of cinnamon before taking a bite. The first taste actually made his mouth sting a bit from the anticipation and hunger forcing tongue and glands to work a bit faster than normal. Then came a low "ummm" from deep in his throat. He had to wipe his mouth with the cheesecloth to stop himself from drooling. The second bite was all gummy texture and hints of cinnamon. The third was the sweetness of the glaze. Delicious. *So you finally got one thing out of Twin Chin.*

Too bad the swordmaster had to get it for him. Too bad she had to give it to him after he was done being a cad. *Too bad that now you feel too much of an idiot to thank her for it.*

"It's good. Really good."

Leandra smiled, a full smile rather than one of her little tic-smiles. She tossed him a hunk of bread, then a piece of cheese. "Chew on some of this. The trail is easier if you eat food that sticks with you."

Cymric reluctantly dropped what was left of the cinnamon roll. The cheese was a little hard for his taste, but it went well with the bread. Leandra pulled a waterskin from her pack, popped the plug. Remembering his own ale skin,

Cymric scrambled for his pack as well. He offered some to Leandra, who shook her head. Cymric unscrewed the cap, took a sip, then felt his face freeze face as his stomach let him know the last batch of ale was not yet forgotten. When Leandra laughed, Cymric felt the heat rising in his cheeks. He returned the ale to his pack, thinking how he must look. His laugh was quieter than Leandra's.

"Nice face," she said.

"We wizards pride ourselves on communicating volumes through subtle nuances of expression. For example, that was my 'thank you, but I don't think ale is an appropriate companion for this meal' expression."

"I thought it was 'try it and it's going to come back up'."

"You are obviously not well-versed in the facial ciphers of wizards. Fortunately, you have a master expressioner at your disposal."

"Along with a wizard, at no extra cost?"

"Indeed, milady swordmaster. Plus so much more."

Leandra laughed again. Cymric smiled. This was certainly better than this afternoon. He had an idea. Taking a piece of bread in one hand, he topped it with a piece of cheese in a flourish of the other. Then he raised and lowered his eyebrows over eyes narrowed into his "crafty" expression. Speaking in a whisper, Cymric named every type of cheese he could think of, his voice gradually rising through the list. Then he cast the spell he had used on the logs, and the cheese burst into flames. He put out the flames with considerable huffing, along with a lot of unnecessary pantomime. The cheese melted more or less evenly along the length of bread.

Cymric broke the bread into two pieces and offered one to Leandra, a thin strand of cheese trailing back to his own piece. Leandra waved him off, then accepted the piece when Cymric gave her his puppy-dog expression. The two sat silently for a moment, enjoying how the melted cheese had softened and warmed the bread. Leandra raised the bread over her head, cheese side up.

"A toast to the things wizards can do."

Cymric laughed, then hoped the pun was intentional. Her expression was back to its usual inscrutability.

"My thanks. A toast to the swordmaster who rescued me from Twin Chin and introduced me to whitewater."

Her eyes flickered at that. Cymric put forward his piece of bread, and Leandra brushed hers against it. Then both bit into their breads simultaneously. Dinner ended cordially, the small talk made cozier by the fire and the dark that surrounded the camp. As Leandra was spreading out her bedroll, Cymric went to get the axe, grunting as he pulled it from the ground. Seeing her quizzical expression, he stopped and gestured clumsily toward the trees.

"I thought I'd replace the logs I used for the fire . . . so you wouldn't have to do it."

"Ever chopped wood before?"

Cymric shook his head.

"Then you've never chopped wood in the dark. It's a bad idea."

"Ah, I defer to your swordmaster's wisdom."

"No, you defer to my common sense. I am a swordmaster who has actually lived in the world. Plus so much more."

Cymric cleared his throat, then gently set the axe back in place. Leandra was climbing into her bedroll, turning her back to the fire. Cymric was puzzled.

"You sleep in your chain mail?"

"Sometimes."

"I've heard that sleeping in armor is really uncomfortable."

"It is."

"Oh," he said. "But one more thing. I was wondering if I could look at the necklace. This time I'd like to examine it while I'm sober."

Leandra rolled over to face Cymric, her scrutiny making him blink. "The necklace is all I have of my past. It's important to me."

"But you've offered it to me as payment," Cymric insisted softly. "Am I not entitled to examine it to know more of the nature of its magic?"

Leandra's face darkened. She delayed a moment before

the torrent of words began. "I don't know who my parents were. I don't know my birthday. I have only a *rough* idea of where I was born. But I do know that necklace has been with me ever since—" Leandra caught herself. Cymric suddenly wanted to apologize even though he had no idea what he'd done wrong. He kept his mouth shut as he watched Leandra struggle for control of her face. Then her expression softened. She watched the fire for a few moments before reaching a hand under the neck of her armor to extract the necklace. She tossed it to Cymric, who leaned off-balance to catch it.

"Take good care of it."

Cymric nodded. Leandra looked him over once more, then rolled over again. Her breathing slowed almost instantly. Cymric stared at the fire, letting his thoughts dance in time with the flames.

Leandra seemed agreeable enough, if prone to the occasional outburst. Dinner had certainly been more pleasant than the trip to camp. But she asked for reason to trust him—and she wanted it before they left Corthy. Was this job worth kowtowing to someone who demanded that Cymric demonstrate his trustworthiness? Besides, how could he do it? She'd saved him a cinnamon roll. That could mean she was either a basically decent person or else needed him enough to maintain a front of decency. The outburst confirmed that there was a lot Leandra wasn't telling him. Her ritual looked sophisticated, her blade mastery most impressive; she was probably more accomplished in sword magic than he was with spells. Why did she hire an only partially successful wizard passing through a nowhere river village? She offered the necklace as payment. The necklace was intriguing, a deep magic, a valuable magic. Cymric didn't think it was something he could ever bring himself to sell. The magic within the necklace could prove more valuable than any coin he could earn hawking it.

Then there was the whole aspect of adventure—traveling with a swordmaster to unravel a deep mystery. When younger, Cymric used to spend hours huddled in the kitchen waiting for the ovens to be fired, keeping himself warm listening to tales of the heroes of legend. He had wanted to be a hero. The idea still tugged at him, but he now knew that heroing didn't pay as well as the legends suggested. Nor did the legends usually mention all the would-be heroes who failed before the saga's hero came onto the scene, their lives and efforts written off in a line such as, "He entered the kaer alone, passing through the gates as had hundreds before him; no one had yet returned."

Cymric examined the necklace, dazzled by the reflections of the silver chain in the firelight. The chain gleamed with a colder, more distant light; a crescent moon on hard-packed mountain snow. The hand seemed unremarkable, for all its gold and silver sheen. The crystal sphere was cool to the touch of Cymric's probing finger, and remained so even when the fire's heat warmed the chain. The rune inside continued its cycle of change, the rhythm and speed seeming to respond to the heat.

Cymric looked over at the sleeping Leandra. Experimenting with someone else's enchanted property without permission was always a breach of etiquette. Cymric knew that it was also a crime in parts of the Kingdom of Throal, places such as the city of Tuakan, for one. Knowledge of the link between the pattern of an item and the pattern of the wielder could yield an advantage for an unscrupulous investigator. Cymric was feeling somewhat scrupulous today, enough so that he wouldn't try to harm Leandra should he stumble across any key knowledge. One more glance at her told him she was sound asleep. She would never have to know.

He looped the necklace around the end of his staff, then carefully lowered his staff into the flame, leaving it there for as long as he could hold his breath. He took a clean breath, spit on his finger, touched the crystal. His finger sizzled against the hand and he winced reflexively, but the sphere itself was cool.

Someone had bothered to enchant the sphere to resist fire. Or else the sphere was so fortified by its basic enchantment as to remain unscathed by natural flames. Either way, a good sign of value.

What did the necklace do? Cymric studied the rune inside the sphere. It changed on a regular basis. Taking his pulse at his neck, Cymric timed the rune's changes to every twelve to fifteen heartbeats, though he couldn't determine any sequence to the change. He licked his lips, glanced once more at Leandra, then cast a spell.

His astral sense could crudely see the rune's changes. Each time it changed, Cymric saw a rough sphere, as if someone had wound glowing blue threads of wildly varying widths into a ball. The exact moment the rune changed, dozens of strands pulled away from the spheres as if yanked by invisible hooks. By the next heartbeat, the sphere would snap back into shape.

Those must be threads similar to my spell threads; perhaps my wizardry can pry a thread or two apart just long enough for me to see inside the sphere. Cymric formed tendrils of thought, slowly insinuating them across the astral space between him and the sphere. He tried to move his thoughts in time with the pulling-strands on the sphere. Four times he tried, four times the sphere closed tight again before Cymric could prop it open. The fifth time he succeeded, but again the sphere snapped back into shape, cleanly severing his tendrils of will. The shock popped Cymric's vision back into the external world. He was sweating.

The rune changed, this time tinged by a red glow. Cymric blinked in disbelief as it changed once more, the red glow becoming even stronger. His hand trembled as he watched. A change, another, then another, the red glow appearing every time. It did seem to be getting stronger. Cymric forced himself to calm, then back into astral sensing. He watched the glowing yarn pull and re-form a sphere. *Spectacular work, wizard. You've broken the necklace; now Leandra is going to have your guts for breakfast.*

Maybe he could undo the damage he'd done. Cymric tried to weave a thread. He failed. Then failed again. He had to calm down, but that seemed an impossibility. Cymric pushed his thoughts away, concentrated on seeing the thread. Wispy, shaky, but of one piece; Cymric finally wove a thread through the pattern of his spell. He cast to dispel the magic now working on the necklace. Maybe he could undo his mistake.

When the red glow finally vanished, Cymric grinned widely, suppressing a laugh. Now Leandra would never have to know how deeply he had pried into the necklace. He was just congratulating himself on wizardry triumphing again when the red glow suddenly returned brighter than ever with the rune change. Cymric froze. Did he wait, hoping the effect would diminish on its own? Did he wake Leandra? Did he let her sleep and deprive her of a chance to save the necklace? Did he let her sleep, hoping to get a decent head start before she could hunt him down? The necklace pulsed red, bathing his face and chest in its light.

Cymric shook Leandra. She opened her eyes groggily, giving him a dour look. The necklace pulsed red. Snapping upright like a trap snaring prey, she grabbed it from an unprotesting Cymric.

"Damn it, how long has this been glowing red?"

Cymric gargled something inarticulate, then shrugged his shoulders to indicate he hadn't the faintest idea. He was working on a feeble protest of his innocence when Leandra spun her bedroll into a tight bundle.

"Run, wizard! They're almost on top of us."

7

While Cymric was sliding his backpack over his shoulders, Leandra began to kick dirt on the fire, then seemed to think better of it. She swung the necklace to her left. Pulse. Ahead of her, up the rise. A brighter pulse. Cymric saw her fiddle with the back of the chainmail near her neck, then she jerked her head downward from the rise, indicating the direction opposite the brighter pulse.

Scurrying down into the darkness, Cymric stumbled in the tall grass at the bottom of the rise, then caught himself with his staff and kept running. There was only enough moonlight to see dark outlines, not enough to pick up small variations such as fist-sized rocks or small indentations in the ground. Cymric banged his knee against a rock when his left boot stuck in one of the latter, but he managed to keep his oath to a medium-loud grunt. He heard footsteps from ahead. It was Leandra come to pick him up off the ground.

"Walk now. Keep off the hills. Keep quiet. I'll walk just behind you."

Cymric took several deep breaths, exhaling as evenly as he could. When Leandra tapped his shoulder, he started to walk. Behind, he heard an indistinct babble of voices, then one rising above the rest. The voices spoke a language he didn't recognize. Cymric kept moving, trying to pick spots where the grass was lower, hoping for less rustling noises and better footing. When his robes occasionally snagged on the grass with a scratchy sound, he cursed silently.

He never heard Leandra at all. When he turned to be sure she was still behind him, his eyes widened to see that she followed less than an arm's length away. Leandra nodded, perhaps affirming that Cymric was going in the right direction. He resumed his progress.

Fire jetted upward from the campsite, the flame providing a dull light that bleached the world of color. Individual blades of grass turned a dull gray, and Cymric's robe seemed a lighter shade of gray, with occasional shimmers. Leandra tapped his shoulder.

"Stop. Get down."

Cymric dove to the dirt, but Leandra remained standing with the necklace cupped against her chest. A pulse of red diffused through the rings of her armor. She began to recite the words of a dwarven poem, interspersed with nonsense words that had the right guttural dwarven sound. She was asking the grass what it was like to be grass, how the rock felt in the earth, wondering why the river ran as it did, how the sjornich knew when winter came. Perhaps it was an elemental spell that would conceal Cymric and Leandra by blending them with the earth. Perhaps she was asking the elements for help.

Cymric sat up. The fire in the campsite rose to become a column half again as high as the trees. Dozens of fluttering specks swarmed around the flames. Bats? Cymric decided he needed a different selection of spell patterns than he currently held in astral space. He released his ignite spell. More reluctantly he also let astral sense slide back into his mind. That part was easy.

Assuming that Leandra was trying to avoid a fight rather than preparing for one, he thought that enhancing his ability to get out of the way of an attack would be a good idea. He selected a spell pattern to increase his ability to dodge a blow, then moved it from his mind to one of the spell matrices tucked into astral space. As Cymric concentrated, the pattern slid down the thread like a bead on a string, neatly folding into the matrix.

If there was a fight, he would also want offensive magic. Something fast with short range, or perhaps a slower spell with greater range? The group at the campsite were no doubt using spell magic on the fire, probably the same to summon the bats. Leandra seemed to have an idea of who or what was chasing them; it was reasonable that their pursuers had some idea of who they were hunting. *If I were engaging Leandra, I'd want to hit her from as far away as possible.* So the longer-range spell made sense.

The spell was more difficult to move into the matrix. The pattern stuck on the thread, requiring several attempts to loosen it. Then it resisted folding into the matrix. Cymric didn't want to force the spell pattern, fearing he might damage it and then have to start with a fresh pattern from his mind. As he continued to twist the pattern delicately, it finally snapped into place.

Bats beat their wings overhead, hundreds of them flooding the field. They joined together into fluttering clouds, then broke out to sweep individually over areas of the field. One swooped low, flying between Cymric's staff and his face, then turned back, passing within a wingspan of his nose. Other bats wheeled close, then darted up into the night. It seemed to Cymric that they didn't react at all to his and Leandra's presence; her magic must be working.

The bats clustered nearby, luminescent points bobbing among a swirl of wings like night lanterns on fishing boats in the Aras Sea. The points hovered together for a moment, then split apart. The bats soon followed. One of the glowing spots darted toward Leandra. Her chanting continued, even-voiced, clear.

Cymric saw that the spots were small glowing sacs on the back of each bat. Trailing underneath the bat were dimly luminescent tentacles, making the whole thing look like a cross between a jellyfish and a bat. The tentacles moved independently of the bat's movements, following a different, invisible force. When the tentacles lashed one of the bat's wings, the bat lurched, falling a good man-height before recovering. Then the bat altered course, away from the direction of the sting. Cymric rubbed his chest in sympathy with the bat. Those glowjellies had to be astral creatures, attached to the bats as the spiritcatcher had been attached to Cymric.

The bat flew close, then past. The glowjelly whipped it again. The bat flew past again at an angle. Leandra kept chanting. Her eyes followed the arc of the bat until it passed behind her field of vision. Cymric kept the bat in sight. It fell, turned again, passing closer. As it came almost close enough to touch, the glowjelly's tentacles radiated out, marking a circle like the notches on a sundial. It lashed the bat again. The bat fell too close to the ground, became tangled in the tall grass. The glowjelly went into a frenzy; the bat flapped and squeaked. It tore itself free with a spasmodic jerk, arced airborne for a brief moment, then plummeted to the ground not two paces from Cymric.

Cymric reached back into his mind. His wizardry spun a thread from the stuff of astral space, reinforced the pattern of his spell. The glowjelly jammed its tentacles into the nose, eyes, and mouth of the bat, which flopped wildly for a moment, then lay still. Cymric sighted the spell along his outstretched arm. *Goodbye, you little floating piece of snot.*

The spell spun through astral space along a path corresponding to the one Cymric sighted. The pattern of the spell merged with the pattern of the glowjelly. Cymric clenched his fist reflexively. Amplified by the spell, Cymric's will tore at the mind of the creature.

The glowjelly's shriek startled Cymric. Even Leandra stopped chanting. As the creature slid off the back of the bat, Leandra drew her sword. Cymric pulped the creature with his staff. Other glowjellies pinwheeled slowly toward them. Cymric heard excited shouting from the camp.

"What the hell were you doing?"

"Start chanting again!"

"They know we're here. Run!"

"Start chanting. I'm casting. Leave and you can buy yourself another wizard."

Leandra took two steps away, then spun and knelt on the ground. She clasped the necklace with her left hand, keeping her sword in her right. She kept her eyes on the swarm of bats and glowjellies, her face set in a scowl as she chanted.

Cymric had more hope than a plan. If Leandra's magic really had kept them hidden, then the glowjellies were reacting to the shriek. Cymric wove another thread, finishing just as the swarm arrived. He targeted a glowjelly on the edge of the swarm, about twenty paces away. Cymric felt his will envelop the creature; it shrieked when Cymric tried to crush its pattern.

The swarm flew over and through them. One bat caromed off Leandra's sword-arm, fell stunned, then took off again. Several brushed against Cymric's robes. Squeaks, squeals, and the whirring of hundreds of wings made a din beyond anything Cymric would have imagined such small creatures could produce. He wanted to cover his ears, but was already weaving the thread for his next spell.

The glowjellies hesitated, then began to flow in a wider pattern. The swarm broke into dozens of small groups of bats, each darting around the location of a glowjelly. Cymric chose one about fifty paces away, further from the campsite than the last one. The glowjellies reacted more decisively this time, swirling toward the position of the latest shriek.

Cymric's hands were shaking. *Not yet, can't stop now . . .* He wove again, then hit a glowjelly eighty paces away. The first spell arced too inexactly, the spell missing the thing by a fraction. Cursing softly, Cymric wove another thread, this spell hitting the glowjelly squarely. A luminescent burst of goo erupted at about ninety paces.

Someone in the pursuing party must have noticed the pattern Cymric had established; there suddenly came two flashes, then two circles illuminated by brightly glowing spheres. The spheres appeared further along the path Cymric had suggested with his attacks. They were moving toward the last downed glowjelly at the pace of a slow walk. *Now that you're looking for us where we aren't, it's time to leave.* He tapped Leandra.

"They're going to be looking into the lighted area for a little while. They'll have a hard time spotting us moving in the moonlight."

Leandra nodded. She slipped the necklace over her head, then tucked it under her armor. The sword was still in her hand. "I'll lead," she said, moving off at a slow trot.

Cymric followed as best he could. Every hundred paces or so, Leandra turned for just a moment and Cymric would spot the red glow from the necklace and correct his course. After a time, one too long for the comfort of Cymric's legs, the red glow dimmed to a point. Cymric caught up again as Leandra slowed down to a walk. He strode up alongside her, ignoring the stitch in his side.

"Now that we're out for an enjoyable evening stroll, would you mind telling me who those people were? Perhaps even why they were after you? You know, just to help pass the time."

In the dark Cymric saw only her silhouette, but he could hear the steady tap-tap on the pommel of her sword even over the quiet rustling of the grass.

"That can wait until Corthy."

"You must be joking."

"I shall decide if I can trust you. You can decide if you want to work with me. If we're still together, I'll tell you everything you need to know."

"Wizards are keen judges of what they need to know. This wizard thinks he needs to know who those people were."

"I'm sure you do."

Cymric stopped and threw up his hands. "Leandra, this isn't going to work unless we tell each other what we know."

Moonlight caught one of Leandra's quick, quirky smiles. "Agreed. How about telling me why you took so long to wake me up? The red glow must have seemed odd to a wizard."

Cymric dropped his arms. He leaned on his staff, feeling a slow, ragged grin spread over his face. He gave his best bow, one hand sliding down his staff, his other arm held out stiff behind him.

"So we agree to a common mistrust, softened by uncommon courtesy, at least as far as Corthy?"

"At least as far as Corthy."

Cymric nodded, then hobbled over to Leandra. He held out one hand in their direction of travel, and took an exaggerated first stride. Leandra took a normal step. Staying an uneasy distance apart, the two traveled silently through the long, rustling grass until the moon began to set.

8

Two days of peaceful travel ended when Cymric caught sight of a column of smoke over Corthy. He and Leandra moved off the trail and up a hill about five hundred paces outside the farming town. They could hear the shrieks and oaths of fighting, but the sounds were muted, nearly lost in the wailing of the wind. Cymric could barely see figures moving about on the outskirts of the village. It looked like adults fighting spindly youths, although the youths were a little more numerous. Leandra studied the battle carefully.

"Ogres," she said.

"I assume we wait?"

Leandra adopted her blank expression, but her eyes narrowed for a fraction of a second. She started down the hill. Cymric blinked, then hurried after her.

"Are you serious about charging into a melee in the middle of a burning town?"

"Yes."

Cymric stopped for a moment to stare at Leandra as she walked past him. Then he picked up his robe so he could dash ahead of her a ways. Then he turned to face her and talked while walking backward.

"Wizards hate fighting, particularly when the wizard isn't convinced it's completely necessary and the fight is against opponents three times his size."

Leandra bunched her hair together with her left hand while pulling two hairpins from the lining of her scabbard with her right. One pin went into her mouth, the other into a mass of hair. She never broke stride. Cymric stumbled, then righted himself, trotting to catch up. Leandra pulled the other pin from her mouth, talking to Cymric without taking her eyes off the village.

"The calendar is in the village."

"What do you think are the odds that ogres would be interested in stealing a ritual calendar?"

"Too high for me. The person who has the calendar is a friend of mine."

"Now, some wizards could begin to see that as a reason."

Leandra reached behind her neck. She rubbed a few links of her chainmail, then pulled. A yellow shimmer played over her hand, then the links expanded into a camail, a chain link collar to cover her neck and shoulders. Another touch, another shimmer, and she pulled a mail coif over her head.

"We saw no refugees along the trail," she said while adjusting the coif under her chin. "That must mean the townsfolk stayed to defend their homes. I have to admire that kind of courage."

Cymric threw his arms to the sky and screamed in exasperation.

"My lady swordmaster, wizards wearing robes find talk of courage most suspicious when coming from skilled fighters armored in magicked mail. Those best protected from physical danger seem least fit to suggest it to others."

Cymric did not see Leandra draw her sword, but he felt the jolt shooting from his left wrist to his elbow. His staff flew several feet, spinning and bouncing end to end. Cymric looked at Leandra in surprise, then flinched.

"'I was talking about *them,* not you. I didn't mean the courage to face danger. I meant the courage to believe in something bigger than *yourself.*"

While Cymric scrambled for his staff, Leandra was sheathing her sword, the shushing sound carrying over the battle noise from town. When he looked up, she had her eyes closed and was breathing deeply. When she opened her eyes again, they looked as sharp as her blade.

"The necklace and I are going into Corthy. Come in. Stay out. Whatever."

She walked away. As Cymric hopped to his feet and began to race after her, he saw two figures heading in their direction away from a burning building. They wore over-lapping pieces of leather, crude helmets, and carried large clubs. *No question that those are ogres; at least we don't have to smell them yet.* Cymric slowed, the urge to run away flooding his legs, chest, and groin with nervous energy. "Leandra, wait."

Leandra altered her course slightly, making directly for the ogres. She matched each step with a single tap on her sword pommel.

"Wait, damn it! I need the right spells in my matrices. Asking me to walk into that inferno without good spells is like me asking you to walk in naked and unarmed." Cymric stopped, breathing more heavily than justified by mere exertion.

Leandra looked from Cymric, to the town, to the approaching ogres, then back into the young wizard's eyes. To his own surprise, he bore the weight of the gaze well.

"No jokes. No clever lines. No fancy words. Just 'yes' or 'no'. When you get the right spells in your . . . things, will you go with me into Corthy?"

Cymric licked his lips, looked at the ogres.

"Are you going to keep those big boys off me until I get my spells?"

Leandra nodded.

"Then I'll go with you into Corthy."

Drawing her sword, Leandra stood between the ogres and Cymric, who sat down, staff across his lap. He calmed his breathing as best he could. *Ogres—big, fast, not the most clever or coordinated of creatures. An illusory attack would probably work against them. I need a defensive spell, but probably won't need to dispel magic. A spell for quicker movement might serve me better.* Cymric chose ephemeral bolt, coaxing the pattern into astral space, hooking it onto the thread leading to one of his spell matrices. In his mind's eye the thread looked kinked and looped rather than the smooth curve it should have made. Fear must have distorted it. Chastising himself for losing his nerve, Cymric maneuvered the spell pattern along the thread to the matrix, but the pattern snagged on a kink in the thread.

Cymric gently increased the pressure of his will. The spell pattern didn't budge, but the thread shimmered and coiled under the effort. Then Cymric visualized a hand slamming the pattern into the matrix, but it slammed too hard. The pattern spun along the rest of the thread, hitting the matrix at a bad angle. A flash of energy poured from the matrix into the spell, vaporizing the pattern. The flux traveled upthread to Cymric, who had just enough time to shield himself, but not enough to keep the magic from leaking out and scalding his neck with an internal heat. Cymric could smell the burned hair on his nape. He frantically checked his other matrices, but all three came up empty. The flux had ruined the patterns in every one of his matrices.

He returned his focus to the external world. The two ogres were perhaps fifty yards away, dragging spiked clubs that casually mutilated grass and flowers as the pair approached. Cymric choked back a cry as he was struck by the full pain and realization of what had just happened. Leandra looked back at him, eyebrows raised.

"I lost all my spells. I blew them out of their matrices."

"Meaning?"

"I can't cast anything until I replace them."

Leandra looked at the ogres, who seemed to have increased their pace slightly. Cymric got up on one knee, then brushed off his robes and wiped away the tears streaking his face.

"Sorry. Time to run, I guess."

"Get your spells back. I'll take care of them."

As Leandra walked toward the ogres, one of them began to scratch vigorously at a patch of greasy black hair. The other raised his club. Cymric tried hard to focus on his internal sight. He relaxed his face, allowing more tears to flow down his cheeks. Once again he chose the ephemeral bolt spell, summoning the pattern in his mind. An ogre growled nearby, spitting out something in passable dwarven.

"Pays Hokf and me, shiny woman?"

"You pays, we not bruise you badly."

"Not badly, but maybe just a little."

Ogrish laughter. The sound of a rapid double-swipe of Leandra's sword was followed by a many-toned "Ooohh" from the ogres, then another deep laugh. Cymric calmed enough to see the thread leading to the matrix. Trying to slide the spell pattern toward the matrix felt like trying to move a delicate glass bead along a rough, uneven wire.

"I have a different deal. You walk away from Corthy, and you can keep all your limbs at no extra charge."

Cymric gently wiggled the pattern over the worst of the kinks and loops, then took the time to let it settle at its next natural resting place on the thread before pushing it any further. The spell pattern moved away from Cymric like a wispy-edged snowflake sinking into a pool of turbulent water.

Cymric heard a scuffing sound in the dirt.

"You pays now, or we breaks much."

"Maybe we break some, and see how the rest fits."

"Bets it fits snug."

"You two use whatever you want me to cut off."

The scuffing sound was followed by a light step. Cymric was floating the ephemeral bolt into the matrix when a roar snapped his sight back to the external world. The ogre's first blow missed Leandra by two club-widths; Leandra parried the second, then instantly followed up with a deep cut across that ogre's weapon arm. The howl preceded the flow of blood. Leandra whirled away from the ogre, placing herself behind him. The first ogre went around his companion, who turned. Both brutes now faced Leandra, and had their backs turned to Cymric. The wizard decided to risk placing one more pattern into a matrix.

Turning his sight inward, Cymric chose his leaping spell. The threads to his matrix appeared blue rather than white, more difficult to see in the gloom of astral space but with fewer kinks in the threads. He started to slide the pattern down the thread. He flinched when an agonized bellow sent a shock up and down his spine, but Cymric

kept his concentration on his internal sight. The spell slipped neatly into a matrix. *Do I go for three?*

"Cymric!"

Leandra's shout brought him back to the external world. The ogre with the wounded arm had switched the club to his other hand. The ogre swung wildly, clipping Cymric in the shoulder and spinning him around. Cymric cast a spell. The spell zipped along the shortest astral arc to the ogre. In the external world, a green wriggle of light flashed from Cymric, and struck the ogre's chest. The ogre staggered a step, then regained his balance and brought the club whistling down onto Cymric's head. Cymric's timing was better than the ogre's; the club smashed into Cymric's footprint.

Cymric again cast his bolt. The flash was far brighter, and Cymric saw spots for a few seconds. His eyes adjusted quickly, though, showing him the ogre lying unconscious on the ground. Leandra's ogre threw his club at her, but she deflected it easily. When the ogre turned and ran fulltilt back toward Corthy, Leandra hesitated, then turned and walked over to the ogre lying unconscious. She prodded him with the tip of her sword.

"He's not dead?"

"No, illusion spells can merely . . ." Cymric watched Leandra's swing cut through most of the ogre's throat. He swallowed reflexively. The ogre convulsed, shooting speckles of blood several feet off from the large pool forming by his neck. The ogre stopped moving. Leandra cut a pouch free from his rope-belt, then looped the drawstring over the point of her sword. She swung the sword toward Cymric, dangling the pouch about a foot in front of him. The sword point was even closer.

"We should have settled this earlier. You dropped the ogre, so this pouch is yours. Or do we split whatever we find?"

Cymric eyed the bloody sword edge, then the pouch.

"Splitting the take is fine with me."

Leandra smiled. She lowered the sword point, letting the pouch fall at Cymric's feet. When she withdrew the blade, Cymric snatched up the pouch.

"You have your spells. Ready to hit Corthy?"

I don't have all my spells, but I'm not crazy enough to tell you I'm not ready. Cymric bowed.

"After you, milady swordmaster. By the bye, who or what are we looking for in Corthy?"

"An elven spellcaster named Gelthrain. Her house is in the center of Corthy, and she has the calendar."

Leandra walked in the direction of the town, Cymric at her side. After a few strides he saw that her expression had changed from grim to scowling. When she broke into a trot, he stayed with her. Thirty paces ahead was an ogre dragging a pulped townsman from a smoking building. Leandra sprinted toward the ogre, shrieking as she took the last few steps like an eagle diving onto its prey. The ogre dropped the corpse, but wasn't able to unlimber his club before Leandra struck. The blow landed on the side of his knee. Cymric heard a cracking sound and then a scream before the ogre fell over, clutching his wounded leg. Cymric cleared the thrashing ogre with a clumsy leap. Leandra was still opening the distance between them.

When she hesitated for an instant, Cymric closed the gap. To their left was a blazing building. His eyes stung from smoke, and the heat from the flames immediately raised a sweat. Leandra was coughing, trying to peer through the thicker smoke ahead. She nodded to her right.

"This way to the center." She took off at a sprint again. Cymric sneezed on a whiff of smoke, following as best he could. The closer they got to the center of town, the more burning buildings they saw. Blistered wounded lay moaning in the streets; blackened and cracked corpses sprawled in the doorways where they had fallen. Desperate townspeople fought in defensive huddles against enraged ogres. Other ogres were dashing in and out of burning buildings seeking loot. They seemed content to ignore a swordmaster and a wizard.

Leandra stopped, and Cymric also came wheezing to a halt. Seeing her look of puzzlement, Cymric decided to cast his leaping spell, the better to avoid any over-enthusiastic ogres. Just as he began his casting, Leandra nodded and started running to her right. A sharp right, but

too sharp a one. She was heading straight into the thick
flow of smoke, away from the center of town.

Cymric's throat was dry. With his concentration so focused on the spell, the most he could manage was a feeble
croak of protest. Leandra was well into smoke by the time
Cymric could move again.

"Leandra!" His shout was hoarse, none too strong as he
followed her into the smoke. The fiery ruins of a house
glowed on his left, and other dots of flame outlined the
street. Cymric chose a path as near to the middle as he
could. To his left a shop groaned and crackled. Support
beams collapsed, sending thousands of sparks riding out
on a wave of heat. Cymric leaped sideways, the magic
carrying him yards clear of the sparks, straight into a startled ogre.

Cymric rolled to his feet just as the ogre shouted his anger. The ogre was armored in chain mail, and carried an
axe that looked like a troll design. His left hand held bolts
of shiny cloth now smudged with smoke. His hair was tied
back in a war braid. His nose ring was adorned with a gar-
net half the size of Cymric's thumb. *At least I'll die at the
hands of an important ogre.* Cymric leaped back, out of
the path of the ogre's attack.

The ogre's eyes widened. He bellowed, "Koffra, Haggs,
ji hav lig cortomanc!" Cymric did not speak ogrish, but he
decided to translate the ogre's words as "Koffra, Haggs,
please fetch me that wizards intestines." Two large,
leather-wrapped bodies rushed from out of the smoke just
as Cymric was attempting another magically powered leap
over a burning house. The spell rushed energy to his legs.
Cymric somersaulted slowly as he gained height, but he
saw that he wasn't going to clear the building.

He crashed through brittle shingle and weakened roof
supports, then slammed into a burning window frame. The
flesh on his forearms burned at contact with the fiery
wood. Then his chest hit the frame, stamping a dark brown
line across his robe. The ogres bellowed excitedly. Cymric
screamed and leaped through the window frame.

He landed in the street, across from two stone buildings
constructed with dwarven masonry. The roofs were on fire,

but the rest of the structures had yet to catch. Cymric
could see ogres looting inside the buildings. There must be
money here; he must be close to the center of town and to
Leandra's magician. Short, skittering jumps took him to
the alley between the two stone buildings. Crouching beneath a window, he paused to re-cast his jump spell.

Koffra and Haggs must also have made it to the street,
because he could hear a pair of ogres shouting. The voices
of ogres inside the buildings answered them. As Cymric
finished casting, one of them opened the window above
him. The huge, pimpled face looked down the alley one
way, then the other. The ogre grunted, an eyebrow went
up, then he looked directly down at Cymric. The ogre
smashed the window in his attempt to grab Cymric; the
wizard's bound left the ogre holding only pieces of glass.

Other ogre-shouts sounded around Cymric as more of
them apparently joined in the chase. Cymric dove into another alley to give himself time to think. The upper story
of the storefront across from him was engulfed in flames,
smoke pouring through every window. Soot and heat
blackened the stone forming the storefront's lower story,
but some of the stonework stubbornly refused to get as
dirty as the rest. Cymric hunched a few inches from a
wall, not wishing to touch hot stone. A shift in air currents
swept some smoke into the alley; Cymric coughed. An
ogre pounded past the alley. Their shouts were everywhere.

The structures here were built along concentric circles,
roads ringing the circles, alleys cutting between the circles.
The buildings were more substantial than the outlying
houses and shops, many of brick or stone, most more than
one story. If Cymric's guess was correct, he was now in
the center of town. Leaving Corthy would mean having to
get past a lot of ogres. Finding the magician would mean
having to spot a clue to her location. Sitting here would
mean just waiting for an ogre to find him. Cymric decided
to keep moving. He crawled beneath the level of the
smoke to the edge of the alley, then took a leap that carried him across the street.

Ogres were busy carrying barrels out of a tavern. One

spotted him, shouting to the others, but none seemed eager to drop a barrel just to chase a spindly human. Cymric disappeared between the buildings before those searching in earnest had a chance to spot him. He kept moving from building to building, looking for one that might suit a magician.

Cautiously circling the center of town, Cymric saw ogres trapped in a burning building surrounded by dozens of infuriated townspeople. He saw ogres smashing all the valuables in an abandoned clockmaker's shop, while others carefully looted the sausagemaker's shop next door. He skirted a spirited melee between twenty or so ogres and the dwarf and ork defenders of a temple. He flitted down an alley as ogres leapt overhead; the brutes were assaulting the roof of a goldsmith's shop, looking for a weakness in the well-fortified structure. The shop's defenders had enough arrows and accuracy to wound their attackers as well as produce a solid thunk against Cymric's backpack.

Finally he found a building that might be the one. The still-intact shop had a sign showing a gentle-faced woman with a golden aura around her long white hair. The face didn't look particularly elven, which Cymric chalked up to either artistic license or inexperience. One ogre was carrying an astrolabe out into the smoke-filled street. Others stood by the steps of the same shop, arguing loudly. Perhaps the magician was still holed up in her shop, and the ogres were unhappy about the prospect of taking her on. But then why did the one ogre go in and take the astrolabe? Perhaps the magician was holed up where the ogres couldn't find her. Looting the shop of a magician whose whereabouts were unknown—that could create some confusion, as well as explain the one theft of the astrolabe. *Of course, with my luck, they're probably just arguing about where to go for some ale.* He might be able to sneak inside. He might also trigger a defensive ward of some kind.

Cymric hid as best he could near his building, which, judging from the burning odors, must once have contained considerable stores of green tea. If the magician were hiding, where would she hide? Cymric scanned the building. The upper story was white plaster, now dingy from smoke.

Fire from the neighboring building had tarnished the stone walls, streaking them with soot. All the buildings around here were either on fire or stained by the ash of a neighboring structure. Cymric felt a small thrill shoot up his spine. One building had been a little different, possessing a wall section that seemed to resist the smoke and soot. *Just like my clothes do after I cast my 'tailor' illusion.*

Cymric got his bearings. The building with the suspicious wall would be on the other side of the magician's shop, kitty-corner across the street. Cymric recast his leap. He bounded out from the cover of his building, past the surprised ogres arguing by the steps. He quickly went around the shop, cleared the street in a single bound, then scurried into the alley.

The building was now burning on both floors. Cymric found the cleaner section. He licked his fingers, touched the section; hot. Studying the wall carefully, he saw that it looked natural, whole, with the variations one would expect from organic rock. But the soot just didn't stick quite right. It was a good illusion, but Cymric was sure that was all it was. He summoned a spark of life energy to power his will. *You aren't the real wall; leave so that I might see you as you truly are.* The first attempt didn't affect the wall. The second produced a white shimmer as the wall went out of focus.

Then it came back into focus as a sliding stone door with carved handholds. The door was hot. Cymric reached into his backpack for the ale, which he squirted onto the handhold until it stopped sizzling. Touching the handhold as lightly as he could, Cymric slid the door open. It moved easily and quietly, revealing a passageway that sloped down to his left and was only tall enough for a stooped walk. Bending over, Cymric stepped in, then closed the door behind him. The door choked off the outside light, leaving him in darkness.

Moving along the passageway, he kept his left hand on the wall while probing the way ahead with his staff. The tunnel was cool after the inferno above, but the air was stale. His body, which had not yet cooled, dripped sweat. Moving slowly gave him time to realize how thirsty he was, how much the burns on his arms and chest hurt.

Cymric stopped, fumbled for his ale. He drew four slow swallows. He continued down the dark tunnel until he heard a single step, then felt a sharp prick at the base of his spine and a cold edge at his throat.

"Twitch or speak in a way that displeases me, and you die."

9

Cymric swallowed hard, an act that only increased the bite of the blade at his throat. He raised his left hand in the air, only to have it jam into the ceiling of the tunnel. The pain from his jammed fingers almost forced a curse from his lips, but Cymric's will kept his tongue silent.

"Gently lay your staff on the ground." The unseen assailant spoke flawless dwarven, except for a hesitation in the long *a* of "lay," almost breaking it into two pure *a* sounds. That was typical of elven speech. Cymric rotated his staff until it was about hip-high and horizontal to the ground. He touched one end of the staff to the ground, then let the other fall into the dirt with a *whump*.

"I'm looking for Gelthrain."

"Many different people are looking. For whom might you be doing your looking?"

"My name is Cymric, I am a wizard. I am working with . . ." Cymric hesitated, then was angry at himself for the hesitation. The blade tightened on his throat, nicking his skin when he swallowed. Cymric had assumed that his captor was Gelthrain. If he was wrong and the person was actually working for the bat-summoners, mentioning Leandra could get him killed. Then again, if his captor was Gelthrain, she might also want to kill him because he'd delayed suspiciously in mentioning Leandra. A jab from the blade at his back interrupted his reasoning.

"I'm working with someone interested in finding a piece of the past, a piece the magician Gelthrain is said to have saved for us."

"Cymric, I need your help. Vague answers make my

wrist twitch. Given where I am holding my sword, a bad twitch could . . ."

"I came to Corthy with Leandra."

"Thank you, my wrist feels better." The point at his back pulled away, the edge at his throat held. Light shone from behind him. A slender, almost bony, hand holding a light crystal by a leather thong appeared next to his face. Tattoos covered the person's wrist, illustrations of lizards and beetles entwined in a chain.

"Take this, hold it above your face," said the person behind the wrist. Cymric used two fingers to take the thong. The person behind him hissed.

"You are young, spell boy. Leandra never struck me as a cradle-robber. How long ago did you complete journeyman?"

"I left my master nearly five years ago," Cymric said. *If I'd stayed another three years, I probably* would *have completed journeyman. But best not bore your host by volunteering information.*

"Leandra's choices never did sit all that well with me. I considered our differences of opinion one of my survival traits. But I do believe you are her choice." The sword moved away from his throat.

Cymric turned his upper body a few inches to the left, turning around completely when the blade-wielder did not object. By the glow of the light crystal he saw an elven woman with white hair cut into two levels, the top full but cut short around her ears, the lower part cut close to her head, with strands of hair hanging over her shoulders. Her jaw ended in a rounded chin that seemed out of place in her otherwise angular face. The eyebrows had been arched and braided in the old fashion of Blood Wood, her left ear scarred at the back. Her expression was smooth and ageless, except for the eyes. The lines around them seemed more like runes than crow's feet. That was certainly possible, for Cymric knew elves had strange habits. The padded cloth of her drab clothes were also stitched with myriad runes. Seeing how comfortably she handled her short sword and dagger, Cymric felt profound relief that she hadn't tried to kill him; she would most surely have succeeded. The elf woman gestured with her sword in the direction Cymric was heading.

"We can go back to my workshop. The calendar is still in there."

"Why did you leave the workshop?"

"I had prepared my day's spells for research and possible defense against the Ristular."

"Ristular?"

Gelthrain glanced at Cymric. She extended her lower lip, then sent her bangs flying with a poof of air. "Leandra has left a few gaps in her explanations," she said.

"She seems to have glossed over some important details in her haste to get here."

"Then I will not deprive you of the joy of personally extracting the story from her."

The elf led the way up a sloping passage. Slender beams supported the roof, and these were covered with runes similar to those on Leandra's scabbard. Gelthrain stopped at the passage's end. She sat down cross-legged, gesturing for Cymric to do the same. Overhead the floorboards vibrated with the sound of heavy footsteps.

"My spells were inadequate to defeat the five-hundred-pound marauders with small brains who entered my shop. Most of the valuable items in my shop are warded; the wards would discourage at least the first ogre to touch each item. I thought I could hide here until the townspeople drove them away. I apparently overestimated the abilities of my neighbors."

"You underestimated the number of ogres. There are too many of them out there."

"The mistake cannot be unmade. If you are willing to retrieve two items—the calendar and my grimoire—I would waive my fee for the calendar."

"Most noble of you, but that gesture only benefits me indirectly, if at all, while the risks are most certainly mine."

"Without my grimoire I cannot choose new spells. I think you need those spells to dispatch the ogres."

"I do not think my need is that dire."

"I think it might be. You came looking for me. You

sought out this tunnel rather than enter my ogre-infested shop. You cannot handle the ogres without me, and I cannot handle the ogres without my grimoire."

"Why did you leave your grimoire? Mine fits neatly in my backpack."

"My knowledge is no doubt a bit more extensive than yours, and the book is no longer so compact. Besides, I warded it to the lectern on which it sits. I couldn't move it without dispelling the ward."

"And you couldn't dispel the ward with your current mix of spells," Cymric concluded. Gelthrain nodded. Cymric ran his hands through his hair. Footsteps continued to sound heavily on the floorboards above. An ogrish shout sounded from further off. Cymric didn't need his grimoire to use spells he had already learned; inscribing them in the grimoire was part of learning the spell. Perhaps Gelthrain's magic worked differently, but he doubted it. What wasn't she telling him?

"How do I get past the ward?"

"Earlier screams tell me some ogres have already triggered the ward by removing the grimoire from the lectern. It should be lying close to the ogres slain by the ward. The ward has no more power until the book is returned to the lectern."

Perhaps, perhaps not. Cymric still believed Gelthrain was lying to him. He decided to go up, retrieve the calendar, then assess the situation. If the grimoire looked too dangerous, he could claim not to have seen it. Besides, the ogres might already have made off with it.

"What does the calendar look like?"

"It's a stone disk, one knuckle thick and three handspans across. But it's much lighter than you might think to look at it. It's on a shelf."

"The grimoire."

"Large book in blue lizard-hide; three silver bands along the binding."

"All right, Gelthrain, you've got a deal. I need one more spell, then you can open the floor up."

Cymric assembled the pattern for an illusion of an undisturbed room, a spell that would mask his movements within the room—as long as none of the ogres were too discerning. The illusion slipped easily from his mind into the matrix in astral, waiting to be cast. He returned to the external world, gently touching the floorboards. Gelthrain spoke two words, and a dozen strips of wood separated from the rest of the floor, lifting less than an inch.

Cymric surveyed the room. It was empty of ogres, but the walls were lined with oddly shaped jars suspended in translucent green fluid and boxes sealed with wax. Shelves to his right held metal masks and serrated knives, while directly below were racks of familiar herbs, the foxglove and basil Cymric had seen in use by other town magicians. In the corner to his left lay an overturned lectern, a mahogany piece flowing with carved faces and hands. Cymric touched the floor and cast his spell, levering himself out of the hole, the dozen pieces of flooring floating just above him as he emerged. Once he was in the room, the boards settled back into place.

Cymric could hear the ogres' argument growing louder near the entrance to the shop as he walked slowly along the shelves, examining them. He saw no stone disk matching the calendar's description, but he saw something else. Lying just outside the door was the twisted body of an ogre, none of his limbs in a natural position and with two extra bends in the left arm. A few inches from his left hand lay a large book bound in blue skin. The binding was as thick as his finger, and the book had more pages than his hand would cover. *Mighty thick grimoire you've got there, Gelthrain.*

Four ogres entered the shop. They unstoppered flasks of oil, then shook the oil over every table and cushion in the front room. Cymric sped up his search, looking for a box big enough to hold the calendar. The first one he popped open held neatly folded piles of skin—ork by the look of the hair on it. The second was filled with the heads of snakes, some tanned, the others reduced to skulls.

By now the ogres had tossed two torches into the room, igniting the cushions in a flash. Only two boxes big enough to hold the calendar remained on the shelves. The wax seals on the first were stubborn. While Cymric was stripping away pieces of wax, one of the low tables in the front room caught fire. Ogres hurled unstoppered flasks through the doorway to the shop. The flasks bounced, flopped, and spun, spattering oil all over the floor. Cymric pulled open the box, and found in it butterflies with all but the edges of their wings carved out. He grabbed the other box. It seemed too light, but hadn't Gelthrain said the calendar didn't weigh much? He popped open the box. Inside were painted beetle carapaces.

Beetle shells scattered everywhere when Cymric threw the box across the room. Gelthrain had toyed with him, sending him up here to get the grimoire all the while knowing he wouldn't find the calendar. The room was beginning to heat up from the fire in front, but Cymric checked the shelves one more time. Nothing. Not a single unexamined container big enough on the shelves or anywhere else in this room. Then he had a thought. The grimoire. Might not it be large enough?

Its binding was thick, and Cymric thought he saw a curved indentation of just about the right size under the front cover. Annoyance gripped him, irritation at Gelthrain for having played some stupid game with him. If she had told him the calendar was in the grimoire, he would have gone straight for the bloody thing. Gelthrain was just putting him through a test—which Cymric realized he had just failed. Had he picked up the grimoire, he would have noticed the calendar immediately. Instead he'd spent all this time searching the room. Perhaps he could talk his way clear later. For now he needed the grimoire.

Gingerly stepping over the ogre's body, Cymric knelt by the book. He didn't have time to prepare another spell that might tell him whether the book was warded. On the other hand, Gelthrain's test would have been simply to choose the book. He probably had only to pick it up.

Hearing more ogres shouting, Cymric looked up to see two of the huge beings staring at him. He winced; he must have stepped outside the area of his illusion. Cymric recognized the ogre on the left from the encounter outside of Corthy. On the right was either Koffra or Haggs. From their shouts, Cymric assumed the recognition was mutual.

He grinned broadly. The ogres were plenty angry, but he was separated from them by a fire that was growing with every passing heartbeat. They were ogres, but the weren't that stupid.

When Cymric picked up the grimoire, he could feel a disk in the front cover. He laughed when Koffia (or Haggs) threw a stone that narrowly missed his head, then waddled to the doorway with his trophy. He had paused to stick out his tongue at them; the ogres immediately burst into the shop after him. Cymric's jaw slackened, but he made for the floorboards by which he'd entered. They had sealed tight.

"Gelthrain, open up! They're on my tail! I've got your grimoire!"

The floorboards raised a bit, then floated upward. Cymric dropped down just as the ogres were entering the room. The floorboards sealed behind him, and Cymric handed over the grimoire.

"How close are they?"

As though in answer, a club smashed through the floorboards. Gelthrain led the way down the tunnel. The light quartz bobbed up and down around her neck, throwing dizzying shadows against the tunnel wall. Cymric picked up his staff and followed just as quickly. A glance over his shoulder showed him the ogres forcing their way down the tunnel on their hands and knees. Gelthrain slowed at a point where the tunnel shortened.

"Once we're outside, I can choose some spells that will even things up a bit for Corthy."

"Perhaps you could even cast something that would find Leandra. I expected her to be here by now." Gelthrain nodded agreement.

When they reached the tunnel's upslope, Gelthrain tried scrambling up while holding onto the grimoire, but feet alone did not provide enough purchase. She had to hand the book down to Cymric, then climb up. Cymric gave the book back to her, then climbed up himself. Gelthrain was staring at the sliding stone door that closed off the entrance.

"The illusion concealing the door has been dispelled."

Cymric had forgotten to mention that detail.

Gelthrain put her ear to the door, Cymric hardly daring to breathe as she listened. Only when she nodded did he start breathing again. The elf opened the door a crack to take a look into the alley. The door slid all the way open with a resounding crack. Standing there was the ogre with chainmail, war braids, and the very large axe. Lifting the axe, he gave them his most toothful grin.

10

Gelthrain clutched the grimoire, then threw herself back as the axe swung inside the door. She collided with Cymric, sending them both down the slope. Dirt filled Cymric's sleeves and plugged his nostrils, but Gelthrain was already on her feet. She was heading down the tunnel at a hunched run, the light crystal swinging wildly from the cord around her neck. Cymric sneezed, then also staggered to his feet. Behind him, the ogre leader grunted with effort, sending dirt cascading down the slope. Cymric cursed his luck at running into an ogre not afraid of engaging a wizard in constricted quarters. He followed Gelthrain down the tunnel. She had a head start, but there was only so far she could run.

Indeed, Gelthrain had stopped running. She was seated on the ground, the grimoire open on her lap as she flipped through its pages. She would stop to glance over a page, then skip ahead or retreat back toward the beginning. Cymric was nearly bent over double by the time he reached her.

"What are you doing?"

"Looking for a spell that can get us out of here. I know I've got one in here."

"You can't find a spell in your own grimoire?" Cymric's voice rose in indignation, and Gelthrain shot him a look. He'd have sworn he saw the lines around her eyes move, crawling on their own rather than conforming to the movements of her face. Meanwhile the ogre leader was grunting his way down the tunnel. Cymric thought that now he understood, which only made him feel an idiot for not having figured it out earlier.

Gelthrain wasn't working with her own grimoire. She was working with one she had recently acquired, one whose wards, spells, and capabilities she still had not yet fully deciphered. She knew there was a ward on the grimoire, because it had destroyed the ogre who must have taken it off the pedestal. But Gelthrain hadn't wanted to risk seeing if the ward was finished. Neither did she want to abandon the grimoire to the ogres.

"You were quite fortunate that a wizard happened along when he did. I solved your dilemma rather nicely."

Gelthrain smiled but didn't look up. She kept scanning the pages, turning them more slowly now, running a finger along a line of text.

"I would be even more fortunate if you would delay those ogres long enough for me to cast this spell. I can create a gate that will get us both out of here."

Cymric tried to throw his head back and his hands to the sky, a move that resulted in a shower of dirt and an unpleasant oath. He said, "You mean you're going to cast a spell that will get *you* out of here, leaving me as ogre bait."

"I have no compunction about leaving you to die. But Leandra might have some objection to losing her pet wizard—and the calendar. So you're coming with me." Gelthrain looked him in the eyes. "But only if you give me the time to cast this spell."

Cymric nodded. He headed up the tunnel toward the ogre leader. What did she mean about Leandra losing the calendar? The ogre was crawling along, his body scraping dirt from the sides of the tunnel. Until this moment Cymric had never appreciated just how wide an ogre could be. It made him extremely thankful to the excavator of low, narrow escape tunnels. Seeing Cymric coming, the ogre jabbed his axe at him, but the clumsy attack missed.

Despite the length of the ogre's arms and axe, Cymric discovered that his reach with the staff was slightly greater. He began using the staff to knock dirt down from the tunnel ceiling and into the eyes of the ogre. The ogre roared, rammed himself forward, then flailed the axe at

Cymric. The blade brushed Cymric's robes, but struck nothing that couldn't be mended with thread.

"Careful, broadbellied one. A wizard's robes are expensive."

The ogre grinned, his eyes narrower than arrow slits. He bent one shoulder forward, then said, "I be sure to take it off, fold it nice, before I impale you on your staff. Koffra! Haggs! *Ji erda lig cortomanc tunul geft!*"

Fine luck. I face an ogre bright enough to know the dwarven word for "impale." Cymric kicked some more dirt at the ogre, then doubled over to hurry back down the other end of the tunnel. He squeezed past Gelthrain, who was lost in inner sight. She could probably still hear him, though.

"Does this spell of yours have a large number of threads? More succinctly, how long do I have to hold these brutes off?"

Gelthrain's eyes flickered rapidly, almost randomly. Her lips twitched, "Yes."

Cymric decided that meant yes, this spell had a large number of threads. He wiped his face on a dirty sleeve, then headed up the tunnel toward the shop. The lead ogre from this group had made good progress, getting to within fifteen paces of Gelthrain. The ogre stopped crawling to brandish his club at Cymric, who had stopped about five paces short of the ogre. Taking a deep breath, he cast his ephemeral bolt.

The green wriggle of light surrounded the head of the crawling ogre, whose grunt of surprise was followed by a scream of pain. Cymric cast the spell again, and the ogre began to back up the tunnel. Good enough for this side. Cymric turned back toward the ogre leader.

"I hope you're casting a really good spell," he muttered as he passed Gelthrain. The ogre leader had advanced perhaps twenty paces from his last position, but he still had twenty or more to go to Gelthrain. The ogre leader watched Cymric advance, raising his axe to counter the wizard's attack.

As Cymric cast the ephemeral bolt, the ogre leader tried to twist out of the way, but the wriggling energy struck him between the shoulder blades. The ogre gave a short cry, bowed his head for a second, then looked up at Cymric with a wild grin.

"Little fire wrong, robe man."

"I rather think it is the right spell at the right time." Cymric cast the spell again. The green bolt shimmered, fading into white mist a hand's-breadth in front of that grin. The ogre's grin got wider in response. The leader had disbelieved the illusion. Cymric's gut tightened.

"Koffra! Haggs! *Vird yric cortomanc zu vith chatna!*"

Now they would all disbelieve it. Cymric cast the spell again out of spite. The ogre concentrated and the illusion faded from view, quicker than before. Cymric knocked some dirt down on him, more to vent frustration than in hopes of stopping the ogre. The ogre laughed loudly, and continued to worm his way along the passage. Cymric turned again. He couldn't take the chance, or the time, to reattune a more effective spell.

"It's up to you," he whispered as he passed Gelthrain. He stumble-ran to the other side. The ogre saw him coming and growled. This one would try to disbelieve the illusion as well, even though it had worked twice before. But maybe this ogre wasn't quite as bright as the leader. Indeed, he was trembling. Perhaps the spell would work. Perhaps Cymric should try something else.

Cymric sidled closer to the ogre. He wiggled his left hand, cast the ephemeral bolt, but the spell glanced off the ogre in a cascade of sparks. The ogre stopped trembling, squirming forward a few feet. Confidence made his expression nasty. Cymric sidled a step closer, then wiggled his left hand. The ogre braced for the spell, but Cymric smashed him on the nose with his staff. The ogre collapsed, his head hanging just off the ground as his shoulders wedged into the tunnel. Cymric whacked the ogre's head one more time, wanting to make sure that he didn't wake up anytime soon.

With the obstacle blocking one end of the tunnel, Cymric headed back to the other side. The leader had gotten to within ten paces of Gelthrain. Cymric stopped just four paces in front of her, digging frantically at the sides and top of the tunnel, hoping to loosen enough dirt to make the ceiling collapse. The ogre pressed forward as dirt fell in streams from the ceiling.

"Almost there," Gelthrain mumbled. A flash of light from behind made Cymric glance back. A wavy ring of blue light had appeared in front of Gelthrain's face, giving her the look of an ice sculpture. Cymric gave a visceral whoop, then doubled his effort on the dirt. The ogre began trying to dig his way through the last few paces. Cymric wasn't sure which of them was doing more damage to the tunnel.

The streams of dirt became a downpour. The groaning ceiling caved in on the lead ogre, but the collapse was only partial. The crystal and Gelthrain's spell suffused the tunnel with shafts of light through the swirling dust kicked up by the collapse. Cymric breathed through his sleeve, which filtered most of the dust, but made breathing laborious. He saw the ogre's right leg protruding from the dirt. It was still moving. Beyond the leg was a small opening to the tunnel behind him. The ogre could probably dig himself out, but Cymric and Gelthrain would be long gone by then.

Through watery eyes Cymric watched the blue ring waver, grow in size, then waver some more. Through the circle he saw a row of tombstones shaded by an overhang of rock. The headstones looked old and weathered, the graves neglected, but to Cymric they were beautiful. Behind him earth shifted as the ogre continued to extract himself. Ahead he saw an ogre flatten himself as much as possible, using one hand to help pass the unconscious ogre over the top of his head to his companions in back. Cymric crouched, ready to leap through the portal on Gelthrain's signal. The ring grew. Gelthrain opened her eyes. Cymric tensed his legs.

With the sound of tearing paper and a tiny *pop*, the wavery ring of light disappeared. Cymric looked where the ring had been, then at Gelthrain. She stared down at the grimoire.

"The spell failed."

"What do you mean, the spell failed? You spent half a lifetime casting the damn thing."

Gelthrain closed the grimoire just as a spray of dirt freed the head of the ogre leader. Dirt flowed around him as he began to move toward the elf and the human. Cymric stared wild-eyed at Gelthrain. She shrugged wearily, then drew her short sword.

"Time to carve an exit for ourselves." Cymric thought their chances of hacking their way through a line of ogres was pretty small. Did Gelthrain not have any other spells, spells of her own? Gelthrain moved toward the ogre nearest her shop who was wielding his club before him as he moved down the tunnel. The leader had freed his axe. Gelthrain took a tentative stab at the ogre, then withdrawing her arm quickly from the counterstroke. Cymric's mind worked frantically as the ogres closed in.

"Wait!" Cymric shouted at the top of his voice. The ogres hesitated and Gelthrain looked at him. He had talked his way out of more situations than he had cut his way out of. He had sold Twin Chin on his prowess, he had at least kept Leandra guessing. His magic flowed more to words than weapons. He let the magic flow through him, adding some of his life energy to augment it. The magic gave a wild gleam to his eye.

"Your spell did not fail. It's just that we started it when the ogres were too far apart." Gelthrain's eyebrows furrowed, but she said nothing. Cymric smiled broadly, letting the magic add the confidence he did not yet feel. Working feverishly, he turned to his inner sight to replace his useless illusion with a simple spell. It snapped easily into place. Cymric's grin became genuine.

"Observe. The enchantment still has force, for when I place my hands near our victim's face we still get a spark." He moved toward the leader, keeping his eyes on Gelthrain as if the ogre were no longer of any consequence. He snapped his fingers, casting his ignite spell. The jet of flame appeared by the ogre's ear. Cymric dropped his staff and waved both hands excitedly.

"See? The etheric arc is clearly intact, and the mystic potential has yet to be realized! The spell is merely awaiting completion. All it needs is a better means of targeting the ogres." The ogre leader froze briefly, then took an angry swipe at Cymric, who stood just out of reach. Cymric snapped his fingers, this time without the benefit of a spell. He turned to face Gelthrain. She looked expectant; Cymric thought she understood the ruse. He poured all the effort and energy he could into his next words.

"All we need is to draw two or three targeting runes on the foreheads of the lead ogres in each column. The spell should then strike them all, before they can crawl back out of range." The lead ogre froze again, staring at Cymric in indecision. *I have the hook, but I have not yet closed the sale.* Gelthrain rubbed the tip of her ear, looking like she was taking in all of Cymric's spurious magic theory.

"Sounds reasonable. But remember our agreement; the spell only liquifies their organs and muscles. Those are yours, but the skin and bones are mine."

Cymric nodded enthusiastically. He wondered if there really was such a spell. Gelthrain turned toward the ogre nearest the shop, and Cymric faced the ogre leader. He picked up his staff with one hand, while curving the fingers of his other hand into a "come here" gesture. The ogre leader's expression held for a moment, then broke in a spasm of fear. He backed away. Cymric followed.

"No, no, stop that. It's too late to think about backing out now. You'll have to be well clear of the tunnel before you're safe."

"Haggs! *Ji deks lig tunnul theert! Asta! Asta!*"

The ogre was backing up frantically now, throwing dirt at the wizard. Cymric made a few attempts to touch the head of the ogre, more interested in maintaining the show than risking getting too close to the ogre in his fear-crazed frenzy of thrashing and axe-swinging. Hearing bellows from the other direction down the tunnel, Cymric judged that Gelthrain's efforts must be equally successful.

The ogre backed out with greater speed than he came in. A few more half-hearted feints at his forehead had the ogre back at the slope. Seeing that crawling backward up the slope was proving problematical for his oversized opponent, Cymric had to dawdle as well. He murmured a

few dark-sounding phrases, licked his finger as if tasting
the air, and sighted the ogre along the length of his staff
while saying, "Yes, that is nearly *perfect.*"

Cymric checked on the footsteps behind him. It was
Gelthrain, struggling along with her grimoire. She dropped
the book, which hit the ground with a loud plop. Wiping
dirt from her face, she stage-whispered, "The other side is
ready. He is the last one."

The ogre shouted, then poured on enough extra effort to
push himself up the slope. Seeing the sliding door shut, he
gave it two kicks that sent shattered stone flying into the
alleyway. A heartbeat later, the ogre scrambled out. Cymric crawled up the slope. Gelthrain handed him the book,
then followed. When she reached the top, she snatched the
grimoire back, but Cymric only grinned at her.

A quick look outside showed the ogres running down
the alley. Cymric pulled himself out of the entrance into
the alley and stood up to his full height. It felt wonderful.
He raised both hands to the sky, uttering a screech of wild
triumph. The ogre leader turned, saw the wizard. The powerful creature whirled his axe at Cymric, then resumed
running. Cymric's brain screamed at him to move. As his
body started to lunge across the alley, the whirling axe-
handle smashed into his neck. He did a half-spin, then
crashed into a nearby wall. As his staff rattled to the
ground, Cymric slid down into the dirt of the alleyway.

11

Cymric felt a gentle slap on his face. He mumbled and rolled over, but didn't open his eyes. The second slap was harder, drawing a more coherent objection "I just sat down," he said fuzzily. "It cannot be time to make the bread."

"We are the ones in the oven, wizard." Cymric recognized Gelthrain's voice. His eyes stung from the smoke that filled the alley and made Gelthrain look more like an angry apparition than a real person. Cymric started to sit up, but was only able to accomplish it with the elf's help. She pulled him to his feet, but he could barely stand, his wobbly knees not helped much by his wracking cough. As if by spell, Gelthrain also began to cough. In that sorry state, the two staggered out of the smoky alley following a path Gelthrain had cleared through several burning bales of garbage. *I must have been out for quite awhile; she took her time coming back to get me.* As the smoke thinned and rose around them, Cymric took in their situation.

Hundreds of citizens ringed the center of town, which was in flames. Some were Corthy militia, dressed proudly in studded leather armor and carrying shields and respectable swords or spears. Most were angry shopkeepers or apprentices armed with family heirlooms from the Empire War or makeshift and make-do weapons: smithy hammers, pump handles, torch-holders, ladles, garden shears. One strapping troll-lad was brandishing a captured ogre club.

The townspeople had reclaimed a wedge of the town center before the ogres could react. The ogres were moving slower now, most of them burdened by sacks and packs bulging with loot. The outnumbered ogres had grabbed carts to block the streets and alleys. Some of the carts were empty, overturned and with their axles broken to make them harder to move. Others were loaded with ogrish baggage and loot. The carts did not form a complete barricade, but they slowed the rush of the townspeople. Frantic ogre defenders smashed those daring enough to cross.

The mob surged at one barricade, pushing carts and debris onto the ogres. At first the ogres responded by pushing back, beating at anyone close, trying to preserve the barricade. But then the ogre leader shifted tactics by sending a few wounded ogres to build a new barricade further back along the street. Tables, sacks of rice, pots and water barrels, smoldering beams and shingles, all were piled into the street.

The defenders of the first barricade were overwhelmed, the mob howling as they poured over and through. Four ogres turned quickly enough to race back to the new barricade, but three did not. One fell to an attack by three townspeople, another was caught under a cart, then bludgeoned to death. The third disappeared under a crush of people as the air rang with their vindictive cries and his agonized howls.

"I know my neighbors. Their bloodlust will not let up until all the ogres are either dead or driven away."

"And it seems that the ogres don't want to leave without their goodies."

Gelthrain nodded. She and Cymric stayed as close to the burning buildings as heat and smoke would permit, trying to avoid the desperate ogres. Cymric noticed that they were also making their way back to Gelthrain's shop.

"If the leader falls, I'm sure the other ogres will flee."

"Go right ahead and take him on, your elfness. I'll be right behind you."

"I think that is more in Leandra's line of work. I thought I saw her in the crowd, but she turned away. She probably can't reach this area because of a ward I put in place a few months back."

"What sort of ward do you put up against a friend?"

Gelthrain didn't answer. They had reached her shop,

whose ground floor was burning bright. Smoke poured
from the upstairs, but no flames showed through the roof
or the upper windows. Gelthrain gestured for Cymric to
enter, and he felt the sting of smoke as his eyes widened
in surprise.

"I'm not going into that shop. I'm no stupid ogre."

"I need your help in removing the ward. It's centered in
the room upstairs. I fireproofed the room."

"How terribly unfortunate that the bottom of your shop
is not fireproofed. What happens upstairs when the beams
collapse?'"

"Well be out of here by then. We either take out the
ward or we hope to avoid encircled ogres whose circle
keeps shrinking. Or maybe you can try to sneak past them
into a blood-crazed mob that has no idea who you are. I'm
sure they'll treat you most hospitably."

Cymric's head buzzed. Gelthrain was right: the ward
was the best of three bad choices. She made a sweeping
quarter-circle with one hand, ending in a palm-up "after
you" gesture. Cymric made a mocking bow in return, but
entered the shop. The stairway up was not burning—
apparently it had been fireproofed along with the upstairs.
But the floor and walls between the entrance and the stairway were writhing sheets of flame.

Cymric cast his leaping spell, crouched like a frog, then
jumped. He sailed over the burning tables, past the glowing wall posts, and then landed on the stairs. He hit so
hard it knocked the wind out of him. Trying to regain his
breath in this heat was like trying to outdraw a bellows
over a white-hot forge; the air was too hot, and all it
wanted was to go somewhere else other than Cymric's
lungs. Cymric struggled up the stairway. Gelthrain followed, her normal leaps carrying her from floorboard to
creaking floorboard.

Two light crystals went on when Cymric walked into
the room, which was filled with smoke but cooler. The
wizard could barely see the volumes in the floor-to-ceiling
bookcases that lined the rear and left walls. The wall to his
right was covered with movable brass hangings that resembled the constellations in the night sky. The wall of the

doorway was covered with an oval mosaic assembled from broken bits of colored glass and mirrors.

Gelthrain stumbled on a warped stairboard, but caught herself on the doorframe. She levered herself around the doorway into the room, then drew her dagger and sliced a shallow cut across the palm of her hand. Pressing her bloody palm imprint against the mosaic, she whispered a brief incantation. That done, she pointed to one of the higher bookshelves. "You start memorizing the five books with the owls embossed on the covers. I'll start removing the ward."

Cymric slammed one of the shelves with his staff and glared angrily at Gelthrain, who looked unperturbed. "Wizards are trained in book memory, are they not?" she said. "I thought that was one of their specialties. I lack that ability."

"Wizards," said Cymric, before being interrupted by a coughing fit, "do not work favors for elves who trick them. You said you needed help with the ward."

Gelthrain nodded absently, tracing a pattern on the mosaic. "The books are warded to this room. I believe I only have enough time to remove the ward from either the books or the one stopping Leandra. But with you, I could do a little of both."

"You *could* have done a little of both. I choose not to reward your deception." Cymric crouched once again, cast his spell. Gelthrain paid no attention. Cymric tensed his legs. "I will be interested in seeing which you choose, books or Leandra."

With that, he leapt out the door, heading for the shop entrance. But his forward motion suddenly slowed, then stopped just long enough for a burning pillar to singe his robe. The next thing he knew, Cymric was being hurtled back up the stairs and slung with great force against the back wall of books. His staff rattled away. That none of the books fell on him was the only stroke of fortune Cymric could find.

"The power of my blood presents you from leaving this room without me. Memorize those books and we leave together."

Cymric remained slumped against the books, trying to regain his breath and poise. His breath came back, but the anger and shame did not go. His mouth was too dry to swallow. "I'm sure Leandra will be pleased with your treatment of me," he croaked out.

Gelthrain stopped working on the mosaic to face him. "She has to see you again to know."

"If I die, you lose those books."

"If you die, you can be sure I will craft a suitably heroic tale of your death. I will help Leandra grieve for you. We will both miss you."

The floor groaned, followed by a loud crack as the room tilted toward one of the back corners. Cymric's staff began to roll slowly toward that same corner, but he snagged it as it was going past. Rising carefully to his feet, he toyed briefly with the idea of attacking Gelthrain to force her permission to leave. She turned away, her hands fluttering along the mosaic, raising crackles of light with her touch.

"I'll be interested in seeing which you choose, pride or life."

"Elf, you would make the bitch queen of Blood Wood proud."

Gelthrain turned and took a step, hands clenched into fists at her side, but when the floor groaned again, she didn't attempt to come any closer.

"You have no idea what it means to say that, spell boy."

No, but I'm certainly glad it hurt you. Had Gelthrain's expression been magic, it could have frozen the room. Instead she was sliding back up the room to the mosaic. Cymric worked his way to the other book wall, panting from the heat and hurting fiercely from all his little cuts and burns. The bookshelves to which Gelthrain had pointed were completely wreathed in smoke. Cymric reached up one hand, his fingertips feeling the books along their spines. He found five with identical embossing, something that felt like a feathered head and beak. He pulled them from the shelves, letting them drop loudly to the floor. Then he sat down to examine the books, flipping open volume one of *Omens of the Obedient Spirits*.

He glanced up briefly to see Gelthrain wreathed in

twisted bands of smoke, the bands rolling and moving in time with her hands. A blue aura sparkled off her skin, the sparks increasing and decreasing with the sound of her voice. The elf was completely lost in her spell. Cymric knew she must be seeing patterns of power and intricacy beyond any he could work. When the room suddenly pitched even more precariously, Cymric returned to the books.

Slowing his breathing, he looked deep into the inner world of the first volume, which appeared to be a series of globes, one inside the other. The globes looked to be made of gossamer wire, with larger metallic or crystalline portions at the junctures of dozens of the wires. Cymric selected a juncture that seemed the best connected on the outer sphere, letting his inner eye travel along the wire globe, his force of will moving him past uneven or thorny passages. Cymric guided his sight toward the innermost sphere, the core of the book's ideas. Once there, he released a bit of his own magical life force, which struck and flared like candle flame on a dwarven fuse. The flame raced along the wire. Cymric eased back on his inner sight, then returned to the external world.

He began flipping pages of the book, dipping into his inner sight to see how the various pages related to the pattern of the book. If the page seemed important, Cymric directed the life flame over the pattern-wires more than once. He paced his page-study to the speed of the life flame over the pattern, reaching the last page just as the flame was finishing its circuit of the outer globe. Cymric plucked up the life flame, placing it back into his mind.

A pleasurable wave rolled up and down his body. A wholeness of understanding permeated his mind. Then the understanding faded and fragmented as the knowledge was parceled into familiar packages and symbols to be stored deep within his mind. It would wait there for the wizard to recall it, but only as a piece at a time, never again as the whole. Cymric sensed that he had enough to reconstruct the first volume word for word.

Gelthrain was still working at the ward, the mirror fragments now reflecting things or places not in the room.

Cymric opened the second volume and returned to his inner sight. He was also aware that the room was getting hotter, the tilt becoming more extreme, the groaning more ominous.

Having finished memorizing the second volume, he looked over at Gelthrain, who gave him a nod. Pure petulance made him open the third book. As he dove into his inner sight, Gelthrain's objection was a distant noise, a counterpoint to the roar of the fire.

"That's all, human," she was saying as he surfaced from his inner sight. "Leave with me now or stay here and roast."

And lose your precious books? I think not. Cymric threw open the fourth book, but a hard slap from Gelthrain made him wobble a bit into his inner sight. The pattern of the book appeared fuzzy, as if the globes were growing a layer of copper moss along each of the wires. Cymric concentrated. He felt a pain in his jaw, a jolt that went up his ear, then to the top of his head. He kept reading. Cymric finished the fourth volume to find Gelthrain standing over him.

"Ward is down, time to *go*." Cymric reached for the fifth book. Gelthrain waved him off. "Leave that here—unless you want your bones to sprout thorns." Cymric decided she meant it.

The two made their way to the doorway, which was not tilted upward. The stairs had finally collapsed, as had much of the roof and most of the front wall. Cymric saw a grimace of pain in the flames along a pillar. He blinked. He saw a face, that of a young man with a neatly trimmed moustache and long hair in the Landis style. The face burned along the floor of the shop, its screams the lively crackling of the burning wood. Then other faces also formed and dissolved in the wavering flames.

"What have you trapped in this place?"

"Spirits of the dead no one would miss. Cast your spell. Jump."

"They are in pain." Cymric added a pang of guilt to the list of his injuries. Spiting Gelthrain had hurt these poor bastards.

"Fire hurts. The dead are lucky to feel anything."

"Why. . . ?" Cymric grabbed the doorway. As Gelthrain did the same, he felt the spell constraining him to the room fade away.

"What do you think held this shop together through all this fire? Jump!" Cymric hesitated. Gelthrain shot him an exasperated look, then jumped herself. While she landed, then began to pick her way through the flames and out onto the street, Cymric saw moustache-face's eyes widened, his jaws trembling uncontrollably. Cymric acted impulsively. Pain tore through his head as he wrenched himself to inner sight and grabbed a spell pattern. Marshaling his anger to power his will, he fired the pattern into a matrix like an arrow into a target.

Cymric leaped into the flames and landed by moustache-face. Immediately he cast a spell to dispel magic, but felt his teeth ache as the spell bounced off the enchantment binding the spirit. Cymric tried to ignore the pain, the smell of singed hair. He cast again; the spell bounced. Gelthrain's enchantment was too strong. Moustache-face screamed once more. Cymric could no longer avoid his own pain. Dry, wracking sobs seized him. He staggered out through a gap in the shop wall, clutching his staff close to his body. He made it less than a dozen steps before dropping to the ground. The next moment the shop collapsed in a roaring groan of sparks.

"I would get that robe off. It's smoldering."

Cymric snorted, but unshouldered his backpack and inched out of his robe. He tried to beat out the flames with his staff, but the effort only tired him out. Weary, he reached into his pack and doused the robe with his remaining ale. He sat for a few breaths. Nearby, the street was filled with townspeople passing buckets of water to pour on the fires of the less-ravaged buildings. He counted four ogre bodies, two of them stripped clean. An elderly woman with a green kerchief held the belt of the third, and was eyeing the boots. The fourth corpse was badly burned. Cymric sighed, grabbing up the wadded, wet mass of his robe. He struggled to get it over his head, almost strangled

by the odors of sweat, burnt cloth, and ale. His right arm
probed for a sleeve.

"Gel!"

Cymric poked his head out of the robe to see Leandra
run up to Gelthrain and then throw her arms around her.
The two women squealed like children, then Leandra took
a half-step back, wiping her hands on her leggings.

"I'm sorry. Here I am all covered with ogre gook . . ."

"Doesn't bother me. Never did."

"You've gained weight."

"You think so?"

"Yes, definitely. It looks good on you."

"Really?" Gelthrain smiled brightly. Cymric mimicked
her expression, silently mouthing the elf's words. He
stopped, realizing that mocking Leandra's friend was not a
healthy pastime for a half-burned, semi-naked wizard. He
went back to working on his robe, with better success.

"Really. I was always afraid you were trying to look
like a skeleton, not just work with one. This is better."

"Thanks. You look healthy as always. Speaking of
healthy, you still seeing Brius?"

"No. He left after one of our arguments."

"Too bad. He always had the chest I wanted to cry on.
So, is there anyone new?" Gelthrain's eyebrows rose as
she made a quarter-turn to face Cymric, who was brushing
off his robes with slow, deliberate strokes. He looked from
Gelthrain to Leandra, then back to Gelthrain. He raised his
left eyebrow. Leandra grinned.

"I see you've met Cymric. He is a wizard I hired to
help with the calendar. Speaking of which?"

"Ask the hero with the scrawny buns; he's the one who
retrieved it from the flames."

"*Scrawny buns* politely suggests that the pointy-eared
witch is lying. She has the calendar."

Gelthrain's eyes narrowed. Leandra stepped in between
the elf and the wizard, raising her hands. "Shut up, Cymric. Ease off, Gel. Please. Where is the calendar?" The
three silently gauged each other, the light of the flames
from the burning shop making them look angrier than they
felt. Cymric sighed and shrugged.

"It's inside the front cover of a grimoire Gelthrain had me bring out of her hellhole of a shop. I gave her the book, but she doesn't have it now. Perhaps she gave it to an ogre as a parting gift."

Gelthrain's expression hardened, but softened again at the pleading look from Leandra.

"I do have the grimoire," she said, "but I certainly did not put the calendar inside." Gelthrain's hands moved to about waist-height, then she pulled them apart to create a glowing opening in the air. She drew the grimoire from the glowing pocket and put it on the ground. She knelt, rubbing the front cover with her hand, then suddenly jerked her hand away.

"Wizard's right. The calendar's in there!" Cymric gave a satisfied snort. Leandra also knelt by the grimoire, lightly moving her fingertips across the surface. She pointed to Gelthrain's knife and held her hand out for it. The elf gave it to her, and Leandra carefully slit the skin of the book's cover, cutting it away from the front. Then she handed back the knife. Ever so gently, she began to edge out the calendar, holding her breath as she pulled.

The next moment there was a flash followed by a loud boom. Cymric's ears rang, his eyes were blinded. He felt something rasp upon his skin. He dimly heard Leandra shout and a relentless hiss nearby. Cymric's sight adjusted in time to see a shadowy serpent-head the size of his chest open its jaws. Gleaming, metallic fangs glowed with drops of luminescent venom as the thing attacked him.

12

Scales scraped against Cymric's shoulders as he twisted away from the attack. Continuing his turn, he backpedaled as fast as he could while trying to maintain his footing. He had no intention of making himself an easy target by falling. He gripped his staff tightly in case he had to prop the serpent's mouth open.

The monster seemed made of near-perfect darkness. Though Cymric had felt the scales, he couldn't see them. Only the fangs reflected any light. Like a many-headed hydra, the creature had five necks and heads. The necks split at the base and then joined together in a complicated knot, which began to weave around Leandra's legs and torso. Three of the heads faced her, while one apiece confronted Gelthrain and Cymric. The heads changed their facing by rippling and flowing around the neck. Apparently the resemblance to serpents did not include bones to support the neck and head.

The elf had backed away from the creature and now had the large grimoire open. Cymric was frantically weaving a thread for dispel magic, though he was sure it was probably a poor choice. As the serpent heads bobbed around her, Leandra swung furiously, hitting the ones that came closest. The one on her left struck in a blur of motion, its jaws engulfing her left shoulder, fangs poised just above her chest. As red light flashed from under Leandra's armor, the serpent's jaws worked, but could not close on her. Leandra's face broke into a sweat. The creature hissed and pulled back.

Cymric put all his effort into his spell, draining a little

life magic from himself to increase its effectiveness. Starting at his fingertips, the spell whirled along the astral arc between Cymric and the monster. The dispel magic slammed into the creature, breaking like an egg hurled against a basalt block.

Leandra struck a solid blow to one of the serpent necks. The attached head shook back and forth. The cut gleamed wetly, and what looked like a wisp of steam rose from the wound. Cymric moved around the creature toward one of the heads attacking Leandra. He slid his hands to the end of his staff, then swung it overhead before bringing it down full force with a crack. But if the blow had any effect, the monster ignored it.

One of the heads was now taking a bite out of Leandra, who screamed as its fangs crunched into her crystal armor. Cymric held the staff like a quarterstaff, windmilling the monster. Leandra stabbed it in the mouth, and the hissing head withdrew.

"Wither!" Brow furrowed, sweat dripping down her ash-streaked face, Gelthrain pointed a long finger at one of the necks. The neck swayed for an instant, a charmed cobra of immense size. Then its skin tightened with a slow creak, only to sag and loosen all along the neck. The head screamed, a sound like red-hot steel dropped into a tempering bucket. The tongue lolled. The neck quivered, toppled, and crashed to the ground.

The other heads exploded with motion. The body rotated, gaining speed like a potter's wheel. The four live heads rose, the fifth flopped loosely. Leandra spun in the center. One of her hairpins flew by Cymric. Hair soon splayed out through her coif. The creature moved like a whirlwind, spinning after Gelthrain, who grabbed the grimoire and closed the covers as she ran. The creature slowed its rotation. Two heads attacked Gelthrain, the first one's neck caught her on the shoulder, spinning her around. The second head struck. Gelthrain flinched, raising the grimoire to block the fangs, which sank deep into the book instead of into her. The head rose a few feet, but Gelthrain hung onto the grimoire. The head shook vigorously to free itself from the book, and that made Gelthrain's grip give out. She screamed as the creature flung her a dozen paces down the street.

Most of the townsfolk reacted to the scene by either gaping or fleeing. Others fell to their knees in prayer. A few approached the serpent creature cautiously, careful to stay out of range. A mustached man in a bloodstained smock shook a butcher's knife at the thing. Two boys in the aprons of smithy work threw rocks, darting in for the throw, then out to reload. A red-faced woman used both hands to carry a burning window shutter aloft, shouting a prayer to Garlen. The creature turned two of its heads toward the townsfolk, hissing at the man and woman, striking at the apprentices as they came in to throw. The thing's first attack missed, but the wide-eyed boys did not come as close for their next throw.

Leandra held her sword with both hands. She stabbed at a neck, sinking the blade into a third of its length. The neck arched up and back, the head making a high, whistling sound. Leandra tried twisting the blade. When that failed, she withdrew it for a second strike. Black ichor covered her blade, vanishing like mist in sunlight as she raised her sword to strike.

Cymric backed away a few paces, then took a deep breath, filling his lungs past the point of merely full. He exhaled slowly, forcing himself to inner sight before he took a second breath. Finding the spell pattern he needed, he gathered a piece of his life force to help propel the pattern into astral space. The new pattern flew into the matrix holding the jump pattern, dispersing the old spell pattern like wind scattering dandelion seeds. Cymric took another deep breath and spun a thread, this time to cast a light spell. A globe of light glowed from the tip of his staff.

Cymric returned all his senses to the external world. One serpent head threatened the townsfolk, two faced Leandra (although one had the grimoire impaled on its fangs), and one struck at Gelthrain. None threatened the wizard. Cymric circled the creature until he saw the deep wound Leandra had made, then he charged, plunging his staff into the wound like a spear, the light as the speartip. The creature's skin reacted like thick ooze hit by a huge boulder, the flesh frothing and rippling away from the light in waves, flesh nearest the light boiling off as mist. The attached head screamed, the sound of ten thousand bats squeaking and shrieking at once. The head flowed around the neck to face him, and Cymric jabbed the staff in as hard as he could. The head hissed, jaws unhinging to swallow him whole. Cymric stabbed again. The head descended in a wobbly strike, then hit the ground with a wet sound, splattering ichor but still shattering bricks and raising dust.

All three heads flowed to find Cymric. The wizard ran, a leaping step carrying him just out of reach of the two nearest heads. The creature began to spin again. Cymric wove a thread for another light spell, this time targeting Leandra's sword. The arc was difficult to see, twitching and twisting as the sword spun around with Leandra. A nearby hiss told Cymric the creature was ready to strike. He cast the spell, withdrawing from inner sight as the pattern zipped along the arc to its target.

Cymric dove forward, under the neck of the head attacking him. The head flowed to face him, and Cymric raised his staff defensively, keeping the light-globe pointed at the creature. The mouth spasmed open as the head gurgled its death cry. Leandra withdrew her sword from the neck, then quickly plunged it in twice more, once into each remaining neck. Both heads crashed to the ground. One head still twitched, the grimoire still held firmly in its mouth. The butcher approached in a frantic three-steps-forward, two-steps-back run. He swung his knife three times, hitting the head twice. The head stopped twitching. The butcher raised his arms and howled. The apprentices slapped hands and forearms together. The red-faced woman spoke her thanks to Garlen.

The knot holding Leandra loosened as the creature's entire body began to bubble and effervesce. She slogged her way out of the black goop while Gelthrain struggled to pull the grimoire out of a similar pile of goop. Covered with tarry ooze from the waist down, Leandra moved slowly, her left leg not supporting her full weight. The ooze slowly turned to mist as she made her way toward

Gelthrain. Cymric followed, his pace slowing as the women's voices rose.

"You know I don't like that tone of voice," Gelthrain said.

"Your message said the calendar was genuine. Genuine *and* clean."

Cymric stopped a few paces from them. Leandra stood, her hands behind her head, trying to untangle her hair from the coif. Cymric's eyes widened as he saw the red stain over the front of her crystal chain. Gelthrain was on her hands and knees, using her dagger to scrape tarry ooze off the grimoire.

"The enchantment ran deeper than I thought. I'm sorry." Anger flared in Gelthrain's eyes as she glanced up at Leandra, then back at the book. Leandra knelt down and touched her friend hesitantly on the wrist.

"Stop scraping that book for a moment and look at me. Please? Gel, what's happening?"

Gelthrain looked up. Her face was taut, her lips tight. "I don't know. I would tell you if I did, truly. We can talk later. But I can't let the book get damaged."

Cymric cleared his throat, but only Leandra looked up. "I can clean off the book." That got Gelthrain's attention, but her face showed more suspicion than relief. Cymric felt an odd embarrassment, as though he'd crossed some unseen line. He cleared his throat again. "My magical light ought to work better than a knife on that ooze. Probably better for the book, too." Gelthrain considered the statement. Her nod of agreement was slow, reluctant. She put one foot out, then levered herself up, hands on that thigh.

"We can talk over by what's left of my shop."

"I plan to stay at Silver Keb's," Leandra said. "We could talk there."

Gelthrain shook her head. "We stay here until your wizard finishes cleaning up my book."

"Fine. I'll join you in a minute."

While Gelthrain was walking back to her shop, Leandra turned to Cymric and nodded toward the book. "Thanks. And thanks for sticking with me during the fight."

Cymric grunted as he pivoted his staff so the light faced down. He took the staff in his hands like a broom, preparing to sweep darkness from the grimoire. Leandra took hold of his shoulder, made him look her in the face.

"You all right?"

"I'm not the one bleeding. What about you?"

"No. But I've been hurt often enough to know I'll get better." Leandra slid her hand from his shoulder, still looking at him intently. Cymric found it hard to swallow under that gaze. She softened her expression. "You dodged my question. Are you all right?"

Cymric blinked. *Your crazy elf friend used me to within two inches of death. Maybe you, too. Don't trust her.* His breath came hard. "No. Gelthrain and I don't get along. She's . . . I think she's dangerous. Very dangerous. But she's your friend." Cymric ended the sentence with a half-shrug he hoped didn't look as awkward as it felt. Leandra gave him a tic-smile. Then a slower, broader smile.

"Yes, she's my friend. But I'll be careful." Leandra turned to join Gelthrain, then stopped to face Cymric again after going maybe half the distance. "Go to Silver Keb's," she called out. "Tell Keb I sent you. Get us a couple of rooms. They have really good bread, great soup. Stay away from the lamb."

Cymric watched Leandra turn back to Gelthrain. Fresh food sounded good; a bed sounded better. He realized a fraction of a second too late that he hadn't thanked Leandra for the suggestion. Now he felt foolish shouting his thanks out across the evening.

He tilted his head down and resumed sweeping the grimoire clean, the black ooze wisping away at contact with his light spell. Cymric lightly brushed the top cover, then the pages, finally the spine. When the light flickered, he pulled the staff away. The spell glowed brightly again and he moved it slowly toward the spine. The light flickered, shrank, then disappeared with a sharp pop. A single word glowed, visible for only a heartbeat before fading. *Maeumis.*

13

In the four days since the fight with the ogres, Cymric had forgotten Leandra's warning about the lamb at Silver Keb's. Now he sat before a plate holding a piece of gristly, boiled meat. He had already eaten the four or five bites containing more meat than fat before gamely trying to chew on the next bite. Deciding it wasn't worth the effort, he picked up his napkin, looked to see whether anyone was watching, then spit the meat into the cloth. At least the bread and soup had been good and the ale passable. He drained his tankard.

The tavern was crowded this evening. News of the Corthy battle had reached a caravan bound for Marrek, and the caravan master knew an opportunity when he saw one. Being the first merchant to arrive in a town intent on rebuilding was too good to miss. So now Keb's was filled with dwarfs who wore nose rings and braided their beards into complicated loops. Cymric concluded that the number of rings through a dwarf's nose corresponded with his importance to the caravan—and a three-ringer was someone important, indeed. A few of the dwarfs also had elaborate tattoos covering the backs of their hands, including their thumbs and fingers. But one finger remained unadorned, though it wasn't always the same finger. Cymric had seen a plain thumb, two plain middles, and a plain ring finger. Out of curiosity he inquired of the bartender about the tattoos. The old dwarf told him to forget about it, forget he'd even asked the question. Cymric dropped the subject.

The newcomers were loud, and liked to sing trail songs at the top of their lungs. The songs had simple melodies, but complex percussion accompaniment. They also had a choreographed clanking of tankards, pounding of fists upon tables, stomping of feet, and clapping of hands. The rhythms impressed Cymric, but he was surprised how many of the trail song lyrics dealt with getting out of the caravan business.

The locals took refuge at tables in corners or along the wall. They groused to the wait staff about the intruders, their objections growing in proportion to the ale consumed. Cymric was seated at a table along the middle of the wall. Not very private, but good for observing the rest of the main room.

A blond-haired boy in a blue apron with silver stitching skittered to a stop in front of his table. "Are you finished with that, mister wizard, sir?"

Wincing a little at the title, Cymric pushed his plate toward the boy. "Thank you, Warris." The boy beamed at hearing his name, but Cymric was still hungry. "Could you bring me some of that pudding I saw Keb preparing?"

"Yes sir! Right away!" The boy almost lunged in his eagerness to clear the table, gathering up everything with a loud clatter. Cymric held out his hands, his expression one of mock-surprise. Warris grinned sheepishly, then his eyebrows shot up and his eyes widened.

"Oh! This afternoon Leandra told me she would finish with the elf-mage tonight. She wants to talk to you. She asked that you not wander off in a drunken stupor."

Great, I drink too much the first night here. Now I have a reputation as a spellcasting lush. Levitating the statues of the town fathers had not helped him reputation, except with those apprentices and journeymen who'd seen him do it. Warris had been among them, and he still had that eager-puppy look.

"Thanks for the message. Next time tell the sword lady to bring it to me personally."

Warris looked confused. His mouth worked for a moment before any sound emerged. "You said no one dare disturb you in your room. That your work with the spirits was delicate and dangerous."

Cymric had made the excuse to keep Warris from knocking on his door every half-hour, asking if the wizard needed anything. The excuse would have to be modified. "Leandra has a charm that makes it safe for her to enter my workshop even during my most delicate ritual. I assumed you would have noticed the charm, for you seem knowledgeable about magic. My mistake."

The boy's face radiated excitement as he seized upon the backhanded compliment, "I will tell Leandra the next time I see her. You can count on me, mister wizard, sir!" Cymric dismissed Warris with an elaborate wave of his hand. The boy nearly flew into the kitchen.

The caravaners were roaring together, starting another song. Cymric listened as the first elements of the beat were added, a two-beat and a five-beat. Just as they were beginning to warble out the chorus to the song, Leandra entered the tavern. But if not for her distinctive, firm stride, Cymric wouldn't have recognized her. Her hair was braided into a complex knot, and she wore a high-collared red blouse and colorful skirt-pants instead of chainmail. She still carried her scabbard, however, which hung from a dark brown belt at her waist. She scanned the tavern, spotting Cymric just as he raised one arm to attract her attention. She deftly avoided a caravaner's fondling grasp, her eyes never leaving Cymric as she passed among the tables. She kicked a chair into position and sat while Cymric looked her over once more.

"You look . . . quite different."

"You look just the same. Don't you have more than one robe?"

"I keep this one clean."

"Tattered, burned, but clean."

"I have a tailor's illusion to take care of those inconveniences."

Leandra shifted her weight forward. "Don't you ever get tired of wearing the same thing?"

Her eyes suggested that the question was important. Not knowing the right answer, Cymric only shrugged. Leandra poofed air with her lips, then ordered a cup of tea when Warris arrived with the pudding. The boy bowed low enough to graze his forehead on the table, and Cymric winced in sympathy.

"Tea? No ale for the conquering hero?" he said.

"I like tea."

Warris hurried back with the tea and a basket of bread. Leandra unwrapped the napkin around the bread, inhaling with a "hmmm" of approval. She tore off a piece, then offered the basket to Cymric. He declined, taking a big spoonful of pudding instead.

"Have you finished Gel's books? Made much headway on the calendar?"

Cymric swallowed hastily. "The books, yes, but I'm just starting on the calendar. It's jammed with odd magical shorthand, and parts of it have been carved and recarved, perhaps more than a dozen times."

"Think you can crack it?" Again Leandra watched him with those eyes; Cymric blinked under the intensity of her gaze.

"Give me time, and I'll give you a translation."

Leandra sipped her tea. Then she tilted her head from side to side, and lowered her shoulders. Her gaze became less fierce, her expression wearier.

"Cymric, I have to leave Corthy soon. I want to know if you'll be going with me."

"So now you trust me to tell you the truth?"

"No. But I thought we might swap truths until we can each make a decision."

Cymric's eyebrows raised a little. He considered, then ate some pudding. Leandra took a sip of tea and waited for Cymric's answer. He sighed.

"Telling the client the whole truth goes against the standard wizard contract." He leaned forward, a conspiratorial look on his face. "But if you promise not to tell any other wizards, I might be able to forget that clause, just this once."

"You've got a deal."

"Fine. You can start." He began eating his pudding in earnest.

Leandra laughed. She pursed her lips, took another sip of tea. "I knew you were lying to me back in Twin Chin. That tale of your visit to Skypoint started wrong. Skypoint rests on four pillars, not three. And not a sight you're likely to forget if you've ever seen it."

Cymric grinned and nodded, saluting with his spoon. "So why did you bother with me?"

"Your description of the dark market was accurate, despite never having seen it. I hope your research into the calendar produces information as accurate."

"What is it you're hoping I'll find in the calendar?" Cymric asked between mouthfuls of pudding. Leandra smiled, broke off some more bread, began chewing slowly. Seeing Cymric about to take another bite of pudding, she waved him off. She pointed at him, then moved her fingers and thumb together in the "talking" gesture. Diverting her with questions had been worth a try. Cymric tried to order a few truths in his mind.

"The monster in Twin Chin was a spiritcatcher. I didn't kill it. My magic was only just enough to wriggle me off its hooks."

"You do seem better with words than spells."

"Perhaps you're right; I should have asked that thing to let you go rather than hitting it with my light spell." Cymric's voice had more of an edge than he wanted.

Leandra poofed air into a long sigh. "Gel said she suspected your training was spotty."

"She said a ward prevented you from reaching her shop. Warding against a friend makes no sense. I do not find your elf a very reliable source." Cymric scraped the pudding bowl, showing his irritation in the noise he made.

Leandra finished her tea in one quick swallow, then looked directly at Cymric. "The ward was meant to prevent those touched by a Horror from reaching the shop. It's possible I am Horror marked."

Cymric's scraping stopped dead. He tried to think of something to say, something that would prove he was a wizard of the world. *Horror marked? Happens all the time, nothing that can't be handled with the proper enchantments.* "Have you ever been possessed?" The sadness in her eyes made him regret the question.

"Let's go outside. I want air with fewer ears," Leandra said. She stood up, brushing crumbs from her lap, then

Cymric followed her through the crowd of caravaners. The door rasped as a heavy spring pulled it shut behind them.

The night air was cool, damp with the promise of rain. Cymric followed Leandra down the street, then into an alley. Sailcloth and sheets were stretched over brooms, lampposts, and charred pieces of wood to create makeshift tents, shelter for those who had lost their homes in the fire. Flickering lamps glowed through the sheets, the shadows expanding to fit the sheets. A forlorn woman in dirty gingham sat in the opening of one of the tents. Two young boys bounded around Cymric and Leandra, using them as obstacles for their game of tag. The boys pointedly ignored the seated woman's tired efforts to scold them. During one loop, the taller boy tried to anchor a tight turn around Leandra by grabbing her sword. He had just touched the pommel when she broke his grip, then yanked him off his feet. Even in the poor light of the alley her anger was obvious. His playmate gawked as Leandra carried the boy back to the woman.

"Is this one yours?"

The woman smiled quickly, but not fast enough to cover her concern. "Yes, mistress. Thank you for returning him."

"He should know better than to touch a soldier's weapon without permission."

"He does, and I am sure he will remember better in the future. Won't you, Nalil?" The boy's head bobbed emphatically. Leandra set him down, then knelt to speak to him. She pointed her thumb over her shoulder, indicating the wall behind her.

"If you had pulled the sword out, even just a little, the runes of the scabbard might have blown you through that wall. Understand?" The boy's wide eyed indicated he did. His playmate eyed the scabbard, then the wall with an expression of wonder and perhaps a tinge of disappointment. Leandra rose, bidding the woman a curt good night.

Leandra and Cymric passed down the alley, emerging into a street lined with burned-out buildings. A few were empty husks, but many had been cleared in preparation for rebuilding. Work was proceeding on one that night. Scaffolds of brass and wood rose along the walls, permitting workers to replace mortar and brick all along each one. Illuminating their work was the greenish glow of flawed light crystals. One worker spotted Cymric, and alerted his fellows with a shrill whistle.

"That's him, that's the one who dumped the guilders' statues on their heads!" The other worker added their whistles. As Cymric bowed low, and the workers increased the volume of their whistling. Leaving Leandra standing there impatiently, he wove and cast a levitation spell on a pallet of bricks, raising them to the height of the workers. Cymric then walked away, leaving applause at his back. Leandra threw him a disapproving glance, which Cymric answered with his what-is-your-problem expression.

"The town fathers are already angry with you over the statues. Gel had to call in a number of favors to calm them down."

"What an amazing coincidence she calmed them down long enough for me to rescribe her books. Very charitable of her."

Leandra stopped, her fingers doing a rain-patter on the pommel of her sword. "Did you decide to be a bastard because I said I need you to work on the calendar, or are you this way all the time?" Cymric started to shrug carelessly, but Leandra's expression stopped him. Her eyes glittered, her pain just barely held in check.

"Sorry." Cymric rubbed his eyes. "You and Gelthrain get along, she and I do not. I seem to remember we left Keb's to talk about you, not the elf."

Leandra sat down, leaning back against as ash-smudged wall. Moonlight washed the life from her face as she turned her dark eyes up toward Cymric. He plopped down cross-legged a few feet in front of her. Elbows resting on his knees, hands clasped under his chin, he was ready to listen.

Leandra closed her eyes for a moment, then opened them and locked her gaze to his. "The Horror who may have marked me is known as Ristul. A few years ago, I tried to hunt him down and destroy him. Not just me; Gelthrain was there, too. So was Ragnar, the stubbornest dwarf I've ever met. Husak the ork, he had a taste for very expensive wine. A few others, but they're all dead, except for Gel."

"They died facing the Horror?"

"They died trying to get to Ristul. We never even saw him."

Cymric shifted a little. Confronting a Horror was the subject of many legends, not too many of which turned out well for the hero of the story. Cymric had never had any personal desire to fight a Horror one-on-one, a lack of desire that he considered full proof that he still had some common sense.

"What made you decide to take on a Horror?"

Leandra blew a strand of stray hair one way, then blew the same strand in the other direction. "There is a prophecy. It says I was born to kill this Horror."

"Prophecies are notoriously fuzzy on the finer points. Any hints about how you're supposed to kill it?"

Leandra's smile was narrow and tight. "No. The story is scant on details."

Cymric shifted again. He was feeling uncomfortably warm despite the cool night. "Probably prophesied by a wizard. We specialize in the vaguest prophecies in the business."

Leandra laughed, a short, sharp sound filled with tension. After that, her smile relaxed. "I'd pretty much given up until I heard a rumor about the calendar."

"It's a ritual calendar. What else can you tell me?"

Leandra leaned forward, expression intense. "Rumor says the calendar originated with the Ristular, followers of Ristul. It's supposed to fill in the gaps in the prophecy."

"Including how you're supposed to kill him?"

Leandra nodded. "The calendar is the key to the prophecy. You are the key to the calendar. Together we can kill the Horror."

14

Cymric sat on his bed, the stone calendar before him on the mattress. The rim of the calendar had three hundred and sixty-six notches. The outer edge had thirteen enameled pictographs representing the months used in the calendar. Each month had four weeks of seven days; the end of the year was a festival of either one or two days, chosen by a procedure Cymric had not yet translated. The pictograph depicting blue vinca and white camellias translated as "days when the flowers first bloom." The calendar started the year during this month. Cymric's reckoning placed today as fireday, third week, second month. Or perhaps it was waterday near the end of the first week. Flowers started to bloom at different times in different places. Cymric wished he knew where the calendar system had been created and that he had paid more attention to the plant lore his master had tried to teach him.

The center of the calendar was filled with oddly twisted writings. The writings seemed to be arranged in a flower shape, as if the viewer were looking head-on at a flower starting to bloom. Cymric had spent hours of futile effort trying to translate the writing. He had played with it, distorting the letters, looking for words within shapes. All he got for his efforts were tantalizing fragments of almost dwarven or slightly ork, or possibly Theran. He had done everything he could think of—everything, that is, that was possible in the external world. Looking at the calendar with his inner sight was the next logical step.

Cymric remembered the five-headed shadow hydra, which had appeared at Leandra's mere touch. Why wouldn't the calendar also have additional protection against magical investigation? Even though that was certainly a danger, Cymric knew that he'd run into a dead end. If he were going to make any more progress, he would have to use his wizardry.

He rose from the bed and shuffled along the polished hardwood in his bare feet. He opened the door to see Warris sitting there, hugging his legs to his chest. The youth shot to his feet with an eager expression. The boy wanted to learn magic, that was no secret, but Cymric's use for him was more mundane.

"Would you fetch me some ale, boy? And some braided bread if there's any left from lunch." Disappointment flickered and died on the boy's face. He bowed, then scrambled downstairs to the kitchen. Cymric walked to Leandra's door, which was next to his, and knocked. Only on a second knock did he get a muffled, irritated response. When Leandra finally opened the door, her hair was disheveled and her expression sour. She wore a green tabard with big shoulders and long sleeves; from her reluctance to open the door, Cymric guessed that she wasn't wearing much else.

"Did I wake you?"

"Yes, you did."

"Social convention states that you should say 'oh no, I was awake', even if we both know differently."

Leandra blinked open her eyes, forcing sleep away. From inside the room, the creak of a bed let Cymric know she wasn't alone. Surprise widened his eyes. Leandra hooded hers in response. He hesitated. Leandra slid her lower lip over the top one, stared at him, waiting.

"I need to use some magic on the calendar. I was hoping you might armor up and watch over me, just in case."

Leandra leaned her cheek into the door. "You have to do this now?"

"I'd like to do it while it's still light."

"You really need me for this." Her statement held a hint of question.

"I'm not sure. If I do, I probably wouldn't even have time to yell for help."

Leandra tapped her fingers about waist-high on the

door, but Cymric guessed that she was probably not wearing her sword.

"Give me a few minutes," she said. "Don't start without me." She shut the door quietly. Cymric stood long enough to hear snatches of quiet conversation. He walked back to his room, but halted at the threshold and turned back into the hallway. He put his back to the wall and slid down into a sitting position.

As Warris came pounding up the stairs with a tray holding two tankards sloshing ale onto a mound of bread, Cymric pointed to the floor beside him. He had meant Warris to set the tray down, but the boy took the gesture as an invitation to sit. Cymric took a long drink, then smiled at Warris.

"Tell Keb this barrel is the best so far. But why two tankards?"

"I wasn't sure how thirsty you were. Or how hungry. Keb said it was all right."

Cymric raised a tankard in salute. "Thanks for thinking of a wizard's thirst." Warris' smile engaged his face from eyes to chin. Cymric took a piece of bread and began to chew slowly and thoughtfully.

"What are you going to do next?"

Cymric waved his free hand nonchalantly. "Attempt to penetrate the mysteries of an arcane object through my force of will and knowledge of magical weaving."

"Is it dangerous?" Warris suddenly had that look Cymric had seen dozens of times before, a hunger for vicarious adventure. In other circumstances Cymric would have seized that look as an invitation to a tidy profit. But he was beginning to like Warris. He also doubted that kitchen help was any better paid now than in his days of tending ovens.

"It might be. I hope not. If you hear any suspicious noise from my room, warn the kitchen. Then leave the building."

"I want to help."

"Then stay alert for trouble, and warn downstairs when it happens."

Warris looked unsatisfied. Cymric shrugged. "Really. That would be the best thing you could do."

The door to Leandra's room swung open. Out stepped a man slightly taller and a full chest broader than Cymric, wearing the leather jerkin, hose, and half-cape of a Landis courtier. His head was covered with dark curls, and a neatly trimmed moustache adorned a nearly perfect face. The flaws were a slightly cocked left eye and a dent in the bridge of his nose. As he was closing the door, the man saw Cymric and Warris, who threw the wizard a questioning glance. Cymric spread his hands out before him in a gesture that said he had no idea. The man saw the gesture and laughed. Reaching into his cloak, he pulled out a handful of silver, which he flicked to Warris, a coin at a time.

"Boy, set me a table with some lunch and a mug of your best brew. Keep the change." Warris snatched the coins, then leaped up and caromed off the banister in his haste to get downstairs. The man stood looking down at Cymric, who took a sip of ale.

"Wizard, we talked quite a bit about you."

"I hope the conversation was pleasant."

"Not really." The man squatted down, which gave Cymric an even better idea of just how big he was. *Maybe he has some troll blood. Or bulls on his father's side.* "Leandra says you can use the calendar to unravel her damned prophecy."

"We wizards are versatile."

The man's gaze was feral. Cymric swallowed hard, quite against his intention as the man continued to stare him down. So tremendous was the weight of the gaze that Cymric had to prop his head against the wall behind him. A strong hand pried the tankard from Cymric's nerveless fingers. The man took a sip, then a long draw. Then he wiped the ale from his lips with the back of his left hand while setting the tankard down with his right. Cymric startled at the clatter of tankard against tray. He immediately regretted showing his loss of nerve.

"I don't care what the prophecy says. If she follows it,

she will die. There's no way Leandra can kill Horror Ristul."

"She seems to believe otherwise."

"I know. I've been trying to talk her out of it for a long time. A very long time."

The man's eyes softened for a moment, giving Cymric the opportunity to reclaim his ale. The gaze hardened again, but Cymric defied the look with a noisy gulp. The man smiled briefly.

"Wizard, I want you to promise me something."

"The promise entails . . .?"

"You decipher the prophecy and go along to help her out of all the trouble it's going to cause. And if she dies, make sure you die with her."

"I presume there's an 'or else' in there."

The man laughed. He tried to grab the tankard again, but Cymric wouldn't let go. He looked down at the man's massive hand, then up to his face. The man withdrew his hand.

"Or else I'll find you. I'm very good at finding people." The man stood up, then quickly and silently descended the stairs without a backward look. Once he was out of sight, Cymric tilted his head back and exhaled sharply.

Leandra's door clicked open. She was wearing her armor, now clean and carefully polished. Her scabbard looked recently cleaned as well. Cymric had no doubt she had also sharpened her blade. She nodded her head toward his room.

"Ready?"

Cymric answered by carrying the tray into his room, with Leandra following close behind. Cymric set the tray against the wall opposite the bed. He waved toward the bread and untouched tankard.

"Help yourself."

Leandra took a mouthful of ale and a handful of bread. She sat down next to the tray. Cymric took one last slug of ale, smacking his lips as he finished.

"Who was that nice young man who so politely threatened my life?"

Leandra stopped chewing for a moment, then finished. "Brius. Old friend. He doesn't want me hunting Ristul."

"He thinks you're following this prophecy to your doom. Do you have any reason to believe you can succeed?" Cymric crossed his arms.

Leandra took a small sip of ale before answering. "The legend says that Ristul slithered about in a ruined city, using his powers to lure travelers to their deaths or lifelong servitude of him. His minions began raiding surrounding villages and towns, often taking prisoners to increase their numbers. Under the guidance of priests several people from many farming villages sacrificed their blood magic, storing it for use by a hero. When I was born, the village elders declared me that hero."

Cymric kept his arms crossed. "Or so the story goes."

Leandra closed her eyes in a brief moment of resignation. She had apparently heard that line many times before. "Their magic will strengthen me in my fight against Ristul—if I can tap into it."

"You don't know how to use the magic?"

Leandra shook her head. Cymric whistled quietly. He thought for a moment, then snorted.

"You faced Ristul the first time without the help of the magic?"

Leandra rocked from side to side. "The legend suggested the magic would aid me in my time of need."

Cymric thought about what it must have been like to march into battle against a Horror, counting on magic that never came. Grudging admiration for Leandra slowly seeped into his thoughts. Even though she'd already lost one grim battle to a Horror, she was willing to try again.

"I had given up until I heard about the calendar. I hope it holds the key to tapping the magic."

Cymric sat next to her, slowly chewing on a small piece of bread. "Is that how the revised story goes?"

"I don't think the story changed. I think it's that I now know more of the story."

Cymric tore another piece of bread. He toyed with it, passing it from hand to hand. "Why doesn't Gelthrain translate the calendar for you?" he asked finally.

Leandra shifted her weight, looking uncomfortable. "Wizards are better at languages and deciphering texts than nethermancers."

Cymric reached for his ale. He sipped slowly, looking at Leandra over the rim of his tankard. "You want to tell me the rest of the truth?"

"No. Gel and I went through a lot together. Some of it she doesn't want to go through again. Leave it at that."

Cymric stared into his tankard, sloshing the ale around. "Not very forthcoming from someone who wants a wizard who speaks the truth."

Leandra's eyes flashed anger. "Maybe I don't tell you everything, but what I do tell you is true. When we met, you lied to me."

Half-truths do very well as lies, thank you very much. Cymric looked at Leandra. Her expression had calmed. His eyes wandered over her hair, so efficiently tucked under her mail coif, her gleaming armor, the Throalic honor-patch on her shoulder, the scars on her face. Then he looked down at her polished scabbard. "Would you mind letting me look at your sword?"

Leandra looked surprised. Her hand hesitated for a fraction of a second above the pommel, then she drew the sword out across her body in one long, smooth motion. Cymric gingerly took the sword, holding two hands under the blade. He held it up. The hawk's-head pommel had been cleaned; no grime showed between any of the finely etched lines. The hawk's eyes were polished, and the blade had recently been sharpened. If the recent fighting had left any scratches on the blade, they were gone now. Leandra had ground the edge until it was smooth as water on a still pond. *She keeps her tools in top shape. She keeps herself in top shape. She wants to face down a Horror.* Cymric decided that Leandra really was the sort of person who lived her life more by what was right than what was convenient. A pang of envy shot through him. Life must be simpler when it was so focused.

He turned the sword over in his hand. *Of course, I would focus my life on something other than hunting down a Horror.* Something like unlocking the magics in the calendar and the necklace. Still, heroes of legend took action just as Leandra took action. Cymric handed the sword back, and Leandra sheathed it with just a whisper of a rasp. He picked up his tankard.

"Leandra, you have more magic woven into your life than anyone I've ever met." The look in her eyes was soft but questioning. Cymric tried to meet her gaze, but found his eyes drifting back down to the ale. "Your necklace is deep magic. That calendar is so full of magic it practically overflows. Your life is tied to a prophecy and a Horror."

He took a drink, holding the ale in his mouth, stalling for time to decide what he was going to say next. *When words desert a wizard, trouble soon follows.* He swallowed. "My life has been the magic of the moment. The key has been to move on before it fades." Leandra didn't interrupt him, though he'd been hoping she would. She just continued to listen patiently, her eyes alert. "I may not be the wizard for the job of unraveling the meaning of the magic in your life."

"Are you willing to try?" Leandra's question was calm, but Cymric caught a hint of tension.

No, thank you, your magic is wonderful, but I'll stick to selling spells to know-nothing locals and sampling local ales. Far safer, even if you have to relocate several times a month. A peculiar chill ran down Cymric's spine. "Yes. I will. This wizard promises to keep trying until he succeeds."

Leandra bit her lip. "Even if it means confronting a Horror? I can't ask you to do that for a necklace."

Whoa, reverse oars! She's giving you a way out. Prudent wizards always leave themselves a way out. "We wizards specialize in avoiding Horrors, but this could be one of those rare exceptions." Cymric saw the shine in Leandra's eyes. *Oh no, you're about to do something really stupid.* "In fact, I'm sure it is. If necessary, I will face down the Horror with you."

Leandra's smile was brief. Her eyes began to fill with tears. "You have no idea what you're promising. Take it back now." She closed her eyes and wiped away the tears. "I don't want to count on you, then have you cut and run."

Cymric stood, surprised that his legs were trembling slightly. "My lady swordmaster, I have only the *slightest* inkling of what I am promising. Just enough to scare me spitless." He laughed, throwing his arms to the ceiling. "Still, it feels right. I mean every word of my promise."

Leandra rose and came over to put her arms around Cymric in a grateful hug. Cymric flinched, expecting a bone-crushing grip from those muscular arms, but the embrace was gentle. Leandra tucked her head beneath his chin, her left hand holding him near the base of his neck, the other low on his back. An awkward moment later, he gave her a squeeze in return. The cool links of her chain armor pressed against him, but he could also feel her warmth underneath. Then he felt as well as heard her sniffles. A tightness grew in his codpiece. Embarrassed, he tried to shift his hips so Leandra wouldn't notice the hardness. They held each other for another five or six breaths, then Cymric let go. Leandra had tears in her eyes again, but this time she didn't wipe them away.

"All right, Cymric. Let's go hunt a Horror."

Cymric grinned despite the jolt the words sent through his gut. He walked over to the bed and looked at the calendar. *Perhaps with a little luck, this will maim me. Then I won't have to keep my promise.* Cymric took the calendar in his hands, then reached back in his mind for his inner sight.

15

Cymric slid his inner sight along the rim of the calendar. The rim pulsed with change, threads expanding and contracting in a regular rhythm. Each pulse shifted the color of the thread, yellow to amber to green to blue then back to green. The threads wove or expanded over the center of the calendar, over the flower-shaped region with all the writing.

Maneuvering his inner sight through the thread was like bobbing through a thorny thicket to find a rose in the center. Twisting his way through to the center, he found himself looking at a bright orange flower. It certainly was no rose. Dozens of thin, blunt-edged petals surrounded the head.

Cymric blinked, stared again. The petals looked peculiar, as if formed from twisted lines of nearly identical orange rather than a smooth surface. He pushed his will, moving his inner sight closer. Some of the lines were slightly darker than the others. He rotated his viewpoint and examined a petal. The lines flickered and pulsed, making them hard to keep in his mind's eye. The lines flowed and merged together. Looking carefully, Cymric could just make out . . . words. Every line on the flower was a line of script. Different languages, different styles, but every line a sentence.

A burst of realization made his inner sight waver as his mind absorbed the thought. The visible symbols in the center of the external calendar were portions of the writing, overlapping and at an angle. It was as if he were trying to read a book with transparent pages, five pages at a

time, holding the edges of the page nearly level with his eyes. No wonder the symbols blurred and merged but still looked like language. His inner sight would allow him to read the message, one petal at a time.

Where to begin? He started with the nearest petal, with a sentence in dwarven. *So was Loben Creek devoured by Ristul, just as the other places of dwarfs had been devoured, for the hero was not yet ready to face the Horror.* The next sentence was in a troll dialect; it said much the same thing about a village named Kettrid. Other sentences supported Cymric's conclusion that this petal contained a list of settlements ravaged by the Horror.

He hopped his sight over to another petal, choosing the brightest, most vibrant one he could see. As his sight fixed upon the petal, a tinge of excitement swept through him. This one felt good, important.

The first sentence was in low elvish: *The hero Leandra followed the prophecy to the heart of Ristul.* Cymric tried the next sentence, which was in dwarven, but it made no sense with the first sentence. He searched for another low elvish sentence. It said, *The fight went poorly, for Leandra felt full the doom of Ristul.* Cymric glanced over the next two sentences, but they seemed out of order. Then he read, *Her time was not yet come, for she shall slay Ristul in a year of sevens, within seven days of the day her destiny as a hero was proclaimed.*

Cymric skipped around the sentences, trying to find the right ones in the right order. He read the low elvish section, then the dwarven, then the Uzbck. Parts didn't make sense, but Cymric pieced together a coherent story from what he read and what Leandra had already told him. The blood magic given by those opposed to Ristul could only be tapped within seven days of the day she had been proclaimed a hero. Elders had proclaimed her a hero at birth; the blood magic could be tapped within seven days of her birthday. The legend told of a cycle of blood magic called the Week of Years, a seven-year period. Blood magic was stronger, far stronger, when tapped in the same portion of the cycle as the original birthday. So Leandra should tap the magic when she was seven, fourteen, twenty-one, twenty-eight years of age—any age that fell in the same portion of the Week of Years as her original birthdate. Then she would be strong enough to defeat Ristul. *We hope.*

Cymric's inner sight began to waver. He had been concentrating for some time. He backed his sight away from the petal, his force of will flagging, his sight dipping, falling into and through the petals. When he recovered, his sight was under the petals. A soft scratching tickled him along the base of his neck. He was starting to move his sight back up when he noticed a silver-white design on the back of one petal. The petal's brightness told him that this was the back of the petal he had just read. Rotating his sight, he could see similar designs on at least four other petals. The silver designs ran along the back of the petal to the stem. He moved his sight along the silver trail. His throat began to tickle. A nudge of will sent the sight down along the stem, gathering speed as it descended.

Something stung Cymric in the face, but he pushed the pain aside, concentrating on his sight. The stem flared to roots, the roots spread into astral space. The silver threads formed a web, spiraling around the roots. Head pounding, he thought he heard Leandra shout. His throat hurt, a stabbing pain, a sensation of choking. His breath became more difficult. His sight wavered. He focused on the web. Strands of the web formed runic letters, spelling the same word over and over again through the spiral of the web. *Maeumis.*

Cymric's head snapped back. His sight floated. His vision rounded and popped as if someone had tried to paint the image on a soap bubble. He felt pain, great pain in his face and throat. He tried to speak. That made the pain worse, so he cried out. Which only made the pain worse.

"Cymric! Can you hear me? Raise your right hand if you can." Leandra's voice was level, but strained. He raised his right hand. He tried to open his eyes.

"Don't! Keep them shut until I get some of this off you." Cymric felt Leandra's hands on his head. As her hand moved, the pain became more distinct. His face and throat were pierced as if by hundreds of sharp needles. Something was choking him. It had needles too. Leandra pulled near his eyes, pulled something out of his eyelids. Cymric tried not to scream, holding the noise down to a bubbling gurgle. She continued to work around his face. Cymric heard snaps like the breaking of a small twig, felt bits of his face pucker then release their hold on whatever was piercing his skin. He tasted blood. A tongue-probe of pain in his left cheek discovered four sharp tips protruding through his cheek into his mouth. One by one, Leandra pulled them out. More snapping sounds preceded a relief in the pressure on his throat. Leandra touched his shoulder.

"It's all off." Cymric opened his eyes. Leandra held pieces of vine studded with thorns. The vines and her hands were bloody. Cymric imagined what his face must look like. Tears began to stream down his face. Leandra dropped the vines and took his hands.

"I've got to get help," she said quietly. Cymric choked back a sob, nodding that he understood. "I'll be back. Soon." Leandra rose slowly, but hurried to the door. Flinging it open, she shouted, "Warrls!"

Cymric tried to calm his breathing. The pain in his face and throat seemed worse. It was as if his body knew the worst danger was past, and so now could let him feel the full pain. He tried to concentrate on something—anything—else. He needed a plan. The first step was to tell Leandra what he'd discovered. No, that was second. Feeling better was first. Then Leandra. The third step—he swallowed the taste of blood, took another breath. He clenched and unclenched his hands. The third step would be a talk with Gelthrain.

A broad-shouldered woman in a carpenter's smock stopped her hammering long enough to look Cymric over as he entered Gelthrain's shop. His robe was freshly cleaned, but his face and throat were swabbed in bandages. The salves helped the swelling, but his right eye was still red and puffy, no more than half-open. Other workmen also gave him quick glances. In answer to Cymric's question, the woman pointed her hammer up the stairs. The steps were still blackened and rough, but Cymric thought they didn't creak so much as make a half-crack under his step.

Gelthrain sat between piles of books, next to a pile of rags and ceramic bottles. She was applying fluid from one of the bottles to the pages of a thin book, then daubing up most of the discoloration with a rag. The pages were becoming cleaner. The elf's hands, face, and hair were streaked with gray, brown, and black. She set the book down.

"Ah, the conquering hero," she said. "I understand that Leandra had to save you from an attacking rose bush."

"Your sympathy is appreciated. However, your facts are skewed."

Gelthrain poured some more fluid on a page, then spread it evenly with a clean rag. She continued to look at her book while speaking to him. "You mean you were experimenting with how it feels to be a blood elf? How broad-minded of you."

"If so, I've found I greatly prefer being human."

Gelthrain had all her attention focused on the page in front of her, carefully daubing it clean. At this pace, the elf had weeks of work ahead of her. She ignored Cymric as he moved among the pile of books.

"I must ask you some questions," he said.

"You have one good eye; I assume it sees that I'm busy."

Cymric sighed. "If you can answer questions while cleaning, then I can clean while asking." Gelthrain stopped. She tilted her head, regarding him with curiosity.

"Such a short time, and Leandra is already beginning to rub off on you?"

Cymric sat down and grabbed a rag. He gestured at a pile of books. Gelthrain considered, then handed him one with a skeletal horse embossed on the cover. She followed that up with a bottle.

"Pour it on, spread it thin, then soak it up before it dries."

Cymric nodded and followed her instructions. He cleaned the pages up to an illustration of an elf reading the omens of a horse suspended by its entrails, complete with Gelthrain's notes in the margin. "Who is Maeumis?"

A page crackled stiffly as Gelthrain turned it. "A dwarven nethermancer. He's lived longer than a dwarf ought to—is probably still alive. Very knowledgeable, with a mean streak."

"He wrote that big grimoire I retrieved for you."

Gelthrain glanced up, her look suggesting that she was reevaluating Cymric. He was pleased and decided to push his luck.

"And the wards on the grimoire are your personal testimony to his mean streak?"

Gelthrain smiled, tossed him a clean rag. "Good guess, spell boy, not quite right. The grimoire has a 'key' spell, one you have to learn and cast before you can read any of the other spells. This one had a side effect; it ripped out every spell matrix I had. Tore them clean away, then sucked them into the grimoire. I've yet to figure out how to get them out."

A chill prickled up and down Cymric's spine. He hadn't even imagined that such a thing could be possible. So that was why Gelthrain had been so desperate to get the grimoire and so helpless without it. Also a fine reason not to go face a Horror with Leandra.

"You couldn't use raw magic against the ogres because . . .?"

"Because if that book isn't tainted with Horror magic, then you and I are siblings. Facing an ogre with a sword seemed preferable to taking the chance of casting raw within a mile of that book and having a Horror take interest."

Cymric nodded in agreement. He wiped another page clean, and saw that the facing page had an illustration. From what he could see through the smudges, he decided to skip it. He flipped to the next page of text.

"Maeumis worked on the calendar," he said.

Gelthrain's guarded expression suggested that was news to her. Her face hid a number of emotions, but not well enough. She snapped her book shut. "Talk Leandra out of going. Please."

"I've promised to unravel the prophecy." Cymric carefully finished cleaning the page. "I've promised to go with her and face the Horror if necessary."

Gelthrain laughed, a shrill, bitter sound. She covered her face with her hands. "You have no idea. Listen to me, Cymric." Gelthrain waited for him to meet her gaze. There was pain in her eyes, elven emotion so visible it brought heat to his face. "We never saw Ristul," she said, "but I knew he was close. His presence fouled and warped astral space. When we entered his conclave, it was so bad I could barely cast a spell. I couldn't see any of my matrices to weave my threads. The spells I cast took erratic arcs, vanishing from sight long before hitting a target." Gelthrain tapped Cymric on his chest. "Go in, and your spells will be completely useless."

"I'll find other ways to make myself useful."

Gelthrain laughed again, then slapped him hard. She spat out her next words like a cobra spitting venom. "Ask Leandra how Ragnar died. Here's the truth. Ragnar was picking a lock on the door we thought led to Ristul's chamber." Gelthrain's breathing became shallow, more rapid as she talked. "I didn't know anything was wrong until *scrack*! Leandra suddenly cuts Ragnar's hand off at the wrist. Then she took his arm off at the elbow on the back swing. Before I could move, she strikes three more blows—*wham wham WHAM*! Completely pulps his face. He convulses, lets out a kind of bubbling shriek while Leandra sheaths her sword and walks down the corridor. I look him over, but there's nothing I can do for the poor bearded bastard."

Cymric licked his lips, regarding Gelthrain warily as she began to weep. "I caught up with her at another door. She asks me, 'Where's Ragnar? We've got to get through.' I knew then she was doomed. I grabbed her necklace, pumped every bit of blood magic I could through it. She screamed, went unconscious. I dragged her out, but I don't know how we made it."

Gelthrain pounded the nearest book with an open palm. Her tears had slowed but didn't stop. "She had no idea Ristul had controlled her so easily, so completely. She still doesn't know. The prophecy says Leandra can kill Ristul. I say the prophecy is so much horse shit. But she won't listen to me."

Gelthrain's voice broke, then recovered. She had regained a measure of calm. "You lead Leandra to Ristul, and you lead her to her doom. What's more, she'll kill you for your trouble."

16

There was an unreal quality about the next few days in Corthy. Leandra and Cymric kept busy, as much to avoid empty time as to get things done. Cymric plunged into work, with Leandra watching him the first few times he entered the calendar. With practice, he learned to dodge the ward, but still got hurt on occasion. The longer he stayed inside the pattern the greater were the odds of the thorns being able to track him. Cymric sensed that Leandra had unfinished business with Brius; he assured her he no longer needed her help. It was a lie he wished she could see through.

He spent hours hunched over the calendar, spinning it in his hands or holding it still for his inner sight. He discovered a puzzle, seventeen broken patterns, or clumps of patterns, buried around the Maeumis-root of the calendar flower. The pieces were blurred, indistinct. Because of the calendar's thorny defenses, Cymric didn't dare let his inner sight linger over the patterns. He had to be nimble in his movements, quick in his perceptions. He took pride in escaping these forays with no more than a few scratches on his hands and arms. He took refuge in this work, not permitting himself time to think about what Gelthrain had said.

One such night was surprisingly hot for this time of spring, with only the flimsiest breeze coming through Cymric's unshuttered windows, just barely enough to occasionally flicker the flames of the candles he'd set on his bedposts. The etchings on the calendar had filled with shadow in the dim light of the room. Cymric concentrated, his breathing calm, measured, perhaps a tad shallow; he moved his inner sight carefully around one of the broken patterns. While gently prodding with his will in an attempt to gather and merge the pieces, Cymric felt a tickle brush across his lips.

He plunged his inner sight beneath the roots of the flower, forcing speed from his will. He snapped his course upward, looping and twisting as he raced along the stem. The mystic thorns forked, grew, and trailed his convoluted path. Cymric could see them at the periphery of his inner sight, purple-streaked brown with dark tips. He could almost feel them along his arms; it was like the times when the bakers used to hit him with their measuring rods. There was that moment just after a blow, an instant of a stunned non-sensation just before the pain began. As Cymric maneuvered to elude the thorns, that moment was drawn out. It would last until he either escaped or the thorns caught him.

He spiraled up, swerved his sight out left, then veered back in toward the heart of the flower. He threaded over, around, and through the petals. Experience had taught him that the thorn defense became confused around the central flower pattern. There, he stopped dead. The thorns shot past him, growing as they went. Cymric watched them split, move, split, slow down, then fork again. They stopped. They had lost his trail. He relaxed.

He caught a scent, faint at first, then increasing to a pleasant presence. Confused, he breathed deeply, catching the sour sweat of his unclean robe and the cheap, heavy berry-smell of the candles. This other smell was different, something like a mixture of fresh orange rinds and old black tea, but the scent was nowhere in the room. It wasn't even coming in through his nose. It was lodged directly in his mind, like a memory made real, no longer needing the senses to perceive it. The scent had to be coming from the pattern.

Cymric gave a short, joyous laugh. He remembered some of the aphorisms often muttered by his master. *Sight and mind create recognition, touch and heart create knowledge. The proof of a pattern is in the tasting.* Cymric slowly let any external odors fade. He reveled in the scent of the pattern. It came in two parts, the orange quick and sharp, the tea slow, full, and lingering. He swallowed as he imagined the taste, but the taste never came. Suddenly, he recognized the lip-tickle, but the awareness came a fraction of a second later than before. He immediately jerked his inner sight up and out of the pattern in a straight line, as quickly as he could. Pain stabbed his right hand as he emerged into the external world.

Cymric dropped the calendar, tearing his hand away from a vine of thorns. The vines quivered, then shriveled to become as small and flat as the etchings on the calendar. Sitting cross-legged on the bed, Cymric sucked at the biggest hole in the back of his hand, trying to numb the pain. All he could smell now was his sweat and the perfumed smoke in the room. He watched the calendar for a few minutes; saw not even so much as a twitch. He leaned forward to pick it up, then lowered it to the floor. He loudly blew out all of the candles except one, then lay back in his bed to think.

Cymric had never come that close, or that connected, to a pattern. He had been taught that pattern knowledge was power, but confusion warred with satisfaction in his mind. *How can the scent of orange rinds and black tea make me more powerful?* The scent did not seem the kind the flower would produce, at least not in nature. Was the scent even important? Or just what Maeumis happened to be drinking while creating the pattern of the flower?

A throaty moan escaped from the adjacent room, followed by other sounds of sexual arousal, which began to arouse Cymric. *Brius and Leandra must be done arguing for tonight.* The walls had muffled most of their discussions, but Cymric had heard the shouted parts just fine. Brius wanted Leandra to stop her foolishness. Leandra wanted him to come with her. The pair would quiet down, regain their breath, then start all over again. From what he could hear, they never seemed to resolve the question, but he figured that the loud gasps of "I love you" meant a truce had been reached. He would inquire in the morning. Now he needed to block out the sounds, to think.

He rolled over onto his side, laying his head in the

crook of his elbow. His other hand tapped an irregular rhythm into the mattress, the hand casting soft shadows on the walls. Cymric focused on the shadows while he concentrated on his thoughts. He had promised to accompany Leandra in her hunt for Ristul the Horror. He had made very few promises in his life, and even fewer were those he'd felt compelled to keep. Promises were good intentions contingent upon events. Gelthrain's revelations certainly counted as a reason to reconsider his promise. If he could believe the elf.

Cymric knew he should get Leandra's version of Ragnar's death, but he was at a loss about how to bring up the delicate, perhaps dangerous, subject. He pictured the two of them seated by a campfire along the trail, spooning the last bit of dinner out of their dishes. Cymric wipes his mouth on his sleeve, puts his plate down and asks, "So how did Ragnar die?" Leandra looks pensive, then puts her plate down. She stares Cymric in the eyes, then calmly says, "His death was a lot like this." A flash of fire reflected on steel, *snick-slash*, and one screaming wizard dies writhing in the blood-stained dirt.

Cymric rolled over to his other side, then stretched an arm to extinguish the candle. He took his robe off in the dark, tossed it where he thought the table was. The breeze had picked up some, felt good on his back.

From Leandra's room came the sound of a bubbly laugh, then muffled conversation. It wasn't the laughter of a woman who hacks her comrades to bits. On the other hand, the laugh came from the mouth of a woman who'd just enjoyed a romp with a lover who apparently refused to accompany her on the most important mission of her life. There were still a few pieces of the Leandra puzzle missing. Cymric snorted. *Most* of the pieces were missing; he just hadn't considered many of them important until now.

There was no question the woman was steeped in magic. That she was driven, Cymric believed that she believed she was destined to kill this Horror. Cymric wanted to believe too. Perhaps some part of Leandra suspected that not everything was as the prophecy said it would be.

She hired me to tell her the truth. All I have to do is find it in time. Cymric decided to keep working on the calendar. To keep working on his promise.

A *rattatat* knock woke Cymric from a dream. Half-awake, he mused over whether or not his arms were strong enough to support Leandra in the position he'd been dreaming about. Probably not for the time necessary—not if she were moving half as wildly as in the dream. Four more sharp knocks sounded at the door. He shook his head like a wet dog, trying to awaken fully.

"It's me," said Leandra curtly.

Cymric glanced down ruefully, then looked for his robe. It lay a good two feet short of the table. He plopped his feet down, then padded barefoot across the floor. He wriggled into his robe, remembering its condition only after the smell reached him. He opened the door to see her in full regalia. Her morning readiness was not an endearing trait.

Leandra pushed the door open, bumping the wizard before he had time to step back. She came in and shut the door. "Brius caught one of the Ristular early this morning."

The news managed to open Cymric's eyes to full wakefulness. Leandra walked over to the window, nodded down toward the alley. "He was down there, probably watching us."

"Probably?"

"Brius is still questioning him. We should know more in a bit." Leandra picked up Cymric's pack, nodded toward the calendar. "Time to go."

Cymric nodded. He packed while Leandra watched, but he found her presence a bit unnerving. As a result the pack was somewhat bulky and not as well balanced. He shouldered the pack, then grabbed his staff. "Where to, sword lady?"

"Marrek, but the first order of business is finding that Ristular's companions. They rarely travel alone."

Cymric nodded, more slowly this time. "Correct me if I'm wrong, but aren't these the same people we tried to get away from on the way to Corthy?"

"I doubt they're the same ones, just others of the cult."

Cymric pursed his lips into an *O*. He said, "What I meant to ask is why are we attacking them *now* when we ran away from them before?"

"Well, first," said Leandra, "this group knows for certain who we are and probably some of what we've been up to. If they haven't reported back yet, I want to stop them. And this time I can prepare an attack rather than letting them take us by surprise."

Cymric didn't think Leandra's reasons were compelling enough to go looking for a fight. But it did sound like the fight was already on its way to them. He conceded the point with a heavy sigh.

Brius sat at a table downstairs, the tavern's sole customer this early in the morning. He grunted a greeting to Cymric, then rose and kissed Leandra. She kissed back—pretty well, in Cymric's opinion. The three sat down at a rough table warmed by the full sun of morning. Warris spread bread and tea on their table, bringing knives and jam a few hasty steps later.

"The rest are down at the first traveler's camp on the southeast trail," Brius told them. He tore a hunk from the warm bread. "They're waiting for the one I got to report back tonight." Brius popped the bread into his mouth, chewed twice and swallowed.

"They were watching us?" Leandra asked.

"They had word to look for me, you, and Gel. Your wizard wasn't on their list."

Leandra clapped her hands, then squeezed Cymric warmly on the shoulder. "Maybe the stones are finally falling our way."

Cymric wasn't sure he represented a solid strategic advantage in a fight against a Horror and its cult. He tried to smother his doubts by spreading his bread with a thick layer of jam.

"There's at least one more group, patrolling closer to the river. I figured I'd try to give them something to chase while you head toward Marrek." Brius looked briefly up at Leandra, then back down at his bread. Leandra gave one of her tic-smiles, followed by a slower, sadder smile. She took Brius' free hand in both of hers.

"I'm ready. Cymric is a good wizard. This time it's going to work." She looked imploringly at Brius, who finally met her gaze. His eyes were sad too. Cymric decided to become fascinated by the crumbs in his lap.

"You think so. Gel doesn't. And I'm not sure. If your wizard can't find a way . . ."

"I won't go in after Ristul. I promise."

Cymric looked back up. The two were staring intently at one another. Brius broke contact first, clearing his throat.

"All right then. Time to pay this food the attention it deserves."

Quiet dominated the rest of the meal. Cymric crunched on the crusty end of a loaf, self-conscious of the noise he made. Tea was sipped silently, bread chewed softly. The clink of a knife against the jar of jam carried through the room. Cymric's thoughts drifted, snapped back by the long scrape of a chair. Brius stood up. He clapped his hands, officially ending the silence.

"We had best get started. In the fights to come, may Thystonius find amusement in supporting our side," Brius said.

Leandra was four steps to the door before Cymric had cleared his seat. Brius started to follow quickly, then slowed suddenly. He turned to Cymric, blinked, then set his face. Brius' black eyes were hard and certain, but the twitching in his right cheek revealed uncertainty. Leandra's tic-smile was a similar expression. *I wonder which one picked up the expression from the other.*

"Cymric, can I talk to you for a moment?"

"Certainly. It must be serious if you're using my name instead of 'wizard'." The flash in the bigger man's eyes made Cymric regret the comment. *Sometimes I should just say yes.* Leandra turned at the tavern entrance, but Brius waved her on. She took a step back inside, then she and Brius locked eyes. Leandra broke the lock, giving Cymric a softer look before leaving. The tavern door creaked shut behind her.

"As long as I've known Leandra, she could take care of herself," Brius began.

"Seems she still can." Cymric slowly twirled his staff between the palms of his hands.

Brius smiled, ending in the warmest expression Cymric had seen from the man. "She does what she needs to do, so she can get done what needs doing. She's neither rash, nor a fool, nor a coward." Brius looked toward he door. "But something is working against her, working very hard. And I don't think she sees it. Or at least, she doesn't see all she needs to."

Cymric twirled the staff faster. He thought he knew where the conversation was going. He already had more than enough responsibility, thank you.

Brius turned back to Cymric, "I woke up during the night and saw her necklace on the table, glowing red like a lantern at Year's End." Brius started a gesture, but his hands froze near his waist, his face locked for the same moment. The hands dropped. "She slept through it. This is the same woman who would come alert in camp if an owl perched too close. I tried to wake her. She just mumbled."

Cymric stopped twirling his staff, and started batting it from one hand to the other. Brius looked away again, smoothing his moustache with the first two fingers of his right hand.

"The Ristular was standing underneath our window. I managed to slip outside and nab him. The scuffle wasn't particularly noisy, but it wasn't silent." He shrugged, sending ripples through his demi-cape. "Still no Leandra. I knew then that Ristul—or something—had a hook hard and deep into her." Brius looked directly at Cymric, waiting until the wizard met his eyes. "I need you to be her eyes, to see where she is blind. Will you do that?"

Cymric stopped playing with the staff. Perhaps Leandra had a number of blind spots to the dangers of Ristul. Being her eyes seemed a more appropriate role for her lover than a trail companion. Cymric felt overburdened by the promises he'd already made, promises he now doubted he could keep in full. But, then again, Leandra could be blind to perils that could tear a wizard apart. Being her eyes could be self-serving. But promising to be her eyes—perhaps he could just say yes, not anger Brius, then let events sort themselves out.

Cymric spun his staff like a top. As it started to wobble, he grabbed it with his right hand, raised it and brought it down with a resounding bang upon the floor.

"That's not a promise this wizard can make." He nodded curtly to Brius, then slammed through the door to catch up with Leandra.

17

Concealed by the tall grass and the dim light of a late-afternoon storm, Cymric and Leandra squatted just behind the ridge of the hill overlooking the traveler's camp. The trail wound among the hills, following the low ground as surely as a river. Just off the trail at the base of the low hill across from them was the travelers' camp. Notched logs formed a segmented windbreak at the northwest corner of the camp. Probably a lifesaver in late winter but rather useless against spring rain.

The Ristular were camped below. There were four of them, two human, two dwarf. Five bedrolls and packs sat on the soggy ground, indicating that this was the group to which the captured Ristular belonged. They had a big campfire going. Given the rain, Cymric assumed one of the Ristular must have known elemental magics.

The Ristular were not the only ones using the camp. An ork family was also camped there; mother, father, one who was shawled and veiled—probably grandmother—and four children ranging in ages from hyperactive to bellicose. Most of them huddled under, or ran around, a makeshift tent, a tarp supported by two poles and a large hand-drawn cart loaded with belongings. Mother and father were arguing over his unsuccessful attempts to start a fire. The occasional buffet looked none too affectionate.

"They aren't sharing the fire with the Ristular. They cannot be that friendly with them," Cymric concluded.

"But they're sharing the camp. If we attack the Ristular, they might think we pose a threat to them."

A dwarf Ristular rose and walked deliberately over to the orks. He bowed courteously to the mother and father, but all Cymric could hear of their conversation were muffled sounds. The father ork handed the dwarf an item, maybe a dagger. The dwarf took two steps back, then gestured with his hands to conjure a small flame in midair. The flame slid onto the item, which the dwarf placed in the fire. The wet wood hissed and smoked, but some of it caught fire. The dwarf bowed, refusing whatever the ork offered him.

"Damn," Cymric said. Now the orks had reason to like the Ristular. Why did the Horror-servants have to be so reasonable and observant of trail etiquette? Why couldn't they be frothing, gibbering maniacs Leandra could slaughter without fear of reprisal from the orks? "I'm open to suggestions."

"They're going to tire of waiting for their spy. We have to strike soon." Leandra gripped the hawk's-head pommel. Staring into the camp, she asked, "Can you handle the orks?"

"Please clarify 'handle', if you would."

"Stop them while I take care of the enemy."

Cymric felt a chill run up his spine. He looked down at the overstuffed wagon. "I'm not the sort of wizard who butchers traveling families, if that's what you mean."

Leandra twisted her neck for a long, slow look at Cymric. Water droplets gathered on her coif. The puddles soon broke, flowing in thin lines down her face. She blinked reflexively when the drops got into her eyes; the reflex was the only motion on her face. She gripped the pommel more tightly. "Can you prevent that traveling family from butchering me while I've got my back turned?"

"I'll talk to them. I can probably convince them to stay neutral."

Leandra nodded. "I'll give you a little bit of time to talk before I attack. If it's not going well, or if the Ristular move suspiciously, I hit them. You're on your own with the orks."

Cymric nodded, then slowly crawled backward until he could no longer be seen from the camp. He trotted around the hill, his movement hindered by his staff. When he splashed in a puddle far deeper than it looked, he worried that the sound might somehow carry to the camp. He circled wide to intersect the trail at a point out of sight of the camp, a point on the trail from Corthy.

While he stopped to catch his breath and straighten his robe some, adopting a more wizardly demeanor, Cymric ran through possible openings with the orks. *Excuse me, but were you aware that the kindly dwarf who started your fire actually serves a ravening Horror? Would you mind standing idly by while my companion carves him to pieces in front of your children?* He strode confidently forward, but Cymric suspected his mud-spattered clothing probably diminished the effect. Taking the last turn in the trail before reaching the camp, he paused as if to consider which campfire to approach, then made for the orks. Cymric could smell the stew now simmering in their cookpot. Mother, father, and young bellicose looked up as he drew near.

"Excuse me, gentlefolk, but I was wondering if you might be kind enough to help a wizard on a mission from Corthy?" Cymric bowed. The rest of the family turned to regard him, although the youngest did so from behind grandmother.

The father spoke, "Corthy? They still needing good, honest hands for mending and fixing?" The mother ladled out some stew, giving the first bowl to grandmother, the second to father, and offering the third to Cymric. She had to stare down bellicose, who was in mid-reach for the food. The boy spat, then leaned back on his elbows. Mother glared, lip curling to show a little more tusk than usual. The boy shrugged, then took an interest in scratching designs in the wet dirt just beyond their tent. Mother turned a composed face to Cymric.

The stew did smell good, if heavily peppered. Cymric was wet, cold, and in need of convincing the orks he was on the level. He sat down, and accepted some stew. "Many thanks. Corthy can use hands, and still has coin to pay them."

The father slurped stew from his bowl. Noting a lack of utensils, Cymric did the same, but his eyes bulged and his tongue screamed in agony at the hot, spicy oils in the stew.

He grunted involuntarily; eyes watering, he managed to turn the grunt into an "uuh-uumm" of approval.

The father grinned. "Marta doesn't cut it down to dwarf strength when she's not expecting company."

As the burning subsided, Cymric noticed flavor rather than sensation. "This is quite good. You might want to add 'cooking' to bolster your 'mending' and 'fixing'."

Marta did not react, ladling out soup for her children and herself. Grandmother smiled, clucking approval. *Now I know who your child is, old mother.*

The father laughed. "Corthy runs on dwarven silver, and their tastes don't run to honest food. Although their ale is stout enough."

"Perhaps, but I still think it worth a try." Cymric took another slurp. His tongue had to wrestle a big piece of lamb into his mouth, while carrots and potato came of their own accord.

"You said you had a mission from Corthy," Marta reminded him, her voice deep and gravelly.

Cymric touched his cheeks to indicate his mouth was still full, then he took his time chewing to create some suspense. "I'm looking for a band of robbers who prey upon travel to Corthy."

"Robbers?" asked bellicose, sitting up in interest.

"Robbers," confirmed Cymric, "and vicious ones at that. Oh, they seem helpful enough at first, offering food, helping with fires, that sort of thing."

Marta and father exchanged glances. Grandmother watched Cymric with eyes that made him nervous. Bellicose sat crosslegged, thumping a knee in excitement. The other children watched with wide eyes, although the littlest turned her face halfway to grandmother.

Cymric took a small sip as they looked at each other, then continued. "They wait until the travelers are asleep. Take what they want, kill anyone who wakes."

"How do you know the robbers are on this trail?" warbled grandmother.

"I don't for sure. But we captured one who was scouting ahead, and he said his four companions were on this trail." Bellicose turned to look at the Ristular. The boy's eyes narrowed and his nostrils flared. A convert, thought Cymric.

"Why did they send you out alone after a band of cut-throats?" wheezed grandmother.

Good question; time to modify the story a little. "I'm not alone, just a member of a party charged with the duty of arresting these villains. They sent me in first because we believe one of the robbers is a magician, one who works with fire." The father licked a tusk, then looked at his oldest boy. The mother looked at the father and then the grandmother. Cymric thought it time to cast a net and see what he could catch. "I noticed the four over there. Have you seen any of them work magic with fire?"

The mother and father looked at each other, then apparently reached unspoken agreement. The father turned his head toward Cymric, kicking at a burning log with the sole of a wet boot. Sparks flew as the log hissed. "Dwarf came over. Magicked a broken dagger with flames. Started this fire," the ork said.

"Working with flames does not make you a robber," grandmother said. She gave Cymric a stubborn look.

Cymric met her gaze, nodding sagely. "My good woman, you are certainly correct. But I think you will agree it makes that party worth further investigation."

"They had five bedrolls," Marta said to grandmother.

Cymric blinked. Grandmother ignored him. She gently ran bony fingers through the coarse black hair of the child nestled against her. She nodded. "The wizard claims Corthy captured a spy, their fifth."

"We certainly did, we certainly did," Cymric said. This was going well. He would suggest the family move. Just temporarily, if they wished, but long enough for him to conduct his "investigation." They could come back when it was over.

"If they are the robbers, what will you do?" Marta asked.

Cymric put on his best grim-portents face. From the father's puzzled look, the expression must have been a little off. He was just leaning toward them when a flash of light bathed the group. Flames from the Ristular fire roared into the sky, three times the height of a man and growing. The other Ristular were positioned between the orks and the flame, apparently protecting the dwarf as he cast his magic.

With a piercing yell, Leandra attacked the camp.

18

A powerful sweep from Leandra's sword caught a human Ristular in the midsection. Perhaps the man was wearing armor under his robes, for the blade didn't bite deep. Leandra spun, hit him in the back for her second blow. This one struck hard, sending the Ristular sprawling not two feet from the fire. The other two guard Ristular howled as they drew curved blades from slits in their robes.

The dwarf magician cut his spell short. The flame shrank considerably, but still rose to human height. The dwarf extended his left hand toward the flame while gesturing wildly with his right.

Marta howled for her children to take cover under the cart. Father went to the cart and drew out a battered mace and a club. He handed the mace to Marta, kept the club for himself. The largest boy also rummaged in the cart, extracting a bent brass bar perhaps fifteen inches long. Grandmother stayed where she was, her body not moving, but her eyes darting everywhere.

Marta and the father took defensive stances near the cart while the boy started toward the Ristular. With one quick step, the father caught up to the boy, grabbing the hair tufts and top of the boy's left ear. A growl and a yank dropped the boy to one knee. The ork boy screeched in protest, suddenly sounding much younger than he looked.

If the orks were going to defend their cart, Cymric thought he might chance helping Leandra, and began to weave the thread for a spell of powerful mental attack. His inner sight remained calm and unwavering; the thread slid smoothly and evenly into the spell pattern.

Cymric kept part of his attention focused on the external world, saw the dwarf magician twist his left wrist. Flame leapt from the fire to his right hand, forming itself into a spear longer than the dwarf. Leandra saw the spear, dodged while deflecting a slash from the other dwarf Ristular. The magician hurled the spear. The shaft of flame followed a clean, smooth curve, straight into Leandra's side.

Leandra screamed as she was blown back a good three yards, impact with the ground dislodging the sword from her hand. She scrambled, recovered her sword on hands and knees. The blade-wielding Ristular moved in for the kill.

As Cymric let fly his spell, he felt a rush of energy pour through him, then relief as the pent-up magical charge flew along the astral arc to its target. The blade-dwarf was clutching his head and stumbling to the ground while Leandra's other attacker spun to see what new threat had appeared. The dwarf magician scanned the campsite before locking his gaze on Cymric. Cymric licked his lips and inhaled, trying to control nervousness. He started to weave another thread.

Leandra rose, began to travel in crab-fashion, facing the human Ristular while moving around him. The Ristular struck. Leandra knocked the blow aside, then riposted to leave a gash on her opponent's weapon arm.

Cymric delicately stippled the thread throughout the spell pattern, resisting the fierce impulse to hurry. Blood throbbed in his head, the spell pattern wavering in his inner sight in time with his heartbeat. The thread glowed evenly, providing a comforting point of stability. Cymric completed the weave.

Smoothly meshing external sight and inner sight, he saw the dwarf reach for the fire, apparently preparing another spear. Cymric's inner senses matched an astral pattern with the dwarf's position. As the dwarf began to draw fire for his spear, Cymric imagined the arc between the spell pattern and the fire's position. Then he released the spell, the fire flying upward as Cymric levitated the logs. The dwarf did not complete his spell; the fire he had gathered flickered and died.

The Ristular campfire hovered a few hundred feet above, bathing the battle in a dim light. Cymric heard the clank of Leandra's parry as much as saw it. He moved forward cautiously, holding his staff firmly with both hands, looking for the dwarf magician. The rain made the task more difficult, the drops diffusing the light from above. A few drops caught the light just right to sparkle or flash randomly, distracting Cymric.

A Ristular collapsed in a death wail, the sound sending prickles over the skin of Cymric's neck and arms. Leandra shouted, then he saw her silhouette leap high over the sweeping blow of the last Ristular fighter, landing just behind her attacker's right shoulder. He twisted frantically to counter an expected attack, but Leandra spun as he turned, a tighter spin that put her on the Ristular's unprotected left. Her sword blade caught the light on its descent, disappearing from view into the dark form of the Ristular. A hissing squeal turned bubbly, and Leandra wrenched her blade free. The Ristular fell, thrashing in frenetic, staccato splashes. A final blow stilled him.

A whizzing noise passed close to Cymric. He spotted the dwarf twenty or so paces away, standing in the middle of the trail south. The dwarf stood behind a low spot in the trail, which was now filled with rain and muddy runoff from the adjacent hill. Firelight shimmered off ripples in the puddle, indicating that the water-covered ground was perhaps five paces wide. Cymric advanced cautiously. If the dwarf could work with fire, he could probably work the other elements as well.

The dwarf scooped up trail mud, then began to gesture as if weaving a thread. Cymric wove as well, imagining the force of his will crashing into the dwarf's mind. A shadow streaked by him, Leandra on her way to attack the dwarf.

"No!" was all Cymric managed before Leandra hit the puddle. She sank like the weight on a fisherman's net, sank impossibly far into the puddle, disappearing under the water.

Cymric hesitated, losing his thread. The dwarf flung the mud into the air. At the top of its arc the mud transformed into crystalline darts. Two hit Cymric, staggering him. As the dwarf scooped up another handful of mud, Cymric started his thread again. The surface of the puddle broke with sudden turbulence. *Leandra is struggling down there. Make this one count.*

As the dwarf gestured, Cymric slid the thread into place, adding some of his life force to the casting. The dwarf tossed the mud into the air, and Cymric's inner sight saw his spell streak forward, trailing a luminescent tail like a comet. Crystalline darts formed in the external world; Cymric dodged out of the way just as his spell hit the dwarf. The Ristular fell to one knee, and Cymric could have sworn he saw sparks in the dwarf's beard.

Cymric ran toward the puddle, but the dwarf had stumbled to his feet and fled down the trail. Cymric debated one final spell, but decided on the puddle instead. It looked as though the trail had been stretched and curved, pulled down to make the puddle far deeper than it should be. Leandra was a vague outline struggling along the side near Cymric. She was trying to climb out of the puddle, getting close enough to the surface that Cymric could see her features, but then she would slip down the slope once more. As she tried to swim up, the water churned like rapids, bouncing her down to the bottom.

Again Leandra tried the slope, and Cymric lowered his staff into the water as far as he dared. Leandra grabbed the staff. Braced and leaning back, he tried to pull her out as the water frothed and roiled. Breaking the surface, she gasped for air as Cymric's grip on the staff began to slip. Water pounded down on Leandra's chest and arms, pouring through her armor, then spun into a whirlpool trying to pull her down.

When Cymric finally lost his grip and his staff, Leandra sank with a shriek. He pounded the dirt along the trail in sheer frustration, then slapped his forehead; he felt mud stick to it from his hand. He took a cleansing breath before quickly and surely weaving the thread for a levitate spell. The water churned and roiled, shooting spouts of water like a fountain gone berserk. Cymric kept his palms up, gesturing for the spell to keep lifting Leandra from the water. She lurched free with a slurping pop.

Leandra coughed, suspended a few feet above the water. She shook her head, releasing a spray of water. She looked exasperated. "Stop admiring me like a trophy and put me down!"

"The spell goes up. The spell goes down. Nothing more. Down would be a bad idea, and up would be only for as long as the spell lasts."

Cymric held his left hand with the palm facing Leandra, holding her in position. His right hand gestured up. The staff jumped from the water, spraying both of them.

Leandra muttered, "The sword is mine." A moment later, Leandra's sword followed, slicing cleanly from the water. Cymric grabbed the staff, offered one end to Leandra. He pulled her to the edge of the levitate spell, then lowered her onto solid ground. Her lips fluttered in a sigh of relief. She grabbed her sword, then pointed the tip at the camp.

"Maybe we have a survivor who we can question."

They trudged the few steps to the camp, where they found all three Ristular dead. Two had wounds to show they had died at Leandra's hand. The first one's single wound didn't really look deep enough to be fatal, but Cymric could see no other obvious cause for the Ristular's death. That spooked him.

Leandra searched the bodies and their packs. Aside from personal effects she found several silver coins and enameled brass medallions, which she left to Cymric. The wizard bent to examine the oblong medallions. On the front were etched three serpents intertwined into a knot. Two had blue backs and white bellies, the third was an iridescent green. Slivers of clear crystal formed the green serpent's fangs. The blue serpents had forked lightning for tongues.

Flipping the medallion over, Cymric saw the smooth brass back finely carved with writing he could not read in the dim light. With a casual gesture he lowered the flaming logs back down to the ground so he could study the back of the medallion by their light. The language itself appeared to be an ancient form of dwarven, and the wavy lines of writing formed a design that was naggingly familiar. Cymric worked through the words, absent-mindedly speaking two of the more difficult ones aloud. After the fire flared, hissed, and popped in response, Cymric decided to keep his lips very still while reading. *The seventeenth shall come, shall expire, and we shall be made whole as our lord and majesty Ristul is come.*

The seventeenth what? Or should it be the seventeenth of when? Cymric put the medallions in his pack. He looked up to see the orks giving Leandra a double-earful. She stood, shoulders raised, arms crossed. He decided she could use a little help in extracting herself.

"The trail is once again safe for honest travelers!" boomed Cymric. He walked toward the orks, his best wizard smile on his face. Leandra dropped her shoulders, stretched her neck from side to side.

"Voig here was telling me how surprised he was that those pilgrims over there turned out to be the robbers," said Leandra.

"Pilgrims?" Cymric blinked as his face lost its smile.

"We have seen their kind many times on the road from Marrek," said the father, who Cymric assumed was Voig. The ork tugged at the hair-tufts in his right ear. "They travel to Marrek for worship. Or so they said."

"I bet the robbers only took the disguise of a group of pilgrims. Not all those pilgrims could be robbers," said Marta.

"How many—"

Leandra cut off Cymric's question. "Our friends here say they have seen dozens along the road." Voig and Marta nodded in unison. Leandra stared pensively at the ork's fire. Cymric leaned against his staff, trying to decide their next move.

The grandmother sat on a rough gray blanket, slowly rocking the youngest ork in her arms. She looked at Voig and then at the eldest boy. "Voig and Spat will help you bury those bodies. Bury them far enough way that scavengers don't come sniffing around camp."

The boy looked at the rain, the soft ground, and started to grumble. Voig went to the wagon for three serviceable shovels and a rusty pick. He handed the pick to Cymric, who dropped his staff to take it. Cymric, Leandra, and the two orks each took a limb of the first dwarf body, then lifted it with a grunt, carrying it about sixty paces from the camp, up slick grass to a saddle between the hills. The pick was more useful at tearing through the sod than Cymric might have imagined, but was useless for digging in the exposed dirt. The three shovels descended into the dirt with a rhythmic *shhuuk,* then rose again with the sound of tearing roots. As the grave deepened, it filled with water, making further digging difficult.

Voig paused to measure the depth against the length of his shovel, then grunted in satisfaction. "Deeper than a dog will dig," he said. Spat pushed the body in with his right foot. The Ristular landed with a splash. The four quickly filled the grave with soggy dirt.

Voig gestured down the hill with his thumb. "Spat and me will get the other two. You start digging."

Leandra gave her assent by plunging her shovel into the nearby grass. The two orks took giant, slippery strides down the hill. Leandra flung the first shovelful of dirt a good twenty feet, making Cymric halt his pick-stroke.

She lowered her head. "Sorry, botched that one. I let the dwarf get away from you."

Cymric shrugged, then swung his pick. It hit with a squishy thump. The impact shook water from his soaked robe. "Perfection is not the mark of an adventuring life."

Leandra nodded her head, but drove the shovel into the ground with a hard stamp of her foot. "Now the other Ristular on the road know I'm coming." She took a whirling step away from the grave, sending the dirt flying out into the night. "Now they know that you're traveling with me."

Cymric once more drove the pick into the dirt.

19

The clean smell of the calendula grew more pronounced as Cymric's inner sight lingered around the pattern of the calendar. His inner sight moved languidly in the flow of astral space, like tall grass in a gentle breeze. The flower itself moved slightly, Cymric patiently mimicking the flower's motion, exaggerating one sway or another to actually make progress along the pattern. Traveling this way along the pattern seemed to fool the ward. The thorns did not detect the motion of his inner sight.

Cymric positioned his inner sight underneath the petals that described Leandra's legend. He drank in the shape of the petals, imagined how this alignment of petals would manifest itself on the external calendar. The wizard thought the petals might align with the day Leandra was declared a hero—her birthday. A mental shrug made his vision waver. His guess was two parts hope, one part wizardly deduction. Events important to the pattern of the calendar seemed tied to dates on the calendar. Leandra's birthday ought to be one of those. Cymric memorized the position of the tips of the petals, imagining rays along the lengths of the petals.

The wizard then drifted down the stem of the calendula, falling and wafting toward the roots, which spelled "Maeumis." His inner sight landed softly. While Cymric was adjusting his inner sight, he felt a tingle across the back of his neck. *The ward must be sensitive to this part of the pattern.* He kept his sight motionless, holding his breath until his lungs forced him to inhale. The tingle again passed over his skin, starting at his neck, slowly washing down his back, bouncing up again, then cascading

down his right arm to fade in his fingertips. Cymric waited
through twenty slow breaths; no more tingle. He took one
deep, lingering breath, preparing himself for a flurry of action.

Noting an open spot along one of the Maeumis-roots, he
delicately spun a thread with his wizardry. The thread
caught the flow around him, and Cymric played it out like
a fishing line, weaving more as the thread grew taut. His
will whip-snapped the thread to where the end was over
the spot of the Maeumis-roots. Astral space rippled on one
attempt. The tingle returned. Cymric stopped everything
for several more breaths.

The end of his thread bobbed in the motion of astral
space, just above the *s* in the Maeumis-root. *Come on,
Cymric, nothing to it. Attach the thread. Invest some of
your life energy into it, and behold! Your pattern is joined
to the pattern of the calendar. Couldn't be simpler. Well,
maybe it could be, say, if I'd ever done this before.*

Every legend Cymric had learned as an apprentice told
him this was the way to gain the magic from an item. But
those items of legend had always been scrolls or wands,
swords for the brawnier heroes, items meant to be wielded.
This was a calendar. Perhaps he would just lose that life
energy, wasting it by attaching it to an item with no power
to be used. On the other hand, the calendar was clearly important to the nethermancer Maeumis. Knowledge of the
nethermancer's pattern was surely worth something. Especially if, as Cymric suspected, the nethermancer were still
actively involved. Cymric swallowed. *All right then—*

Wizardry knotted the thread into a quick double-hitch
around the *s*. He released a portion of himself, his life, his
legend. His face warmed, his chest and groin tickled.
Cymric gasped as the life energy released from his pattern
began to pour along the thread. Inner sight saw the energy
thicken, strengthen the thread as it pulsed along the thread
in rhythm with his heartbeat. Milky-blue splashed from the
end of the thread, flaring to jets of brilliant white where it
touched the *s*, fusing Cymric's thread to the pattern of the
calendar.

Cymric leaped upward with his inner sight. He continued to weave, lengthening the thread woven into the pattern. His ears felt pressure and began to ring furiously as he rose. Peripherally he saw three lattices of thorns growing as they dove toward the roots.

When the thorns hit the roots, the turbulence disturbed the astral space around Cymric's sight. His image of the calendula wavered, distorted, and magnified, then shrank to normal. Cymric wove as fast as his mind would allow, the thread rising in a straight line toward the petals he'd observed earlier. Tilting his inner sight below, he saw two tendrils of thorns spiral up and out, searching for him. The third coiled near the roots. He tilted his sight back up.

The petals of Leandra's legend loomed just above. Cymric sighted a good spot for a knot at the base of one of the petals. His inner sight suddenly veered and slammed into the calyx, just underneath the petals. Surprise flooded his mind as pain erupted from his wrists, elbows, and knees. Gathering his bearings, Cymric saw that the petal he wanted was now above and to his left, receding bit by bit in jerky motions. He looked down to see thorns racing up his thread. As they rose, the thorns snared and kinked the thread, making it shorten, one sharp jerk at a time.

Cymric spun thread, adding his fear to the substance of the thread, anything to make the thread longer in less time. A burst of speed looped the thread around the base of a petal. As his sight rotated, Cymric saw another thorn-lattice bearing straight at him. Sucking in his breath, he timed the approach of the thorns. He turned, rotated, then dove through a gap in the lattice. The thorns on the thread behind collided with the thorns Cymric had just threaded. Waves from the collision caught his inner sight, threatened to carry it far away from the pattern. Cymric stopped spinning thread to hold on. Pain lanced through his neck. One of his shoulders popped audibly, the hurt coming soon after the sound. When the waves finally subsided, Cymric spotted the petal he wanted. He spun and tied the thread before the thorn-ward could recover. Cymric popped his inner sight, returning to the external world.

He was kneeling in soft, wet ground, with the calendar between his knees. The rain had stopped. Sweat trickled

down his forehead, and his robe clung wetly to his under-
arms and sides. Leandra stood above him, sword in hand.
The silhouette of the ork's cart stood in the distance. Cymric tried to defuse her look with a smile, but it didn't seem
to work. *Can the thorns follow the thread after I exit the
pattern?* Cymric waved off Leandra. She took a single
step back. Cymric panted as he waited. Nothing happened.

"Wowowooowooooow!" Elation filled Cymric. He
pumped his arms furiously at his sides as he howled. "Yes!
Yes! I did it!" He threw his arms up into the air. Still
grasping her sword tightly, Leandra looked as though she
could use some convincing. Cymric laughed, and Leandra
relaxed enough to lower her sword. Cymric swelled to
carry the full pomp of his lofty position as wizard.

"If I'm right—and I would stake my reputation as a
wizard that I am—we shall soon know your birthday. The
best day for you to kill Ristul."

Leandra's expression went to stone, but her eyes flickered with emotion. "For us to kill Ristul," Leandra said.

Cymric's tinge of regret was quickly overwhelmed by
the euphoria of his triumph. "Yes, the two of us against a
Horror. I must tell you, my dear sword lady, that this is the
first time I've honestly thought we might win." Leandra
sheathed her sword. Her face looked grim in the dim firelight.

Cymric fell into his wizard-patter. He raised the index
finger of his right hand. "Only a few moments more, and
then this transcendent mystery shall——" Cymric caught
Leandra's expression, now even tighter. He fell back
against the ground, face covering his hands. He snorted a
laugh. His hands fell away from his face. He exhaled, sat
back up, then stood, practically leaping from a cross-
legged position. He looked into her dark eyes. "Leandra,
I'm sorry. The patter is part of me."

Leandra closed her eyes for a moment. She shook her
head, opened her eyes. "It's not the wizard-words . . . it's
that they delay the answer. Do it."

Cymric slapped himself mentally. Leandra had been
waiting for a way to use the prophecy for years. He sat
back down and cast his astral sense, finding his thread

glowing white in the pattern near the surface of the calendar. He traced his finger along the stone petals over the thread, following the line to the edge of the calendar.

"Third month, eighth day," he said.

Leandra choked back a soft cry. She raised her face to the sky, blinking several times. "We still have time?"

Then Cymric remembered her outburst the first night they camped. She hadn't known the date of her birthday. She couldn't have known if she were in time for the prophecy. She had simply plunged ahead after a Horror, in the wild hope that she wasn't simply throwing her life away. The thought, and the day's exhaustion, began to eat away at the energy of exhilaration. Cymric rolled up to his feet beside Leandra. Seeing tears starting to streak her face, he fumbled for her hand, then found it. Leandra drew the hand away, shaking her head. An instant later she must have changed her mind, for she grabbed his hand and squeezed hard. Then she relaxed her grip but continued to hold on, crying softly.

Cymric stood awkwardly beside her, then reached over with his free hand to brush away the tears. Fear stopped his hand before it touched her cheek. His hand flopped back to his side, making him feel even more useless. *Why aren't there spells for this sort of thing?* Cymric cleared his throat. "We've got time. I'm still not sure of the exact date the calendar starts."

Leandra's breathing became more ragged, her crying louder. Cymric's mind raced to say the right thing to reassure her. "I've narrowed it down. Today is between the twenty-first and twenty-fourth of their second month." More tears. Cymric's voice rose a little in pitch, his words coming closer together. "We have thirteen to sixteen days. The prophecy gives us a week on either side, so—"

Leandra shook her head and waved him to silence. "Talk about it tomorrow, yes? Not tonight."

Cymric carefully watched her face, those dark eyes bright with tears. He squeezed her hand. "But you're crying *tonight.*"

Leandra made a noise in her throat, an almost-laugh. She touched her forehead to Cymric's right eyebrow, then hugged him. He put his arms around her, which only triggered a new flood of tears. The sobs were louder this time, more violent. Cymric felt a lump starting in his own throat, but Leandra was soon calmed to sniffles. Cymric tried to rub her back, only to snag a finger in a link of her chainmail. His protest brought a quick laugh from Leandra, but then she quickly bit her lip. Looking at her, Cymric felt his throat still tight. His words caught in the constriction, coming out as a croak. All he could do was give her a lopsided smile.

Leandra kept her eyes on Cymric's, while rubbing gently along the side of his neck with one hand. Cymric felt his throat relax enough to let out a long "huh." Leandra dropped her hand to his chest, and she patted him gently. "Thanks. A lot." She kept her eyes on him.

Cymric felt a full smile stretch across his face, but he dropped his eyes, feeling a little embarrassed. He bent down to pick up the calendar, and Leandra picked up his staff. They walked around the puddles, heading for the ork's makeshift tent.

Enough for tonight, thought Cymric. Tomorrow their fight with Ristul would begin in earnest.

20

Cymric awoke from a deep sleep, cold under his blanket. Early light of day washed the color from his arm—which was wrapped around Leandra. Shock woke him completely, but his arm suddenly felt like lead. Move too quickly and Leandra would wake up. Not move in time and Leandra would wake up with his arm around her. Sunlight gleamed off the pile of Leandra's chainmail, next to her padded shift and pants. *That means she's not wearing much more than a blanket.*

Cymric no longer felt so cold. His face felt flushed, and he was almost afraid to breathe. Swallowing silently, he made his decision. He lifted his arm stiff and straight, as if it were a dock crane on the Aras Sea. He swung the arm over his side, rolling onto his back as he flopped the arm to the ground.

Grandmother ork sat watching him, her smile making the warts on her face bunch up with those next to her eyes. The two littlest orks leaned against grandmother, both looking at Cymric with wide eyes, their tongues flicking against short tusks. The bigger child, the one with long, dark hair, looked up at grandmother ork, who nodded. The child grinned, then scampered over to Cymric on her hands and knees.

"Good mohning, mizzer vizard," she said. Her dwarven was a little off, but the shine in her eyes told Cymric how proud she was.

Cymric managed what he hoped was a smile, considering the time of morning. "Good morning. What is your name?"

The ork girl thought for a while, her lips forming silent

words. She broke into a huge smile, her upper lip clearing her tusks. "Leeba!"

"Arak croz visard ved allo Leeba," said grandmother. The girl looked back at grandmother, gave Cymric one more smile, then rushed to bury herself in grandmother's breast. From the safety of grandmother, Leeba took an occasional shy glance at Cymric. Grandmother chuckled. "Leeba's a good girl, smart like her mother. I'm teaching her dwarven, so she can earn her living as her parents before her."

"She will be fortunate if she can someday speak as well as you do."

"She already does. Just not yet in dwarven." Grandmother's wide smile could not conceal all of her distaste for dwarfs. Cymric thought it best to grunt noncommittally, then stretch and scratch his head as if just now fully waking. He sat up, looking for his robe. It lay wadded into a ball, compressed under the indentation of his head. Taking it by the shoulders, Cymric shook it out as best he could. Then he tried to modestly shimmy into his robe while still covered with his blanket.

Leeba's giggle told him how futile was the effort, but Grandmother rapped one of the girl's tusks with a sharp nail. Pouting, Leeba jutted her lower lip to cover her tusk. Seeing Leeba punished made the little ork boy giggle, until he too was silenced by a sharp look from grandmother. Her look became kinder when she turned back to Cymric. "The rest of the family is out repairing a provisioner's wagon that rattled on by before dawn. Earn some decent food to thank you for saving us from the robbers."

Cymric blinked once to remember the story he had told them, then squinted with a thin smile that he hoped expressed grim satisfaction. No giggles; he must have been close.

Grandmother looked at him, tilting her head slowly to the left and behind her. "There are some covered wasteholes just over the ridge of that hill. The lime hasn't been replaced for some time, but there you are."

Cymric followed the line of her nod, then trudged up the hill. Flies buzzed around the warped, stained covers over the three waste-holes. The covers did little to contain the odors of the pits, which had rough wood pieces marking the proper foot positions for each one. As he uncovered the nearest hole, the stench of rotting garbage and human waste rose quickly in the morning air. Cymric's eyes teared, and his nose protested. The wandering life does have its inconveniences, he thought ruefully.

When he was done, he replaced the lid, then wandered further down the backslope of the hill. He faced the fresh morning breeze, which carried with it the scent of wet sweetgrass. The tall fennel had still to flower. Black-winged delks hopped along the ground, their blue-tipped beaks snatching up crickets and other insects. The birds kept a wary eye on Cymric, but none took to the air as he passed through their midst. The wizard walked through the fields, in general heading toward a patch of orange on an adjacent hill. Once at the base, he sprinted up to the flowers, the grass rustling and scraping off his robe.

Calendula carpeted the hill, the same flower stylized in the Ristular calendar. Cymric stopped, spun, then flopped onto the ground. He lay on his back, face warming in the sun. *Talk to me, tell me what the next step should be.* The flowers did not answer. Cymric lay back for some time, half-mulling over problems, half-enjoying the sunshine. He felt his skin soaking up the warmth of the sun, down into muscles sore from a fitful night's sleep. As he steeped his body in sunlight, he let his dilemmas soak deep down into his mind. Some, such as how they might actually kill Ristul the Horror, seemed insoluable, given what he knew now. Cymric sorted through the problems, choosing one he thought needing solving today.

The calendar indicated that Leandra's birthday was some time in the next two weeks. Marrek was perhaps eleven days by road, and the road was perhaps another two days away. That would get them there in time. But the orks had seen more Ristular on the road to Marrek. Trying to go around them would slow him and Leandra down. Once the dwarfs had warned the others, confronting them might be much more dangerous. The road looked like a bad choice.

The river would be quicker. It was three days away, and Marrek was perhaps six days downstream, less if they could find a boatman willing to risk the river at night. Patroling the river would be more difficult for the Ristular than patroling the road. But the river was water. The Ristular obviously had elemental water magic. So the river could also be a bad choice.

Then again, earth magic could help them patrol the road. Cymric pressed his head against the cool, damp ground. When his hair felt wet, he propped himself up on his elbows. He watched the bees busily working around the flowers. Their bulbous bodies dipped, flew, jerked to a stop, changed direction, hovered, alighted, circled, or buzzed in a straight line into the distance. Their movements were fascinating—and hard to predict. *Now that makes sense.*

Why not travel by both river *and* road? They had enough time. Anytime the Ristular spotted them they could switch to the other method of travel. Or go off-road for a day. Or backtrack for half a day. Anything to make their approach erratic and hard to predict. If the Ristular broadened their search, Cymric and Leandra could make a beeline for Marrek. Cymric thought they should start by heading for the river.

Cymric stretched, arms overhead, hands spread, legs extended, toes pointed. He yawned, sat up slowly. Solving a problem before breakfast was the sign of a good day. He walked briskly back to the camp.

He crested the last hill to the smell of fresh biscuits and seasoned sausage. Descending into the camp, he walked around a metal tub filled with water and set near the cart. The fire had been rebuilt several feet away from the tent. Leandra was sitting between Spat and Grandmother. Beside grandmother were the two youngest orks. Across from them sat the parents and a middle child, who delighted in stealing bites from her parents' plates, ignoring her own. Spat had decided that the hand-long sausages were conveniently bite-sized, though the juices and bits of gristle on his tusks and chin suggested that his estimation was wrong. Leandra ate hearty bites. The grandmother cut the sausages into small pieces, feeding herself and the youngest. A drinking flask was in front of each person. The only sounds were knives against plates, childish giggles, and Spat's loud chewing and swallowing.

The father gestured toward a pair of skillets by the fire, then reached down to a cloth beside him. A wobbly toss later, Cymric had a tin plate. A knife followed on a higher arc. Cymric speared two sausages and three burned biscuits, returned to sit by Leandra. As he sat down, the wizard brushed Spat. The ork glowered, which turned his eyebrows into a single, long line, but he did scoot over a few inches. Marta handed a flask to her food-stealer, who promptly brought it over to Cymric. Cymric thanked her in slow dwarven. The girl smiled.

"Good to see you could find the camp from way over on the other side of the hill," Leandra said.

Cymric swallowed. "I was thinking about the road ahead."

Leandra soaked up some of the sausage juices with a biscuit. "Our friends were kind enough to let me use their wash basin to bathe." She nodded at Grandmother. "Gran knows a heat spell. Got the water plenty hot." Then Leandra batted her eyes rapidly at Cymric. "Spat made sure I didn't get cold. He brought me pitchers of hot water. Four times."

Spat's shoulders shook from his whispery laugh. Cymric looked over at the adolescent ork, then back at Leandra. On the way he caught Voig's fatherly smirk. *Oops.*

Leandra tore off a piece of biscuit. "So I was just wondering what took you so long." She tossed the piece into the air, caught it in her mouth without taking her eyes off of Cymric.

"I also took advantage of the sunshine," Cymric said, "to soften muscles the night left stiff." He tried to shrug away the vague sense of guilt beginning to coalesce; it didn't work.

"I shouldn't doubt you would be stiff," Grandmother said as she slid sausage from her knife into the wide-open mouth of the youngest. "You had half your body exposed to the night air, holding Leandra as you were."

Cymric felt his cheeks warm. "It wasn't a conscious act, believe me," he said.

"Gran thought the same thing." Leandra cut the last of her sausage. "I threw your hand back a few times. But ev ery time I did, you would start whimpering." She took a bite of sausage, watching Cymric carefully.

Cymric felt his eyes bulge. From the strange warm pressure in his face, he knew he was blushing. "I did not!" he objected.

The two youngest children nodded solemnly. Spat laughed again, his whole upper body shaking in exaggerated mirth. Leandra made a slow, deliberate turn toward Spat. Her smile was not particularly pleasant. Spat convulsed somewhat less.

"Gran suggested I let you be so we could all get some sleep."

Cymric drank from his flask, then took a long time to wipe his mouth with the back of his hand, which allowed him to compose his expression. He was also trying to think of something to say.

Leandra flashed a tic-smile, then her expression softened. She brushed Cymric's hand with her own. "Your face tells me what I needed to know." She removed her hand, took the last piece of biscuit from her plate. "Eat up. We've got some traveling to do." She popped the last piece, then drank the remains of her flask.

Cymric nodded. He paid a lot of attention to his sausage and biscuit, while Spat paid a lot of attention to him. The ork bent a sausage sideways into his mouth, then burst it with a savage bite. Bits of juice and sausage struck Cymric. The human looked over at the ork, met his gaze, then looked back to his own plate of food.

"Spat Kaerbreaker!" said Marta. "You apologize this instant."

"Sahhy," said Spat, with all the compassion of a crocodile. He swallowed, then grinned. Pieces of sinew and skin dangled from his tusks. Marta stood up, the green of her face growing darker with anger. She looked down at Voig, who seemed totally unconcerned. Spat rose languidly, facing his mother from the vantage point of one head higher. The other children became very quiet.

"Clean yourself up. We have company," Marta said crisply.

Spat grunted. He started to tie down the flaps on the cart, ignoring his mother's orders. Grandmother coughed. Marta looked over. Grandmother looked at Leandra. The three women exchanged a flurry of glances, the final glance being a long, questioning look from Marta to Leandra.

Leandra tapped her pommel, then nodded. She rose. She rotated her shoulders back, rolling her neck to limber it. One step put her two strides away from the rebellious ork. Leandra smiled widely. "Say, Spat—"

"Uhh?" Spat looked up with a lopsided smirk.

Cymric did not see Leandra's sword clear her scabbard, but he heard it. He also sensed twin pulses of magic resonate like a gong one could feel but not hear. Sunlight glinted off the metal slashing past Spat's face. The *whish-whish* of the blade created a spray of saliva and flying bits of something.

"I like a boy who listens to his mother." Leandra's sword snicked back into her scabbard. Wide-eyed, Spat reached a trembling hand to touch his lower lip. Two trickles of blood oozed from the base of his tusks, now clean. Cymric blinked slowly. *Her sword is too big to do that without taking out half of Spat's teeth.* Leandra must have altered the nature of her sword through her magic. Perhaps it was the nature of the sword. Perhaps it was the nature of all swordmasters. Cymric thought it was something peculiar to the nature of Leandra. Cymric found hope for a large impossibility building from witnessing this small one. *Perhaps there is something to this prophecy after all.*

Marta's stunned expression led Cymric to believe Leandra's action was not quite what she'd had in mind. Grandmother's quiet "mmm" said just the opposite. Voig's eyebrows rose, then settled as he nodded slowly, tongue on his left tusk. Three children stared in awe as Leandra walked over to Cymric, then tapped him on the shoulder. "Ready?"

Cymric took a last bite of food, then finished most of his flask. He quickly shouldered his pack and hefted his staff. Voig broke the tension with a booming laugh. He smiled while shaking Leandra's hand. Cymric bowed to grandmother, then to Marta, flourishing his staff behind him and kissing the back of her hand. The girls squealed at that. Spat sulked. Leandra waited a few steps away.

Voig clasped Cymric's arm, the cords of his muscles set in a firm but cordial grip. "Good luck traveling with that one."

"My luck has held so far."

Voig grinned, then dropped his voice. "My boy says Leandra does a bath proud—for a flat-tooth."

"You will understand if I don't pass on the comment," said Cymric, letting go of Voig's arm. Voig laughed again. Cymric walked over to Leandra, then paused to release a blast of flame from his staff. The children cheered and waved. The wizard and the swordmaster then walked from the camp.

When Cymric could no longer hear the child-orks, he moved a step closer to Leandra. "Had you thought at all about what you would say to Marta if you had just happened to miss and ended up carving up Spat's face?"

Leandra set her face. "No. We're now dueling the Ristular." Her stride picked up a little.

Cymric let his tongue slide along his upper lip as he pondered her words. He waggled his staff as he looked at her. "Perhaps you would care to elaborate?"

Leandra's tic-smile hung around longer than usual. "There is no point in thinking about the consequences of failure. We only live if we succeed."

21

Cymric split open the pomegranate, following the cut Leandra had made. They were sitting at the edge of an impromptu market set up at the intersection of five trails. Farmers had gathered that morning at a campsite in the wedge between the northern and northeastern trails. Camping there were a group of Astendar pilgrims, nearly seventy strong. Though their purses were not heavy, they weren't empty either. Once the market began, it quickly grew in size because almost every traveler stopped to peruse its wares. Now other peddlers had set up shop as well.

Cymric and Leandra had arrived in the middle of the afternoon, coming south from the ork campsite. Strolling around the market, Cymric estimated that seven hundred or so people had gathered. He knew that the warm weather and the serendipitous nature of the event had elevated spirits and loosened purse strings, but he forced himself to suppress his mercenary instincts. An Uzhbek woman had set up shop as a soothsayer with a patter that made Cymric wince. Astral vagaries indeed! Her clients devoured every word.

Searching about for Leandra, he turned around, only to spot four Ristular, their robes opened at the collar because of the heat. All were dwarfs, but the dwarven elementalist was not among them. The four were examining a human farmer's stock of herbs. The shortest was haggling the price with the ruddy-faced farmer, whose arms flailed wildly in ritual indignation.

Cymric stopped to look at some candles at a nearby cart with a blue awning. Though his disinterest wasn't feigned, the pudgy candle mistress took his nonchalance as an opening move. He tried to ignore her pitch, wanting to listen in on the dwarf and the farmer, whose bargaining was, fortunately, being carried out in full voice. They were haggling over the farmer's entire stock of borage. Was that herb used to increase courage? Or was it only that its name sounded like courage?

Cymric left to find Leandra, vaguely surprised to discover he was walking away with three candles, his purse a few silvers lighter. The candle mistress gave him a satisfied smile and a friendly wave goodbye. Cymric nodded absently to her.

He found Leandra browsing for some fresh fruits and bread for a meal. When he told her about the Ristular, she hurriedly concluded her shopping. Now the two of them sat at the edge of the market, with five peddler-trolls between them and the rest of the market. The trolls were drinking heavily and dicing loudly, inspiring most passersby to either avert their eyes or glance warily at the trolls. No one paid much attention to the two quiet humans sitting a few paces away.

Cymric finally made it to the pulp in the center of the pomegranate he was eating. He shared some with Leandra, then continued to eat his own portion, sucking the tart flesh off the seeds before crunching them. Then Leandra began to slice a pale-white round of cheese while Cymric checked her cold tea. He pulled the tea ball out by its chain, but decided to leave it in for a while longer. He poured ale for himself, tilting the bottle until its last glug. He took a long drink, licking foam from his lips as he came up for air. Leandra gently knocked the tea ball against the side of her pewter flagon, then wrapped the ball in a well-stained cheesecloth.

"Staying here for the night is out," said Cymric.

Leandra nodded as she sipped her tea. Layers of cheesecloth muted the glow of her necklace. "Southwest of here is a shrine to Garlen. It's a hike, but we can make it by a few hours after nightfall."

"Speak for yourself, ironlegs." Cymric was used to walking, but he had still not adjusted to Leandra's pace, which was more of a forced march than a walk. He crunched on a crust for emphasis.

Leandra curved a smile around the rim of her tea. "You should try Landis blend instead of ale. Keeps you moving."

"Perhaps one day I might enjoy the taste of bitter, burnt bark. When that day comes, I'll be happy to take your advice." Cymric peeled the soft wax from a slice of cheese, then ate more than half the piece in a single bite.

"One night you may find yourself winded, with Ristular raising a cloud of dust one hill behind you. Then you'll wish you'd taken my advice." Leandra looked toward the market, then back at Cymric. He took one more sip of ale, made a face, then dumped the rest of his ale. He rinsed out the tankard with a squeeze of his water skin, then handed it to Leandra. "Go ahead, murder my tongue. Please."

Leandra unwrapped the tea ball. She held it in her right hand, gesturing to it with her left in an almost wizard-like flourish. She unscrewed it, added some fresh tea from a pouch, then plopped the ball into the tankard, hanging the hook over the edge. "I think we can stick to the smaller trails as long as we head for the river. Any river village ought to have a boatman for hire."

Cymric nodded, took a suspicious glance at the dark stain spreading through the water in his tankard. "I was wondering if I might examine your necklace tonight."

Leandra's face blanked for a moment. "Why?"

Cymric swirled his tankard as he talked. "It's the one piece that doesn't fit the puzzle. There's no mention of it in the calendar."

Leandra cocked her head, reached behind her ear to twirl a strand of hair. She looked tired and a little scared. "The Ristular are practically crawling into our backpacks. I need the necklace for protection."

"I understand." It was true that he did, but Cymric also needed to wrap up some loose ends before they reached Marrek. "If we go to a shrine of Garlen, that should offer some protection."

Leandra crossed her arms. "Not enough. I am no questor of Garlen."

Cymric held his hands out, patting down the air in a gesture intended to calm Leandra. "You've had the necklace all your life. You don't even remember when you got it. The necklace is practically strung on magic. Yet a prophecy based on your life makes no mention of the powerful talisman you carry. Not even an oblique reference."

"Prophecies always come up short on details. This prophecy certainly has," said Leandra. She took a gulp of tea, then reached over to pluck the tea ball out of the tankard even as Cymric was fidgeting with it.

Cymric sipped the tea, which passed the tip of his tongue without incident, then gagged him with its bitterness on his first swallow. Cymric sputtered and coughed, wiping his lips with his sleeve. "Damn, this tea keeps you up because you can't sleep until you forget its taste."

Leandra took a thoughtful sip of hers, then looked at him with full, open eyes and a slight shake of her head. "I thought it was the magic in the herbs. But I guess it takes a wizard to figure these things out."

"We wizards are quick to figure that if it burns the tongue out of your mouth, you may not want to drink a gallon of it." Cymric sloshed the tea around in his tankard. Leandra drained hers. Cymric screwed up his face as he decided to take another sip. He drank, surprised to discover the taste wasn't as bad on the second swallow. His surprise must have shown, for Leandra laughed.

The trolls exploded into an argument, conducted entirely in trollish except for select elvish and dwarven obscenities. The argument escalated into a shoving match, and one of the peddlers reached into his sack for a breadboard. A roar, a swing, then the breadboard broke with a terrific *crack*! over the skull of the shortest troll. When the troll's knees hit the ground, it was like a signal for the start of a general melee among the trolls. Pots clanged against sheet pans, a pepper grinder deftly deflected sewing shears. The trolls were destroying merchandise at a great rate, but other than the surprise strike on the short troll, not harming one another.

A crowd gathered to cheer, place wagers, and hope for

more blood. One too-thin young woman even went so far as to throw her walking stick to a disarmed troll, screaming for him to crack the knees of another combatant. At that, Leandra and Cymric hurriedly gathered up their lunch, packing what they couldn't carry by hand. They edged around the crowd. Not seeing the Ristular, they hastily took the southwestern path.

Once they'd put a few hundred paces behind them, Cymric tried again. "Your necklace is the puzzle piece that doesn't fit."

"It fits my neck. That's enough."

Cymric laughed and Leandra shot him a hard glance. "I suppose you're right. The fields are crawling with Ristular." He sighed, one of his best sighs.

"It's not an *effective* pout unless you use your lower lip," Leandra said tartly. Cymric extended his lower lip, quivering just so. Leandra laughed once, then shook her head. "It's not going to work."

Cymric nodded, then sighed again. "So close," he mumbled.

"Keep it up and I'll thump you with your own staff," Leandra said. Her voice rose in annoyance. She kicked some trail dirt at Cymric.

That's enough for now. The level of Leandra's annoyance was probably a good sign. No rage, not a lot of fear, just annoyance; Cymric might yet get another look at that necklace if he switched tactics later. *And you, my magnificent piece of jewelry, can tell me whatever it is the calendar cannot.*

The shrine to Garlen sat in a pool formed by a natural spring notched into a rocky formation. Orange, red, and yellow rock striped the pool, mineral deposits the spring had brought up from deep within the earth. Rimming the pool were smooth, round rocks approximately two handspans wide, and set around it were three light quartzes set on six-foot wooden poles. Two were cracked and flickering, one still beamed brilliantly. Surrounding the glade were tall birch trees, home to a colony of squirrels.

The shrine itself sat by the edge of the pool farthest

from the spring. Rising about waist-high from the water
were limestone slabs piled atop one another. Set on the
slabs was an alabaster statue of a woman of middle age
seated in a cross-legged position. Her face was angular,
but her smile and eyes kept her expression from being se-
vere. She wore a robe whose shoulder sash was still
flecked with a few bits of the original blue paint. Around
her were alabaster renditions of a loaf of bread, a mortar,
and a pestle. There was also a copper flask, which had
long ago succumbed to verdigris. At the base of the shrine
were offerings of bread, fruit, and grains—which explained the shrine's popularity with squirrels.

Leandra crossed the glade to the spring. She washed her
hands, then cupped them to catch the water. She turned to
face the shrine, raising her hands in gratitude, then drank
the water. "Thank you, lady, for inviting us into your
home," she said. "Your hospitality is always a light for the
heart." She stepped away, looking expectantly at Cymric.
"Garlen has blessed these waters. I suggest you thank her
for them."

Cymric cleared his throat. He had never really inter-
acted with any of the Passions. He knew you never bar-
gained with a merchant wearing the symbol of Chorrolis,
that a warrior devoted to Floranuus fought fiercely and
rarely surrendered, and that you should seek healers who
worked by the grace of Garlen. The Passions were real
forces, as real as the King of Throal, and just as distant.

Cymric glanced once at Leandra, then stepped up to the
spring. He quickly washed his hands in the chilling-cold
water, dashed some on his face to rinse off the trail grime.
He stopped, water dripping from his face, when he realized Leandra had not washed anything other than her
hands. He hoped Garlen didn't stand on ceremony or at
least wasn't prone to punish ignorant transgressors of her
rituals. He cupped his hands, filled them with water,
turned to the shrine. Cymric was certain the statue smiled
in amusement.

"Say something you mean, and you'll do all right," said
Leandra from behind him.

Cymric nodded. He raised his hands, then drank. The

water had an iron-y taste, but was still fresh and good. He swallowed the last, licked his lips, opened his mouth, closed it again. "Thanks for having us," he said, running a hand through his hair. "I'll try not to make too much of a mess of things."

Cymric winced. *Good going, oh wizard of the spoken word. I'm sure Garlen is quite taken by your charms.* He backed away from the pool, turned to face a perplexed Leandra. "First times are always awkward," he said with a shrug. She nodded and rubbed his shoulder affectionately, then started to set up camp.

Dinner was lunch again, eaten at a more leisurely pace. Cymric tried the Landis blend once more. He decided he could become a drinker, but not an enthusiastic one. Leandra did not take any tea. Cymric raised his tankard. "Is there a reason you're not having tea with your dinner?"

Leandra stripped the wax from her cheese as she answered, "This blend is really strong. I want to sleep tonight."

Cymric stopped in mid-slurp. He thought for a heartbeat, then continued drinking, finishing the tea in a series of gulps. "Well, as long as I'm going to be up, I should be productive. Say, by examining the necklace?"

Leandra frowned, an expression Cymric hadn't seen before. She molded the cheese-wax with her fingers, turning it into a small cube, which she then tossed into the air. She caught the cube while looking at Cymric. "You're sure this is necessary?"

"To be absolutely honest, I don't know. My instincts say 'yes'."

"Do your instincts tell you how long it might take? Can you finish before I go to sleep?" Leandra now picked at the cube. Her face was tight.

"I'll do what I can in the time you give me."

Leandra ate the cheese, taking bites from each edge, nibbling her way around toward the center. When she finished that one, she started another. Cymric ate silently, letting her consider her options.

"After dinner," Leandra announced. "Let me get ready, then you can wizard away on the necklace."

"Thank you. I'll do what I can in the time. At least I won't be starting from scratch," said Cymric. He stopped chewing for a second as he realized what he'd said. He took a few more bites, then looked up to see if Leandra had noticed. She sat cross-legged, then gave him a tic-smile when he caught her eye.

"The first night out of Twin Chin?" she asked.

Cymric nodded. "When it glowed red, I thought I'd broken it. The more I tried to fix it, the redder it got." He started a nonchalant shrug, aborted it in mid-gesture. He exhaled deeply. "I'm sorry. It was a stupid thing to do."

"Yes. It was," Leandra said. Her eyes said quite a bit more, most of it angry. She crossed, then uncrossed her arms, finally putting her hands on her knees.

Cymric felt horrible. But that was such a long time ago, he told himself, then realized not so many days had passed. During that time a lot had happened, a lot had changed. "I've changed," he said.

Leandra's eyebrows raised slowly. Her skepticism showed from the top of her eyes to the bottom of her lips. Cymric snorted, then hung his head. "Look, I'm not saying I'm perfect. Being with you has made me see things a little differently."

"How so?" Her words were flat and cold, like ice over a still pond.

"You don't take the easy way out. I usually do. Or did. Seeing who you are makes me think a little more about that."

"Makes you *think* a little more," said Leandra. "You *think* enough to change the way you act?"

Cymric felt the tension in his neck and shoulders as his anger rose. He leaned back a few inches and shook his hands to release the tension. "No, at least not until Corthy."

Leandra relaxed a little. She rubbed her hands along her thighs, continuing to read Cymric's face. "What are the results of your thoughts in Corthy?"

First, I'm sitting here with you, on my way to a spot on a Horror's dinner menu. Cymric didn't voice the sarcasm, however. He listened to the squirrels leaping from branch to branch until he'd composed his reply. "I like you. I admire you for strengths I don't have and for other things I can barely understand."

Leandra blinked a few times. Her face lost its tightness, but remained unreadable. Her hands kept moving, but more slowly now.

Cymric found his own breathing had become tight. "I think—I'm afraid I'm going to get to know you, to like you more, just in time to see you carved to pieces on Ristul's altar." He threw his arms in the air, then clapped loudly, and brought his hands down to clasp them behind his neck. "Brius and Gelthrain couldn't dissuade you. I'm not entirely sure I want to, because your decision is one of the things I admire about you."

Cymric stopped. The tightness he felt in his chest had gotten worse. He dropped his hands and took a deep breath. Leandra reached out and held his left hand in her right. Her touch was warm, reassuring. The next breath was easier. So was looking back into her eyes, which were now open, gentle.

"I'm—going with you. I don't know if I can find a way for you to kill Ristul, or even survive. But I'm going to try. But to try my best, I need to probe your necklace." Cymric thought back for a moment, then gave a half-smile. "I guess I didn't quite answer your question, did I?"

Leandra squeezed his hand again, looking him directly in the eye. A faint smile crept into her expression. "Close enough. Let me get ready."

Leandra prepared her hair for the coif, sharpened her sword, did some stretching exercises. Cymric thought about the necklace, the calendar, the Ristular. Things still didn't make a whole lot of sense. There were gaps in his knowledge, dangerous gaps. He certainly hoped the necklace could yield some of the answers.

Cymric seated himself against the shrine, drinking one last tankard of Landis blend. I should be alert enough, he thought, but my hands seem a little shaky. Leandra walked up and knelt next to him. Reaching behind her neck she unclasped the necklace. The stones clacked against one another as she placed the necklace in the palm of Cymric's hand. She squeezed his hand with both of hers, eyes smiling more than her lips.

"Just so you know, I like you, too," she said, then let go with her top hand to knock a strand of black hair away from his eyes. She returned that hand to Cymric's. "You're funny. You're smart." The tic-smile flickered for a couple moments. "You've got some growing up to do. But I like you."

Cymric felt a tingle up and down his arm. Leandra's eyes followed every movement of his face. He licked his lips. She released some of the pressure of her grip, but kept contact with his hand. "If you can find a way to take on Ristul, that would be fantastic. If you cannot, I want you to leave me at Marrek."

Cymric felt a chill spread across his chest. "I can't send you in alone."

Leandra nodded. "I appreciate that." She locked eyes with him. "But I can't take you with me just to die."

"You wanted to take Brius in with you, enough so I could hear it through the walls."

Leandra laughed, then released Cymric and cupped her face in her hands. Cymric looked down at the necklace, watching it catch the light from the quartzes, until she looked back up. "Brius and I have more of a history. More promises between us. I thought . . ." Her eyes were sad, her face drained. Life slowly flowed back into her expression. "You're not Brius. This is not your prophecy or your fight." Leandra sighed, looked beyond Cymric into the pool. "We'll talk more later."

Cymric squeezed her hand. There had to be a way for her to survive this. If only he could find it. Cymric let go of her hand, let Leandra and all the rest of the external world slide away as his inner sight dove into the pattern of the necklace.

22

Cymric's inner sight hovered just above the blue surface of a sphere of threads. The threads pulsed, expanding with an irregular rhythm. In between the gaps Cymric caught glimpses of the pattern of the rune, the magical heart of the necklace. The pattern was a coppery horn, spread and flattened at the bell, wavery and twisting near what would be the mouthpiece. The horn was filled to the top with a milky mist that spilled over the boundary formed by the horn.

Cymric took his time searching along the outside of the blue sphere. He centered his inner sight at a spot close to several areas that formed gaps when the threads pulsed. With each pulse he looked to see how long a gap remained open, but the gaps existed only for a moment. *Your choices are a quick wizard or a caught wizard.* Cymric remembered how the sphere had easily snapped his threads the first time he'd tried to pry his way in. If the sphere snapped down upon his inner sight. Cymric assumed that a savage headache was the best outcome he could anticipate.

Threads snapped out, creating a gap. Cymric dove. He could hear a crackling hum, then a whoosh as the threads rushed back into position. Cymric's inner sight blurred as exertion of will pushed his sight just ahead of the threads. The threads twanged shut behind him. His inner sight was inside the sphere.

As he approached the center pattern, he saw that it appeared to be a cross between a horn and a tornado. Rather than presenting a solid surface, coppery lines whirled

about the axis of the horn. As the whirling sped up, the milky substance in the horn was sucked down into it. As the whirling slowed, the white mist overflowed the bell of the horn. Cymric noted a musty, sweet odor each time the mist poured forth.

He nudged his inner sight closer to the horn. When the whirling slowed, the wizard saw what looked like writing formed along the lines, as if a flowing script had been fashioned out of wire. The script looked to be a form of high Elvish, the kind reserved for ancient court dramas and proclamations. He approached until he heard a *whiskwhiskwhisk,* like the sound of a rapidly moving wire brush over a smooth plate. He steadied his position, reading the words as they spun by: *freedom's passage for the soul on the bell.*

Cymric carefully backed his inner sight away, and floated toward the bell. He swung up and over, positioning himself over the middle of it. As the whirling increased, Cymric felt a suction, a force dragging at his inner sight, his will. He could resist the insistent pull by mentally anchoring himself to his point of view. He envisioned his inner sight connected to his body by a thick metal chain, the kind t'skrang riverboats used for their anchors.

As the milky substance was sucked down into the horn, the drop in the level of the mist revealed writing on the horn. The writing looked fragmented, vague shapes not quite complete. Cymric steadied his breathing, then envisioned extending the chain one link at a time, moving his inner sight closer to the bell. His inner sight hovered a hair's breadth above the rim. The writing was jumbled, pieces of letters rather than whole words. As the mist drew deeper into the horn, the letters formed a word, the same word repeated dozens of times: *Cymric.*

Each link of his mental chain shattered. Cymric's inner sight spun down into the horn. He strained, threw life energy into his will, but his efforts didn't even slow the plunge. He was quickly enveloped by the mists inside the horn.

Your pain is over. You are free.

Who said that? Or thought that? Cymric's mind strug-

gled to move of its own accord. A wave of pleasure hit
him, catching him by surprise. Cymric could feel his arms
and legs again. Delicious feeling rippled smoothly along
his back, warm feathers brushing across his skin, a spreading, liquid sensation eagerly absorbed by every muscle.
Cymric's breath caught as the feeling raced up his spine to
erupt inside his head. He was left with a feeling of calm,
of relief.

Your pain is over. You are free.

Cymric spun faster, but the feeling was not unpleasant.
The world was right, what was happening was right and
long overdue. *Snap out of it, wizard! How can this have
anything to do with you? You hadn't even seen the necklace until a few weeks ago.* The urgency in Cymric's mind
dimmed to a point. His inner sight was filled with a white
glow, a comforting glow, a glow he felt inside his mind
more than visualized with his sight. Serene, floating, now
barely aware of the spinning, Cymric stopped struggling.

Your pain is over. You are free.

Extreme acceleration jolted his inner sight. The white
glow disappeared. Cold air rushed past Cymric, as if he'd
fallen off the back of a dragon flying above the clouds.
The pressure stopped, and Cymric began to warm up. He
moved his inner sight gingerly. Distant spots of white,
blue, and green dotted the blackness. Some of the spots
moved, most of them slowly, a few rapidly, all traveling
from his left to his right around him.

Where am I? Cymric decided that answering the question was not as important as getting back. He marshalled
his will to tap his wizardry, breaking his inner sight. Nothing happened. His inner sight continued to float in blackness. The image of a promenading star field blurred as he
panicked. Four more attempts at wizardry left his inner
sight in the same place.

Has my spirit been severed from my body? Cymric had
been told all the standard horror stories about magicians
who sent their souls to wander astral space, only to lose
contact with their bodies. The magician's physical self almost always died in those stories, leaving a wailing spirit.
Cymric had listened lackadaisically; he *knew* he would

never roam too far from his body or spend too much time in astral space. So he never paid much attention to what a wizard should do if he lost contact with his physical form.

Cymric's thoughts raced as his inner sight floated in the void. *First, see if your spirit has been completely severed from your body. Try to reestablish contact.* Cymric's inner sight occasionally activated other senses as well. Which sensings were from his sight, which from his body? When the horn had expelled him, he'd felt cold air and then a gradual warming. Cymric recalled the sensation. He'd last felt warm, his face had felt warm. Could he feel his face now? Cymric concentrated. *Eyes moving under closed lids, slack jaw twitching the lips of an open mouth.* His body—he was still connected to his body!

All right, then, things weren't completely hopeless. The magic of the necklace had probably jettisoned his will and inner sight to some point of astral space far away from the external world where his body still sat. He would have to close the distance, get close enough to pop out of his inner sight. So which way was closer?

Cymric urged his inner sight toward the promenade of stars. One of those points might be the necklace. Cymric traveled at good speed, but the field of stars did not grow appreciably closer for some time. As he traveled, he attempted to reconnect with his body. Once he felt his back against the cold stone of the shrine. He felt someone shake his shoulder. Another time he smelled birch on the night air. Another time he felt the necklace held loosely in his hands. He tried to order his hands to wiggle, to move the necklace, hoping for some corresponding movement in the field of stars. No luck.

Cymric was now close enough to the field of stars to see that it had depth. The nearer, larger points of fire passed in front of and obscured more distant dots. Some of the "stars" were smooth, glowing spheres with no visible flame. One of them might be connected to the necklace.

Cymric heard a moan from the external world, a voice that sounded like Leandra's. His inner sight saw a nearby sphere shimmer and blink out. Cymric whirled his sight over to the spot, searching frantically. There! There in the blackness was a pinhole of light. As he watched, the pinhole began to close. Cymric plunged toward it, trying to compress his inner sight to become smaller than the pinhole. He failed. He tried to loosen his sight, to play it out like a thread.

He penetrated the pinhole. As he extruded enough of his inner sight through it, Cymric became aware of his new surroundings. He was back inside the horn. It had stopped spinning, and now glowed an angry red. The horn began spinning again, but this time Cymric felt himself propelled toward the bell of the horn. He exited to see the threads of the surrounding sphere had also turned red and were pulsing wildly, creating huge gaps in the surface of the sphere. Cymric darted through a gap, then popped his inner sight.

His eyesight was blurry. He rubbed his eyes, saw a red glow, then an exultant laugh erupted as Cymric realized he was back in his own body. He heard the *snick* of a blade being drawn. He stretched his arms high over his head, then looked left to see Leandra drawing her sword. He stood letting the blood rush into his legs. His left leg had fallen asleep, so he shifted his weight onto the right. Leandra advanced, sword in hand. She was squinting. Cymric snorted: "Relax. It's me."

Leandra nodded, but kept advancing. Her squint looked strange. Cymric held out his hands; he was about to say something when he noticed the fierce red glow from the necklace. Leandra swung her sword in a high, overhand swing. Startled, Cymric dodged. His left leg collapsed under him, the circulation not fully restored. The sword blow rang off the shrine.

Cymric scrabbled to his feet. Leandra's next blow was a swipe at waist height. Cymric threw himself back, ankle catching on a smooth round stone. He splashed into the pool, the crab-walked backward in panic. *Which is stranger, her attacks or the fact that both missed?* Cymric knew he was lucky to be alive. Leandra knelt, examining the pond carefully.

Cymric stood up. He touched his left hand to the drenched robe covering his chest. "I'm fine." He held the necklace in front of him. "This glow has nothing to do with me. There must be Ristular very close by." Leandra regarded him carefully, but she still squinted. Cymric ran his left hand through his hair; drops of water spattered the pond below. "We should get out of here."

Leandra nodded slowly. "Of course. You're right. Let us be off." She gestured with her sword to their packs, then turned to walk that way. Cymric sloshed out of the pond, lifting water-heavy boots over the rim. He left a rail of puddle-prints as he walked over to Leandra.

"I'm not sure what your necklace does, but it sure is impressive doing it." Cymric grinned, flipping the necklace from his right hand to his left. Leandra nodded absently. Cymric raised an eyebrow toward her. Getting no response, he bent to grab his staff and pack. "I think—"

Cymric caught the movement just in time to raise his staff defensively. The sword bit into the staff, the momentum of the swing tearing it out of Cymric's right hand. He scrambled and backpedalled. Leandra followed. Cymric tried to balance his weight evenly between his feet. He tried faking left, running right, but Leandra didn't buy it. Her sword slashed once, catching him on the left wrist, near the palm of his hand. Pain lanced up his arm as blood oozed over the necklace. Cymric continued to back up, dodging as he went. Leandra's second blow nicked his left arm near the elbow.

As Cymric neared the pond, Leandra began to squint again, as it was hard for her to see him against the background of the pond. What was going on? *Leandra hit me in the wrist and elbow. Gelthrain said Leandra had killed her dwarf companion by cutting off his arm at the wrist and elbow. When Leandra was possessed by Ristul.* Whatever was inside her now did not like looking at the pond. A pond filled with water blessed by the Passion Garlen.

Cymric practically belly-flopped into the pond, avoiding the sword blow, which rang off a limestone slab supporting the statue of Garlen. Spinning around in a spray of water, he readied himself to dodge again. Leandra stood at the edge of the pond, shading her eyes with her left hand. She didn't follow him into the water.

Cymric breathed heavily until his lungs were sated and

his heart slowed a few beats. Then he stood and called out, "The water is a bit brisk, but invigorating. Come on in—Ristul."

Leandra threw her head back and laughed. She shook her head slowly. "Good bravado. Bad guess. Ristul could just boil away that water, you along with it."

Cymric sloshed around the pond in a circle, holding his arms out wide in one of his most theatrical gestures. "I apologize for not knowing the names of all of Ristul's servants. And you would be?" He bowed in a slow, exaggerated manner. Leandra might be possessed by Ristul; a Horror could obviously lie. But Cymric felt that a simple shrine to Garlen probably would not stop a Horror that had penetrated the protection of one or more kaers. Leandra probably was possessed by someone else.

Leandra's smile was slight, showing a sliver of her front teeth. "Introductions are not necessary, wizard. I already know you are Cymric."

Still clutching the necklace, Cymric crossed his wrists over the front of his chest, bowed again. "Then, madam or sir, you have me at a distinct disadvantage."

The smile on Leandra's face grew a bit wider. "Yes." Leandra sheathed her sword. She walked over to a birch tree, snapped off some branches. Cymric began weaving a thread, enhancing the pattern for disrupting magic. *Worth a try.* Leandra began moving her hands, cracking pieces of the branches as parts of the motion. *Uh oh—hope I finish my spell first.*

Cymric flung the spell along a flat line. The spell passed through Leandra, hesitating only briefly. No effect. *Damn.* Cymric began weaving for another try.

With a dramatic crack from a twig in her left hand, Leandra pointed at Cymric. The necklace flared red. Cymric felt a jerk at the base of his skull, then the middle of his back, accompanied by a pop. Then the sensation faded, as if drained into the pool. *That was close.*

Cymric finished his second weave. He glanced with inner sight along the path to his target. The spell pattern pinwheeled away from him directly toward Leandra. Then the spell pattern struck, changing its form to something familiar, then faded away quietly. *That was not so close.* Trading spells looked like a bad idea. Leandra grinned, starting cracking more branches.

The necklace had practically expelled his inner sight, first into astral space, the second time hurtling him toward the external world. *Perhaps the necklace propels spirits away from it or its wearer?* Slipping the necklace back onto Leandra might expel the spirit, or help her own will kick out the spirit.

But trying to get the necklace around her neck would mean leaving the relative safety of the pool. If the spell caught Cymric while out of the pool ... The wizard exploded from the pond, spraying water everywhere. Soggy boots pounded the ground, propelled by fear-crazed legs. He watched Leandra's eyes grow wider, her hand motions faster. Cymric skidded around her, avoiding the fitful flailing of her stick-filled hands. He slipped his hands over her head, as if the necklace were a garrote. He snipped the fastener into place.

Leandra stiffened for a second, then fell to her knees. "Aaiiaahh—there is nothing to be done then," she gasped. She snapped a final twig, then grabbed her head with both hands. As her body went limp, Cymric sensed a rush of astral energy away from her body. He knelt beside her, grabbing her hands to restrain her if she were still possessed. He formed a wild idea of dragging Leandra to the pool, realizing a fraction of a heartbeat later that if anyone would be doing the dragging, it would be her. Then he heard a snap, felt a pop at Leandra's left wrist.

She screamed. Her body convulsed, easily breaking Cymric's grip. The number and volume of the snaps increased. Her forehead dented inward with a loud crack. Her eyes bulged as a ripping sound traveled down her spine. Cymric covered his ears at the scream.

Leandra lay quivering, her face returning to a more normal color as the necklace stopped glowing red. She heaved twice, the second time ending in a drool of vomit. Cymric ran to his pack, pulled out cheesecloths, came back to clean her up. She looked up at him, dazed. He daubed her face.

"You're crying," she said.

Cymric had to blink to realize she was right. "Sorry I took too long with the necklace." He picked up what vomit he could with one cloth, tried wiping her face clean with another. "Something possessed you while I was— gone."

Leandra nodded wearily. "I felt it. Could resist it some. When it used my body. Not the spells."

Cymric rinsed the cloths in the pool, then returned to Leandra. He finished cleaning up her face. Pain creased lines around her mouth and eyes. He went to his pack, emptied a flask, filled it with fresh water from the spring. Cymric propped her head up gently with his arm.

Leandra sipped slowly, taking ragged breaths between each sip. She blinked as she looked at Cymric. "My left arm is broken. I can't—" Leandra closed her eyes, drew her mouth tight. Then she opened her eyes again and exhaled sharply. "I can't feel my legs."

Cymric looked into her eyes, then down at her legs. They looked normal, not jutting out at odd angles. He gently prodded the nearest leg. No response. He lowered her head to the ground. "I'll figure something out. I promise." He stood up. *Perhaps the shrine could help.*

"You could get me some blankets," Leandra said weakly.

Damn it, he couldn't even do the simple tasks right! Cymric berated himself, kicking his pack before opening it. He retrieved Leandra's blanket as well, then carefully placed the two layers of wool over her. Leandra managed a slight smile.

"I'm going to see what the shrine has to offer," he said, brushing stray hair out of her eyes. Then he stood up and ran to the shrine.

Cymric looked up at the serene, angular face of Garlen. *I apologize in advance for any rituals I do not observe, but I need your help.* He waited to see if there would be a reply. He heard none. Cymric carefully reached for the copper flask, now streaked green and aqua. The flask swished when he pried it loose. He tried to twist open the top, but it was solidly gunked into place.

Cymric took two steps toward Leandra before remembering her broken arm; opening the flask one-handed wouldn't work. Cymric tried again, grunting with effort. The top didn't even budge.

The wizard sat down in front of the pond. Setting the flask in the cold water, he quickly dipped into his inner sight to place a new spell in a matrix. He concentrated on the spell, trying to place it precisely. The flame flash appeared finger-wide, just licking the top of the flask. Cymric applied the spell a few times more. A hissing squeal and a pop told him his plan had worked. The top sizzled as he dunked it into the water. It was still hard to turn, but it came off. The syrupy fluid inside smelled of peppermint. Cymric stuck his finger into the flask; the taste was cool, a stronger mint flavor than the scent suggested. He refilled his flask with water; Leandra would need some to wash this down.

Leandra drank nearly half of the Garlen flask, then polished off the water. Sated, she lay her head back, closed her eyes, breathing evenly. Cymric sat down beside her. A short time later, Leandra cracked open her eyes. "Doesn't hurt as much."

"Can you feel you legs?"

Leandra shook her head, but was asleep by the fourth shake. Cymric rubbed his arms. He was wet and cold, but Leandra had the blankets. Nor could he burn the birch wood, as that belonged to Garlen. He sighed and reached into his pack for a slab of cheese, then ate slowly from it as he watched Leandra sleep. It was going to be a long night.

As the hours passed, Cymric spent much of the time wondering how a lame hero and an inadequate wizard could kill Ristul when they couldn't handle even one of his servants? When morning finally came, he still hadn't found the answer.

23

Leandra gave a quiet grunt of pain almost drowned out by the bang of the wagon wheel hitting a rut in the road. Cymric looked back at her from his seat up front. Leandra lay in the afternoon sun next to three barrels filled with farm tools to be fixed. She smiled weakly. Cymric shifted to his knees, facing her in the back of the wagon. He unstoppered the Garlen flask, then gave her a sip. When she nodded that she'd had enough, Cymric switched flasks, letting her polish off the water. He sloshed the Garlen flask experimentally; there was perhaps an eighth of a flask left. He turned back to face front. The excited farm boy urging on the oxen was too wrapped up in his monologue to notice the behavior of his passengers.

"—until well after the harvest, what with all the bad goings-on. My ma said Liffick is no place for honest workers these days, with all kinds of trouble floating in from the river. But here I am, taking you and the tools. Life works itself out. That's what gramps always said."

Cymric caught the shine in Colin's blue eyes at the mention of "all kinds of trouble." The boy was broad-shouldered enough to handle most ruffians, and probably believed that was the commonest sort of trouble in a river town. Cymric looked at Colin's brilliant red hair and smooth, freckle-free complexion, and thought of river rats procuring slaves for exotic Theran tastes. Probably what Colin's mother had thought also. She had waved to the wagon for a long time, too long for a simple two-day errand, long enough to bring a blush to Colin's cheek.

As they neared Liffick, flat land became hillier, greener as the use went from tillage to pasturage for sheep. The

wagon stopped as a few hundred sheep decided that the
pasture to the left of the road looked more inviting than
that on the right. In the distance, Cymric saw a broad hill
covered with fleecy dots, perhaps five times as many
sheep as were crossing in front of them, perhaps more.
Cymric kept looking at the sheep until the wagon crested
their hill.

Down the road lay Liffick. The center of the town was
walled, probably representing the town's original bounda-
ries. New buildings sprawled in every direction. The
larger, more permanent ones extended up and down the
river; orange terra cotta or blue and green tiles covered
their roofs. Further away from the river and the town center, the buildings were smaller, roofed with slate, mud, or
sometimes tar paper. Across the river was a crowded landing, serviced by a continuous stream of poled ferries.
Cymric squinted, for he thought he saw one of the ferries
skim across the surface. A float ferry meant Liffick attracted enough money to keep such an operation profit-
able. Cymric snorted, and revised Liffick's standing in his
list of possible future sites where he might sell his services.

The wagon bumped along the road into Liffick, drawing
some cold stares from orks who lived in the first few
shanties they passed. Juvenile orks harassed Colin, calling
him "seed spitter" and "weed head." Colin's tight smile let
Cymric know things might have proceeded differently if
he and Leandra had not been in the wagon. The road became less bumpy, the buildings a little nicer the closer
they got to the town walls. Dwarf cobblers looked up from
their outdoor work tables, a human tailor raced from his
shop to measure Cymric, suggesting a whole new cut and
cloth in accordance with the new Throal fashions. Push-
carts edged the street. Maneuvering the wagon became
more difficult as they neared the walls.

At one intersection Colin locked his wheel with that of
an ale wagon heading in the other direction. The dwarf
driver stood on a cask, alternately screaming and biting his
brown beard. He grabbed his green felt cap, repeatedly
swatting Colin about the chest and shoulders. Colin stood

dumbfounded, not even trying to ward off the dwarf's blows. Cymric's efforts to calm the dwarf only won him similar attentions from the felt hat.

Two spear-carrying trolls waded through the growing crowd. The tabards they wore over their chainmail bore a white shield embossed with a blue animal, either an eel or a very fat snake. The crude tailoring suggested that these two did not rank high in whatever organization they represented. The dwarf immediately proclaimed his innocence to one of the trolls, vehemently placing the blame on Colin's cart-handling.

The second troll looked into Colin's wagon. He grunted, pointed to Leandra's armor, then pulled aside his tabard at the shoulder. His armor had a small brass medallion, similar to Leandra's. She and the troll clasped forearms. Her smile was broad, the troll's huge. The dwarven driver quieted as he watched the troll and Leandra.

"Good to see some others got out," the troll rumbled, "I was with Frohl."

Leandra nodded, wincing. "Cedric, then Brius once Cedric fell."

The troll snorted like a bull, then tugged on a long nose hair. "You had the hard way of it then," he said quietly, "What you need in Liffick?"

"Healing."

"We've some just come to town. We had serious problems with a magician, more than our herbalist could handle."

"What sort of problems?" said Cymric.

"A nasty dwarf. Found removing parts from ancestors buried in the guild mausoleum. When we tried to nab him, he broke the bones of half a dozen men. Three more he burned—from the inside out. Their skeletons fused together from the heat." The troll's eyes narrowed. "Still there; city council hasn't decided how to bury them. The dwarf then injured some guild officials. The guild put up the money for the healers from Marrek. By airship, no less."

"The dwarf is gone?" said Cymric.

"We believe so. Cursed a few hundred sheep, then left."

The troll shrugged and slapped the side of the wagon. "We'll get you to the healers." He walked to the front of the wagon, bowed curtly to the dwarf driver. "The human oaf apologizes for delaying your august dwarfenage. Please move your wagon. Now."

The dwarf's eyes darted from troll to troll. Muttering under his breath, he drew out copper coins from his money pouch. He held the money aloft with one hand, pointed to the locked wheels with the others. Five of the grubbier dwarfs scrambled from the crowd and began pushing the ale wagon. Once they had disengaged the wheels, the driver snapped the reins, and the ponies started to move. The five helpers jogged alongside, receiving payment as the wagon rolled away, the trolls clearing a path through the bystanders. Colin followed their lead.

The streets narrowed until they reached the walls. The gate towers were covered with copper and brass sigils, enchantments to ward off Horrors. Liffick must have been established soon after the Scourge, when the world no longer had to live in kaers, but when Horrors were still more common than they were today. Six dwarven guards in better-looking tabards manned the gate, watching those who came and went. The medallion-troll talked to the guards, who then looked over at the wagon. Two of them crisply slapped fists to chests in a Throal honor-guard salute.

The wagon rolled down the town's main avenue. Colin followed the trolls to a large building. Stone arches rose every six paces, supporting curved, ivied walls. Between each arch sparkled a stained glass window, curved to fit the wall, each window two or three times Cymric's height. Each window showed dwarfs drinking, dwarfs eating, dwarfs singing, each a picture of celebration. As Cymric passed one window, a stained glass figure tapped a keg, offering a foaming mug to the wizard. The arm and mug broke the plane of the window. Cymric blinked; the illusion was excellent, an expensive touch.

The trolls guided the wagon to a pair of massive wooden doors, the left of which was open and stopped

with a statue of a unicorn on a cliff. They instructed Colin
to stay with the wagon, told Cymric to come with them.

The interior was lit by multicolored streams of light
pouring through the windows and by the gentle glow of
rose light quartz in sconces clustered near the top of supporting pillars. Rows of long tables had been overturned
and stacked atop one another to make room for cots. There
were perhaps a hundred cots in the hall, all full. Muslin
sheets covered a few of them, shrouding those now beyond a healer's power. Guild apprentices, still in their
smocks, had been pressed into duty as orderlies.

The healers had set their gear on the hall's polished red-
wood bar, which was lined with decanters, tubes, fire
rings, gems, amulets, books, furs, bones, scrolls, sprigs of
herbs, scorched beakers. Two dwarfs sat behind neatly
stacked parchments, a steady *scritch* coming from their
quills. Each wore a gray and white tunic, but there the resemblance ended. The thin male dwarf looked older than
the bones on the bar. The plumper female looked about
Leandra's age; Cymric corrected for dwarven life span and
guessed she was about forty or so. Her left eye had been
replaced by a streaked yellow agate. She looked up as the
trolls approached with Cymric.

The two trolls bent to one knee. Cymric bowed, perhaps
a little late. Both trolls cleared their throats, looked at one
another. The dwarf raised her eyebrow. Finally the
medallion-troll spoke. "Mistress Pouika, we request you
look at an injured sword sister. She is not bonded by the
guild—"

"Then she will have to pay for our services," said
Pouika.

"—but she has a Throal commendation," said the troll,
his voice rising a bit.

Pouika switched eyebrows. "She shall have our full attention, but she is still required to pay."

The trolls rose and bowed. One gestured at Cymric.
"Her wizard can negotiate the fee. Thank you, mistress."
They clacked their spears on the floor, turned and marched
in step to the doors. Cymric blinked. Pouika waited patiently.

"Leandra has no feeling in her legs, a result of spell damage. I think—"

"I think, master wizard, that you should allow *me* to do the diagnosis." Pouika slid off her stool to walk around the bar. As she traveled its length, she picked up three herb clusters, a round carnelian, and something that looked like a cobweb. While she was making her way through the jumble of cots, the look of one patient stopped her, a young dwarf with swollen eyes, yellowed skin, and bald patches in his beard. Pouika knelt, whispered softly to him. He slowly shook his head. Pouika sighed, looked at the herb clusters. She got up, fetched a pitcher of water from beside another patient's cot. She persuaded the dwarf to drink, chew an entire cluster of herbs, then drink a little more. She whispered again, smiling as she ended. Patch-beard returned a weak smile. Pouika started for the wagon again.

"I'm low on supplies, wizard. The guild is only so generous with its funds." Pouika's voice was level, neither bitter, nor angry, just stating the facts. "Unless you can pay for what your sword sister needs, I may not be able to help her." She got to the wagon, hesitating at the human-scaled step. Colin helped her up with a smooth lift, then Pouika climbed into the back with as much dignity as she could muster.

"How are we today, my fine stretch of a sword woman?" She placed the carnelian on Leandra's forehead.

Leandra's face became a polite mask, her smile courteous but without warmth. "I need my legs back."

Pouika nodded. "We shall see what we can do. First I need to know what has been to done you." She took the carnelian in her hand and slowly ran it down the length of Leandra's body. Pouika stopped to make circular motions above Leandra's hips, then moved a hand-span or so back up. The healer put the carnelian down, then placed both hands on either side of Leandra's waist. Cymric sensed threads being woven, a slight waver in astral space, then the spell was cast. Pouika closed her eyes for a few moments; her breathing synchronized with Leandra's. When the healer opened her eyes, they were huge, with eyebrows high. She looked down at Leandra.

"You are fortunate to be alive. You should be dead. Your spine is broken in two places, and you have damage to intestines and liver."

Leandra swallowed slowly. "How long until I am whole?" She stared directly at Pouika.

The healer avoided her gaze. "It would help to know how you are holding yourself together. If we can augment that, we have a good chance."

Cymric reached into his pack for the Garlen flask. He showed it to Pouika. "We were attacked at a shrine of Garlen. I took this potion from the shrine. It seemed to help Leandra."

Pouika glanced at Leandra, stared at the flask, back to Leandra, her gaze finally settling on the flask. "The flask was full?" Her voice was husky. When Cymric nodded, Pouika gestured for the flask. Cymric hesitated before handing it to her. The healer opened the flask, wafted the scent with her hand. She then rimmed the flask with her finger, sampling the fluid. Pouika closed her eyes. She kept them closed as she announced, "The breath of Garlen."

Cymric presumed her reverential tones meant the breath of Garlen was a good thing. He reached for the flask, but Pouika did not give it up. Instead she signaled to a pair of orderlies with a stretcher. They carried Leandra; Colin picked up her personal effects. Pouika turned to Cymric.

"Your friend's life force was not enough to absorb the damage of the spell. She would have died but for the grace of Garlen and her gift to you. Garlen's life is sustaining your friend."

Cymric knitted his eyebrows. "I'm not sure I understand."

Pouika wrinkled her nose. "When your friend reached the threshold of death, Garlen gave of her own life force to satisfy death's demand for a spirit. Through the breath of Garlen, she continues to do so. But the gate to death remains open until the damage can be healed."

"Can you shut the gate?"

Pouika nodded absently. "We have most of the supplies. When the guilds hear that Garlen has chosen life for your friend, I doubt they will risk angering Garlen by denying her aid." Pouika closed her eyes for another moment. "As for payment, we will accept the remainder of the potion, plus four hundred silvers for supplies that other patients may live."

Cymric opened his mouth to object, then thought better of it. "Any idea where an enterprising wizard might raise four hundred silvers?"

Pouika looked annoyed, then her face cleared. "The nethermancer cursed a large number of sheep. They lie listlessly on a hill outside Liffick, not moving, rarely eating. Strike a deal with the Farmers Guild to remove the curse if you are able in such magics."

Cymric stretched himself to his full height, a move not quite as effective as he hoped, for Pouika was still in the wagon. "Wizards know curses."

"Then I shall send for a guild representative to come talk with you." Pouika climbed back over to the front of the wagon, and Cymric helped her down. The healer returned to the bar with the Garlen flask while Cymric went to find Leandra's cot. She was just conscious enough to acknowledge his presence, perhaps having relaxed her will once she felt the healers would treat her. Cymric sat beside the cot, talking of an interesting bakery he'd seen on the way into town, the sheep problem, how Leandra would be on her feet in a few days. Cymric's monologue trailed off. He sat holding Leandra's hand until the Farmers Guildsman arrived.

The guildsman was a dwarf of enormous girth and officious expression, dressed in russet velvets and fashionably cut boots. He introduced himself as Worthro, and offered to take Cymric to the hill to inspect the sheep problem. Cymric accepted.

Cymric, Worthro, and four dwarf guards to shield them from what Worthro called "the warty element in town" took a packed dirt road out of town. By road the journey was only three miles, but Worthro stopped so frequently to haggle that Cymric was sure they could probably have

used the same amount of time to cover nine miles if they'd
only kept up a steady pace. Cymric set his price at five
hundred silvers. He wouldn't budge, despite verbal gym-
nastics from Worthro that would have done a courtier
proud. Worthro grumbled about the recalcitrant tall, but
agreed to the price.

The hill was perhaps a quarter-mile across, rising about
fifty paces. Lying in the grass were hundreds of sheep,
some baahing piteously, others languidly chewing the
grass in front of them. Several farm hands stood watching
the sheep. A few tried to coax the sheep at the edges of
the group to move. No one wandered out into the group of
sheep. Cymric saw why; about a hundred paces away a
swarthy farm hand, beard matted with sweat, lay on his
back. He would move his arms or legs occasionally, crying
out as he did.

One of the farmers came over to them, saluting Worthro
when he stopped. "Jol went after that ram of his. Got
stuck early this morning. Ram's still there too."

Worthro nodded sagely, looking out across the hill.
Then he slapped Cymric in the small of his back. "Arak,
I brought you a wizard to lift this blight." The guildsman
beamed at Cymric. "Go to it, son."

Cymric saluted with a tap of his staff to his forehead,
then faced the hill. He slid a pattern into a matrix, wrap-
ping the spell around his own pattern to enhance his astral
sense. The hill appeared as a blot of darkness that made
Cymric feel queasy as the back of his mind began digging
up a memory. He added some of his life force to a second
casting that let him penetrate the darkness.

Catching a shift in astral energy, he saw three huge,
coppery helix-arms extending beyond the range of his astral sense. Where the arms converged were hundreds of
barbed lines, like rose bushes bent into hooks. It was the
spiritcatcher from the well. Only now it was ten times as
big.

24

Astral images of barbed tendrils faded, replaced by the scene from the external world. The sheep, and poor Jol, lay on spots corresponding to the positions of the tendrils. The spiritcatcher had hooked them. Some of the sheep were dead, others lay at varying distances from death. *So, monster, what are you doing here? Besides killing sheep?*

Cymric walked around the perimeter of the hill, again seeing through his astral senses. He kept a prudent distance from the nearest tendrils. Last time he'd used dispel magic to weaken the creature's hold upon him. This time the creature held hundreds of other creatures. Cymric would probably have to dispel the magical hold on each one while also avoiding being snagged by the spiritcatcher. The odds of success were too long for his liking.

Perhaps he could convince the creature to leave, dropping the sheep and Jol as it did so. He doubted the spiritcatcher was much of a conversationalist, let alone a connoisseur of the finer points of debate. Cymric would have to use a somewhat cruder method. He mulled over his options. He wanted to do five things: sense astrally, disrupt the creature's magic, keep out of its grasp, and have ready a quick, short-range mental attack and a slower, longer-range, more powerful attack to shred the creature's will. He only had three matrices. Casting raw magic next to a spiritcatcher seemed really stupid. Time to alter the plan.

Cymric wandered back to the waiting farmers. Preoccupied with his own thoughts, he gestured idly to the hill with his staff. "The problem is not a curse; it's an astral monster about the size of that hill." Worthro blanched while the other farmers looked at Worthro. The guards fidgeted, a couple toying with the hafts of their axes, another paying attention to the arrangement of his helmet. "I have defeated this creature once, but it is even more powerful now."

Worthro rubbed his moustache with one finger. "Seven hundred and fifty silvers if you defeat it this time."

Cymric was annoyed. He really didn't want to renegotiate his fee. He wanted to know why the spiritcatcher was here and how to drive it away. He threw Worthro a leave-me-alone, I'm-thinking glance.

Worthro misinterpreted the face. He tugged on the sleeves of his fancy dress shirt, looked around him, then ahemed loudly. "Very well, then, fifteen hundred silver pieces to defeat the creature. That is our final offer."

Cymric smiled ruefully. Certainly a better rate of pay than the twenty-four and a half at Twin Chin. He tried to commit the scene to memory, to see if there was anything he could learn to make commanding higher fees easier. His delay made Worthro even more nervous. "Fifteen hundred sounds fair." Worthro smiled in relief, taking a step forward to shake Cymric's hand. "But I'll need the help of some of you."

Worthro stopped, his hand extended in front of him. "What sort of help?"

"As I free some of the sheep, they may be too weak or too injured to move on their own. You'll have to move them while I distract the creature's attention."

Worthro looked dubious, licking his lips as he stalled for a response. One of the farmers came up, clapped Worthro on the shoulder, and said, "Don't tangle your beard over it. We'll help the wizard." Worthro nodded sagely, but relief showed through his expression.

Cymric sat, maneuvering patterns in his mind before he hit the ground. He slid the patterns for the quick attack and disrupting magic into matrices, taking the time to precisely align each pattern so there was no chance for a repeat of the mishap outside Corthy. He again enhanced his astral sense, hurriedly replacing that spell pattern with the pattern for his leaping magic. Cymric didn't breathe as he slid the last pattern into place. It held. He stood, nodded casually to the group of farmers. They watched, stolid as cattle, as Cymric walked along the bottom of the hill.

He decided to start with sheep. That way, if his technique required a little refinement, the result would be mutton rather than a dead farmer. He walked slowly, watching a nearby ewe. Her eyes had nearly dulled to the black of her face, but she still breathed. Cymric wove a thread to his dispel magic pattern, the astral perturbation attracting the attention of the spiritcatcher. At the first hint of a change in astral space, Cymric backpedalled furiously, losing his thread. Barbed tendrils shot through the earth, ripping a hole in the aura of the living earth, though still invisible in the external world. The tendrils spun upward, then retracted and vanished from Cymric's astral sense.

The farmers cried out at Cymric's sudden retreat, but he raised his staff and waved it slowly. The farmer's huzzah sounded half hearted. Cymric then returned his attention to the problem. The thorn-tendrils were familiar, moving in a way similar to the thorn-ward on the Ristular calendar. It made Cymric think that Maeumis was behind both the magic of the calendar and that of the spiritcatcher. The magics had the same structure, almost the same style to them. Perhaps Maeumis patterned the defenses of the calendar after the spiritcatcher. Perhaps both were simply the result of one ancient tome. Maeumis probably created both of them. Cymric quickly swallowed his doubts; the answer felt right as much as it was reasoned right.

He tapped the thread he had tied to the calendar some days ago, his neck and chest tightening as he directed the energy from the thread to his own pattern. His pulse quickened and grew stronger; Cymric could feel it in his head and throat. His knowledge of the calendar and its creator, Maeumis, became a tangible, tingly cold zinging along his limbs, strengthening his magic against Maeumis and the nethermancer's constructs. The cold flowed outward along his limbs, reflecting off the tips of his fingers and toes to race back to his head. Cymric felt an impact on the top of his skull, as if someone inside his head had thrown a snowball. That solid cold melted and dripped from the top of his head to pool around his heart. His heartbeats didn't ripple the pool, but did warm it. When Cymric could no longer feel the pool, he knew his knowledge of the calendar had become a part of him.

Cymric cast his leaping magic, blood pulsing through his legs. He smiled, wiggled his eyebrows, and walked back toward the ewe. *So, monster, let's see if you're still connected to Master Maeumis.* He wove a thread to the dispel magic pattern, heartened that the thread seemed surer, stronger. The perturbation again attracted the creature. Cymric held his ground, releasing his spell upon the ewe. Astral sense detected a flash, then the flail of a tendril disengaging from the ewe. Cymric leaped as the tendrils tried to snare him, doing his best to mimic the motions he'd used to avoid the calendar's thorn-ward. The tendrils missed.

The ewe bleated, rose to her feet, fell again. Cymric unleashed a blade of mental energy, striking a moving tendril. Triumph flooded his limbs with energy as the spell struck. The mind dagger flared more brilliantly than normal, drawing power from his knowledge of the calendar. So Maeumis *was* responsible for the spiritcatcher.

Cymric leaped straight into the air and whooped, which the farmers took as a signal to intervene. Two of them raced for the ewe, their stocky legs pounding the ground with jarring strides. Cymric leaped and tossed mind daggers at the tendrils while the farmers effected the rescue. As the two were carrying the ewe to safety, Cymric wove for another dispel magic, feeling a soothing coolness as the thread neatly fit into the pattern. He had to leap midweave, maintaining his concentration through the air and the hard landing. Then he unleashed the spell, freeing another sheep. This one had the energy and sense to run downhill, away from the creature. Seeing other sheep also beginning to bleat and a few more staggering to their feet, Cymric reasoned that the creature must have had to withdraw tendrils from the spirits of those animals in order to deal with him.

His life energy was running a little low, but it did the dead no good. Prudent use of his life force to bolster his magic might make the difference. Astral sense warned him a fraction of a second ahead of the attack. Adding some of his life energy to his leap, Cymric somersaulted through a thicket of tendrils. He landed on his feet, then continued moving up the hill in erratic skips and bounds. The farmers hurried to rescue sheep from the slope below. Every time Cymric sensed the movement of a tendril, he targeted it with a mind dagger.

He moved quickly, trying to avoid any pattern in his movements. The increasing number of tendrils made dodging more difficult. Before his leaping spell could lapse, he cast another. The farmers were retreating, carrying the sheep they had to and herding what they could. Cymric bounded downslope toward Jol. His leap became a flying spin as he avoided the creature. He landed close to Jol. "Are you strong enough to get away if I release you?"

Jol nodded, face red from hours in the sun. Cymric wove and cast, touching Jol in the chest. Inner sight saw a gentle blue light infuse Jol's pattern; he began to crawl away toward the other farmers. Cymric cartwheeled in the opposite direction. His back flared pain as some of the creature's barbs raked across his spirit. Screaming angrily, he responded with a mind dagger boosted by a sizzling packet of his life energy. The spell impact nearly blinded Cymric with the astral flux, wave after wave of brilliant white fire. The fire rolled over him without heat, but his spirit bobbed like a bottle in an ocean storm. Disoriented, he stopped for a moment to get his bearings in the external world. He had never thrown a mind dagger that potent before, and it had left him a little dizzy.

The spiritcatcher responded a bit differently. Everywhere sheep were bleating or staggering to their feet. Cymric knew where all of those newly freed tendrils would be going. He leaped up the hill, heading for the center of the creature. He hoped the creature would be reluctant to risk striking itself, choosing instead to slacken its attacks on him.

The creature frenzied, tendrils and limbs striking everywhere. They collided, deflected off each other, tangled

with one another. Cymric panicked, nearly leaping into a tangle of thorny limbs. But then he realized the spiritcatcher was dumber than he thought, and he tried to think of ways to exploit the weakness. He lay perfectly still for a while, hoping the creature would thrash randomly rather than continue hunting him. He looked down at the maw of the creature, which flared with changing colors, copper to orange to yellow to emerald to sapphire. There was a strange configuration to its maw, an outline formed by its "teeth", which in turn was repeated by the shapes of threads woven around the maw. The whole reminded Cymric of the metal puzzles Throalic merchants loved to peddle, except this puzzle had the center piece missing. The spiritcatcher was meant for one particular purpose, completed when a pattern of the correct shape filled its maw.

The creature's color changed again, drifting from sapphire back down to its coppery hue. The limbs began to disentangle. The maw began to move away. Cymric waited as long as he dared, then leaped through an opening in the thorn tangle. Only after he had leaped about sixty paces did he pause to look.

The spiritcatcher was slinking off. Cymric followed cautiously, keeping the creature just at the edge of his astral sense. He trailed the monster until he saw it slip beneath the shimmer of flecks of elemental water carried in the river's current. Cymric stood for a moment, then raised his staff to shout to the sky, "Flee, you misenchanted amalgam of astral filth! And don't come back!"

A sound at his back made Cymric turn around. Two of the dwarf guards stood there, along with Jol and another farmer. The rest of the farmers were probably busy with their sheep. Worthro must have decided that following a wizard who hopped like a flea was not a dignified pursuit. The shorter guard stepped forward. "It's gone then." Cymric nodded. The dwarf harrumphed in a manner Cymric couldn't decipher, but then punched Cymric in the arm as befitted warrior camaraderie. Cymric winced, glad Leandra didn't express her appreciation this way.

Jol stepped forward, steadied by the hand of the other

farmer. As he reached for Cymric's hand, his grip was strong, but his hand trembled. "Thank you. We have a saying that spellcasters will go to any lengths to avoid bending their backs in an honest day's work. Jol Cathcart now knows that the saying is a lie, and I'll say so to any who try to defame you." Jol's mouth hung open for a second, but he found nothing more to say. Embarrassment silenced Cymric as well. Jol released his hand, then walked away, one hand on the shoulder of the other farmer.

The guard nodded toward Liffick. As Cymric started to walk, the guards fell in alongside him. The story must have preceded him, for the look of the townspeople was more curious, more furtive than hostile, when they got back to town. The shorter guard nudged Cymric in the hip. "Worthro is going to try to cheat you, you know. He likes to pay with a single, large pouch, thinking you won't count out fifteen hundred silver pieces in front of him. He'll probably try to shortchange you by a hundred, maybe two."

Cymric blinked. He'd completely forgotten about the payment. Other than the need to pay Pouika, the money hadn't mattered. But now that someone was trying to cheat him, he got angry. "I'll count every silver. Slowly, to watch Worthro sweat."

The taller guard pretended not to hear the conversation. The shorter one grinned. "I've got a better idea if you like, and more fitting, I think. Old Ilka counts the money we pay out. She doesn't like the guild shaving its promises. I can get her to let you know how much is in the pouch."

Cymric raised his eyebrows. "Then I can announce the exact amount in mysterious wizard fashion. And let Worthro sweat doubly as the coins are counted." The guard's grin widened. Cymric laughed. "Thank you, sir guard. If I may be so bold as to ask, why are you so helpful to itinerant wizards?"

"Don't like defending people who break promises; more trouble than it's worth." The guard's expression became crafty. "My sister is a wizard, and she has dealt with Worthro's kind. The trick is from her. You know, kind of wizard to wizard."

Cymric's smile started small, then stretched to the limits of his face. "Then I shall consider it an honor to continue such a fine tradition."

They came to the walls, and were admitted with no small amount of quiet side chatter between the gate guards. Cymric asked his escort to lead him to Leandra. They saluted, and moved a step ahead. Cymric mulled over what he'd learned, and considered what he already knew in light of new suspicions. "Tell me, is the mausoleum within the city walls?"

The question surprised the guards, their expressions suggesting wizards were a bit more mysterious than previously expected. The taller guard answered. "Yes sir, right next to the guild hall."

The guards dropped Cymric off at the healer's with a stomp of their boots and a flourish of their axes. There, Cymric sought out Pouika, finding her hard at work distilling a new concoction. He interrupted, but her look of annoyance changed to pleasure when she saw it was him. "Your news arrived ahead of you. Good work."

"Thank you. I shall give you your silver tomorrow after I extract payment from the farmers' guild."

Pouika nodded, then tapped the copper still with a glass rod. "The breath of Garlen is enough to form the basis for better than a dozen potions. The guilds coughed up most of the other ingredients. Your arrival helped me save a lot of lives."

"Including Leandra's?"

Pouika puffed her cheeks. "She will certainly live. She's tough, and Garlen's grace goes with her. I would say she'll be walking in a week, at full speed in maybe a month, maybe three weeks."

"Why the face?"

"Your swordmaster gives me the impression she plans to leave in a day or two, whether or not her legs work."

Cymric snorted. He rolled his staff between his hands as he decided. "Let this wizard try his bedside manner. Perhaps she can be persuaded to linger a while longer." He bowed to the healer, who immediately resumed her work. Cymric walked carefully among the cots. He had to explain to one delirious dwarf that he was not a healer, trying to break as gently as possible from his grasp.

He found Leandra resting comfortably by a pillar. Her chainmail was piled beside her cot, but the necklace was still around her neck. Her sword lay across her lap, and she had her right hand draped over the hilt. She stared at a stained glass window, watching the illusion of a dwarf couple performing an intricate folk dance. She smiled when she saw Cymric. "They seem to think they can keep me here for days. They don't know me very well."

Cymric knelt beside the cot. "No, they don't. But I think they're right, that you should take the time to heal."

Leandra propped herself up on one elbow. "They want me to rest for weeks, maybe a month. We don't have that kind of time."

Cymric looked down, trying to be sure about what he was saying before saying it. "I think we do."

Leandra studied his face carefully. Her suspicion was evident. "You now think the dates are different than the ones given in the calendar?"

Cymric shook his head. In his heart he felt he was right. But his confidence melted when he looked into the quiet fierceness of Leandra's expression. Her eyebrows rose and her eyes widened as she waited for him to speak. If he didn't say something soon, his courage would fail him altogether.

"Leandra, the prophecy is a lie."

25

Leandra slapped him hard, leaving a searing sting on his left cheek. Her face froze in pain, her arm thrown across her body from the blow. She gingerly laid herself down on the cot. Her teeth gritted, then her jaws relaxed. "You talk to Brius about this?"

Cymric nursed his cheek. He considered her question, trying to determine whether there was more to what she was asking. "No, if you mean did we hatch a plan to dissuade you before you got to Marrek."

"You did talk to Brius about the prophecy."

Cymric waved his right hand, warding away her assumptions. "Not in so many words. He just said that if I determined that the prophecy meant to send you into the clutches of the Ristular, then I had better be ready to walk into them alongside you."

Leandra's eyes widened briefly, warm spots of brown surrounded by luminescent white. Her gaze lost focus. "But he wasn't willing to walk into Marrek with me."

Cymric hesitated, slowly rolling his staff between two hands. "I cannot speak for Brius or for what happened between you." He shifted his weight, uncomfortable with his position. The shift did not help the discomfort. "I am speaking as the wizard whose truth you wanted. The prophecy—" Cymric felt frustration well up within him. He had only a few facts, his magical training, and a nagging intuition. With these he confronted a driving force in Leandra's life. "The prophecy has a hollow ring to it."

Leandra's face could have been chiseled from ice—sharp, clean, cold. Her arms were crossed, her right hand reflexively rubbing her upper left arm, "Just what sounds false to you?"

"I just drove the spiritcatcher away from Liffick, the same one from the well in Twin Chin. Bigger now, more powerful, but the same one." Cymric laid his staff on the floor, held his hands up in a circle. "This time I saw the center of the beast. Its pattern is incomplete, needing another pattern to complete it. I'm sure it needs your pattern. If you would let me read your aura, I could find out for sure."

"Not today, wizard. Too much effort; I need my life energy elsewhere." Leandra closed her eyes for several breaths. Her face relaxed with each breath. "So the Ristular have a creature meant to kill me. The prophecy says I will kill Ristul. I have to believe the Ristular will bust their scrots to stop me."

"The spiritcatcher has yet to attack you even though it's been in your area at least twice. Odd for a creature conjured specifically to kill you." Cymric tapped Leandra's elbow. "I think the nethermancer Maeumis created this prophecy. The Horror Ristul may not be involved at all."

"You've been sniffing Pouika's herb pouch!" Leandra said angrily.

Cymric began to tick his reasons off on his fingers. "The calendar is Maeumis' doing; his name is part of the pattern. Knowledge of the calendar's pattern helped me against the spiritcatcher. The spiritcatcher is therefore also Maeumis' doing."

Leandra blinked; theoretical magic was apparently not her strong suit. She listened intently, but her expression was wary.

Cymric gestured to the other cots. "The people were struck by nethermantic magic, powerful magic, the sort I would expect Maeumis to have." Cymric held up both index fingers, moving first the left and then the right. "The nethermancer leaves, the spiritcatcher appears. Too much for coincidence. I believe the nethermancer who did this is Maeumis."

Leandra thought this over. She nodded slowly. "So this

nethermancer is working for a Horror. The legends are filled with such perversions."

Cymric shook both index fingers simultaneously. "I don't think so. Maeumis was found in the mausoleum. Inside the walls, inside of Liffick's wards against the Horrors. If he were possessed, tainted, or wielding significant Horror magic, the wards would have picked him up. But nothing happened. For a servant of a Horror, he is remarkably clean of its influence."

Leandra began to look annoyed again. "So his servitude is completely voluntary. We are talking about a dwarf who melts people's bones from the inside out."

"Perhaps." Cymric opened his hands wide, holding them up just beyond his shoulders. "But another thing that strikes me odd is the . . ." Cymric struggled for the right words to convey the meaning to someone not versed in the discipline of wizardry. ". . . similarity, the flavor of the magic. The thorn ward inside the calendar, the shadow hydra, the spiritcatcher." Cymric snapped his fingers. "And those glowjelly things on the backs of the bats. All many-limbed, all able to sense or capture the spirit of the target. These seem to be taken from the same section of a nethermantic grimoire—related magics."

Leandra looked puzzled, then winced. Cymric had forgotten that he was talking to an injured woman. He excused himself, offering to go get Leandra something to drink. An orderly responded to his request by giving him a mug of fresh lemon water. Cymric walked back slowly, giving himself time to think. He offered the mug to Leandra, tilting it for a few sips at a time while she drank. He composed his thoughts, threw out some finer points of logic. He could give her more details later. When Leandra indicated she wanted no more, he set the mug on the ground.

"I believe Maeumis created the prophecy to lure you into a trap."

Leandra's eyes darted over to the pictures in the stained glass window. Breathing evenly, slowly, blinking infrequently enough to make Cymric uncomfortable, she watched the illusion of two dwarf dancers clogging atop a table. A tight, lopsided smile appeared on her face as she sat there watching the window. The smile disappeared as her eyes found Cymric's. "You won't mind a few questions?"

Cymric shrugged. Leandra swallowed carefully before asking, "The miracle from Garlen?"

"You mean the potion?"

"The breath of Garlen is part of the miracle. Pouika believes the Passion gave me part of her own life force, keeping me alive until the potion took effect."

Discussion of the Passions, their motives, their miracles made Cymric nervous. Religious talk invariably led to an issue of faith. Leandra and Pouika had faith that Garlen had intervened on Leandra's behalf. All Cymric could confirm was that the Garlen flask was full when he'd needed it. It may have lain there for days or weeks before they'd arrived at the shrine.

"I'm willing to say that Garlen intervened at the shrine, creating that potion." Cymric spread his hands and raised his shoulders. "But I cannot honestly say Garlen created the potion for you. The flask could have been prepared long ago, for the first traveler who needed it."

Leandra let a tic-smile cross her face. She tapped her necklace with her left hand. "And this? Is this the nethermancer's doing as well?"

Cymric rubbed his head vigorously enough to throw his black hair into total disarray. The necklace didn't fit his theory of the prophecy; it didn't fit any theory he had at all. Why did Leandra have the necklace? Where did she get it? What was she supposed to do with it? "I don't know. But I don't think Maeumis created the necklace. The magic feels different."

Leandra's smile returned to stay. "So, wizard, there are two facts—" She caught herself in time to cut off Cymric's objection. "And at least one of them is at odds with your explanation of the prophecy: the necklace."

Cymric plopped himself into a cross-legged position, slumping low to the ground, low enough to look underneath Leandra's cot. He watched the leather-soled feet of orderlies as they went from cot to cot. He listened to their whispered inquiries, the patients' controlled responses. An orderly stopped to ask Leandra if she were comfortable, then left when she grimaced a reply. Cymric straightened his posture. He tapped Leandra on her right wrist, considered a moment, then let his hand rest on hers.

"Leandra, you tried to kill me when you were possessed."

She flicked her eyes away from his, then quickly brought them back. "I don't remember much. I do remember it was using my body to try to cut you up. I tried to resist."

Cymric kept his hand on hers, keenly aware of the warmth of the touch. "You tried to cut off my wrist, then my elbow on the back swing. That's how Gelthrain said you killed Ragnar."

Leandra pulled her hand away. Cymric followed, again placing his hand upon hers. She did not pull away again, but started to cry instead. "You are . . . saying I killed Ragnar."

Cymric licked his lips, considering his words. "I think you did." He clasped her hand in his as he began to rush his words. "I think that whatever possessed you back there is what possessed you seven years ago. This time it possessed you even though you were standing in the middle of ground supposedly consecrated to Garlen."

"I wasn't wearing my necklace."

"Not this time. But the first time you were." Leandra's tears began to flow in earnest. Cymric felt like a cad. He'd expected to have to root around for the truth, but he hadn't expected to have to dig through Leandra's entrails to get it. He started to speak again, thought better of it, and let Leandra cry. He continued to hold her hand, occasionally stroking her head. He discarded the idea of hugging or holding her; her injuries would probably make such gestures excruciating. Leandra soon cried herself out.

"Ristul has the power to make me kill my friends," Leandra said hollowly. "Good reason to send me in alone, Cymric."

Cymric sat silent for a while, just holding Leandra's hand, being with her. "I am asking you not to go in, with me or without me." He raised his other hand. "Look, the prophecy smells of Maeumis. I think he possessed you now *and* seven years ago. I don't think you have ever encountered Ristul."

Leandra lay quiet for several minutes. She stared at the light quartz, the stained glass windows, the other cots, the pillars, the orderlies, pretty much everything except Cymric. She sighed, finally turning her attention back to him. "If the prophecy means nothing, why do the Ristular hunt me every seven years? Why not all the time?"

"I have no idea. The thought processes of Horror-worshippers have never made sense to me."

Leandra slowly turned her head toward Cymric. She grabbed his shoulder. "If the prophecy means nothing, why is Maeumis hunting me?"

"Leandra, you're the best swordmaster I've ever seen. Sacrificing you for your blood magic makes perfect evil sense."

"Did it make sense seven years ago, when I hadn't yet carved a legend for myself? Does it make sense to conjure some hideous spiritcatcher just to kill me?"

No, it did not. There were still too many loose threads to the pattern. Leandra must have read his face, for her grip relaxed. Cymric cocked his head, raised an eyebrow. "We wizards hate unsolved puzzles. Particularly the ones that might kill us."

Leandra managed a long, sad smile. "I'm asking you to solve it for me. I figure you have a week. That leaves us enough time to make it downriver to Marrek."

Cymric raised both eyebrows. Leandra raised hers back. Cymric clucked his tongue repeatedly. "Pouika says you need more like a month to heal."

Leandra wiggled both eyebrows at once, a gesture Cymric sometimes used. She didn't do it very well. "She's used to healing guild journeymen, not swordmasters. I'm good at putting my body back together after a fight."

Not much of a fight, Cymric thought. His doubt must have shown, because Leandra pressed her point. "Garlen wants me out of here. A week should be plenty." Cymric rolled his tongue in his left cheek, but said nothing.

Leandra tugged at his sleeve. "Cymric, you may be right about the prophecy. But if you're wrong, this is my last chance to kill Ristul. To avenge kin and neighbors. To stop Ristul and his followers from killing more people, destroying more villages. I cannot walk away from that simply because a nethermancer is trying to kill me."

Cymric snorted, then shook his head reluctantly. He wiggled his left hand. Leandra released his sleeve. He stood, stretched his back, then looked down at Leandra on her cot. He kicked his staff up to his hand, tapped his forehead in salute. "To a most productive week for each of us." He walked from the hall, ignoring the complaints when he accidentally brushed against two cots.

Cymric found lodging, then spent the rest of the evening trading on his freshly won status as sheep-saver and monster-defeater. He inquired about the town's magic workers, as well as Liffick's merchants of the arcane. He wandered from tavern to tavern, careful not to crowd out his newly learned information with too much ale. Still, the day was long enough, the ale strong enough for sleep to come as soon as his body hit the bed.

He spent the next morning visiting the merchants, pricing everything he thought he would need. The firewort was far too expensive, but that was because the cagey old herbalist saw no reason to drop his price so early in the season. Cymric had more luck with the silver lime, the mat of espagra hide, the spiced wood, and an especially delicious lamb and peppers kabob given him by an aunt of Jol, the farmer he had saved.

That afternoon he wandered down the Boulevard of Spring, which ran east from the center of town. He stopped in front of a gate with two blue dolphins. He'd been told that this was the residence of Yleesa, an elementalist. When Cymric placed his hand on the hand-imprint in the gate, a gong resonated just beyond. The gate opened onto a deep pool with pillars set into it for steppingstones. Cymric tested the footing. Finding it sound, he started across the pool.

Columns of leaping water startled him. The columns darted across his path like eels trained to jump through hoops. They erupted from the water with a loud splash, yet slipped back silently into the pool with barely a ripple. Cymric heard a giggle when one of the water-eels hit the pool. None touched him, but they became more numerous, their leaps more choreographed as he approached the door. A pair shot low in front of his ankles, while another two leaped over his shoulders, front to back. Others then shot in crossing arcs to form the shape of a dome over the next step. At the final step, they leaped, hovered, and crossed. The effect was like walking through an arc of swords formed by an honor guard, but without the guards and with quite a bit more giggling. The knocker on the cedar door was made of silver and shaped into a lion's head. Cymric rapped twice.

The dwarf woman who answered the door wore a beautifully embroidered robe covered with stylized renditions of wind, rain, and surf pounding against jagged cliffs. There was a stretch of ash-black flecked with red and lined against a fiery orange glow that Cymric guessed to be a beach somewhere along Death's Sea. Other scenes and glyphs wove through the robe, scenes about which Cymric couldn't have ventured even a guess. The whole blended together impossibly well, he thought, the true sign of an artisan's hand. He felt ashamed of the plainness of his own robe. He would have to change it someday.

Cymric introduced himself, asking for Yleesa. The woman made a graceful move of her robe, saying that she was Yleesa, invited him in. As she poured him some tea, he explained his need for a small elemental spirit, perhaps an air or fire sprite. Could she provide him with a scroll of the appropriate spell, and if so, what would she ask for such an item?

Yleesa smiled, demurring on the answer. Instead she talked about her training with the renowned elementalist Releana, asked about his own training, about his travels, then told him an anecdote of her own wandering days. Cymric fell into his patter. Seeing her reaction, he shifted to a more genuine voice. Yleesa never laughed at his tales, but smiled often. After the fourth cup of tea, she offered to put quill to a fire sprite spell, and to teach him the necessary words in the elemental tongue for that one spell. She wanted one thousand silvers.

Cymric sipped for a while, debating whether to try to negotiate. He drained his fourth cup, then announced that the price was high for such a spell, but that combined with Yleesa's hospitality, it was more than fair. Her smile told him he'd chosen the correct response. He left, taking time to step back and forth, even leap over a few of the steps in the pool. The water-eels went wild, cavorting and dancing in time with Cymric's movements. He lost his balance by the gate, but a barrage of water eels propelled him out the gate before he could stumble into the pool. Cymric grinned and whooped, then bowed to the pool. A dozen columns leaped from the water, bowing back.

Cymric headed back to his lodging, totalling up how much he would need for what he had to buy. One thousand for Yleesa, two hundred and thirty for the firewort, one hundred fifty for the silver lime, another hundred for the spice wood, plus another hundred or so for the espagra hide. Oh yes, and four hundred for Pouika. All told that was more than he had, even with the fifteen hundred the Farmers Guild had promised to pay him.

He walked back along the Boulevard of Spring, whistling happily as he raced through possible solutions. Ah, this was just like old times. Alone, several hundred silvers short, a deadline staring him in the face. Only this time, Leandra's life rode on his luck.

26

Cymric smiled at the dwarf trying to cheat him, raised his tankard in salute across the huge desk separating him from the guildsman Worthro. On the wall behind Worthro were fifteen plaques covered with gold leaf, each inscribed in stylized ancient dwarven. The lettering was difficult to read from this angle, but said something like "functionary distinguished by no notable failures for the year fourteen ninety one." Cymric's smile broadened. Every little bit he learned about his opponent helped.

"Care for some more? We use only the finest barley." Worthro poured himself another, but Cymric put his hand over his tankard. Worthro tilted his head in a questioning expression, then wriggled his beard in a facial shrug. The dwarf began to slurp the head off his ale. Cymric sipped his.

A stooped dwarf clad in a threadbare blue shawl and faded floral dress entered the room, taking small, steady steps. She carried a money bag that jingled with each step. The bag was closed with a gray velvet ribbon that had a series of elvish characters etched into it in a spidery hand. The elderly dwarf placed the money bag on the desk in front of Worthro, who smiled perfunctorily. "Thank you, Ilka. Glad you could be so prompt so early in the morning."

Ilka made the start of a courtsey, then slowly backed out of the room. As she was leaving, Cymric stole a closer look at the ribbon. It was covered with runes. Repeated over and over again, as if the figures were a decorative pattern for the ribbon, were the runes for the number 1,144. Three hundred and fifty-six less than Worthro had promised him. Cymric made some last-minute alterations to his speech.

Worthro opened his expression to something approximating innocence, handed the bag to Cymric. "Well done, Wizard. The Farmers' Guild is pleased with your work. Take this silver and our gratitude."

Cymric avoided snorting. He pretended to examine the bag carefully, then dropped it onto the desk, where it landed with a splat-jingle. "Your silver is three hundred and fifty-six pieces short. I'm afraid the gratitude of those who would break a contract is not worth much. I'm going to have to ask for additional restitution." Cymric worked hard not to let his satisfaction show. He leaned back in his chair, took a long drink, and watched Worthro over the top of his mug.

Worthro's expression was even, unsettlingly so. No trace of either shock or dismay. As Cymric waited, he thought he caught the trace of a predatory smile on the dwarf's face. The delay made Cymric uncomfortable. Unaccustomed to negotiating with dwarven guilds, he wasn't sure if speaking first in this situation was a sign of weakness. He sat a few moments more. "I suggest you make an offer quickly. The wrath of wizards is not something to be taken lightly."

Worthro's smile turned vicious. He toyed with the fingers of his right hand, cracking the knuckles of his index and middle fingers. "You have been well paid, wizard, for what amounted to less than an afternoon's work. The amount in the bag represents more than fair value for all the sheep you saved."

"Not including Jol, of course. I'm sure the farmers will be delighted to hear that their guild values the lives of their members so lightly."

"Be sure to go from pasture to pasture to tell them. You can spare the time. But can Leandra?" Worthro pronounced it as two syllables rather than three. Triumph crept into Worthro's expression, molding his face into a smug collection of wrinkles and folds. It was ugly to see, and uglier to feel. "Oh, try a spell if you wish. The Guild Hall is protected against better magery than yours."

Worthro stood up. He pointed to the bag. "Take it or leave it."

Cymric took the bag, seething at the sight of Worthro's victory smile. The dwarf extended his arm to the door, and Cymric turned to leave. But then he turned back again, part of him knowing that what he was doing was stupid. Coming around, he wheeled suddenly, swinging the bag. Worthro looked astonished, ducking too late. The metal sound of the coins striking each other was a fine counterpoint to the cracking sound from Worthro's jaw. Cymric dropped the bag, which burst, sending silver pieces rolling across the floor in every direction. "No deal, dwarf."

Satisfaction flooded Cymric, followed by regret as soon as he left the room. Worthro's silver was not enough, but now he had far less than enough. He rounded he corner of the corridor leading to the exit, then paused to lean his head against the cool marble tile. He heard someone gruffly clear his throat, looked up to see eight guards watching him. They had their axes drawn. At the head of the pack was the short dwarf from last night.

"Not much luck with Worthro?" The warrior's tone was quiet, sympathetic.

Cymric pounded the wall with his fist, then headed for the exit. The guards quickly flanked him. They clanked down the polished stone floor, a riot of noise in a normally hushed bureaucracy. Those who did not rate an office of their own looked up from simple pine desks as Cymric's procession passed. Pens halted on parchment as the curious stared. The group soon reached the steps and the air and sunshine of outside. He paused for a moment, breathing deeply to find a spot of calm inside himself. The guards stopped, their expressions fearful.

"Begging your pardon, sir," said the warrior, "but none of this is our fault. We would appreciate it if you would allow us to escort you back to your inn without any trouble." The dwarf's tone suggested that trouble was a distinct possibility. Cymric walked slowly as he pondered what to do next. Passing the mausoleum, he hurled a silent curse, asking the spirits of Worthro's ancestors to witness their descendant's shame. A dozen paces later Cymric stopped again. The guards took defensive stances, the short one raising his axe.

"Worthro cheated another magician, didn't he? That dwarf nethermancer?"

The dwarf warrior looked uncertain, but lowered his axe. "Like I said, it's not worth defending folks who break their promises. I lost some friends that night."

Cymric nodded. "Because Maeumis went berserk. He killed a lot of folks, not just from your guild. And left the spiritcatcher to decimate your flocks."

All of the guards raised their weapons. Cymric held out his hands. "This is between Worthro and me."

"Begging your pardon, sir, but we have strict orders," said the warrior.

"Bend them. I'm the best chance you have to stop Worthro from cheerfully risking your lives every time he cheats a magician."

The guards looked at each other. The debate was silent and swift. One lowered his axe, the others followed. The warrior spoke. "You cast a spell, sir, and escaped before we could react. Is that not correct?"

Cymric moved his hands as little as possible to weave a thread. The levitation spell caught all eight guards, sending them up a hundred feet or so. Cymric left them yelping like that, and reentered the guild hall. A few clerks noticed him, but no one seemed alarmed by his presence. He took the corner with large strides, threw open Worthro's door with a bang. Worthro sat there, ale mug to his cheek. A young clerk was busy gathering and stacking the silver.

Worthro glared at him. "You called the deal off, smoothface. There is no silver for you here."

Cymric sat himself in the chair, wrenched Worthro's tankard from his hands, dumped the ale on the floor, poured himself a new mug. The clerk froze. Worthro's face went red. "I have a new deal named Maeumis," said Cymric.

Worthro's eyes hardened. "Where are the guards?"

"Detained. We wizards are a tricksome lot."

Worthro looked the clerk directly in the eye. "Run for help, boy."

The clerk hesitated, looking from Cymric to Worthro. Cymric nodded to the boy. "Go ahead. Master Worthro and I need to be alone for this discussion anyway." The clerk went from a kneeling position to a sprint in a heart-beat.

"No more dealings with you, wizard."

"Twenty-five hundred silvers and details on the services Maeumis provided you."

"You are remarkably hard of hearing for one so young."

Cymric leaned back, sipping his ale and listening for the sound of heavy boots on the stone floor outside; nothing yet. "Your guards tire of dying so you can save a few silvers for your superiors. You made a mistake, a bad one. No plaque for you this year."

Worthro blinked, looked wary before regaining his composure. "The damage has been done. Why should I pay you good silver, plus divulge any alleged dealings with this Maeumis? What do I gain?"

Cymric took a long drink. "A very public song-and-spell, at the end of which I cast powerful magic to rid you of the ensorcelment Maeumis placed on you. The one that has caused your errors in judgement, none of which were actually your fault."

Worthro's moustache twitched. The sound of boots echoed down the hall. A pair of guards peered in around the doorway. Worthro waved them in. They drew their axes and entered, sending Cymric's stomach into flipflops. His face, however, he kept as still as possible, watching Worthro. The dwarf reached for his quill, and scribbled on the parchment. He handed the parchment to Cymric:

Ilka, Please augment the previous payment to the wizard Cymric to raise the total to two-thousand five hundred silver pieces.

—Worthro

Cymric nodded, handing the note back. Worthro gave it to the guards. "Take this to mistress Ilka, and return with the money as soon as possible." The guards looked hard at Worthro, but he waved them off with a confident smile. They saluted and left.

Worthro stood, went to get himself a clean tankard, and poured himself an ale. He drained half the mug before beginning to speak. "Maeumis sold us a ward against a Horror . . . It was missing all the blood magic, of course, but that was all he claimed was necessary to activate it."

Cymric shook his head, looked at Worthro. "He sold you what?"

"A ward. Against a Horror he claimed was loose in the area. But we had Goldquill Guild scholars research the Horror; it vanished at the end of the Scourge, its disappearance confirmed by a number of sources. Naturally, we could not offer full payment."

Cymric's stomach tightened. He turned facts over in his mind, which was beginning to form an ugly suspicion. "Naturally. May I see the ward?"

Worthro shook his head. "Sold it to the Goldquill Guild. It's theirs now. You could take it up with them, but they—"

"Are known for zealously guarding their knowledge." Worthro nodded in agreement. Cymric held his ale in both hands, staring down at the amber liquid but not drinking any more. Worthro drank two full tankards before the guards returned with the silver and an extra bag. Cymric gathered what was still scattered about on the floor, put it in the new bag. Judging the silver the guards had brought to be heavier than the eleven hundred and forty-four left in the room, Cymric figured the payment was close enough for him to count later. As Worthro was pouring his third ale, Cymric rose to leave.

"I'll be back in a couple of days for your—cleansing." Worthro nodded, sipping his ale. The dwarf looked dazed, not particularly caring whether Cymric was in the room. He must have taken losing harder than at first appeared. Cymric rapped on the desk to get his attention one last time. "Worthro, listen to me. Next time you see the Goldquill

Guild, tell them it's a wizard's professional opinion that they had better find the blood magic for that ward."

Worthro blanched, and Cymric left the Guild Hall thinking he was going to have to confront Ristul after all.

27

Illuminated by the soft glow of twenty-three candles, Cymric's scalpel scratched an intricate pattern into the scaly espagra hide. He shuddered at the sound, then sat back on his heels to relieve the sharp pain in his knees from kneeling too long on a stone floor. He laid his scalpel down next to the iridescent green hide. Exhausted from a long day of magic, Cymric took frequent breaks rather than risk ruining the conjuration symbol. Two sides of the triangular design were complete. The third side, the longest one, had the most intricate designs of the symbol. Yleesa had shown him how to carve the symbol, yet the symbol would have been quite beyond him without the vellum copy Yleesa had given him. Next to the vellum lay a large translucent page, inscribed with the spell Cymric would have to use.

This time he needed a longer break than his usual seven slow breaths. He flexed his right hand as he looked to the desk he had shoved into the far corner of the room. He wobbled to his feet and walked carefully, avoiding puddles of congealed wax that had overflowed the candle holders. The desktop held a half-empty pot of cold tea, two bites of rye bread, a chicken drumstick, and one sweet muffin hoarded from breakfast. He plopped himself onto the old cane chair in front of the desk and picked up one of the pieces of rye. Cymric chewed twice before swallowing it. His hand fluttered between the drumstick and the muffin, finally seizing the meat with the vigor of a swordsman drawing for a duel. His mind on magic, he didn't get a clean bite. Indeed, his gnashing, sucking, and drooling sounded trollish, and part of him relished the breach of etiquette even though no one was about to be horrified by his bad manners.

Morning had been spent with Yleesa finishing six hard days of study. In the early afternoon Cymric had performed before a sizeable crowd outside the mausoleum, removing the "curse" from Worthro. The guild dwarf proved quite fond of overacting, frothing and flailing as Cymric spun his song and spell. Cymric thought Worthro's performance entirely unconvincing, but the crowd ate it up. The cheer that erupted when the final flame flashes "destroyed" the curse almost made the sham worthwhile. A limp Worthro was carried away on a stretcher. The back slaps and congratulations were genuine, particularly those from members of the Farmers Guild.

In late afternoon Cymric played the part of a crutch who spoke encouraging words. Leandra could walk a little with help, and could stand unaided for short periods of time. She had taken each step with the kind of concentration Cymric reserved for his most difficult spells. She expressed confidence that she would be in fighting trim within a few more days. Cymric kept to himself the opinion that she would be lucky to make her way to the privies without help. He also kept to himself Worthro's revelation about Maeumis. He didn't yet know what to make of the fact that Maeumis had sold a Ristul ward. He hoped a more thorough delving into the calendar would help.

Cymric grabbed the teapot with his left hand, the cane chair with his right. He scraped the chair along the floor, turning it around the other way. He sat regarding the calendar and the incomplete conjuring triangle. He tipped the teapot, drinking directly from the spout, swishing each mouthful from cheek to cheek several times before swallowing. Cymric imagined each swallow driving his frustration further and further down into his gut, away from his head. He drained the teapot, clattered it down on the desk behind him. He rubbed his hands. This was it, his best and perhaps last chance to crack the meaning of the calendar.

He knelt by the espagra hide. Over and over he rhythmically whispered "fleur," "ochost," "grieve direct," the name of each part of the design as the scalpel cut through the scale. He worked across the length of the hide, one blade-thickness at a time, working continuously until he was less than a finger-width from completion. He took his seven slow breaths, then closed the angle to finish the triangle. Laying the scalpel aside, he picked up the vellum and recited each word carefully, attempting an even cadence. The words became stickier near the end of the spell, a manifestation of the fire sprite's will. Cymric kept his concentration, forcing his tongue through the final syllables.

The flames from all twenty-three candles rose; twenty-three guttering points of light spiraled into the triangle. The sprite flared into existence in the center of the triangles, absorbing the candle flames. The size of the sprite startled Cymric, who'd been expecting something the size of a windling or smaller. The fire sprite had the appearance and size of a robust dwarf, barely contained within the triangle. The sprite smiled, angry-red lips parting to reveal flickering darts of incandescent white heat.

"I am here at the bidding of my summoner."

Cymric began to sweat. He bowed quickly, making sure his hair got none too close to the sprite. "Your summoner needs a task of fire."

The sprite's laugh expelled sparks, reminding Cymric of the collapsing houses in Corthy. The sprite's beard undulated wildly with the laugh, a campfire caught in a strong wind. "You have chosen wisely then, summoner."

Cymric pushed the calendar to the edge of the triangle. "No ordinary burning. I need you to enter the magic of this. There is a ward, a ward of thorns. I want to you dance with it, dance upon it, until it is burnt from the pattern of this thing."

The sprite frowned, the motion of its beard and hair calming to a steady blaze. "Such may not be consumed by my poor heat."

"Occupy it then, move upon it as flames upon a log. Keep it away from me. But burn nothing else of the pattern."

The sprite stroked its beard, the sound like seasoned logs crackling on a winter fire. Its hand lost form where it touched the beard, as if his hand were wax melting. The fingers returned as soon as the sprite dropped his arm. "Seems a poor task to be asked to burn what may not respect flame, while leaving untouched that which concedes graciously. What do you offer?"

Cymric held out four sticks of spice wood. The sprite's eyes flared, and its teeth danced wildly within a burning mouth. As the sprite reached for a stick, a wavery snowflake pattern appeared, then disappeared in a frantic hiss of steam. The sprite cried out, retracted its hand with four fingers and the tip of its thumb missing. A spurt of flame ignited on the remainder of the thumb, and the thumb grew back. The other digits returned with the spatter-hiss of grease frying in a pan.

"Two for keeping the ward busy. Two for burning nothing else but the ward." Cymric's voice was firm, but his hand shook a little.

The sprite gave no indication that it recognized this sign of human frailty. Its eyes remained fixed on the spice wood. "Done. Let us to it."

Cymric whispered *"fyr daevin Cymric kilik ist,"* lowering the protective magic of the conjuring triangle. Then a bright flash panicked him into thinking he'd made a mistake. His eyes adjusted to see the sprite now two handspans high, kneeling on the face of the calendar. The sprite scooted over a few inches, planted a splayed hand on the calender's surface. Its face lost all expression, then its cohesion as the sprite seemed to pour into the calendar.

The room was dark. Cymric crawled forward until his left hand bumped the calendar's warm rim. He seated himself, grasped the notched stone edges with both hands, then willed his inner sight to float slowly down into the pattern of the calendar.

The orange of the calendula seemed dull compared to the brilliant sparking arcs formed by the fire sprite. All three thorn helices had erupted in pursuit of the sprite, growing, climbing, twisting, and diving in a clumsy chase. The sprite's arc reversed instantly, bouncing a trail of sparks down a long section of thorns. The thorns didn't smoke, but pieces fragmented off as if transformed to dust. Cymric caught the acrid odor of green wood burning. A thrill teased Cymric's spine; the plan might work.

Cymric continued to guide his inner sight down the stem of the calendula, serenely floating down to the Maeumis-root. From there he examined the hundreds of tangled roots, which blended and joined to form the stem of the flower. He then followed the twisty, curvy path of some roots to their end. Cymric was astonished to see that no matter how devious the root's path, it always ended up vertically aligned with other roots. Sometimes only two or three roots were aligned, another time Cymric counted fourteen. Each of these root-stacks were evenly spaced from one another. Just like the notches on the calendar.

Cymric took his bearings on the central flower, then drifted around the roots. When he counted ninety-one, he took his bearings again; a quarter-turn around the flower from his starting point. The root-tips must be aligned with dates on the calendar; it was far too even to be a coincidence.

A bright flash drew away his attention. Far above, a thorn ward toppled fiery strings that broke into blazing segments falling toward the roots below. The arc of the fire sprite was still visible as it darted here and there, avoiding the other thorn wards. Cymric still had time.

What were the roots and what was the meaning of their alignment? Maeumis had used the roots to construct the pattern of the flower. The roots were probably conduits or symbols of the power Maeumis had tapped to integrate into the pattern of the flower. A real calendula had far fewer roots than this pattern. Why so many?

Cymric probed the tip of one root with his inner sight. He sensed a brittleness and a smell, as if the root were old and powdery. He tried a few other roots, gaining nothing new. He went back to the first root he had probed. If the roots had been used to draw power, perhaps he could give a little power to a root and see what happened. First he wove a spell thread for levitation, then connected it to the root, hoping it would draw power from the spell pattern.

But instead of casting the spell, Cymric waited to see what the root would do to the spell pattern. Nothing happened. The spell thread faded.

So the roots did not draw power from spells. Cymric's external senses were feeling a persistent itchy spot between his shoulder blades—his willpower beginning to flag. Cymric blocked the sensation as best he could.

Perhaps the roots would absorb blood magic, a possibility that made sense; hundreds of roots suggested a readily obtainable source of magical power. Testing this guess would require surrendering some of his life force to the pattern to see whether it would be absorbed. If the experiment worked, Cymric might never get that life force back. Not to mention what the pattern would do with his magical essence. Maeumis the dwarf had built the pattern, and until now all of his magic had been unpleasant. Adding a bit of wizard's blood seemed a poor way to improve it.

The root image fluttered and fuzzed as Cymric hung on indecision. His will wouldn't last forever, nor would he be able to afford the fire sprite for future trips. Leandra was agitating to move on to Marrek. This might be his last chance to unravel the secret of the calendar.

The image of the root shrank into precise focus. After weaving a thread and attaching it, Cymric then forever surrendered a portion of his life force. This bit of blood magic traveled down the length of the thread, pulsing with each heartbeat, moving forward a fraction with each pulse. The wet sheen of red contrasted with the dull gray of the thread and the flat white of the root. As the gob of blood magic neared the thread, Cymric's anxiety rose. So did his pulse, and the speed of the blood magic along the thread. As the blood magic hit the root, Cymric heard a *crunch-crack* as loud as a boulder falling into a frozen mountain lake.

Even as his inner sight was plunging into the root, dizziness blurred his vision. He felt something pull at his face, fuzzy points of light and then a loud, tired voice.

"You shall be called Heslar, son of Vonnek," said the voice. "I claim your blood as my own." Whoever was

speaking remained out of sight. Or was he that haloed blur
to Cymric's right?

Before Cymric could try to focus his vision, the dizziness returned. This time he saw a huge dwarf face just in
front of him. A spoon also popped into focus, a dollop of
musty-smelling cereal in its bowl. "Come on, Heslar.
Open the vault. Deposits make your wealth grow." The
huge face smiled.

*I am experiencing someone else's memories. The roots
must represent the lives*—then Cymric's thoughts broke as
the spoon jabbed forward. Sticky paste filled his mouth, a
bitter taste that made gorge rise in the back of his throat.
He spit, splattering the face in front of him. Dizziness
grabbed him again.

He spent time playing King of the Mountain with his
friends, especially chubby Bellic. He mastered figures
faster than boys two years his senior. Much later he and
Bellic snuck out of his master's storeroom to conceal
themselves in the high grass by the river, where they
watched a questor of Astendar teach some of the local
youths how to dance. A sharp jab from Bellic drew his attention to a dwarf girl with red hair and moves that flowed
as smoothly as the river's.

A dizzy blur preceded his first kiss with Erin. He was
aware of a feeling that spread from his lips and feather-
fingered its way throughout his body. The feeling lingered
even after her lips had moved away. He heard her giggle,
saw her hair, a red strand caught in her fingers. Her eyes
gleamed, then her fingers opened to release the strand.
"Well?" she asked.

The chisel made its final *chink,* pulling back to reveal
the word *Heslar* below the other names on the bronze
plaque. His pride fired his limbs, made him feel as if he
could wrestle a brithan barehanded. A different pride,
deeper and cooler, filled him as he exchanged vows with
Erin. His voice shook with emotion as he spoke, embarrassment gripped him as he mispronounced the name
Astendar. The witnesses laughed. Erin gripped his hand
even more tightly.

A bead of sweat dropped onto the saddle in front of

him. He quickly wiped it dry, then returned to the dragon design the cavalryman had requested. Erin entered the workshop, face lined with fatigue. She hesitated before speaking. "The questor of Garlen has anointed a hero for the village." Hope surged through his heart, hope that the raids would end and the Ristular could be driven from their land. But Erin's expression, and then her words, dashed the hope. "The signs are clear. Garlen has chosen the human babe. Garlen has chosen Leandra."

Pain coiled around his legs as he fell to the ground. Men in the robes of the Ristular grabbed him. He screamed for Erin to keep running, saw the crossbow bolt drive deep into her left thigh. Nausea choked him just as his sight sparked out from the blow to his head.

The dwarf leaning over him had black eyes and silver lines decorating his face, as if a wire mask had melded with his face. Blood spattered that calculating face, and the hands probing his chest were covered in gore. The face looked over one shoulder and nodded to an unseen captor. "He's ready."

Rough hands lifted him to the altar while the dwarf rinsed out a dagger in a copper bowl. The hilt was the head of serpent, the blade the forked serpent's tongue. He began to struggle; he did not want to be sacrificed.

Whoa, wait, time to leave. Cymric tried to exert his will, to force his inner sight out of the vision.

He turned to look at the dwarf, who was just raising the dagger. "I, Maeumis Weirkin, Thrall of Ristul, bind you to my master, so it may find sustenance and shall find its way."

He managed to pull free from the captor holding his right hand. His blow was weak, but caught Maeumis squarely on the jaw. The dwarf rocked back out of sight. Hands quickly pinned him again, and Maeumis reappeared, hand on jaw.

Come on, come on, come on! Cymric poured more of his life energy into his will, struggling to break free of the vision. Maeumis raised the dagger, plunged it down. Cymric screamed as Heslar screamed. Maeumis placed his other hand on the dagger, steadying the blade as it made the incision. Pain jolted through him with each twitch of the blade.

Cymric screamed as the muscles in his back spasmed. He kept screaming. The pounding on his door became more insistent. The dagger slid another fraction. *The pounding on my door*—Cymric latched onto the sound, the frantic beat thumping through the wood and rattling the knob. Cymric screamed again as he realigned his senses to the external world.

He panicked at the darkness. Someone threw his weight against the door, but it held. Cymric crawled toward the sound, his knee crushing an extinguished candle. He found the door just as those on the other side were slamming into it once again. A quick hand-slide along rough-hewn wood found some splinters and the doorknob. Cymric opened the door.

Two dwarfs in heavy boots stood outside, the one in a green cap vigorously rubbing his shoulder. Their expressions held enough fear to rout a squad of militia, but they held their ground. "Wizard, you're bleeding."

Dazed, Cymric looked down. The light of the hall lamps showed the front of his robe stained with blood. The stain was spreading.

Green cap stepped forward. "Let's us take you to the healers." Cymric tried to wave them off, but they grabbed him under the armpits. A red flare illuminated the room. Shrieking a crackling oath of triumph, the fire sprite appeared in the conjuring triangle. The dwarfs dropped Cymric and fled down the hallway.

Cymric crawled back toward the triangle, picking up the spice wood along the way. While he tossed the wood into the triangle, one piece at a time, the sprite boomed out a laugh. "Best burning I've done in ages! Got two of the thorn wards. Last one is your problem. My thanks for the opportunity. And the payment."

"Welcome," mumbled Cymric.

The fire sprite regarded Cymric, eyes dimming to the color of dying embers. "Seems you went too close to the dark heart of the thing. I avoided it."

"Wise choice." Cymric collapsed on the floor to rest.

His hand probed underneath his robe. His skin had been sliced open, but the wounds didn't seem deep.

"I would make the same choice if I were you. At least until I were a better magician than you are." The sprite laughed again, then vanished in a puff of perfumed smoke.

Cymric lay still. Above the waist he was covered in darkness. The rest of his body was illuminated by light from the doorway. The sprite was right about him needing to get to a healer, but his need to think was even greater. He thought about the calendar, which held the pattern of the flower in the center. The flower had hundreds of roots, each root probably containing memories of the person whose blood magic Maeumis had stolen to build the pattern. Cymric examined the flower carefully. It looked bigger, more fully in bloom than the last time he'd seen it. In some small way Cymric's blood magic had contributed to the pattern's growth.

Cymric didn't know the purpose of the pattern, but in the vision Maeumis had said ". . . so it may find sustenance and shall find its way." The pattern either strengthened or summoned Ristul. Probably both. The problem was that Cymric couldn't be sure.

No, the real problem was that the fire sprite was right about him not being a powerful enough magician to uncover the secrets of the pattern within the calendar. The truth Leandra needed from her wizard would continue to elude him. If she still wished to confront Ristul, she would have to do so without much real knowledge of the prophecy. That hurt worse than the pain in his chest.

Cymric sat up, a motion that set his head to throbbing. Then, when he tried to rise from his sitting position, he fell back down before he'd even managed more than a few inches. Changing his tack, he rolled up to his hands and knees, then pulled his left knee to his chest so he could put one foot on the ground. He wobbled to his feet, fixed his first target as the doorframe, and took cautious steps to his goal. At the doorway, he gripped the frame, pausing to let the dizziness pass. It seemed that standing up got easier every few breaths.

As his next goal he fixed the handrail of the stairway at

the end of the hall. With the little bit of extra energy not devoted to each step, Cymric wondered what he would tell Leandra. He thought about what he'd heard, about how Leandra had been chosen as a hero by Garlen. A weak snort escaped his lips. Cymric grabbed the handrail, steadying his progress down the steps. He tried to think of the words he would use to tell her that it had been her destiny to save a village from Ristul.

At the foot of the stairs he paused as the inn patrons stared at him with a mixture of curiosity and horror. With his next step, Cymric staggered along the wall and the troll barkeep rushed from behind the counter to grab his elbow and steady his progress. Cymric thanked the man, but he couldn't keep from letting loose a wild laugh as the two of them continued toward the door. The barkeep's grip tightened and his eyes narrowed in concern, but Cymric paid him no mind. He was too busy wondering just how he would tell Leandra she had found her destiny nearly twenty-eight years too late.

28

Cymric winced as Pouika pulled the thread through the skin around the deep cuts he'd taken. While she worked, he sat on the examining table, robe across his lap, fist clenching its hem. Dark curtains separated the examining area from the rest of the hall, but the thin fabric did nothing to block the coughing and complaints of the makeshift hospital's other patients. A yellow herbal stain smeared his chest, orange where the blood still oozed. Pouika, continued to stitch a design in the shape of a healing rune that she promised would heal the wounds before the threads fell apart. Leandra frowned as she watched, her eyes flashing anger. Though she was wearing full armor, Cymric noticed that she leaned against a pillar for support. Leandra was just better at concealing pain than he was. At least she'd stopped tapping her sword hilt.

"We leave for Marrek as soon as Pouika finishes," she announced, catching Cymric and the healer totally by surprise. Cymric grunted harshly as the startled Pouika accidentally drove the needle deeper than she'd intended. Tears welled up in his eyes as she pulled the thread through; it felt more like she was sewing a hot wire into his flesh.

Leandra walked over to the table, leaning against it with one hand and covering Cymric's right fist with the other. She looked him in the eye. "I know you ran into problems with the calendar. Thanks for trying."

You don't know the peasant's part of it. Cymric raised his eyebrows as he blinked his eyes clear. "I discovered a thing or two. We should talk about it before you decide to take off for Marrek."

"We can talk about it on the boat."

"You've already hired a boat? So you were going to Marrek no matter what I learned from the calendar."

"All I'd lose is the price of a deposit. Trade season will soon be in full bloom. I needed to guarantee passage."

Her explanation mollified Cymric, but doubt still nagged him. Leandra had probably made up her mind some time ago. Back at the Garlen clearing she'd released him from his promise to accompany her to Marrek. Pouika made another pass with the needle, making Cymric grimace.

"Last one," said the healer.

As much as Leandra claimed to want the truth from him, it now seemed that what she'd really wanted was tactical advice, an edge in her fight against Ristul. She still believed that prophecy directed her to battle a Horror. Cymric doubted that he could say anything to dissuade her. Pouika was running a gentle hand over the stitching, then she nodded, apparently satisfied with her work. Cymric sat chin-to-chest, examining his wounds.

"I'd advise not going anywhere with legs as unsteady as yours," Pouika said to Leandra.

"The journey to Marrek takes only a few days. My legs will be fine by the time I arrive."

Pouika's mouth smiled, but her eyes did not as they searched Leandra's face. She gently touched the scabbard hanging from the taller woman's belt. "I would not presume to tell you how to care for your blade. Perhaps you could extend me the same courtesy for my profession."

Leandra blinked, then knelt down to Pouika's height with some popping of her joints. "I do not mean to offend. Garlen gave me a sign. It's time I leave; we both know that."

Cymric looked up. "What sign?"

Pouika hesitated, then hugged Leandra, who returned the gesture with a flicker of pain passing across her face. Then she stood to her full height and squeezed the dwarf's hand before gesturing for Cymric to follow her. He slid off the examining table while grabbing for his pack and staff, then fumbled with his robe as he hurried around the curtain. Leandra walked rapidly but unevenly to her cot. Leaning against the cot was her backpack; next to it was a small bundle of neatly stacked clothes, rations, and cooking utensils.

Leandra dropped to one knee, picked up the pack and gingerly worked it over her shoulders. "Jam what you can from the stack into your own pack," she said. "And leave what you cannot carry. I want the clothes more than the rest."

Cymric watched her struggle with her pack for a heartbeat, then moved to help her. He lifted the pack from behind, easing its weight while Leandra worked against the straps. The pack weighed much less than when he and Leandra had first arrived. She'd lightened it considerably to carry only what she could manage with her injuries.

While she was adjusting the last strap, Cymric untied his own pack and threw open the flap, eyebrows rising as he looked at the available space and then at the pile of Leandra's belongings. He lifted out the calendar and began to rearrange other items in his pack. Without turning from the task, he asked her, "What sign did Garlen give you?"

Leandra opened a side pouch on her pack, and pulled out a flask. She tossed it to Cymric, who dropped a shirt to make a two-handed catch. "Garlen filled that for me. It's the flask from the spring."

Cymric turned the flask over in his hands, then opened the top and took a taste. It had the same sweet, peppermint taste of the potion at the spring. He capped the flask before handing it back. "So Garlen wants you to get better. Why do you think she wants you to leave before you're healthy?"

"I asked for a way to leave. I prayed for a way to meet the obligations of the prophecy. The next morning the flask was refilled."

Cymric thought Leandra's story was plausible. He also thought it plausible that Garlen refilled the flask on a regular basis or that the flask itself might be enchanted. Leandra's determination was plain. When he finished packing, leaving only a ladle, Leandra made to leave. Shouldering his pack, Cymric struggled for a moment to find his voice, then blurted the truth. "The calendar suggests that Garlen did anoint you a hero."

Leandra slowed but kept walking. "The calendar only suggests?"

Cymric took a few quick steps, careful to dodge the cot holding a dozing dwarf. By then he'd caught up with her. She looked over, wariness creeping over her face. Cymric took the time between here and the hall entrance to think over his next words a little more carefully. "I traveled the memory of a dwarf named Heslar. A questor of Garlen anointed you a hero when you were just born. Heslar seemed to believe you were to protect his village from the Ristular. But—"

He knew he'd made a mistake the instant he hesitated. Leandra's eyes showed her anger first, but her voice was steeped in it. "I failed. Heslar's dead and his village is destroyed. Isn't that how your story ends?"

Close enough to suit this wizard. His curiosity tickled his tongue to ask how she knew about the Ristular killing Heslar. Another look at her face made him think it was more prudent to tell his curiosity to take a reed boat out on Death's Sea.

"I may be Garlen's heroine, but there wasn't much I could do about Ristul for the first twenty years of my life. Now I can at least try." Leandra turned into an unfamiliar street, but her confident step suggested she knew the way. Perhaps she hadn't been confined to a cot the whole time Cymric had been dabbling in magic.

The dockside was crowed. Cargo clogged the riverside streets, as most of the ships had been unloaded earlier in the afternoon. Now captains in threadbare velvet coats haggled with brokers with impeccably coifed hair smelling of lavender. Troll longshoremen inspected damaged lamps already passed over by dwarf merchants. A gust drove the smell of rotten fruit from one warehouse, while outraged poultry cackled and flapped inside wood and wire crates. Poor children darted from crate to barrel looking for something they could eat or sell, but they were driven away by bored militia whose efforts were in proportion to the value of the cargo threatened.

Leandra turned left at a barrel filled with unappetizing red pickled something onto a pier more warped than straight. The boats tied alongside were small, perhaps twenty feet or less. She stopped at one bearing the emblem of a windling trapped beneath a fishbowl.

"Hail Orseth!" she shouted.

The elf who emerged from the cabin surprised Cymric with his greasy black hair split into looped braids and his square-cut white shirt and shiny green pants. The style was human, as was the lack of cleanliness. But the silver and crystal rings on the fingers of Orseth's left hand were unquestionably elven, as were his seemingly boneless gestures. He bent down, lifted the gangplank with a grunt, then dropped it with a clatter. His smile seemed genuine. "Welcome aboard, Leandra. Is this your wizard?"

"This is Cymric," she said, extending a hand his way and nodding. "Cymric, I'd like you to meet Orseth, a friend of Brius, now a friend of mine."

Cymric snorted, then bowed low. Orseth straightened himself with exaggerated motion, then returned the bow. They held their positions until Leandra stomped up the gangplank. When he rose, Cymric saw Orseth pointing to a mooring line. "Would you mind untying that, master wizard?"

Leandra waved him off. "Not yet. Cymric and I have a matter to settle." Orseth shrugged, sauntered back down into his cabin. Leandra stayed on the gangplank, squarely facing Cymric. "I'm off to Marrek, and I've paid for your passage. This is your last chance to back down."

Cymric laughed. "Milady, never underestimate a wizard's ability to find new ways to back down."

Leandra's eyes flashed as she tightened her grip on the hawk's head of her sword. "I mean, I need to count on you. If you step on this boat, it means you're with me to the end of the campaign."

Cymric slapped his staff against a mooring pile. He took a breath. It didn't help, so he smashed his staff against the pile five or six more times. "How can I be with you to the end when I'm not with you now?" Leandra continued to stare at him, but said nothing. "The prophecy you've been following is a lie. I'm sure of it." He pounded his staff into the pier, then tossed it up with his left hand, catching it with his right. "I don't know what the calendar means, except that Maeumis made it, and he used a lot of blood magic to do it. If I could crack the calendar, it might be different. As it stands, you're walking into a den of fanatics without any clear idea either of what you should do or what it's possible for you to do."

Leandra walked down the gangplank. She knelt by the mooring pile, then began to untie the rope. Cymric took a step forward and bent down to talk to her.

"What are you going to do when you get to Marrek? Find the Ristular and charge in their front door?"

"I take it you have a better idea."

Cymric straightened up and threw his arms to the sky. "Yes! Yes, Leandra, I do. Walk away from this one."

"The Ristular seem to be able to find me."

"Fine! That doesn't mean you have to run screaming straight into their stronghold."

Leandra worked the last knot free. "I believe Garlen has made this choice for me."

Cymric blinked, his mouth open. "You're saying the Passion of hearth and healing wants you to attack a Horror and its followers singlehandedly? Leandra, that's *stupid*!"

Leandra hurled the freed rope onto the deck of the boat, and Cymric regretted what he'd said. She got up and walked over to begin untying the other mooring line. Cymric licked his lips, then went to join her. When he reached for the rope, she slapped his hands away. "I don't want to face a Horror by myself. But I will if—" She stopped untying the rope. She sniffed once, then looked at Cymric. Her eyes were shiny, but she had shed no tears. "Cymric, did you mean the promise you made in the inn in Corthy?"

Cymric's stomach tightened. *Damn, there goes the wiggle room.* The answer was no, he hadn't meant the promise. When he'd vowed to stick with Leandra, to face a Horror, he hadn't known what that would mean. *Promises are good intentions contingent upon events.* Events had given him a glimpse of the magic involved, the power arrayed against them. The odds looked bad for him, worse for Leandra. He hadn't been able to fully decipher the calendar because there hadn't been enough time. Before when he'd failed, it had usually meant it was time to move on, to dodge the consequences. Now . . . actually, it still meant it was time to move on.

"You in there?" Leandra's question was soft. Cymric came back to the world to focus on her face. The tears were still there, one having escaped the red rims of her eyes to trickle down the right side of her face.

Now I can at least try. Leandra said it. She meant it. She was going to face Ristul, or Maeumis, or something. Perhaps she was going to die. Make that "probably going to die." Cymric didn't want her to go. And if she went, he didn't want her to go alone.

"I don't suppose I could convince you to let me teach you the wizardly art of running away?"

Leandra eyes opened wide, then she laughed. She bit her lip. "Maybe you could. But only after Marrek."

Cymric picked up his staff and used it to thump his head several times, and none too gently. Leandra meanwhile had finished untying the knots and thrown the rope on deck. "You might find it useful to have someone who can show you how to run away. Even in Marrek." The way Leandra was looking at him as she stood up made the heat rise in Cymric's cheeks. "I'll go to Marrek. Any running away I do will be with you, not away from you."

"Promise?" Leandra's eyes searched his face intently.

"I promise. I'll even make that a swordmaster kind of promise, rather than the sort we shifty wizards use."

Leandra didn't laugh as he'd expected. Instead she clasped her hands over his, which were holding the staff. She stood for some time, eyes closed. Cymric let go of his staff, leaning it in against his shoulder. He held her hands, aware of the warmth and the callouses of her right hand. Leandra released his hands and moved into him, heedless of the staff. She sniffed several times, once breathing in a gasp-sigh. "Thank you," she said.

Cymric opened his mouth for a sharp-witted reply, then decided against it. He only hoped he wasn't going to be scared witless by whatever they faced. He had to keep thinking, especially in those situations where he might prefer to run away. "Hope I can be useful to you when things get bad."

Leandra looked up at him. "Being there is a pretty solid start."

"I personally would like to be something other than dessert for a Horror who's just had you for a main course."

"Oh, I wouldn't worry. I'm sure the Horror will eat you first."

Cymric laughed, bringing a smile to Leandra's face. Grabbing at his staff as Leandra moved away, he then followed her up the gangplank. Orseth emerged from his cabin and picked up a pole. Leandra took another. Together they shoved the boat away from the dock. Orseth moved to the tiller. Shouting poling instructions to Leandra, he moved the boat into the current. Lifting her dripping pole from the water, Leandra placed it back in its notches on the deck. Then she and Cymric joined Orseth at the tiller. On a river ruddy-red with the setting sun, each slap of the water marked another bit closer to Marrek.

29

A fireball shrieked overhead, then exploded in the water
sixty paces away. Warm spray was all that hit Cymric,
who was sitting with his feet dangling from the boat, sipping some of Leandra's Landis blend. Upstream of
Marrek, a flotilla of rivercraft had congregated a safe distance from the two t'skrang steamboats battling outside the
harbor. Both ships had come racing in from the Serpent
River, whistles screaming and elemental engines belching
smoke. The captains must have decided that the race for
first berth was too close to call, because fire cannons
boomed almost simultaneously. A proper frenetic battle for
t'skrang honor followed.

Orseth said t'skrang battles "are big on bellowing and
small on bloodshed." While the boarding actions looked
and sounded serious, Cymric had to admit the fire cannon
barrages were remarkably inaccurate. Two rowboats of
t'skrang rowed furiously for the docks, cheers ringing from
a nearby fishing skiff as one of the boats pulled into the
lead. Someone's wager must be looking more secure.

Leandra sat beside Cymric putting her hair up into a
combat coil. "Which lizards are winning?"

"Fiercely contested, I would say." Cymric pointed to the
steamboat with the red paddles, prow, and smokestacks.
"The rowboat from that ship looks like it will make the
docks first."

Orseth, who was sitting on Leandra's other side, tossed
her some fresh biscuits, two of which she passed to Cymric. "Could be. But even that advantage might not be
enough. Captain Eluchai has several adepts in his crew,
but they'd be better at fighting than rowing, so I bet

they're in the trailing boat." The first boat reached the docks. Its occupants ignored the hemp ropes twined around the piles, preferring to throw their own grappling hooks onto the docks. Their faint "huzzah" was echoed by a much louder cheer from the watching dockhands.

Orseth hastily swallowed a biscuit. "Time to move closer or else we'll miss the show. And the best berths." The elf grinned. He stood, shook his head when Leandra started to rise. "You stay and watch the fight. I'll call for river help to nudge us in."

The elf returned to the tiller, unlatched a compartment in the deck to remove a silver cup. Next came a bottle of wine, but not a particularly distinguished-looking vintage. Orseth poured the wine into the cup, then reached into the compartment a third time and emptied a small burlap pouch of long, dried blue leaves. He swirled the leaves into the wine while singing softly. That done, Orseth raised the cup in salute of the water, then poured the mixture off the stern. Nothing happened.

Cymric looked back toward the docks. The second rowboat had arrived while the crew of the first kept busy throwing off grappling hooks and cutting lines. The few from the second boat who managed to reach the docks were soon hurled back into the muddy water.

A shudder passed through the boat, which canted wildly to port, sending Cymric sliding off the deck. While he scrambled for handholds, Leandra grabbed him with her left hand, the right holding onto rope lashed to the cabin. She let out a grunt of pain with each pull on Cymric, who lifted a few inches at a time. On the last couple of tugs he was able to help haul himself up.

The boat was now slicing through the water at a good speed, throwing up a turbulent wake at the other unmoving vessels. Glancing down, Cymric saw half a dozen translucent corkscrews, like those in Yleesa's front pond—elementals singing in squeaky, high-pitched tones. The water moved in response, propelling the boat forward. Orseth leaned hard into the tiller to maintain direction. "All those fireballs must have gotten them riled," he shouted.

Orseth started singing once again. Cymric hung on tightly to the ropes attached to the cabin, and so did Leandra. Noting that the boat neither slowed down nor continued to gain speed, he watched the elementals until a shout from Leandra drew his attention to the fight on the docks. A t'skrang was leaping about the docks, tail and sword a flurry of concerted motion. Orseth interrupted his singing to yell, "Kricklen, a t'skrang swordmaster! Thought you might want to see one in action."

Leandra nodded, a broad smile stretching across her face and her eyes lighting up each time Kricklen made an acrobatic move. She let go of the ropes to applaud when the t'skrang disarmed two opponents at once. Despite Kricklen's best efforts, the opposing t'skrang were slowly encircling him, but his antics were giving the other crew time to scale the docks. The complexion of the fight changed, breaking down into small clusters of cursing, taunting lizards.

Kricklen was now faring better against a smaller number of foes, keeping them off balance with broad tail sweeps while beating them about their heads and shoulders with his sword. Little by little Kricklen's crew slowly claimed the dock and began to toss the other crewmen into the river. Some of the defeated crew flailed arms, legs, and tails while shrieking full-lung, then fell *ker-splash* with a plume of water rising up to the height of the docks. The victors waited until these t'skrang surfaced, then loudly thumped their tails in approval of the defeat display.

Orseth lullabyed the boat into a choice berth, then bid the elementals goodbye. As they surged off through the water and rushed to the center of the river, they created a wave two men high. Some of the t'skrang got caught in the wave. After a moment of floundering, a chorus of whoops indicated that the wave met with t'skrang approval. Leandra leaped from the boat. After landing she squeezed her eyes shut, then opened them in an annoyed expression. To Cymric it looked as though the excitement of the fight had her blood flowing faster than her thoughts; she had forgotten about her injuries. She exhaled sharply, then began mooring the boat.

A pudgy dwarf tromped down the pier toward the boat, bound book under his arm, sweat beading on his forehead and glistening in his beard. Orseth lowered the gangplank for the dwarf, who came pounding up the plank while opening his book. He tapped the margin of the right-hand page. A quill of pure black peeled from the page and floated to his hand. Pudgy looked at Orseth. "Vessel, cargo, and stay?"

"The boat is *A Troll's Dream*. I carry two passengers and a selection of collectibles. I wished to be berthed for a week."

Pudgy raised an eyebrow. "Nature of collectibles?"

Orseth smiled the way a python smiles at a rat. "The sort of collectibles requested by the Outriggers Guild. I have the contract if you wish to see it."

Pudgy delayed a fraction of a second, then thrust out his hand. Orseth pulled a stained piece of parchment from his sleeve, its seal of silver and purple waxes broken. Pudgy's face twitched, then he shook his head. "Your papers are in order. That will be thirty-five silvers for the week." Orseth attempted to haggle for the price, but Pudgy would have none of it. Orseth planted his hands on his hips, determined to pursue the matter. "You two take off," he said. "Good luck."

Leandra flourished her sword in salute. "Say hello to Brius for me when you see him." Orseth gave her the strangest grin, but only nodded his head before returning his attention to Pudgy.

Cymric and Leandra strolled up the pier to the dockside. Workers were busy preparing for the ships and boats now arriving, but the walkways were clear of cargo. The winning t'skrang steamboat was docking with whistles sounding. Most of the crew did not wait for the ship to stop, swinging on ropes or taking running leaps to the dock. A few missed. Those who landed scrambled for the city gates, which were outlined by a tall archway studded with glowing crystals. Beyond the gate Cymric could see the top of a huge pearlescent dome. Leandra followed the lizard throng.

The four dwarf officials at the gate looked harried even

as the first t'skrang arrived. To Cymric it looked as though each official was accompanied by an unusually high number of guards, six or seven in chain mail, plus one in full crystal plate. All were armed with axes, all had their weapons out and ready. The guards eyed the t'skrang carefully. Taking a guess at which would be the quickest line, Cymric nudged Leandra in that direction. He found himself inordinately pleased that he seemed to have chosen correctly.

Ahead of them waited a group of five t'skrang, the holes in their satin waistcoats showing their painted and polished scales. All five carried daggers, and three were armed with swords. One had studded his tail with green-faceted gems, perhaps peridot, a half-dozen of which had been enchanted to sparkle brilliantly with their own light. The group reached the official, a tired-looking dwarf whose rightmost beard-braid had worked itself loose. Seated at his desk covered with quills, inkpots, seals and wax, parchment documents, and a half-eaten muffin, he asked the t'skrang the nature of their visit. The five huddled and murmured for a moment. When they broke the huddle, Gemtail spoke for the group. "To sample fine dwarven food and finer dwarven ale. To sing the songs of legend. To fight pitched battles in the streets. To loot the wealthiest merchants and raid your holiest places. To carry off your women to our ship for nights of wild abandon. All with your permission, of course."

The guards shifted their weight, looking at each other and the official. The official rubbed his eyebrows vigorously as if to wake from sleep. He grabbed five pieces of parchment and began pouring wax on them, then stamped a seal with vigor. "You may purchase ale and food as you like. You may sing until the midnight bell. All other requests denied. That will be four silvers apiece."

The t'skrang looked disappointed, and Gemtail whipped his tail in a catlike gesture of annoyance. They murmured once more, then paid the fee and took the parchment before bounding past the guards into Marrek.

Cymric stepped forward, toying with the answer to the official's question. Actually, sir, we are here to hunt a Horror and its fanatical followers. We doubt we can harm it, but we can probably anger it enough that it will destroy your city as it has destroyed many villages. What do you say? Suddenly snapping back to the here and now, Cymric found the dwarf official smiling as though he had just caught Cymric in some secret ritual.

"Got a forked tongue longer than my hand?"

Cymric shook his head. "Excuse me?"

The guards grinned. The official stamped two pieces of parchment. "Welcome to Marrek. I sincerely hope you enjoy your stay. That will be one silver apiece."

Cymric's eyebrows rose. The official merely shrugged while one of the guards looked steadily at Cymric. Cymric paid the silver. Leandra nodded to the guards as they passed. Once they were through the gate, Leandra said, "First time in Marrek?"

Cymric nodded. Leandra smiled. "A good city, though silver holds too tight a grip. But I know the best way to see the city for the first time. Come." She took a left, following the gate wall, then passed through an archway with a griffin symbol, and began to climb the spiral staircase inside. The stair ended in a tunnel that made two sharp bends. The second bend opened onto a platform facing a blank wall. Leandra tapped Cymric on his left shoulder. He turned.

The city was hewn from the ground, four gigantic terraces nested like an inverted pyramid. Buildings were packed onto the tops of the terraces, and some were carved into the terrace walls along the zigzag roads that connected one terrace to another. At ground level the "pyramid" was perhaps three miles wide, perhaps more. In the center was the biggest building Cymric had ever seen. The pearlescent dome was its top, supported by a tower and dozens of columns. Beneath the tower was a huge statue of a griffin, more eagle-like than any he'd ever seen depicted. Though its wings were tucked back, they still extended hundreds of yards. Blocky slabs of stone formed walls built around and encasing the griffin. Where the griffin's forepaws rested, the building changed styles. The walls became white, with slender windows, doorways, columns, and

towers. Causeways ran from the terrace levels to this level.
Gigantic stairways descended to the next level. The bottom level was a collection of pools and gardens, illuminated by hundreds of multicolored light crystals. Cymric managed to spot a few arches and a window or two hidden in the greenery.

"The palace. The terraces of the city were built to match the levels of the palace." Leandra pointed to the dome. "Marrek was sealed off from the Scourge by some elemental shield. The dome is heavily magicked, but the people left its top outside the shield for the purpose of observation. The matching part of Marrek is called topside." Her finger moved down. "The griffin is the symbol of the ruling house of Marrek. The largest terrace starts near the top of the griffin, slopes down toward the claws. The terrace is called Beakstreets." Her finger dropped again. "Courtiers live on the next level. The terrace has the same name. Royalty live in the heart of the palace, hidden in the gardens. That whole area is called the palace level."

Cymric nodded. He remained silent for a while. "Throal is larger, but you cannot see all of it at once. This is—" He shrugged, at a loss for words.

Leandra's smile was tight. "This is the home of Ristul."

Cymric snorted. "Thanks for spoiling the view." Another couple turned the corner, two young dwarfs. The girl gasped. The boy grinned, then moved in behind her to hold her as she took in the sight of the city. Cymric looked back at the palace. "Do you know where they are?"

"They have a walled enclave in Beakstreets, on the other side of the palace from here. Same one we tried seven years ago."

"What? The Ristular operate out in the open?"

"They pay their taxes and a little more. They stay clean within the city walls. At least to the extent bribery allows."

"Marrek is big. *Someone* would have to notice a Horror within the city limits."

Leandra's eyes became flinty. She stared at the palace. A giggle, a slap, a protest and then another giggle sounded from the couple behind them. Leandra walked toward the edge of the platform, to increase distance away from the couple. Cymric followed, felt a brief giddiness as he looked at the long fall. The people below appeared to be half the size of his thumb. Leandra lowered her voice. "Gel and I talked to the guilds. They were concerned, but skeptical. The palace told us to shove off."

Cymric grunted. The Ristular must have stronger hooks into the local power structure than he would have thought. He still had a hard time believing that a city that had survived the Scourge would now embrace a Horror. Perhaps the Ristular were brilliantly concealing their activities. Still—

"Seen enough?" asked Leandra.

Cymric nodded, and they turned back to the tunnel. The young dwarf woman suddenly acknowledged their presence, self-consciously removing the young man's hand from her right breast. The suitor's grin showed not the least trace of embarrassment. Leandra and Cymric clacked through the tunnel and clattered down the stairs, then Leandra stopped suddenly, throwing her arm out and back to halt Cymric.

A t'skrang stood at the entrance of the stairway. He wore a blue velvet waistcoat and silk pantaloons, with purple velvet surrounding the sapphires on his scabbard. His hand poised over his long sword. "Draw steel or I'll use mine to make you squeal like the sow who bore you."

Anger flared in Cymric. He could feel the tug of magic behind the t'skrang's insult, which only made him angrier. Leandra stood motionless for a moment, then smiled slowly. "I like a fair fight. I will draw as soon as your sword clears its scabbard."

"You might find drawing your sword difficult once I've cut your scabbard away from you."

"You might find walking through the streets difficult once I cut those ridiculous pantaloons off of you."

"I ignore fashion opinions from those who can stand to travel with someone who looks like he changes his robe once a season."

"I ignore the opinion of anyone stupid enough to pay a gate official more than the one silver piece it really costs."

The t'skrang hissed loudly. He opened his mouth as if to throw another insult at Leandra. He drew his sword faster than Cymric could follow with his eyes. Leandra didn't have that problem. From the sound Cymric judged that she'd started her draw after the t'skrang. But she still struck first, provoking a *squawk-hiss* from the t'skrang. He parried and tried a tail strike, but Leandra skipped over the clumsy tail swing. The swords hit together with a faint clank, as if neither was being swung with full force. Cymric decided this was the way of fights between swordmasters; balance and speed were the key. Putting your strength into a strike risked the swordsman being thrown a fraction off-balance, a huge opportunity for a skilled opponent.

Cymric shook himself from the role of spectator. He flung a mind dagger spell along the path of his outstretched arm. The shard of light flew true in astral space, hitting the t'skrang's pattern near his forehead. The pattern released a flare of green.

"Ahhh! Your magician hit me! Can't take me on by yourself?"

Leandra took a step back, keeping her guard up. "Cymric, did you?"

Uh-oh, guess this is just some kind of swordmaster display. I wonder which one gets the honor of carving me up? "Uhhh—yes. I thought that was part of the wizard contract. Squashing the brains of arrogant t'skrang who attack my companion."

The t'skrang grinned, showing an impressive array of needle-sharp teeth. "A short duel is enough for my purposes. You are Leandra?" Leandra nodded, keeping her guard up. The lizard sheathed his sword and bowed. "Kricklen. I am most pleased to draw against you. You are as fast as I have heard."

Leandra lowered her sword, but did not sheath it. "Who told you about me?"

Kricklen's tail lashed back and forth as he held out a small wooden disk with a red-brown stain. "This token from someone who is very good at tracking allows me to track you."

Leandra's eyes widened, her mouth opened then quickly closed. Kricklen nodded. "He has asked that you stay at the Hostel of Lochost, Courtier's East. He made a substantial donation in the name of Lady DeCorvo."

"Is Brius in Marrek?"

Kricklen's arms and tail went straight up. "I have no idea. He was secretive. That's what you get for spending too much time with someone who lives and breathes court intrigue. He was expecting you to show up several days ago. I've been in and out of Marrek half a dozen times in the past couple weeks. Nothing from the token until today."

Leandra nodded. Kricklen bowed again, came up grinning. "If you will excuse me, I have to torment a certain gate official." He bounded away with a tail slap, then settled into a strut when he landed.

Leandra reached out to squeeze Cymric's hand, her look saying it all. He was annoyed with himself for being annoyed. But a small part of him whispered, *Now the wizard hits the scrap heap.* Cymric tried to shake this line of thought. Brius obviously had some brains to go with his brawn, and at least some wealth and influence. Brius could help them get out alive, if not defeat Ristul. Still . . . he was very annoyed.

It took more than an hour to make their way down to Courtier's East. Guards questioned them as they entered the level, but saw no reason to turn them away. Another half hour of asking for and following imprecise directions put them in front of carved teak doors in the side of an alabaster building. Etched into the left-hand door was a jungle scene, illusion magic making the depicted python slither among the leaves. The right door showed a mountain top, where a huge reptilian bird had landed. The illusion magic here had unraveled slightly, for the bird's motion was jerky. Two orks in leather armor with polished silver studs pulled open the door on silent hinges.

"Welcome to the Hostel of Lochost. Are you questors or visitors?"

"Visitors," Leandra said

The door guards looked around before one of them cleared his throat. "You have made a donation?"

"A generous donation. I am Lady DeCorvo." Leandra smiled and walked past them, leaving Cymric scampering to catch up.

They next came to what Cymric would have called the common room, though he was certain this establishment called it by a different name. Dwarfs sat in overstuffed leather chairs, sipping brandy from what he thought must be . . . snifters. Yes, that was the word. Most listened, while a few talked while animatedly pointing to maps on low wooden tables. Some sat on pillows by other low tables, earnestly rattling dice cups and moving colored chips back and forth across the table. The pillars were of pitted green bronze, taken from some other building for this one. The atmosphere felt relaxing, the effect of a finely crafted illusion. Servants wore bright clothing, but no outfit really matched that of any other. They moved quietly from chair to chair, from gaming table to gaming table. When an ork passed carrying something that smelled of tomato and herbs on a silver platter, it brought a rumble from Cymric's stomach.

To the left of the common room was an uprooted tree lying on its side. Planed into the side was the top of a desk. As they approached, Cymric caught a sharp cedar scent. A dwarf with sleeves rolled up to his shoulders worked diligently on a scroll, quill scratching a careful trail across the parchment. Leandra cleared her throat to attract his attention. He looked confused for a moment before uttering, "May I help you?"

"A donation has been made in the name of Lady DeCorvo,"

"Certainly, Lady DeCorvo. Let me check our questor's records." The dwarf opened a small cabinet, extracted a card. He replaced it, found another; satisfied that this was the correct one, he read it, initialed it, and looked up. "The card recommends the spice suite for you. Suitable?" The dwarf returned his attention to the scroll.

Leandra raised an eyebrow. "Spice suite?"

The dwarf blotted his quill, never looking up. "The

spice suite is among the better, as you might gather from the legends." Then his quill stopped dead, and he glanced up with a distant look. "But then you would know that if you were an initiate. From the size of the donation I presumed you were a follower."

"I certainly believe in Lochost and her passion for freedom," said Leandra, dodging the issue.

The dwarf smiled and resumed his writing. "Most of our rooms are quite different from one another, as befits Lochost, also the Passion of change. The questor decides who is to stay where, a decision influenced by the size of your donation." The dwarf switched quills and began to make finer markings in between the spaces of his earlier words. "The rules of our hostel are simple. You are not to interfere with the activities of any guest in their rooms. You may exchange tales, conclude bargains, game, do whatever you wish with others here in the travelers' room, as long as the others involved wish it also."

"Understood."

"We followers know Lochost is also the Passion of rebellion. Some of our guests feel obliged to break the rules. Our questor is supposed to treat all such infractions lightly," the dwarf said. His grin was broad and slow. "Of course that's just a rule, and our questor is a rebellious sort."

Cymric snorted. Leandra smiled and assured the dwarf that Lady DeCorvo was not here to violate the rules. The dwarf withdrew two slender silver keys and gave them to Leandra, who nodded as she listened to the dwarf's directions. Following those directions she and Cymric came to a polished ebony door emblazoned with an arc of lacquered paintings of herbs and spices. Leandra inserted a key, then the door opened on its own.

The suite had a sitting room with a couch, four chairs, and a table, a private bar stocked with a number of interesting-looking bottles, a private bath with a porcelain tub, a master bedroom and two servant's bedrooms. The wooden floors were covered with elven rugs. The sitting room and master bedroom each had picture windows showing a rugged seacoast. Cymric examined the window in the living room. The image looked too well-crafted for an illusion, but divination magic with a view of the sea seemed a ludicrous amount of magic for a room decoration. Cymric decided to investigate the window after some rest.

Leandra dropped her pack down in the sitting room. She threw open the double doors to the master bedroom, took five steps, then spun and collapsed onto the four-poster feather bed. Staring at the ceiling, she suddenly smiled. "This room is Brius. This whole place is so Brius."

Cymric entered the bedroom. He ran his hands experimentally around the dresser, watching drawers open and close automatically. "It's so Brius that he doesn't even have to be here." Cymric felt foolish the moment he said it, but Leandra's laugh surprised him.

"No. That is Brius too."

There was sadness in Leandra's voice. Cymric felt bad for having brought up the subject, and guilty for being a little glad that Leandra felt as she did. Silence claimed the room for a long time as Leandra continued to stare at the ceiling. Cymric experimented with the magical devices in the room, spending a considerable time playing with water flow in the wash basin. He blinked, thinking he saw a flash of red in the mirror over the basin.

Leandra sighed and sat up. "Here's my plan. Food. Sleep. More food. Hunt a Horror. How does that sound to you?"

Cymric's answer was cut short as the door into the suite sparked, slamming open with a shriek of tortured metal.

30

A harsh word preceded the sudden darkness, to which Cymric reacted instinctively by throwing one hand out in front of him. Just as instinctively Leandra's sword snicked from her scabbard. Remembering that the bed was positioned to his right and behind him, Cymric turned and moved in a crouch across the room, keeping his hand in front of him. His shin banged painfully into the bed frame, the noise startling him. He clenched his fist to keep from grunting in pain.

"Leandra," he whispered, "can you guard the door long enough for me to create some light?"

A terse whisper responded, "Do it. Shut up."

Cymric nodded even though no one could see him. No, that wasn't true. Darkness was nethermantic magic to which nethermancers were usually immune. At least one person could see what was going on. That spooked Cymric more than the darkness itself the thought of someone standing a few feet away calmly watching his frantic efforts. He strained to hear, heard nothing.

Taking as quiet a breath as possible, Cymric decided to place a pattern for light into a matrix, replacing his leaping magic to make room for the new pattern. Triangles of red light burst behind his eyes as he rushed his first attempt. Spots continued to float before his eyes, but he ignored them to concentrate on moving the pattern from his mind into the matrix. The next attempt went smoothly until the pattern was in astral space, following the glowing white thread to its matrix. Then the pattern began to warp and expand. Through concentration Cymric was able to re-

turn the pattern to its proper size, but not its proper shape. The spell pattern hung on the thread just outside the matrix. Cymric tried jiggling it with variations in mental pressure, exerting and relaxing his will, but each effort failed.

He hissed and discarded the pattern, had just willed another to form in his mind when a thump from outside the bedroom distracted him. Perhaps it was Leandra. Perhaps it was the spellcaster's accomplice, one who could not see in the dark. He heard other noises too, the squeak in the floor, a scrape against a rug, the jiggle of glasses as someone nudged the bar. Cymric revised his picture of what was happening.

One assailant had cast the spell, while the others lay in ambush, waiting for him and Leandra to stumble out of the darkness. When he and she didn't come out, some of the team had come after them. If so, it hadn't been the best of plans, a thought that heartened Cymric.

Two more failures brought sweat to his forehead. Beads ran down his face to catch on his lip, pool near his chin, or drip the taste of salt into his mouth. He pulled the collar of his robe over his head, blotting the moisture from his face with his robe. Then he wriggled his head to drop the robe back into position, forming the spell pattern in his mind, trying to make the pattern move in the same manner as his head. He kept bobbing and rotating his head until the pattern moved in synch. He then slid the pattern into astral space, guiding it with head-motions; it slipped easily into the matrix.

Cymric's hands mimicked the weaving of the thread. The thread wove on the first attempt. The spellcasting would be more difficult; there was magical darkness to resist the light. Infusing the pattern with some of his personal energy, he urged the light to drive out the darkness.

Then light flooded the room to the sound of tearing parchment. Braced in the doorway was a Ristular, her hood thrown back, her hands spread to feel the wall. A jewelled dagger glinted from a cord around her wrist. She was young, her pretty oval face framed by red hair that curled beneath her ears. She squinted against the light, then saw Cymric. When their eyes met, he smiled in spite of himself.

Leandra's leap was a blur. Her sword struck high, cutting the woman's throat. Then she kicked the gurgling Ristular out of the way, and charged into the living room with a scream that would have made a hunting cat proud. Several voices cursed in response. Cymric started toward the room, hesitating as he saw the woman flop over to her belly, then rise onto hands and knees. She was staring at Cymric and crawling toward him with a horrible wheezing sound that bubbled blood. It wasn't until she struggled to grip her dagger that Cymric realized she hoped to kill him before spilling the last of her own life blood. He rolled over the bed, putting the big four-poster between him and her.

"Cymric!" Leandra's cry was urgent. Cymric swallowed, rooted to the spot in horror at this woman's determination. He tried to fling a mind dagger, but the spell dissipated listlessly. She had reached the bed, her dying brain addled by the obstacle it presented. With a lurch and a grab she pulled her torso onto the bed whose sheets quickly soaked with blood as she tried to climb over toward him.

"Cymric!" He finally got his feet to move, although wobbly knees nearly sent him crashing to the ground as he rounded the bed. The Ristular tried to grab him, but her trembling body reacted erratically. Cymric bolted, forcing himself not to look back as he left the bedroom. Eight Ristular surrounded Leandra. Individually, their short swords and daggers were no match for her sword and armor, but together they were another story. Leandra fenced them off through timely parries, rapid feints, and by hurling anything not bolted down with her free hand. She gritted her teeth, flinging a chair with a roundhouse toss. Three Ristular ducked.

The first mind dagger sailed into the target's mind, but the Ristular barely flinched. Cymric launched another one at the same moment Leandra was gashing an attacker across the chest. Her Ristular stumbled, dropping his sword. He grimaced with his hand on his temple, then howled as he charged Cymric. Cymric dodged around the low couch. A woman dropped out of the fight with Leandra to help the Ristular chasing Cymric. While Cymric kept moving in a circuit around the furniture, Leandra went on the offensive, doubling her efforts.

An ork servant carrying fresh linen peeked around the doorway. Her eyes widened, her mouth made a big O, then she screamed. One of the Ristular who turned at the sound caught the full force of Leandra's sword. He crumpled, a wet stain spreading across his dark robe. Dropping her linen, the ork fled into the hall, shouting an alarm. The woman chasing Cymric flicked her eyes toward the doorway. The others kept their attention on their attacks.

Cymric wove a spell thread, working through intuition and feel. He couldn't afford to take his eyes away from the external world as he dodged Ristular through the obstacle course of the room's furniture. It was like trying to lace up winter boots with mittens on. He knew where everything was supposed to go, the motions were simple, but he had a hard time getting it right. A clumsy thrust from the woman thunked into the bar as Cymric scooted around behind. The other Ristular moved to cut him off. Cymric flung out his left arm, hand spread, and shouted, "Die at my touch!" The Ristular flinched and spun away. Cymric sprinted on past.

A howl of pain drew his attention. On the ground another Ristular was trying to sidecrawl away from the melee. Leandra's face and arms were coated with a sheen of sweat. Her remaining three attackers had backed off two paces, looking for a way through the swordmaster's defenses.

Heavy footfalls sounded in the hall, followed by two orks appearing in the doorway. They wore the leather armor with silver studs, carried spears with highly polished tips. One pointed his spear directly at the Ristular closest to Cymric. "Drop your Weapons, you robed freaks!"

One of Leandra's attackers dropped his dagger, but the woman chasing Cymric reached into her robe. When she withdrew her hand, it was holding an oily-black ball that she threw to the ground, speaking a word that sounded half-cough, half-growl. Cymric again found himself in darkness. Now he was angry; these maniacs had tried to kill him, and he didn't want them to get away. He sat quietly and wove a thread, then scrambled a few paces to a wall. He urged magic into the external world at the edge of his outstretched fingers, gently laying the spidery levitate pattern onto the floor. He hoped to cover the entire entrance to the living room with the effect of the spell, throwing any stealthy Ristular to the ceiling.

A cry and a thump sent a thrill through Cymric. Someone had entered the circle of levitation, and he only hoped it wasn't Leandra or an ork. He sat with his back to the wall, weaving a thread to again create light, when there came the sound of glass breaking followed by a hideous scream. Arcs of jagged blue light leaped from two points, spreading like a fan as they flew through the air. A single figure was defined in the darkness by the arcs of light crashing into, bursting, and retreating from her body. It was like watching a shoreline on a pitch-black night, the shape of the rocks defined by luminescent waves crashing over them. The figure jerked several times before falling to the ground.

Cymric's first light glowed briefly, then died as darkness swallowed it. The second spell broke the nethermantic dark. The orks had retreated to the doorway, kneeling with spears planted and pointed ahead. A Ristular was pinned to the ceiling, just now experimenting with moving against the force of the levitate spell. Leandra was walking along the wall, her left hand on the wall, her sword out in front of her. Her necklace blazed red. A Ristular who happened to be a finger's-width away from the tip of the blade surrendered his sword. The two others still crawling along the floor followed suit.

On the other side of the living room smoked the corpse of the woman who had thrown the darkness. She had broken one of the seascape "windows" trying to escape. Cymric walked over to the window, breathing through his mouth trying not to smell the burnt odor of the body. The window frame was lined with runes, enough for Cymric to know that the seascape hadn't been an illusion. The window had been a specially shaped scrying crystal, permanently magicked to focus on a scene hundreds of miles away. Breaking the crystal had poured that magic through the woman. Cymric thought about searching the body, but his stomach recoiled at the notion. One more look caused a reflexive heave. He left the body alone.

Leandra talked to the orks across the levitation circle. They had used the blunt ends of their spears to fish the one Ristular from the circle, and bound his hands securely behind his back. One at a time, Leandra grabbed the other three and tossed them into the levitation circle. When the orks finished binding one prisoner, they fished another from the circle.

Cymric looked at the three Ristular still sprawled on the ground. The first was unconscious, barely breathing. Cymric didn't know what to do first: restrain the prisoner or try to tend to his wounds. Leandra walked over to the one whose robe was now one wet, shivering mass. She placed the point of her sword on his neck, driving it through muscle and spine with a *pop-crack*. The robe lay still. Cymric froze, his mind racing for something to say. Leandra killed chest-gash next, finishing the unconscious Ristular last. Cymric gagged, then swallowed the vomit back down. The ogres had been one thing, and the Ristular at the road camp had died in a fight or through enchantment. This was worse. Leandra began to search the bodies.

"Leandra?" His voiced was strained, a little weak. The taste of a regurgitated meal still burned the back of his throat.

She looked up at him, studying his face, then left the body to go fetch a linen towel and a bottle of water from the bar. Cymric rinsed his mouth and cleaned his face while Leandra spoke quietly with the orks for a few moments. They grunted, then herded the four Ristular from the room. Leandra crossed back to Cymric, stepping over the body of wet-robe. She knelt beside him, but he couldn't look at her.

"You didn't fight in any of the wars, did you?" Leandra's voice held no question. Cymric fixed his gaze on a tumbler on the shelf behind the bar. His eyes watered, blurring the outline of the tumbler when he blinked. He shook his head. Leandra sighed. "Well, we're in a war now, Cymric. This is how wars are fought."

"You are in a war," Cymric snapped. "I am on a quest."

Leandra smiled a sad smile. "Seven years ago I too thought of it as a quest," she said softly. "But then it changed for me. I don't know when. Brius didn't either." She tapped Cymric on the wrist. "Cymric, I'm not sure what else the Ristular want to do, but I know they want to destroy me. And I want to destroy them. For me, that is war."

Cymric nodded. He shrugged, spread his hands. His breath caught, hung, then escaped percussively. "It's just not the way I thought it was done. You know"—his voice caught again, embarrassment and shame weighing down his tongue—"the way herocs of legend conduct themselves."

Leandra's laugh was bitter. "I wondered about that. Do heroes act as the legends say, or do troubadours mold the truth for tavern audiences?"

Cymric nodded, spun his staff between his hands, drank some more water, giving his question time to bubble to the surface. "Did you ever hope to be a hero?"

Servants and guards returned to clean up the room, the guards toting away the bodies, the servants trying to clean the blood-soaked rugs and tidy up the furniture. They assiduously avoided contact with Leandra or Cymric, working around them as if they were invisible. Cymric's discomfort grew. He readily accepted the invitation implied in Leandra's nod toward the door.

The desk-dwarf met them in the hallway as they stepped through the doorway. He was apologetic, yet let them know that the questor had decided that the safety of other guests outweighed the hostel's obligation to Lady DeCorvo. There would be no charge for damages. The questor wished to refund most of the donation, provided DeCorvo and her retinue found lodging elsewhere. Leandra graciously accepted the offer. Cymric counted the money in the suspiciously small pouch. The coins were gold, so the sum was more generous than the weight of the

pouch suggested. They returned to their room for their
packs, then headed out.

One of the ork guards caught up with them as they were
crossing the common room. He told Leandra to be careful;
Marrek had many more pilgrims like those who had attacked her. Most stayed in their compound in Beakstreets
East. The pilgrims had made donations for a room at the
hostel five days ago, one of the cheap rooms looking out
onto the street. The questor had not wanted to antagonize
religious visitors, but they had spooked other guests during
their stay. The hostel was now preparing a formal protest
to the Prince, although the guard doubted any action
would be taken. Leandra thanked the man, and slipped him
a few silvers for his trouble. He shook the silver in his
hand, pocketed one piece, then handed the rest back. "Pilgrims have given orks problems. Driven some from
Marrek," the ork said quietly, "Disappeared some others.
Dwarfs don't much care. You might."

Leandra's tic-smile flicked across her face four times.
She nodded, extending her hand. They clasped hands,
drawing a look of concern from the desk dwarf and two
servants. Cymric cleared his throat. The ork released the
handshake, and he and Leandra passed through the teak
doors onto the street.

Leandra readjusted the pack on her shoulders. Her injuries were reasserting themselves, and combat had put a
hitch in her walk. A grimace preceded her next tic-smile.
"The basics of the plan still sound good to you? Food.
Sleep. More food. Horror hunt?"

Cymric stepped aside as a troll merchant in gold silks
hogged the walkway with a drunk swagger. As he turned
up a stairway, tired legs made his boots scrape over each
step. Cymric debated his answer until Leandra gave him a
tight-lipped stare.

"The plan stands without serious amendment," he said.
To himself he added one element to the plan: discuss how
the Ristular knew that he and Leandra were staying at the
hostel and whether Brius might be trying to get them
killed.

31

Afternoon sunlight glistened off the faceted black stone skin of an obsidiman watching five Ristular thread their way through the marketplace. Her iron staff probably weighed seven times what Cymric's did, but she wielded it as if it were made of bamboo. The brass hemisphere on top of the staff had a basket of fruit and a loaf of bread hammered into it, signifying her position as a market guard. Cymric sat five feet behind the guard. Reaching into a straw shopping basket, he took out a piece of three-spice chicken, which he ate as casually as possible while keeping a close eye on the Ristular. He chewed noisily, mouth open, his mind on the robed figures, not his table manners. With the sound of a grinding rumble above, the obsidiman turned, fixing her green eyes on Cymric. He caught himself, stopped chewing, then covered his embarrassment with the new linen napkins Leandra had purchased. The obsidiman turned back around.

Leandra returned, carrying an orange earthenware jug and walking along booths not twenty feet from the Ristular. She smiled, squeaked the cork out of the jug, then took a long drink before passing the jug to Cymric as she sat down. Cymric sniffed; fermented fruit juice plus a hint of lemon. His sip surprised him, the taste much more refreshing than the smell suggested, a light blend of fruit flavors with the slightest tickling kick. He took a full swig.

"It's not whitewater, but it's not milk either," Leandra said. "Drink like that and you'll be sitting here through nightfall." Cymric slowed his pace, but took another swig. Leandra reached into the basket for a piece of chicken, flicking off hunks of pepper before taking a bite. Her face froze in a moment of rapture at the first taste, then she resumed eating with a more tranquil expression. After consuming half a thigh, she paused. "I learned some interesting tidbits from Garoche."

"Who?"

"The ork guard from the Lochost hostel. Guild magicians found a ward in our room. An illusion to prevent us from noticing when the necklace detected the Ristular."

Cymric remembered the glint of red in the mirror shortly before the attack. The illusion had probably prevented anyone from spotting the glow directly, but had not been quite sophisticated enough to conceal secondary sources such as the reflection. "I used an illusion like that in Gelthrain's workshop. Theirs must have been pretty sophisticated if it could squelch the mere glow of the necklace." Plus, the ward must have been triggered even before the necklace started glowing—yes, very impressive. Cymric grew uncomfortable at the thought of yet another discipline of magic serving the Ristular. He should have suspected it, he told himself, taking a savage bite out of the chicken.

Earlier in the day Leandra had purchased two blue scarves. First, she'd wrapped them around the stones in the necklace, then squeezed the whole affair under her armor. The glow was still faintly visible, coloring dozens of links in her armor. The glow slowly receded as the Ristular walked further into the market, vanishing about the time Cymric lost sight of them in the crowd.

The obsidiman guard rumble-lumbered to a new post four booths away, the site of a loud dispute between a potter and a customer. Cymric caught the phrase "Iopos glazing" a number of times, as well as querulous suggestions about what the potter ought to throw next into his kiln. Leandra took the jug back. Cymric chewed slowly. Last night they'd avoided the topic of Brius, avoided most topics other than what to eat and where to sleep. They could no longer avoid them. Cymric juggled the order in his head. He decided Brius should be last, to better the odds of getting through the other topics. He borrowed the jug from Leandra, took a swig and handed the jug back. He wiped his mouth and hands, irritated that his hands had already begun to sweat. "What do you know of the Ristular compound?"

Leandra raised one finger as she finished chewing. "Not much has chanced since I last saw it. They took over the Upandal works in Beakstreets East."

"What sort of defenses has it got?"

Leandra shook her head. "Some must have changed. For what it's worth, Gelthrain said the wards were simple. Ragnar had problems with some of the locks. The Ristular themselves varied."

Cymric borrowed the jug again for a small, cool sip, then thunked it back down in front of Leandra. "Any problems getting in?"

She took a long drink before giving Cymric a wicked smile. "Getting in should be simple. All it takes is a small donation."

"Excuse me, did I hear you right—a small donation?" Cymric's visions of demonic guards and fiendish traps were difficult to adjust to the idea of a small donation. The only images that came to mind made him shudder.

Leandra's smile grew broader. "The Upandal works are something to see, especially the garden. The Ristular maintain it, open to the public for a fee."

"You're joking."

"No, I'm not. The Ristular keep their plans to themselves. Letting folks see parts of the works gives them a good public face and fattens their purse a little."

Cymric grabbed the jug back, took a long drink, then held on to the jug. Risking his life, braving dangers to overcome fiendish defenses before meeting his demise was one thing. Paying for the privilege seemed something else entirely. Not at all in keeping with the heroic image. After he'd taken a few more slugs, Leandra threw him a disapproving look and pulled the jug from his hands. Cymric selected a soggy biscuit from the basket, nibbling on it as he broached the next topic. "Last night I kept waking up, thinking about the calendar, Maeumis, and the prophecy. Perhaps my most important conclusion is that the Horror Ristul isn't in Marrek."

Leandra's eyebrows rose. She corked the jug with a definite thud. "Your reasons?"

Cymric gestured to the griffin face on the palace looming above them. "Well, first, there's so much magic in the palace I can almost smell it from here. It was built to protect Marrek's nobles during the Scourge. If a Horror were in town, I'm sure the magics would activate." He stuffed the rest of the biscuit into his mouth. "Two, you said the gardens and other works are being maintained in such a way that the public wants to see them. Legends strongly suggest Horrors have a more grisly esthetic. And three, Maeumis delivered a ward against Ristul to the town of Liffick. If Ristul were here, I'm sure he would keep the nethermancer under his claw. Developing a ward against one's master doesn't seem like an approved activity for the servant of a Horror."

Cymric reached for the jug, but Leandra slid it away with a nudge of her leg. Still leaning forward with outstretched arm, he met her eyes. "I believe Ristul has not yet been summoned to this world."

"And today's interpretation of the prophecy?"

Leandra's tone stung. Cymric knew that he was working in the ether with some of his reasoning. Well, what of it? He'd been right before. He'd been wrong before. This was just his best guess. "I think the prophecy was part of the bait to lure you to them at the proper time. To kill you, or whatever it is they have to do with you to properly summon Ristul."

"You now think the necklace—?"

Now Cymric was weaving a story from threads slimmer than an apprentice's first. All he had was a hunch, formed from a belief that Garlen would not throw Leandra's life away in a futile battle against a Horror. He had little supporting evidence other than the great power of the necklace. "I think Garlen has chosen you as a hero to stop the summoning of Ristul. I think the necklace is a tool."

"Other than warn us, what does it do?"

Cymric felt the blood go to his cheeks. Instinct drove him behind a barricade of wizard's words. "Its powerful amalgamation of patterns provides a unique platform for spirit portage, most useful in—" He caught himself, swallowed once. "I'm sorry, Leandra. I just don't know."

Leandra nodded. She reached forward to tap him on the knee. "You did what you could." She leaned back again. A tic-smile came and went. "You said the prophecy was part of the bait. What was the rest?"

Cymric looked at the jug, not so much for a drink as for a possible place to hide. His desire to shrink failed to have any affect on reality. Trying to decide how to phrase his next few words, he reflexively glanced at the hawk-pommel of Leandra's sword. Her fingers drummed a rapid rhythm against it.

"You're wrong."

"What?" asked Cymric. Her emphatic statement had snapped the links of his chain of thought.

"Brius didn't betray me. I know him well enough to know he would never sell out to the Ristular." Leandra's face was set. There was to be no argument on this point.

Cymric squirmed a little before deciding to try anyway. "How did the Ristular find Lady DeCorvo's room?"

"The t'skrang messenger, the swordmaster Kricklen. You've seen that the t'skrang aren't the most discreet race in Barsaive."

Perhaps Leandra had a point. But hadn't the t'skrang just come in on the steamboat? Even if Kricklen had walked down the docks loudly proclaiming that Lady DeCorvo planned an extended stay at the hostel, the Ristular couldn't have set up the ward in such a short time. Not even their magicians could be that good. They must have known several days earlier. Leandra's expression hadn't changed, and now she had her arms crossed. Cymric looked at the jug rather than at Leandra. "Perhaps you're right. But you might want to think about what you would do if—"

"Fine. I'll think about it."

Cymric put up his hands to signal defeat, then returned to his meal. Leandra lightened the jug, then handed it to Cymric, who drained what little remained. As they walked through the market, Cymric gave the jug to a young boy, who wandered off happily, drawing people's attention by blowing a deep bass whistle on the jug.

They spent most of the rest of the afternoon preparing to enter the Ristular compound. The tales of legend spoke of planning over maps, fasting and prayer, rituals to strengthen a hero's pattern, his connection to the magic within him. Somehow the stories forgot to mention the shopping. The money from the hostel greatly extended their personal funds. Haggling with an alchemist got them three healing potions at a reasonable price. That accomplished, Cymric figured it was time to head for the compound. He was wrong.

Leandra went shopping for a dress. First she tried to match her scarves. When she found a red dress with puffy shoulders that she loved, she first went back and bought some matching scarves. She modeled her outfit in front of the fawning dwarf seamstress and Cymric. Leandra perplexed the seamstress by insisting that she must try the dress on over her armor. The dwarf protested that it would wrinkle, and no one ever wore a dress over chainmail armor. "I've joined the palace guard," Leandra said with an earnest expression. "They informed me I have to provide my own parade dress."

The seamstress' eyes flicked back and forth, trying to determine whether or not Leandra was joking. Cymric had to bite his staff to keep from laughing. "Shouldn't you be buying your new outfit, Cymric dear?" Leandra asked sweetly. "You wouldn't want to be seen in that old thing."

Cymric was taken aback for an eyeblink. Then he grinned. The Ristular would be looking for him in his blue robe. A fresh look might just buy him some time. Besides, if Leandra wanted to look sharp ... They agreed to meet at the shop of a hairdresser the seamstress recommended.

Cymric hated to admit it, but he was enjoying passing himself off as the wizard of a visiting Iopolan nobleman. His master had told him his outfit simply *would not* do for court here in Marrek. Every tailor he went to readily agreed. He finally settled on one who was familiar with Iopolan fashions, not because he liked the studded boots, velvet vests, or silk shirts, but because it fit his story. The ruddy brown he chose went well with the red swatch of cloth he'd gotten from the seamstress, and he had enough silver to ensure high skill and a little elemental magic for a quick, elegant fit.

Feeling cocky, Cymric followed the tailor's recommendation to a haberdasher. The latest fashion in Iopolan hats was apparently long, floppy things sporting a chakta feather. Cymric didn't know if he looked good in the hat, but he certainly didn't look like the old Cymric. He bought the hat as well as a trim leather backpack that matched his outfit. The haberdasher tried to talk Cymric out of it, saying that such were for the servant of a courtier, whose accouterments must match his master's. Cymric glibly explained that his servant was too busy to be fitted himself and that they were nearly the same size, an explanation that left the haberdasher obviously relieved. The haberdasher's advice next took him to a barber, who cheerfully cut Cymric's hair while passing along gossip on the prince's latest indiscretion—with a member of the Outriggers Guild no less. Cymric was on his way to a fragrancer suggested by the barber when it occurred to him that wearing cologne might permit an enemy to sniff him out should he again be caught in another darkness spell. His final purchase was a brass-handled walking stick. Not as effective a weapon as his staff, but more in keeping with his image as a gentleman.

Leandra was perhaps half-ready at the hairdresser's. The dwarf had to stand on a stool to reach her, but betrayed no concern about the awkwardness of the arrangement. She was currently applying a pack containing "rare essences of elemental earth" to Leandra's face and hair. Cymric took a seat and waited, enjoying the sideways glances he received from some of the patrons. Apparently a well-dressed wizard was a commodity in high demand with well-bred ladies of the court.

The dwarf hairdresser suddenly clapped her hands, then swiveled Leandra's seat to face the mirror with a coo of satisfaction. Leandra nodded, thanked the woman, and gave her a tip that the dwarf seemed to think was more than generous. Cymric rose as the dwarf swiveled

Leandra's seat to face him. He had his bow planned, and he had practiced the flourish with his hat on the way over. But he froze at the sight of Leandra.

She was beautiful. Her hair flowed over two twists in the back, her dark eyes shining with untapped energy, her lips somehow a more luscious red than her dress. The dress moved as a delightful hint to what lay underneath. As she glided closer, Cymric caught a hint of her spicy scent. He couldn't swallow; he could barely breathe. His composure melted in the heat of his face and loins. His mind struggled. "Uhm—that's nice. I mean *really* nice." His voice was rushed and husky, which made the other patrons giggle and the dwarf woman beam. Leandra smiled and presented her arm. Cymric caught his breath and took it.

They came out of the shop onto a broad boulevard leading back to the marketplace, then turned the other way heading for Beakstreets East. Leandra looked at him, smiling warmly. "So the ways of wizards are not always subtle."

"Milady swordmaster, we wizards are always quick to acknowledge a superior enchantment." Leandra squeezed his arm. They returned to the inn to pick up the Ristular medallions from their packs. Cymric wore his medallion under his vest and put the calendar in his leather pack; it filled the pack. He reluctantly left his staff behind, taking the brass-handled walking stick instead.

Leandra drank a little more than half of the Garlen vial, passing the rest to Cymric, who drank as much of the sticky-sweet fluid as he could. The little that was left Cymric decided to keep in his belt pouch along with his healing potion. Leandra carried her medallion and potions in the new court bag strapped to her wrist and lightened by minor magic. On the way out they left several hundred silvers in the inn strongbox. They also left signed statements of what to do with the silver should either one not return after thirty days.

Back down on the street, they passed taverns, walked down a short street lined with scriveners' shops, and then climbed a switchbacked-staircase lined with replicas of the palace griffin. They paused to look at the palace, then climbed to the corner roundabout, which took them to the boulevard heading south on this level of Beakstreets East. In the distance Cymric could see the slender towers of the Ristular encampment.

He looked again at Leandra, feeling something was missing. "How did you hide your sword?"

"The seamstress added a slimming illusion to the dress. Covers all sorts of unsightly bulges. Inexpensive, too, because it wasn't necessary to alter my own contours."

Cymric raised his eyebrows and pursed his lips. He kept his eyes ahead, but a smile slowly displaced the pursed lips. Leandra cocked her head to one side, watching him. When his smile broke into a grin, she laughed. They stepped around a pushcart jangling with copper pots and utensils, waved away a chattering dwarf trying to sell them night crystals, waved to an old dwarf who sat on his stoop watching the world go by. As they neared the Upandal works, Cymric called a halt. He wanted to select the three patterns from which he could create spells. Hiding, disrupting magic, and enhancing his astral senses all seemed good choices. The heavy fighting would be up to Leandra, but looking look at her now, it was hard to believe that was what she had in mind.

As they approached the wall surrounding the Upandal works, they saw Ristular busy trimming the ivy growing along the walls to fit into abstract patterns that complemented the tiling of the wall. Leandra's scarf glowed in spots. They strolled to the end of a long line of sightseers, most of them young couples such as themselves. Cymric spotted the dwarf couple from the platform for viewing the palace. The couple was in the middle of the line, oblivious to everyone around them. Cymric and Leandra settled in at the back of the line, which soon grew into a longer coil behind them. Cymric marvelled at how many visitors were here.

Leandra smiled and leaned over to whisper, "The gardens have a number of private nooks. Useful for hiding bodies of many sorts."

Cymric shuddered. The line moved quickly, splitting

into two at the entrance. Young human Ristular sat on
stools at the entrance, collecting donations in brass buckets. Leandra eyed each boy before choosing one, who
smiled up at her earnestly. "Welcome to the works of
Upandal. The Pilgrims of the High Star ask for a donation
of one silver piece per person to help us maintain this
cherished treasure."

Leandra opened her bag, trickling fifteen or so silvers
into the bucket. She smiled beautifully. "I've been here before, but I was unable to leave a proper token of appreciation."

The boys eyes lit with joy. "May the High Star bless
your evening!"

Leandra's smile continued. "That was about seven years
ago. I had a most enjoyable conversation with one of the
garden leaders. I was wondering if there was any chance
I might find him tonight?"

The boy looked confused, then shook his head. "All our
garden leaders soon move onto a higher calling. If he is
still in the compound, he would be in the Refectory of
Souls doing our most important work. He could not be disturbed." A portly dwarf in Ristular robes was attracted by
the conversation. When he cleared his throat, fear momentarily chilled the boy's expression, then quickly melted in
the warmth of his smile. "Enjoy your evening." Leandra
gave him her brightest smile as they moved into the garden.

The devoted of Upandal had done a marvelous job with
the garden. The only straight paths were polished marble
walkways that led to a delicate castle in the center. All the
other paths curved to show new delights around every corner. Cymric and Leandra spent some time admiring a
flower-strewn pond and the island with a carefully manicured rock garden in the center of it. The burbling turbulence from the waterfall that fed the pond had been
ingeniously channeled to send the flowers into slow spinning paths around the island. A human couple on the
bench a few strides away shared a gentle kiss. Cymric returned his eyes to the flowers. Leandra nudged his shoul-

der, then began to move along a path that sent them back to a marble pathway.

They entered the castle, climbing jeweled stairs to the second level. Leandra nodded toward an unoccupied window, which they approached, making Leandra's scarves begin to glow fiercely. She moved into him, her breasts against his chest, her head nuzzled in his neck to conceal the glow as best as possible. Her scent made his head spin, but he had to pay attention to the four Ristular coming up the stairs. Robes scuffling on the polished floor, they marched to the window behind Leandra. They examined the glass, pointing at this and that flaw. One threw back his hood; the elementalist who had escaped the road encampment. He peered at the glass.

Leandra's lips brushed Cymric's neck, her words buzzing along the skin of his neck. "Tilt your hat. Look down at me," she said. With one hand he adjusted his hat, moving it down a few degrees. Leandra's face was turned up to his, her right hand sweeping down the length of his left arm, brushing across his palm before she took his hand. Then she moved his hand up and out toward the window.

Out the corner of his eye Cymric saw the elementalist wave his hands while another Ristular spoke angrily in a language Cymric did not understand. Leandra stood on her toes to whisper into his ears, her lips catching the lobe of his right ear. "See the building your hand is pointing at?" Cymric moved his eyes to the left. Three rectangular spokes met at a domed hub. "That is the Refectory of Souls." Cymric nodded his understanding, bringing his nose and mouth in contact with Leandra's hair. His breathing deepened, and he pressed against her. His groin felt the thin material of her dress, chafed against the chainmail underneath.

Leandra pressed her thumb into the front of his right thigh, pushing him away gently. "Easy." He bent his hips to break contact. She massaged the side of his hip, continuing to whisper in his ear. "We never made it to the dome, although I think we made it to the last doorway. That's where we have to go."

Cymric nodded again, resisting the impulse to kiss the

top of her head. The Ristular moved back down the stairs.
Leandra moved away, but kept hold of his hand. She
kissed his hand softly, looking into his eyes before letting
go of his hand. Her gaze never left his. "Ready?" Her
voice was strong, calm.

Cymric shook his head. "No. Let's do it."

They left the castle. Leandra took a few misturns as
they wound through the garden, but her memory was remarkably accurate for a seven-year old impression.

A woman's laugh escaped from behind the rose bushes
obscuring the next turn. Then she appeared, clad in
Ristular robes, one hand holding the hem of the robe as
she ran around the turn in the path. Leandra quickly pulled
Cymric into a small rotunda formed from white-flowered
trellises, but not before they saw the robed man pursuing
the woman make an astounding leap to cut her off. She
shrieked and smiled. He bowed, pulling a silver rose from
his sleeve. Her eyes grew wide, then she fluttered her
lashes coquettishly while inhaling deeply the scent of the
flower. As the man stepped forward, she mock-batted at
him with the flower, knocking back his hood. Dark curls
spilled forward, and light fell on the dent in the bridge of
the man's nose. It was Brius.

32

Leandra froze, her hand gripping Cymric's arm hard enough that he had to suppress a gasp. The Ristular woman swiped at Brius, the silver petals brushing across the broad man's moustache. As Cymric tried to weave a thread for astral sense, he felt Leandra's grip tighten when Brius suddenly kissed the woman. Cymric thought his arm might snap when the woman moaned. The pain disrupted his next thread, and then Brius broke from the kiss. The woman slipped from his embrace, disappearing around the rose bushes with the scuffing of soft leather on stone. With a grin Brius loped off in silent pursuit. Leandra's grip gradually relaxed and Cymric was finally able to weave the last thread and cast the spell.

Leandra's expression was fierce, eyes narrowed to arrow slits, mouth clamped tight. Cymric wanted to say something, but didn't know what might be right. Instead he spent the time adjusting his astral sense to account for Leandra's pattern. Leandra opened her eyes wide, blinking several times. The tic-smile fired once or twice, ending in gritted teeth. She relaxed enough to say, "So help me, if you say 'I told you so'—" Cymric reached for her hand. Leandra hesitated then turned into him, starting a hug which he completed. "Damn him! I hope he serves Dis when he dies, and I hope I'm the one who sends him there." She punched Cymric in the arm, the blow drawing a grunt from him. Leandra shook once with a sob, then looked up. "Sorry. It's not you I'm mad at. But I *am* furious."

Cymric "ahemmed" nervously. He wasn't sure if what he was about to say next would help or not, but from the look of pain on Leandra's face it was worth a try. "It may not be what it seems—"

"And monkey farts don't smell!"

"—just as it wasn't what it seemed when you tried to carve me up by the Garlen spring."

Leandra bit her lip then wiped her face. Her composure was returning, but doubt still filled her eyes. "Are you sure, or are you just saying that."

"I'm not sure, but I'm not just saying it. Doesn't it make sense, though?"

"How?" Leandra's desperate need to believe filled that one word.

Cymric sighed. He could be wrong and Leandra might get hurt worse, even killed. Brius could be the ass he appeared to be and deserve carving into myriad pieces. Cymric secretly hoped so. But if he could ease Leandra's hurt, he wanted to. His lips twitched before he spoke. "If Maeumis had possessed Brius, he could have obtained Brius' plans for you as Lady DeCorvo. As Brius, he could hope to fool you, lull you into lowering your guard."

"Can you prove it?" said Leandra defiantly.

I was about to try, but someone was crushing my bones, making it difficult for me to cast the proper spell. The same someone who was nuzzling my neck a few minutes ago, when it was a convenient way to turn attention from us. "My spell didn't come off in time. If I see Brius again, I'll have a pretty good chance. He has to use magic or undergo a shift in emotions, but I would imagine seeing you would prompt one or the other."

"How can you let me know?"

How about I scream "he's possessed!" and we both flee for our lives? "I'll make some obvious reference to water or a spring, mindful of the incident at the Garlen spring."

Leandra nodded. "Thanks," she said, absently rubbing Cymric's upper arm. "If you don't speak within a few moments of meeting him, I'll assume he's not possessed, and I'll cut him to pieces." Cymric raised his eyebrows, but said nothing.

Leandra walked around the rose bushes, Cymric trailing her, but Brius and the woman were gone. The trail to the

Refectory of Souls was tricky. Their first false turn ended at a topiary display of satyrs piping at the moon. The next stopped at a suspended sphere of water filled with live goldfish. Frogs croaked underneath the sphere, jumping up to land in the water. Whatever held the sphere of water together treated the surface of the sphere as the surface of a normal pond. Frogs swam along the surface, and the fish approached from several directions. Cymric spent a minute too many trying to analyze the magic involved. Leandra tugged him away.

The third trail led to a branch lined with willows. Dragonflies the size of Cymric's hand darted in and out of the branches, trailing a luminescent red or gold dust that glittered over the ground and fronds. Leandra hushed Cymric with a motion of her hand, then indicated two Ristular gardeners walking a path that crossed theirs. She took the lead in following the pair; they walked past a series of small whirlwinds that buzzed and whistled as they rearranged a rock garden, a row of lilacs in full, fragrant bloom, coming finally to a polished gray marble wall etched with the outline of a door. One of the Ristular fumbled with his medallion, drawing a laugh from the other. The first held the medallion shoulder-high against a spot in the wall perhaps a hand's-width away from the etchings. A rumble and a shoosh preceded the appearance of a stone door, duller in sheen than the marble, inside the etching. A Ristular pushed open the door, which swung on silent hinges. A short pause followed by another rumble and shoosh as the door closed, the final sound a heavy thud.

Leandra and Cymric waited in what concealment the lilac bushes offered in the deepening dusk as three more pairs arrived and entered. By the time night fell, no more came. Leandra signaled that they should wait a bit, just to be sure, then tapped his shoulder and moved out.

Approaching the wall cautiously, conscious of the crunch of rough gravel under his soft boots, he paused to let his astral sense take in all of the door. Though magic pulsed within it, it seemed to be of one piece, without additional patterns for traps or wards. An advanced magician could of course incorporate those into the pattern of the

door itself. Cymric pulled the medallion from under his
shirt, jerking it so clumsily over his head that it caught at
his hat and knocked it off. He snatched up his hat, then
placed the medallion at the spot where the Ristular had
done so. Nothing happened. Cymric moved the medallion
down half a handspan, and suddenly it chimed softly,
"Hail the High Star all who enter. Hail Ristul."

The doorway ground like pebbles in a polisher, and
Cymric felt a blast of air at his ankles as the shoosh
sounded. The door appeared, visible only in the faint glow
of the etching that surrounded it. As it slid open silently,
Cymric and Leandra stepped into a small white plaster
room illuminated by a single flickering oil lamp in the
center. The rough-plank door had no handle, but the walls
on either side were dotted with brass plugs about twice the
size of a silver piece. The door *rumble-shooshed* shut behind them, sending the lamplight into a wild dance.
Leandra muttered, "This is new."

A half-dozen of the plugs pulsed in Cymric's astral
sense, all part of some pattern. Magical power began to
build. Cymric immediately wove a thread for dispel magic,
but the spell in the ward looked like it was going to be
faster. Dying on Ristul's doorstep wasn't exactly what
Cymric had planned. *Blink.* "Hail the High Star! Hail
Ristul!" His frantic waving prompted the same words from
Leandra. The magic ward stopped, and a bolt snicked free
in the door. Cymric pushed the door open with one hand.

"Jerimdas, is that you? You and Maika checking out the
backs of those hedges agai—" The dwarf sitting on the
stool had his back to the wall through which they entered.
His close-cropped black beard advertised his youth. When
he glanced up, his smile changed instantly to a look of
confusion. Then he peered quickly down both ends of the
corridor to see if anyone might be around to help.

Leandra grabbed Cymric's walking stick and smiled
deferentially. "Excuse me, but I was wondering if you
might help us with this?" The dwarf looked up at Leandra,
then down at the walking stick, just as Leandra turned and
rotated her hands to swing the staff toward his face. The
blow caught the dwarf under the nose, knocking his head

back against the wall. An immediate follow-up to the side of the head sprawled him flat, unconscious. Leandra turned the handle on this side of the door, creaked the door open, and tossed the dwarf inside. She closed the door, her face showing disappointment at the absence of any scream or audible sign of a spell being released.

She looked both ways down the ends of the corridor. Her eyes narrowed, then she nodded to her left. The wooden stairway was made of narrow strips of light wood, perhaps birch, which creaked every few steps. The walls were white plaster, bordered by a red and brown strip broken up occasionally by yellow triangles. Cymric was surprised to see an oil lamp rather than a light crystal providing illumination, until he felt a breeze from the ceiling. Fine wire mesh covered the ventilation ports, a difficult system designed as proof of the builder's devotion to Upandal. Some of vents were clogged, and nearby lamps stained the ceiling with oily smoke. Apparently the Ristular could not maintain all the works of Upandal. Leandra passed two doors, then stopped to listen and peer around a corner.

"It might be helpful if we had some of their robes," said Cymric.

"It might, but we don't. We'll have to depend on stealth and strength now."

Cymric began to weave a spell thread. "If you're willing to travel slow, I've got a way to make us travel unnoticed." Leandra nodded. Placing the pattern of illusion just ahead of Leandra's feet, Cymric urged it to spread out to its full ten paces, infusing the external world with a false pattern. "Take ten steady paces, then stop. I'll recast the spell. With luck no one will spot us."

"That's a little slower than I'd like, wizard," Leandra complained, but she took the ten steps that took her around the corner. Cymric followed behind, crouched near Leandra's feet as he wove, reaching out in front of her as he cast the spell. The false pattern flowed like fog across a field in early morning, and Leandra walked ten paces more to another intersection. Hearing footsteps coming from a hallway leading to the intersection, she drew the

sword from her dress, the blade rasping against the sheath.
Three Ristular crossed the intersection, the woman talking
excitedly about "Ristul's work to come." One of the men
groused that by the time Ristul's mighty work got to them,
it seemed to consist of no more than pulling weeds. Cymric waited until the sound of their footsteps receded.

A loud gong interrupted his next casting. The gong rang
a second time, and a third. Voices filtered through the hallway, growing in number and volume. Doors behind them
creaked open, each one disgorging six or more Ristular.
The Ristular filled the corridor from both directions, but
all flowed to the right when they reached the intersection,
a chattering brown herd. Cymric and Leandra flattened
themselves against the wall so the spell would have to
work no harder than necessary. When a dwarf went past at
a run to catch up with his comrades, he clipped Cymric's
arm with his shoulder, then stumbled a few steps. He
glared accusingly at an oil lamp several feet back and
nearly a foot too high, then disappeared around the intersection. Cymric's heartbeat began to slow, and his breathing became easier.

Stragglers kept the corridor from being empty, but Cymric still had plenty of time on his spell. From the other side
of the intersection came the sound of running feet, then a
woman appeared, struggling to pull the robe up over her
bare legs as she went. Her hair was disheveled, her smile
lopsided, her features familiar. She stopped and blew a
kiss down to the unseen portion of the hallway, then scurried through the intersection. A steady, booted stride
sounded from the hallway. Cymric looked at Leandra.
"This could be a very bad idea."

Too late. The next moment Brius strode through the intersection, robe hiked to his waist so he could notch his
belt. His trousers were no longer tucked into his boots, and
his hair was as disheveled as the woman's. Leandra set her
face and gripped her sword, stepping out of the spell's
range to appear behind Brius.

"Hello, Brius," she said.

Brius spun on one booted heel. His eyes registered surprise, but it vanished as he slipped the end of the belt into

the final loop. With a single motion he dropped his robe and extended his hand to catch Leandra's fingertips to bring her hand up for a kiss. Relaxing her posture, Leandra stepped toward Brius, reached her hand around his neck and lifted her head to kiss him.

Cymric let his astral sense work on Brius, but he had difficulty even spotting the man. The astral space around him bent and curved wildly as if it were a sheet of taffy pulled by a dozen eager hands. Cymric squinted. What had Gelthrain said? That the Horror had warped the fabric of astral space itself? Spellcasting over anything but the shortest of range would be extraordinarily difficult.

Cymric finally locked onto Brius. Two horns swirled up from the other man's cheeks, looping out and around his ears like rams' horns, trailing off into four glittering threads that twitched and jumped like the strings on a marionette. The image dimmed as Brius' emotions steadied, brightened again when magic flowed from the threads through the horns. The horns themselves wriggled with gold runes; they shifted shape rapidly, the pieces fracturing and recombining to form new runes.

Cymric stepped out quietly, hoping the intensity of the kiss would obscure his appearance. He coughed. "Hey, do I have to throw a bucket of cold water on you two? Come on, this is serious business we're on." Brius looked up, and Leandra turned around to stare fixedly at Cymric. The question lingered in her eyes. Cymric nodded to Leandra, and covered it by saying, "Well, it is."

Brius smirked. "Good to see you again, wizard," then promptly put himself between the wizard and Leandra, turning his back to Cymric. "Fine dress, Leandra. Were you expecting to see me here?"

"No. Scouting as usual?"

"Exactly," said Brius. Cymric came around in time to catch the gleam in his eye, a look that gave him chills. Leandra did a masterful job of pretending not to notice. Her necklace blazed steadily, her scarves providing only a pretense of concealment.

Brius indicated the way he had been traveling. "What now? The Ristular gather in hopes that they may complete some hideous ritual. Each night their leader comes and tells them it is not yet time."

"Are they well armed?" asked Leandra.

"No, but they are many."

"What about their leader?" Cymric asked.

"A powerful nethermancer. You probably wouldn't want to cross paths with him." This last Brius said with a wolfish, predatory smile that he would surely have suppressed could he have seen it in a mirror.

"I'm sure we can handle him if need be," Leandra said calmly. "I came here to fulfill a prophecy and slay the Horror Ristul. I say we start now."

Brius chuckled. "That sounds like the Leandra I know. Very well, then, follow me." He spun on his boot and strode off down the hall. Cymric looked questioningly at Leandra, but she was already quickening her step to catch Brius; Cymric hustled in response. "You draw his attention, I get the necklace around Brius to boot Maeumis. The three of us take it from there," she said quietly. She held her sword in her right hand, worked the catch of her necklace with the left.

Cymric nodded, hurried to overtake Brius. It was a plan. Not a particularly inspired plan or one in which Cymric had much confidence, but they had no time to debate their options. He pulled even with Brius, and whispered conspiratorially, "So, tell me, what is this ritual of theirs?"

"You will see, wizard. It is a quite impressive display of falderal." Brius turned left onto a well-worn carpet whose original color was blue. The traffic of thousands of footsteps had trampled it into a nondescript gray-brown. Light crystals replaced oil lamps on the walls. The left wall contained a stylized mural of Ristular on horseback sweeping through a village, burning the buildings and capturing the people. The right wall had a mural of Maeumis, metal rings cut into his face, offering a bowl of blood to the sky. The dagger remained in the throat of the victim, while the Ristular who restrained the victim turned awe-filled faces toward a swirling black cloud behind Maeumis.

The hall ended in a large brass door, about half-again as tall as Cymric and set on hinges as thick as his thighs. The fear on Leandra's face told him she'd seen this door before. Through the doorway Cymric could see dozens, perhaps hundreds, of Ristular forming themselves into lines spread throughout the huge domed room. The dome appeared to be burnished copper, the supporting beams of a luminescent metal that glowed a diffused yellow. The beams topped a marble wall that was fifteen feet tall. It was covered with hundreds of brass plugs like those at the entrance to the building, but these were larger. *Garlen, if you let me get out of this, I shall take up baking again, I swear it.* Deep down Cymric knew that not only was it a lie, but that lying to Garlen was probably not a good idea. As he followed Brius through the doorway, he tried again. *Garlen, if you let me help Leandra fulfill her destiny, you can do whatever you want to with me.* Leandra and Cymric stepped into the room, where they saw three raised altars, one at each door. Then the massive door grated shut behind them, closing with a percussive boom.

Brius raised his hands as the Ristular turned to look. Leandra caught Cymric's eye. "Friends, fellow worshippers, I—," began Brius.

"Am a pompous dwarven dung ant who cannot get a woman without stealing someone else's body to do it!" screamed Cymric

The face of Brius shone with fury, but Leandra was already whipping the necklace over his head. The man's reflexes astonished Cymric; the necklace flashed where it made contact with his forehead, but Brius raised a hand to the side of his face just in time. As the Ristular gasped, he blocked Leandra's attack, knocking her arm out of the way. "She is Leandra!" he shouted, bolting toward the worshippers. "She is the seventeenth, the last of the villagers to elude us! Hers is the blood that shall summon Ristul!"

The Ristular roared, surging toward Leandra while Brius tried to put as many pilgrims between him and her as possible. Leandra cursed, fumbled the necklace back on. Her sword cut an arc of light as she struck the first two Ristular to reach her, an effect Cymric had never seen before. From Leandra's expression, maybe she too was seeing it for the first time.

Cymric dove for cover behind the first altar. Even as he wove his first thread, he noted the grooves leading to the gold bowl. Must be for her blood. He wove the false pattern. Centering the spell on a spot he touched made the casting possible, despite the warped nature of astral space. Magic tingled over and through him. The first Ristular who rounded the altar looked perplexed, glanced up at the altar. Cymric quietly slid out ten paces, cast the spell again, slid, then cast again. He stopped beneath a trio of brass plugs, each wider than his forearm was long. Written in dwarven on each plug was a name. The name on the middle plug was familiar: Heslar.

Leandra was a whirlwind of motion. She leaped, she spun, her screams and battle oaths sometimes carrying over the shouts of the Ristular. Astral lines pulsed from the walls to Leandra, waves turning to jagged flashes as they touched her. Cymric watched more carefully. The pulses started at the brass plugs in the wall, the jagged bolts hitting Leandra high—on the necklace.

His mind raced. The necklace had drawn spiritual energy, his spirit, through it. These lines must contain that energy, energy that was strengthening Leandra. But Heslar? Cymric looked to the center of the room. The flashes ever so briefly illuminated a shape, a shape unfolding familiar petals. Then he looked around the room, and saw that it was like being inside the calendar, all the threads supporting and creating the flower in the center. The threads must be the blood magic of those slain. The flower must be the ritual to summon Ristul. But the flower needed one last thread: the blood magic that would come from sacrificing Leandra.

Cymric never noticed the hand until it had grabbed him by the throat. Brius' laugh was quiet and nasty. "There are advantages to having a beastmaster's body and a nethermancer's eyes. As strong arms slammed Cymric's head against the marble, Cymric tried to cast a spell, but his head rung. A second slam prompted him to swing his walking stick, which bounced off with little effect. Brius laughed, a loud laugh that became a roar. Cymric gagged as Brius lifted his head, strangling him.

"Leandra!" Brius shouted. "Surrender or watch me kill your wizard."

33

Brius casually banged Cymric's bruised skull against the cold, marble wall, and Cymric couldn't see for the spikes of pain. "I can keep this up far longer than your wizard can," Brius told Leandra. "Drop your sword and surrender."

Cymric tried to croak, "This is war" to Leandra, hoping she would leave him. With the help of the spirits of those whom Maeumis had sacrificed, Leandra might actually have a chance to defeat the Ristular. She could almost certainly escape—and Leandra alive meant Ristul could not be summoned.

With one hand, Brius kept an iron grip on Cymric. Cymric felt his body stiffen as Brius began to trace a spell pattern with his free hand. "Not yet," Brius murmured, as Maeumis cast a spell through him. "Be still." Cymric saw a flare around Brius' body and a series of wavy pulses around the nearest altar. Tears streaked Cymric's vision; he wondered if the nethermancer were communicating with the Horror.

Then Ristular lay unmoving on the ground. Perhaps twice that number had stumbled away from the fray, wounded enough to let their comrades carry on the fight. Leandra's court bag lay crushed a dozen paces away, the cut cord dangling from her wrist. Two score or so Ristular ringed her. Perhaps a hundred more still waited in back of that mob. Cymric revised downward his estimate of Leandra's chances. The only good thing was that no spells had been thrown against her, at least none successfully. And it was probably Ristul's warping of astral space that they had to thank for that.

Cymric blinked to focus on Leandra. She kept moving, now in a circle, now in a figure eight, now in a triangle. Her sword moved constantly, whistling at the top of its arc as Leandra kept the mob at bay. Her dress was in tatters, revealing gleaming armor underneath. "Let the wizard go. I will surrender a full hundred beats after you release him."

Brius laughed. "Giving him how much time to sneak back in here or cast who knows what spell? I would rather just kill him." Out the corner of his eye, Cymric saw a swirling motion in the astral space around the nearest altar.

Leandra's blade gained speed. "Without spells, I doubt even all the Ristular could prevent me from getting to you. They can wear me down afterward, but I will kill that body."

Brius smirked. "I have another."

Leandra took a running leap in the direction of Brius, then took to the air, the necklace giving her extra distance; Cymric saw the threads touch her as she cleared the ground. Her blade cut two Ristular, her rush boring down a third. Those on the side moved to close the gap, but those closest to her had to be pushed forward. One simply broke and ran. Brius poured his full strength into pulping Cymric's head against the wall, overpowering Cymric's feeble resistance. Through a shower of pain, Cymric foggily wondered why he wasn't dead yet, then vaguely remembered drinking the Garlen vial. He spit blood in a choking laugh; Brius might get to pound on him for some time before he went down.

Leandra cleared the crowd, pushing them back with a scream and a whirling blade. She stopped two paces from Brius, who swiveled Cymric in the way as a shield. Her sword snicked into its sheath. Brius raised both eyebrows as Leandra raised her hands out and to her sides. "Try this," she said. "Brius might be fast enough to grapple me before I draw my sword. If I draw in time, I prune Brius like one of your rose bushes. You grapple me; Brius is stronger and you eventually get me. But to do that, you have to let go—"

Brius dropped Cymric and leaped onto Leandra with a

roar. She reacted an instant too late. Brius crashed into her, toppling her to the ground. Leandra grabbed the hilt of her sword, but Brius seized her hand, trying to pry it away from the hawk's-head. He pinned her other shoulder with his knee, devoting two hands to Leandra's drawing arm.

Then the other Ristular began to close on the pair. Staggering to his feet, Cymric doubted he could awe this crowd by casting any of his spells, even assuming he could somehow target through the twisted morass of astral space. He looked around the room, saw a small shimmer in the center of the room. Perhaps—

He ran bloody and—he hoped—wild-eyed toward the advancing Ristular. He pointed and screamed. "The flower! Look! The flower is blooming!" Eight or nine Ristular ignored him, but three others turned to look. Two saw the shimmering. They also pointed. Now others turned. Prepared for this day, praying and working toward this day, many joined Cymric in shouting that the flower was blooming.

"Ristul is come!" screamed the woman who had been with Brius. Here and there pilgrims fainted. The crowd wavered until a tall man shouted "The ritual! We must ready the ritual." Now the mob broke into small groups. Some tried to stop their comrades, urging them back toward Brius. Cymric saw the elementalist knocked down as he futilely tried to stop the crowd. He couldn't guess how long this charade would occupy the Ristular, but it was at least a respite.

Brius wrested Leandra's hand from her sword, used his other hand to draw the sword and smash the pommel across her face. "You aren't much without this, are you?" Cymric launched himself at Brius, lumbering in uneven steps as Brius pulled his hand back to smash Leandra again.

The runes on Leandra's sheath began to glow. Cymric slipped as he backpedalled on the slick marble, his hands and arms squeaking on the stone as he stopped himself. Three runes lifted from her sheath. Even at less than an arm's length away, the weft of astral space made a rune miss, then vanish in thin air. But one struck Brius in the chest, and the other in the forehead. Brius screamed. Bits of hair, skin, and bone jetted in a dreadful hiss along with drops of blood and white pinwheels of force.

Brius crashed against the wall, pinned by the force of the magic. As Leandra rolled to her feet, the runes bore deeper into Brius, whose screams grew more frantic. She rushed to him, unclasped her necklace and worked it around the beastmaster's neck. Cymric saw bright, oily globs retreat up the four threads, passing through the far door and out of sight. The horns splintered and crumbled. "He's free!" Cymric shouted to Leandra.

"The sword is mine," she said quietly. The runes stopped glowing, and Brius slumped to the ground. Leandra turned around, settling into a defensive crouch, sword ready. "Patch him up. We may need him to get out of here." The Ristular had stopped forming for the ritual, many of them now staring at the three of them.

Reluctance slowed Cymric's movements until he heard someone scream, "The last! The last is still free!" He knelt by Brius, quickly drawing a healing potion from his side pouch. Brius focused his eyes on Cymric. He gritted his teeth, then tapped the necklace. "Give me the potion. Get this on Leandra." Cymric nodded, unclasped the necklace, then handed the potion to Brius.

Leandra was already meeting the first Ristular advance. Her movements weren't quite as flashy without the necklace, but a Ristular dropped just the same. Spotting Cymric as he moved toward her, she extended her free hand behind her. Cymric passed her the necklace, which she immediately put around her neck in an ungainly left-handed move. Then she parried three Ristular short swords, giving ground toward Brius. The Ristular were furious, their expectations of Ristul's appearance having been raised and dashed in too short a time.

Brius stood, his legs steady, but his expression pained. He closed his eyes. A shimmer from his right hand elongated to become a claw, its jagged tips the size of his original fingers. *So that is what beastmasters are like. Certainly explains the look in his eyes.* Brius howled as he

leaped for the nearest Ristular, who recoiled from the
charge. The claw tore deeply into the screaming pilgrim.

The scream seemed to galvanize the Ristular, who
flooded into action. Leandra and Brius fought fiercely, she
swinging her sword high while Brius struck low, often
from a crouch. His snarls were matched by her high-
pitched shrieks, their moves showing the effects of years
of partnership. Their attacks were deadly, but the press of
bodies had them hemmed into a semicircle some nine
paces wide. The Ristular weren't skilled enough to break
through the defense, but they began to wear down Leandra
and Brius, their shouts and frenzied oaths drowning out
even the roar of Brius.

Cymric stood with his back to the wall. He could try to
place attack magic into a matrix. He could also try pounding a few Ristular with his walking stick. Neither seemed
effective. And Maeumis could return any moment. His astral sense was weakening; he wanted a chance to spot
Maeumis should he choose to appear in a different body.
He reworked the pattern to enhance his astral sense as the
Ristular shrank the semicircle to about seven paces wide.
Beginning to smell blood, the mob's howling rose in pitch
and frenzy as they rained daggers, swords, and fists on
their prey. A sword blow got through Leandra's guard, delivering a deep cut to her left shoulder.

Cymric swiped at a hooded head, missed, felt frustration
well up inside him. Leandra and Brius shouted warnings to
one another. The Ristular became even more fierce, climbing over one another, over the living, wounded, and dead,
in order to attack Leandra, who they called "the Last."
Cymric tried to calm himself, scanning the room for anything that might help them out of their predicament. A
dagger scraped his face as it sailed through the semicircle.

He knew the brass plugs held powerful magic, but he
doubted he had the time to investigate them. And the astral
flower was connected to the ritual to summon Ristul; nothing immediately useful. He glanced over to the altar toward which Maeumis had cast his spell. Dull, black
nothing. He looked at the doors, searching for wards or
other spells that he might be able to trigger in desperation.

Then he snapped back to the black nothing surrounding the altar, the familiar black nothing he had seen twice before. Cymric looked carefully, avoiding the sword thrust of the frenzied Ristular. Brius picked the man up and hurled him back into the mob, then shouted something at Cymric, who was deep in spell magic. He deftly slid the pattern for his leaping magic into the matrix that had previously held the spell to enhance his astral sense. Just as Cymric leaped to complete the spell, Leandra looked back at him.

"You with us or off in wizard land?" she shouted. Her parry came a little late, but the sword blow glanced off her armor with a horrible scraping sound. Though her counterstrike forced her attacker to retreat, the circle had shrunk to five paces across, small enough that the attackers were now interfering with each other. The press of bodies would soon pin the three of them to the wall.

"Wizard land," shouted Cymric. "But I'll be back!" He began to weave a thread to dispel magic, keeping it short and tight to the pattern. Then he crouched low before his leap carried him over the startled Ristular to land within a footstep of the altar. Ristular who were too far back to attack Leandra and Brius howled as they saw a chance for a new victim. Cymric cast dispel magic upon the altar, putting everything he had behind it. He felt his spell strike the core of Maeumis' spell, one that held the spiritcatcher in check. Sustaining the mental pressure behind his pattern, Cymric raised his fists in the air as he felt his spell crack through the nethermancer's.

Wild oaths came from the hoarse throats of those behind him, then Cymric crashed face down onto the altar, pinned by the weight of several bodies. Eight hands grabbed him, turned him over, held him to the cold stone surface of the altar. A fifth figure threw back his hood. The battered face of the dwarf elementalist seethed rage as he drew a serpent-tongue dagger from his belt. Cymric tried to wiggle his legs enough to find purchase for a leap; with the help of a spell he might be able to bull his way off the altar. "This is the last time you will cross us, wizard," the elementalist intoned as he raised the dagger. "I, Foromin Earthworker, Thrall of Ristul, bind you to my master, so it may find sustenance and shall find its way." The restraining hands dug into his flesh. Cymric tried a leap, but he managed only to flop one leg free.

An agonized scream accompanied the dwarf's dagger stroke, which stopped just inches from Cymric's chest. The dwarf's body jerked, suspended three feet above the ground, then Cymric saw the astral pulse of the spiritcatcher's barbed tendril push the dwarf a few inches higher. The tendril began to take form, manifesting itself in the physical world as the spiritcatcher entered it from the astral plane. The Ristular holding him froze until a second tendril pierced one of the dwarfs holding Cymric's arms. The other three fled. Cymric sat up and leaped off the altar, eluding the two tendrils bursting through the stone. Tendrils were erupting everywhere, many catching Ristular, most catching nothing. The dwarf's terrified scream increased fifty-fold.

The mob broke as they fled for the three exits. The first to reach them were not those who had the talents necessary to open the brass doors, which had been closed through magic. Panicked humans and dwarfs threw their shoulders against the thousands of pounds of metal, pounded on the doors with fists and weapons, tried to pry open magical runes. The spiritcatcher grabbed a few more with each passing moment.

Brius and Leandra dodged the tendrils, working their way to Cymric.

"What the hell is that?" asked Brius.

"A spiritcatcher. A pet for Maeumis."

"What's it doing here?" Leandra punctuated her question with a swing of her sword, her blow chopping into a tendril with the sound of a pick into ice. Cymric shook his head. Another annoying part of the puzzle he hadn't unraveled. Brius twisted away from a barbed tendril.

When the frantic Ristular finally succeeded in opening one brass door, those behind swarmed through. Those who had clustered around the still closed doors made a break for the open one. Most made it, the spiritcatcher feeding on the few who did not.

"Don't move," Cymric said. He knelt and quickly cast

his concealing illusion. No more tendrils erupted near them, but a few pushed through the floor to probe tentatively at the shimmer in the center of the room. Those tendrils flailed wildly, then quickly withdrew into the ground. The Refectory of Souls was now filled with sixty or more dying Ristular impaled on what looked like jagged icicles. The impalings spilled no blood, even though the tendrils now had physical form. Every so often a Ristular twitched on his tendril. Cymric was breathing rapidly, his stomach turning. Leandra and Brius looked only a little better.

"Now what?" Brius' question was subdued.

Cymric thought a little bit. "We can probably extend a chain of spells to cover our exit, the way we did coming in. But I'd like to find a way to make sure Ristul cannot be summoned. I need to use my inner sight."

Leandra nodded. She tapped the pommel of her sword. "What do *we* do?"

"Keep alert for Maeumis," he said, drawing a grunt from Brius. Cymric walked over to one of the brass plugs, which was inscribed with the word "Valiza" in ancient dwarven. He got control of his breathing, then touched the plug. Inner sight drifted down the length of his arm to view it. A thread attached to the plug, one that ran to the flower form in the center of the room. Then again, the word "thread" was probably a misnomer, just as "rope" didn't do justice to the thigh-thick twines of hemp used to tether Theran sky ships. The thread was as thick as Cymric's wrist and far more durable than those in the calendar or the necklace.

The plug contained a rich pattern of blues and greens within it, much as a spell matrix contained a spell pattern. Studying the pattern, Cymric expected to find the essence of blood magic, all the power that could be drained from the life of Valiza. But the pattern recoiled as he probed, shifting from blue and green to blue and indigo. Cymric pulled back his inner sight. He advanced more cautiously, but the pattern still retreated. He picked up the smell of sweat-soaked sheets, the sensation of terror at the sound of an axe upon the door. Could he be sensing the memories of Valiza, the way he had experienced the memories of

Heslar in the calendar? But memories did not move. People moved. Spirits moved. The plugs contained the spirits of those slain in the Ristular ritual.

Why were they still here? Cymric turned the problem over in his mind. They referred to Leandra as "the Last". All the other spirits were still here; it must be that the ritual required that the spirits of everyone in an entire village be sacrificed to Ristul simultaneously in order to summon the Horror. Or the spirits of three villages, or eight villages, or however many villages were listed in the calendar. That would be a tricksome bit of magic. So the ritual held the spirits until the last person was killed, then released all the spirits to Ristul at once. Cymric pulled back into the physical world.

He let out a triumphant whoop, which made Leandra suddenly spin her swordpoint to his chest. Shaking with excitement, he went through his list of conclusions. "First, the Ristular design the ritual to release all the spirits at once in order to summon Ristul. Second, Maeumis decides to backstab the Ristular. The spiritcatcher makes the ritual fail by catching many of the spirits as the ritual releases them, then Maeumis can later tap the power of the spirits he has captured. Third, Garlen chooses you as the hero who will send these spirits home. I was in there; your necklace can send spirits on to their proper destinations."

"How?" Leandra's question brought him up short because he couldn't answer. When he'd been examining the necklace, moving his inner sight close to the horn within the necklace seemed to trigger the process. He'd been pulled in when the runes in the horn formed his name.

"Put the necklace on the plug. Call to the spirit within, making sure to call her by name."

Leandra removed her necklace, the stones still blazing scarlet. She held it in both hands, pressing it against the plug. Then she scowled as she looked at the plug. "I do not read old dwarven."

"Sorry. Her name is Valiza."

Leandra closed her eyes. "Valiza, can you hear me?" Cymric watched the necklace with his astral sense. The faintest ripples appeared around Leandra's hands, like an insect skeeting across water. Leandra's pattern brightened, the normally staid browns and reds glowing hotter, some burning white. Cymric's ears began to buzz and tickle. "Valiza, I am Leandra. I want to help you. Please come closer." Leandra's face twitched, then set in concentration. A tic-smile broke across her face. "Yes, that Leandra. I am older now—it's difficult to explain." She licked her lips. Her hands trembled. "Valiza, it's time to go."

An ominous creaking sound came from the walls, like a ship battered in stormy seas. The walls seemed to bend, as if made from putty. The ceiling beams curved in and out, the lines on the marble floor bulged apart or puckered up like mere cloth being pulled by an invisible needle and thread.

"Cymric?" Brius dropped to a crouch. He snarled as the ground rolled underneath him. He lashed out although there was nothing to strike.

The walls and beams showed no cracks, no signs of the tremendous stress they must be undergoing. A portion of the copper dome twisted down to touch the floor like an instantaneously created metal stalactite. The whole world was twisting, bending. *But not breaking.* Cymric knew then. Ristul was trying to break through into this world, trying to stop Leandra before it was too late.

The Horror was powerful enough to twist astral space, powerful enough to twist space in the external world. But it could not create a crack or poke a hole into space, a hole through which it could enter. It was as if the Horror were trapped in a sack of untearable cloth; it could grab handfuls of the sack, twist it, stretch it, make it bulge or bunch. But it could not tear a way out of the sack. The ritual had meant to create a hole, the flower acting like a seedling pushing its way through frozen ground to sunlight above. Now Leandra threatened to cut the flower before it broke the surface. Ristul was going into a frenzy.

The red glow wreathed Leandra's hands and arms. Her breathing was rapid, the muscles of her arms strained. She licked her lips. "Call the others before you go. Call them by name, Valiza." Another tic-smile. "Yes, even Kaleb. Garlen grant you a safe home."

The thread attached to the plug glowed star-white, then began to pull away from the flower. Other threads, those tangled with the first, also began to pull away. Leandra gasped. The red glow now washed over her in waves, from her hands to her waist, over and over again. As each wave slapped Cymric with a stinging heat, he could only imagine what Leandra must be feeling. "Remember them. Sing them. Call them. Say the names of those who touched your life." Leandra repeated the phrase over and over again, turning it into a chant. Thread after thread tore free from the flower, passing through the necklace Leandra held. The red glow rolled over her from hands to feet, splashing against the marble like burning oil. Petals fell, the stem unraveled. With a rising shriek, the last of the flower dissipated into strands to flow through the necklace.

The refectory snapped back to normal like an overtaut bow string finally released. The walls and ceiling returned to their solid shapes. The Ristular hung motionless from the tendrils of the spiritcatcher. The only sound was Leandra's ragged breathing. Brius went to her, cradled her as she slumped to the ground. Leandra opened her eyes, looked first to Brius and then Cymric. "Hands burned. Rest just hurts." The necklace lay on the ground. The stones shone a gentle blue.

Brius glanced up at Cymric. "You were right. You work with some wicked magic, wizard."

Leandra smiled. "Looks like you've earned your pay." She gently scooped up the necklace, avoiding the blisters on her palms, passing it to Cymric. Cymric turned it over in his hands, watching it catch the light. The feel of deep magic still resonated within the stones, which he placed gently into his pouch.

With a series of soft thuds the Ristular slid to the marble floor. The tendrils of the spiritcatcher sank into the ground, disappearing from the external world to leave a wispy astral trail. Brius grinned. "Looks as though we've come to end of this battle. A better end than I'd have put money upon." Cymric nodded idly as he tilted the healing potion to Leandra's lips. She drank greedily, and Cymric emptied the vial. His hand froze, the empty vial hovering over his side pouch.

Then Cymric jumped to his feet, letting the vial drop. The sound of broken glass echoed through the empty refectory. Brius looked at him, and Leandra started to rise. Cymric grabbed his walking stick, took five steps, then turned to shout, "You're hurt. Get yourselves out of here. I'll meet you back at the tavern." He sprinted after the trail of the spiritcatcher, a trail that would lead him to Maeumis.

34

Cymric's sleeves caught on thorns as he raced deeper into the garden. Twisting free with a snapping of branches, he scanned ahead for the trail of the spiritcatcher. The creature slowed its pace; so did Cymric. A half-moon and a sky full of stars gave light enough for walking, but Cymric's scrapes and cuts were proof that running was hazardous. He wound his way among rose bushes grown into a deep labyrinth. By day the maze was probably a pleasant diversion for those with time to kill during an afternoon. But now it was night, and Cymric reserved his murderous thoughts for the nethermancer.

The spiritcatcher stopped moving entirely, its trail fading as it ceased expending magic. Cymric noted the spiritcatcher's position as best he could.

The nature of the roses had changed here, catching and reflecting light better than did the flowers forming the outer layers of the labyrinth. Leaning closer, Cymric saw that they were silver roses. The kind Brius had when possessed by Maeumis. He moved forward cautiously, then rounded a bend and gasped softly at the sight before him. Piled in a pyramid shape against a wall of bushes were several ork skulls. Dozens more had been tossed aside carelessly, left to lie wherever they happened to land. Cymric threaded his way warily along the path, careful not make any noise by stepping on a skull.

From around the next bend he heard the splash of water. He stopped to collect his thoughts. Impulse had brought him to the garden, but there was no need to die for it. He listened to the water, trying to come up with a plan.

"Hiding in the bushes of my garden is not really hiding,

boy." The voice was gruff, gravelly. Cymric froze. The voice laughed. "Have it your way."

Cymric cursed himself, then walked around the bend into a small sitting garden. Surrounding the garden was a gravel walkway interspersed at regular intervals with a total of six stone benches. In the center of the garden was a fountain decorated with the statues of four dwarfs seated at a tavern table, tankards raised to different heights. A fifth statue stood pouring a cask for the others. The water poured from the cask, cleverly arranged to hit all four mugs. The splash came from the overflow of the mugs hitting the table.

Bones covered the grass surrounding the fountain in an elaborate design that began as two concentric circles, the first surrounding the base of the fountain, the second just inside the gravel path. Complex lines of bones joined the two circles, the larger bones near the outer circle, the finger and toe bones forming swirling patterns at the inner circle. Maeumis stood on the opposite side of the garden, just inside the bone circle. As he began to approach along the edge of the circle, Cymric saw that the right half of his face was badly burned. As the dwarf got closer, it became apparent that his right eye was bandaged in gauze and that the rings of metal implanted in his face had melted on the right side. His beard, too, had burned away from the side of his face, the first strands of blackened, singed hair appearing on his chin. The white hair of his head was unruly around a bald, blistered wedge. His burning flesh stinking, his cracked skin bleeding, Maeumis stopped in front of Cymric. "So you win. The old dog is whipped by the human pups."

Cymric swallowed slowly. He had to breathe openmouthed to tolerate the stench. Maeumis laughed. "Not very pleasant, is it? Damn sword bitch. You'd think she'd have told her lover about the runes, would you not? She kept that knowledge pretty deep within herself."

Cymric snorted. "The third rune that disappeared—"

"A spellseeker. I suppose in case someone tried to levitate the sword away from her, or some such. After the

Garlen enchantment forced me from Brius, I returned to find my face on fire."

Cymric tested the edge of the bone circle with his astral sense. Magic hummed within the bones, agitated and angry. When he tentatively touched a bone with the tip of his walking stick, the brass head exploded with a shriek of shrapnel. Pieces struck Cymric in the left leg, dropping him to one knee. Maeumis tittered. "Thus our problem is illustrated. You hate me, but cannot penetrate the magic of the circle. I hate you, but am too injured to take on a human pup who has woven a thread so tightly through my calendar."

"Another unforeseen outcome for you. Certainly a run of bad luck."

Maeumis shrugged. "The calendar was a calculated ploy. It did bring Leandra here before the magic of the ritual expired. That you found a use for it only proves that you are not wholly incompetent."

Cymric tried to stand, then thought better of it. "Nice to know that a not wholly incompetent human pup is the equal of the great Maeumis. Oh, I'm sorry, I forgot; I'm only your equal because you had your face burned off by another human pup."

Maeumis bent down to regard Cymric with his remaining good eye, which glittered with evil emotion. "But I will heal. You will still be a pup."

Cymric stood on his good leg. Blood ran down his left; he felt his pants sticking to his skin. "The Ristular have reason to hunt you."

Maeumis laughed wildly. "A group so stupid as to believe I would help them summon a Horror such as Ristul. The summoning required the lifeblood of more than a thousand victims just to create a portal wide enough for Ristul to enter our world. What did they think would be required to sustain it?" The nethermancer laughed again, this time the sound diminishing to a chuckle. He bent to examine a bone, changing its alignment slightly. "Their cult was an ancient one. Their ancestors had more sense than they, or at least more interesting magic. Almost worth the pain of their company to learn." Maeumis nodded to Cymric. "This is goodbye for now. Needa and I must be going."

"You named the spiritcatcher Needa?"

Maeumis walked to the inner circle, then replied without turning back. "I named Needa after the first peasant we sacrificed to Ristul. I thought the event deserved commemoration."

Cymric's breath caught. Maeumis wove a thread, looping it around dozens of bones, creating knots more intricate than any Cymric had ever seen in a spellcasting. He tied the first and began a second. Anger flared through Cymric. He took the calendar from his pack, hurriedly weaving a thread to the pattern for dispel magic. He cast the spell on himself as he dove into the bone circle, holding the calendar in front of him like a shield.

Cymric screamed. Pain wracked his body. He felt a tremendous pressure in his left arm. The bones of his forearm exploded as the walking stick had, bursting his skin in dozens of places and hurling Cymric back from the bone circle. Shock rolled through his body. He sobbed, lying on his right side in a fetal position, rocking back and forth. Slivers of bone projected at odd angles, his wounds soaking his vest in blood. His body shivered in between convulsions. He tried to calm himself, focus on something, anything. He saw the calendar lying a few feet away. The refectory ritual had been one thread short, one wash of blood magic away from completion. The stone disk was the ritual in miniature—and Cymric had already added his thread to the calendar.

He tried to wriggle over to it, but his vision swam from the pain of the effort. The slightest movement brought a cry from his lips. He stopped to catch his breath, but his stomach trembled violently, forcing him to take the air in irregular gasping gulps.

Maeumis clapped enthusiastically. "The blood of Raggok flows through your veins, boy. Tell me, has your madness passed?"

Cymric clenched his teeth as he wormed his way to the calendar. He grabbed it with his right arm, then wriggled his way back to the bone circle. He screamed as he dropped the calendar within a few inches of the circle. His upper body convulsed again, slamming his head into the calendar. Cheek upon cold stone, he stared across the calendar at the dwarf nethermancer. Maeumis grinned in happy disbelief. "You're going to try again? Perhaps I shall linger awhile, then. I would so enjoy watching you kill yourself."

"We wizards are noted showmen. Enjoy," spat Cymric. He rested his shattered arm on top of the calendar, willing his blood magic into the calendar. He panted as the calendar soaked in his life force, then barked a laugh at the puzzlement on Maeumis' face. A glow brightened the center of the calendar, orange petals rising from the calendar as the flower grew. The flower strained against an unseen barrier while Maeumis cursed and began to weave a thread. Cymric urged more of his life force into the flower, and the stem shot upward, the petals opening to full flower. In the center the stamen changed, becoming crystalline and needle sharp. With a pop, the flower poked a pinprick into astral space.

A blast of cold escaped the hole. Cymric held onto the calendar, feeding his life to the flower that maintained the hole. A deep bass roar tore through the garden. Rolling waves of shimmering force expanded from the calendar, scattering bones in every direction. A wave slammed into Maeumis, who was shouting as he tried a spell, the cadenced shout becoming a shriek of fear and pain. Space folded and stretched within the dwarf, stretched and folded again. Maeumis wailed as he became longer and thinner, impossibly thin yet still alive. The waves of force reversed direction, rolling back to the calendar. They carried Maeumis with them, back to the calendar, back to the hole in astral space, back to Ristul. Then Maeumis was sucked into the hole with a sound like somebody tearing off a joint of lamb.

Cymric released the calendar. The noise stopped. The flower vanished. Struggling to stay conscious, he worked his good hand across his body into his pouch. He wiggled the Garlen vial free, fighting to open the top one-handed.

He drank the remaining bit of potion, which tasted clean, tasted wonderful, with only a hint of the peppermint. The pain in his arm subsided a little. The potion stopped the bleeding, forming scabs around the bone almost immediately. Breathing slowly, he lay on his side, a sharp, stinging pain bringing a new ache to his arm. It happened again; this time a scab tore as a bone fragment retracted. Cymric grunted or cried out as each bone fragment retracted into his arm, the power of Garlen mending his arm the best it could. He slid over to a bench, rotated onto his back and pulled himself up to sit leaning against the bench as he tried to catch his breath.

Seated amid a field of scattered bones, Cymric turned teary eyes to the field of scattered stars. Watching the sky, he waited until his arm had healed enough to return to the tavern and Leandra.

EPILOGUE

Leandra drove the pommel of her sword into the boy's stomach. He wore leather to prevent serious harm, but the blow was powerful enough to imprint the hawk-beak and eyes into the armor. He would remember it. His sword fell from his hand as he doubled over and crouched, but he stayed on his feet. Leandra had expected the blow to drop him, but Greely's toughness forced Leandra to reevaluate him. The boy would probably make the cut.

Greely huffed, squinting in the low morning sun that bleached color from the grass of the practice field. Among the thirty-nine others watching attentively, the ork Bjava's face showed a smirk; Leandra would pay more attention to him in the afternoon. As he had been taught, Greely dropped into a hand-down crouch to retrieve his sword. Then he straightened quickly, sheathed his sword, and saluted smartly. Leandra felt her left cheek twitch, for which she inwardly rebuked herself; she made it a point to control her tic-smile during practice sessions. "Guardsman Greely, we do not train for attacks to the head. You are not ready for them. Your attack and my response are all the proof you require."

"Yes, Commander."

Greely stepped back to the others, and Leandra addressed the company. "After breakfast all of you will report to your instructors for extra drill on the defense."

"Yes, Commander!"

The crisp unison pleased Leandra. She needed all the signs of progress she could find. "Dismissed. See you in the afternoon." The company turned a quarter-circle, then jogged off the field in cadence. Leandra waited until they were off the field before she started walking to the drafty shack they called a headquarters. She kicked at the dew on the grass. She'd never enjoyed drilling troops, and these were proving particularly infuriating. Crossing the line of tall pines that bordered the practice field, she delayed a moment to inhale deeply, then turned onto the crushed brick path leading to headquarters. The rough-hewn boards, warped windows, and cracked shale roof looked ridiculous when compared to Mount Throal looming behind it. Leandra's gloom lifted when she smelled the tea through the mesh in the door. For an old troll, Rhior had a surprising social streak in him.

Rhior had his feet up on the desk, head lolled forward, snoring lightly. The tea was brewing on the camp stove under the window sill. Two mugs sat on the nearby map table.

"Reviewing strategy again?" teased Leandra.

The old troll opened one yellow eye to make sure he had to open the other eye. Seeing that he did, he swung his legs off Leandra's desk, rising stiffly to salute his commander. Leandra wasn't sure why he went through the motions at all. She started pouring the tea.

"So which was it this morning, useless or trouble?"

Leandra handed the first mug to Rhior. The troll held it with his last two fingers held away from the handle. Elegance had nothing to do with it; the handle could only fit two of his fingers. Leandra took a sip of her own tea before answering. "The morning they become trouble, I'll buy you whitewater until you think you're falling from the top of Mount Throal." She knocked a strand of hair back into place behind one ear. "I'm not sure why I even bother."

Rhior grinned. "That's what you get for saying 'yes' to a king."

"So it's all my fault. Tell me something new."

"All right. Courier packet arrived for you a few minutes ago."

Leandra's heart skipped a beat. She hoped it was from Brins. He'd been sent to track down persistent rumors of Theran activity in the Caucauvics weeks ago. He'd promised to write, and had already done so twice. That was pretty good for Brius. A third letter would be a sign that he was truly serious in his feelings for her. Or at least a sign that the last few letters she'd written had made some kind of impression.

Rhior reached under the desk to pull out a package that looked much too large to be from Brius. Leandra broke the courier seal, unwrapping the waxed-cloth covering. She smelled something good even before peeling away the last layer. Inside was a pouch of tea, Landis Blend Sun Mixture, and a letter. Leandra opened the pouch and sniffed the tea; rose hips, orange, and some other wonderful unidentified scent wafted up to greet her. She unfolded the letter:

"Leandra," it began in her friend's unmistakable script.

"Corthy is quiet as always, at least as quiet as it can get with Gelthrain in town. When accused of conversing with the dead in the Kolbrenton family crypt, she entered a novel defense. She claimed these dead needed to talk, and would simply find someone else if she became unavailable. Charges were dropped.

"Warris practices his magic diligently and is a fine apprentice, although he tends to push me back up onto the high road when opportunity lures me onto a different path. I have decided it is time to take him traveling and show him a little of the world beyond these circle-streets. His eagerness to see Throal is fitting for a boy his age, and somewhat infectious. By the time you read this, we should be heading upstream on the Coil. We should be in Throal in a few days.

"I very much look forward to seeing you, Leandra. If your new duties prohibit you from leaving camp, I understand. In that case, perhaps your camp needs some expert ward-detection at a very reasonable price, say, a few hours of their commander's time?

"The tea is a small gift for you. During the last few months I have had some time for research. After prying a few facts from Gelthrain's sneering lips, I tackled the calendar a few more times. I located your thread and calibrated the events on the calendar. Your birthday is the

twelfth of this month. Warris and I have planned a proper
party, and are bringing along everything we could think of
that he could carry. He is the apprentice, after all. We
should be in Throal on the tenth. I hope our plans meet
with your approval.

"Say hello to Brius for me, and give my regards to that
warty old troll of yours."

It was signed, "Your friend, Cymric."

Leandra looked out the window for a time, enjoying the
warm emotion that spread through her. Then she smiled as
she folded the letter, laying it beside the pouch of tea.
Rhior looked at her, curiosity showing as plainly as the
stains on his tusks. "You're going to have to handle the
training for a few days next week," she said. "I'm taking
leave."

Rhior's tongue tapped the broken tip of his left tusk.
"Taking leave for where?"

"Just down into the city. Some wizards are coming to
give me a birthday party. But I'm sure you'll be invited."

Rhior's tongue snapped back into his mouth with lizard-
like speed. "You never mentioned you had a birthday coming up. I just thought you were old like me, and willing to
forget them." Rhior looked at the teapot a while before
saying, "So, just how many birthdays *have* you seen?"

Leandra drained the mug, setting it down on the
already-stained border of the map. She began to squeak
her way across the warped floor to the door, then looked
back and smiled. "As far as I'm concerned, this is my
first," Leandra said. "I plan to do it right." The door clattered shut behind her as she stepped out into the sunlight.